READER'S DIGEST

CONDENSED BOOKS

FIRST EDITION

Published by

THE READER'S DIGEST ASSOCIATION LIMITED
25 Berkeley Square, London W1X 6AB.

THE READER'S DIGEST ASSOCIATION SOUTH AFRICA (PTY) LTD.
Nedbank Centre, Strand Street, Cape Town

Printed in Great Britain by Petty & Sons Ltd., Leeds

Original cover design by Jeffery Matthews A.R.C.A.

For information as to ownership
of copyright in the material in this book see last page

ISBN 0 340 21665 4

READER'S DIGEST
CONDENSED BOOKS

IN THE FRAME
Dick Francis

BAKER'S HAWK
Jack Bickham

BRING ON THE EMPTY HORSES
David Niven

LORD OF THE FAR ISLAND
Victoria Holt

THE HESSIAN
Howard Fast

COLLECTOR'S LIBRARY
EDITION

In this volume

IN THE FRAME
by *Dick Francis* (p.9)

A house stripped by thieves of its valuables, a woman savagely murdered, a painting of a horse that was not all that it seemed to be.... This was the trail of crime that led Charles Todd—an easy-going artist —right across the world to the race tracks and art galleries of Australia, and to a final perilous confrontation among the jagged rocks of New Zealand's coast.

Fast paced, wryly humorous, and full of surprises, this is the latest and most engaging thriller from the master of this genre.

BAKER'S HAWK
by *Jack Bickham* (p.131)

It was in the summer of 1882 that young Billy Baker found the fledgling hawk injured in a gully, deserted by its parents. And the only person who could help him nurse it back to health was the old fellow they called "the crazy man" who lived up on the mountain. There was ugly talk around town about the crazy man. And—though Billy was too young to know it—the time was not far off when the talk would be turned to action. Mob action.

BRING ON THE EMPTY HORSES
by *David Niven* (p.241)

The Golden Years of Hollywood . . . David Niven lived them, the gaudy, exciting days of the big stars, the big producers, the big pictures. Himself one of the biggest of the stars, in this intimate and often hilarious book he remembers his friends—Gable, Bogart, Goldwyn, Garbo and many others— and describes the strange, intoxicating world where they chose to work and play.

LORD OF THE FAR ISLAND
by *Victoria Holt* (p.307)

All her life Ellen had dreamt of a certain room, voices, an overpowering sense of horror. Even in the shelter of the magnificent castle on the Far Island, close to the man she loved, the dream persisted. Until the night when she found it was a dream no longer, when the voices were real, and the horror also.

THE HESSIAN
by *Howard Fast*

The Hessians
paid by the
rebellious
two

ublished by Michael Joseph, London

IN THE FRAME

a condensation of the book by

Dick Francis

Illustrated by Michae

The beautiful young wife of his cousin brutally murdered . . . then, a week later, a friend's house inexplicably burnt to the ground. Two acts of violence with nothing to connect them—or so Charles Todd, artist and keen racing enthusiast, thought at first. . . . Until, that is, a chance word put him on to a painting of racehorses that might not have been all that it claimed to be, and set him —for the sake of his cousin's sanity—haring off to Australia and beyond.

The conspiracy he uncovered there was discreet yet merciless. With the hushed, irreproachable world of expensive art galleries as its front, it was to lead him perilously close to a second brutal murder. His own.

In this, his latest thriller, best-selling ex-jockey Dick Francis gives us, as well as his unequalled horseracing expertise, fascinating insights into the international art community. The result is a story full of surprises, topical, fast-paced and marvellously readable.

CHAPTER ONE

I stood on the outside of disaster, looking in.

There were three police cars outside my cousin's house, and an ambulance with its revolving blue light, and people bustling in through the open front door. Intermittent bright white flashes from the windows spoke of photography in progress within. The chill wind of early autumn blew dead brown leaves sadly onto the driveway, and harsh scurrying clouds threatened worse to come. Six o'clock, Friday evening, Shropshire, England.

With foreboding I completed my journey to the house. I had travelled by train to stay for a country weekend. No cousin with car to meet me at the station as promised, so I had started to walk, sure he would come tearing along soon in his muddy Peugeot, full of apologies and jokes.

No jokes.

He stood in the hall, dazed and grey, his body limp inside his neat business suit. His arms hung straight down from the shoulders as if his brain had forgotten they were there. His head was turned slightly towards the sitting room, the source of the flashes.

"Don?" I said. I walked towards him. "Donald!"

He didn't hear me. A policeman, however, did. He came swiftly from the sitting room and took me unceremoniously by the arm. "Out of here, sir," he said. "If you please."

Don's eyes slid uncertainly our way. "Charles. . . ."

The policeman's grip loosened very slightly. "Do you know this man, sir?" he asked.

9

"I'm his cousin," I said.

"Oh." He took his hand off, told me to stay where I was and look after Mr. Stuart, and returned to the sitting room to consult.

"What's happened?" I said.

Don was past answering. His head turned again towards the sitting-room door, drawn to a horror he could no longer see. I disobeyed the police instructions, took ten quiet steps, and looked in.

The familiar room was unfamiliarly bare. No pictures, no ornaments, no oriental rugs. Just bare walls, dusty wood-block flooring, heavy furniture pushed awry.

And on the floor, my cousin's young wife, bloody and dead.

The big room was scattered with busy police, measuring, photographing, dusting for fingerprints. I knew they were there; didn't see them. All I saw was Regina.

Her eyes were half open, still faintly bright. One arm was flung out sideways with the dead white fingers curling upward. I looked at the scarlet mess of her head and felt the blood draining sickeningly from my own.

The policeman who had grabbed me before saw me swaying in the doorway, and took quick annoyed strides back to my side. "I told you to wait outside, sir," he said.

I nodded dumbly and went back into the hall. Donald was sitting on the stairs, looking at nothing. I sat abruptly on the floor near him and put my head between my knees.

"I . . . found her," he said.

I swallowed. What could one say? It was bad enough for me, but he had lived with her, and loved her. The faintness passed away slowly, leaving a sour feeling of sickness. I leaned back against the wall behind me and wished I knew how to help him.

"She's . . . never . . . home . . . on Fridays," he said. "Six . . . six o'clock . . . she comes back. Always."

"I know," I said. "I'll get you some brandy."

I pushed myself off the floor and went into the dining room, and it was there that the significance of the bare sitting room forced itself into my consciousness. In the dining room too there were bare walls, bare shelves. No silver ornaments. No silver

10

spoons or forks. No collection of antique china. Just a jumble of empty drawers dumped on the floor.

Wrenstone House had been burgled. And Regina . . . Regina, who was never home on Fridays, had walked in. . . .

I went over to the plundered sideboard, flooding with anger at all greedy, vicious people who cynically devastated the lives of total strangers. Forgiveness was all right for saints. What I felt was plain hatred, fierce and basic.

I found two intact glasses, but all the drink had gone. Furiously I stalked through the swing door into the kitchen and filled the electric kettle.

In that room too, the destruction had continued. What valuables, I wondered, did thieves expect to find in kitchens? I jerkily made two mugs of tea and rummaged in Regina's spice cupboard for the cooking brandy, and felt unreasonably triumphant when it proved to be still there. The sods had missed that, at least.

Donald still sat unmoving on the stairs. I pressed the cup of strong sweet liquid into his hands and told him to drink, and he did, mechanically. Most of the hall furniture had gone too. The small Sheraton desk . . . the studded leather chair . . . the nineteenth-century carriage clock. . . .

"Christ, Charles," he said.

I glanced at his face. There were tears, and dreadful pain. I could do nothing, nothing, to help him.

The impossible evening lengthened to midnight, and beyond. The police were polite, and not unsympathetic. But there was doubt in many of their questions: it was, after all, not unknown for householders to arrange their own well-insured burglaries, and for smooth-seeming swindles to go horrifically wrong.

Donald didn't seem to notice. He answered wearily, automatically, with long pauses sometimes between question and answer.

Yes, the missing goods were well insured, had been so for years.

Yes, he had been in his office in Shrewsbury all day as usual.

Yes, he had been out to lunch. A sandwich in a pub.

He was a wine shipper.

He was thirty-seven years old. Yes, his wife was much younger. Twenty-two.

Yes, his wife always spent Fridays working in a friend's flower shop.

"Why?"

"What?" Donald looked vaguely at the detective inspector, sitting opposite him across the dining-room table. The antique dining chairs had gone. Donald sat in a garden chair brought from the sunroom, the inspector, a constable and I on kitchen stools.

"Why did she work in a flower shop on Fridays?"

I interrupted brusquely. "She was a florist before she married Donald. She liked to keep her hand in. She used to spend Fridays making table arrangements for dances and weddings."

"Thank you, sir, but I'm sure Mr. Stuart can answer for himself."

"And I'm sure he can't." I said. "He's too shocked."

"Are you a doctor, sir?" I shook my head impatiently. The inspector's gaze wandered briefly over my jeans, faded denim jacket, fawn polo-neck, and desert boots, and returned to my face, unimpressed. "Very well, sir. Name?"

"Charles Todd."

"Age?"

"Twenty-nine."

"Occupation?"

"Painter."

"Houses or pictures?"

"Pictures. Mostly of horses."

The constable wrote down these scintillating details in his notebook.

"And your movements today, sir?"

"Caught the two-forty from Euston and walked from the local station."

"Purpose of visit?"

"Nothing special. I come here once or twice a year."

"Good friends, then?"

"Yes."

He noded non-committally. Turned again to Donald. "And what time do you normally reach home on Fridays, sir?"

Don said tonelessly, "Five. About."

"And today?"

"Same." A spasm twitched the muscles of his face. "I saw the house had been broken into . . . I telephoned . . ."

"Yes, sir. We received your call at six minutes past five. And after you had telephoned, you went into the sitting room to see what had been stolen?"

Donald didn't answer.

"Our sergeant found you there, sir, if you remember."

"*Why?*" Don said in anguish. "Why did she come home?"

"I expect we'll find out, sir."

The careful questions went on and on, and as far as I could see achieved nothing except to bring Donald ever closer to breakdown.

At some point during the evening Regina's body was loaded into the ambulance and driven away. I heard it happen, but Donald gave no sign of interpreting the sounds. I thought that probably his mind was raising barriers against the unendurable, and one couldn't blame him.

The inspector rose finally. He said he would be leaving a constable on duty at the house all night, and that he would return himself in the morning. Donald nodded vaguely and, when the police had gone, still sat on, with no energy to move.

"Come on," I said. "Let's go to bed." I took his arm, persuaded him to his feet, and steered him up the stairs. He came in a daze, unprotesting.

His and Regina's bedroom was a shambles, but the twin-bedded room prepared for me was untouched. He flopped full-length in his clothes and put his arm up over his eyes.

I STAYED WITH Donald for a week, during which many questions were answered. One of the easiest was the reason for Regina's premature return home. She and the flower-shop friend had erupted into a quarrel bitter enough to make Regina leave at once. She had driven away at about two-thirty, and had probably gone straight home, as it was considered she had been dead for at least two hours by five o'clock.

This information was given to Donald by the inspector on Saturday afternoon. Donald walked away out into the autumnal garden and wept. The inspector, Frost by name and cool by nature, stood beside me in the kitchen watching Donald with his bowed head among the apple trees.

"I would like you to tell me what you can about the relationship between Mr. and Mrs. Stuart. How did they get on?"

"Can't you tell for yourself?"

He answered after a pause. "Guilt can manifest itself in an excess of mourning."

"Dangerous bunk," I said. "As far as I could see, the honeymoon was by no means over." I turned away from the sight of Donald. "What are the chances of getting back any of the stuff from this house?" I said.

"Small, I should think. There have been hundreds of similar break-ins during recent years and very little has been recovered. Antiques are big business these days."

"Connoisseur thieves?" I said sceptically.

"The prison library service reports that all their most requested books are on antiques. All the little chummies boning up to jump on the bandwagon as soon as they get out."

He sounded suddenly quite human. "Like some coffee?" I said.

He looked at his watch, raised his eyebrows, and accepted. He sat on a kitchen stool while I fixed the mugs, a fortyish man with thin sandy hair and a well-worn suit.

"Are you married?" he asked.

"Nope."

He stirred his coffee reflectively, "When did you visit this house last?" he said.

"Last March. Before they went off to Australia."

"Australia?"

"Donald had some idea of shipping Australian wine over in bulk. They went to see the vintage there. They were away for at least three months. Why didn't their house get robbed *then*, when they were safely out of the way?"

He listened to the bitterness in my voice. "Life is full of nasty ironies."

Donald came in through the back door, looking red-eyed and exhausted. "The Press are making a hole in the hedge," he said.

14

Inspector Frost clicked his teeth, got to his feet, opened the door to the hall and called out loudly, "Constable? Go and stop those reporters from breaking into the garden."

A distant voice replied, "Sir," and Frost apologized to Donald. "Can't get rid of them entirely, you know, sir. They have their editors breathing down their necks. They pester the life out of us at times like these."

Donald sat down heavily on a stool and rested his elbows wearily on the table. "Charles," he said, "if you wouldn't mind heating it, I'd like some of that soup now."

"Sure," I said, surprised. He had rejected it earlier as if the thought of food revolted him.

Frost's head went up purposefully, as if at a signal, and I realized he had merely been coasting along until then, waiting for some such moment. He drank his coffee while Donald disposed of two platefuls of soup and a chunk of brown bread. Then, politely, he asked me to take myself off, and when I'd gone he began what Donald afterwards referred to as "serious digging".

It was three hours later, and growing dark, when the inspector left. I watched his departure from the upstairs landing window. He and his attendant plainclothes constable were intercepted immediately outside the front door by a young man with a microphone, and before they could dodge round him to reach their car the pack on the road were streaming in full cry into the garden.

I went methodically round the house drawing curtains, checking windows, and locking and bolting all the outside doors.

In spite of his long session with the inspector, Donald seemed a lot calmer, and when I had finished Fort-Knoxing the kitchen-to-garden door he said, "The police want a list of what's gone. Will you help me make it?"

"Of course."

"It'll give us something to do. . . ."

"What about your insurance company? Haven't they got a list?"

"Only of the more valuable things, like some of the paintings, and her jewellery." He sighed. "Everything else was lumped together as 'contents'."

We started on the dining room and made reasonable progress,

15

with him putting the empty drawers back into the sideboard while trying to remember the silver each had once contained, and me writing down to his dictation.

Faced by the ranks of empty shelves where once had stood a fine collection of early nineteenth-century porcelain, however, he baulked entirely.

"What does it matter?" he said drearily, turning away.

"How about the paintings, then?"

He looked vaguely round the bare walls. The site of each missing frame showed unmistakably in lighter oblong patches.

"You probably remember them better than I do," he said. "You do it."

"I'd miss some."

"Is there anything to drink?"

"Only the cooking brandy," I said.

"We could have some wine from the cellar." His eyes suddenly opened wide. "Good God, I'd forgotten about the cellar."

"I didn't even know you had one."

"Reason I bought the house. Perfect humidity and temperature for long-term storage. There's a small fortune down there in claret and port."

There wasn't, of course. There were three floor-to-ceiling rows of empty racks, and a single cardboard box on a wooden table.

Donald merely shrugged. "Oh well . . . that's that."

I opened the cardboard box and saw the tops of wine bottles. "They've left these, anyway," I said.

"Probably on purpose," Don smiled twistedly. "That's Australian wine. We brought it back with us."

"Better than nothing," I said disparagingly, pulling out a bottle and reading the label.

"Better than most, you know. A lot of Australian wine is superb."

I carried the whole case up to the kitchen and dumped it on the table. The stairs from the cellar led up into the utility room and I had always had an unclear impression that its door was just another cupboard. I looked at it thoughtfully. "Do you think the burglars *knew* the wine was there?" I asked.

"God knows."

16

He searched for a corkscrew, opened one of the bottles, and poured the deep red liquid into two kitchen tumblers. I tasted it and it was indeed a marvellous wine, even to my untrained palate. *Wynn's Coonawarra Cabernet Sauvignon.* You could wrap the name round the tongue as lovingly as the product. Donald drank his share absentmindedly, as if it were water.

The old Donald had been a man of confidence, running a middle-sized inherited business and adding his share. He had a blunt uncompromising face lightened by amber eyes which smiled easily. The new Donald was a tentative man, his movements uncertain, as if he could not quite remember how to do things, and I knew it was because with half his mind he thought all the time of Regina, and the thoughts were literally paralysing.

We spent the evening in the kitchen, talking desultorily, eating a scratch meal, and tidying all the stores back onto the shelves. During that time the front door bell rang repeatedly but never in the code pre-arranged with the police. The telephone, as its receiver was lying loose beside it, rang not at all.

We went eventually upstairs to bed, although it seemed likely that Donald would sleep no more than the night before, which had been hardly at all. The police surgeon had left knockout pills which Donald wouldn't take. On the upstairs landing he seemed struck by one particular patch of empty wall.

"They took the Munnings," he said.

"What Munnings?"

"We bought it in Australia. I hung it just there. I wanted you to see it. It was one of the reasons I asked you to come."

"I'm sorry," I said. Inadequate words.

CHAPTER TWO

Frost arrived tirelessly again on Sunday morning with his quiet watchful eyes and non-committal manner. I opened the front door to his signal, and he followed me through to the kitchen, where Donald and I seemed to have taken up permanent residence. I gestured him to a stool, and he sat on it.

"Two pieces of information you might care to have, sir," he said to Donald, his voice at its most formal. "Despite our intensive investigation of this house we have found no fingerprints for which we cannot account."

"Would you expect to?" I asked.

He flicked me a glance. "No, sir. Professional housebreakers always wear gloves."

Donald waited with a grey patient face, as if he would find whatever Frost said unimportant. Nothing, I judged, was of much importance to Donald any more.

"Second," said Frost, "our investigations in the district reveal that a removal van was parked outside your front door early on Friday afternoon. Dark coloured and dusty, sir."

"Oh," Donald said, meaninglessly.

Frost sighed, and started another careful speech about the sitting room being kept locked by the police for a few more days and please would neither of us try to go in there.

Neither of us would.

Apart from that, they had finished their inquiries at the house, and had Mr. Stuart completed the list of things stolen?

I passed it over. It still consisted only of the dining-room silver and what I could remember of the paintings. Frost raised his eyebrows and pursed his lips.

"We'll need more than this, sir."

"We'll try again today," I promised. "There's a lot of wine missing, as well."

"Wine?"

I showed him the empty cellar. "It must have taken hours to move that lot," I said.

"Very likely, sir," he said primly. Then he looked up the cellar stairs and, almost casually, said, "Is your cousin in financial difficulties?"

I knew his catch-them-off-guard technique by now. "I wouldn't think so," I said unhurriedly. "You'd better ask him."

He switched his gaze sharply to my face. "A great many middle-sized private companies are going bankrupt these days."

"I can't help you. You'll have to look at his company's books."

18

"We will, sir."

"And even if the firm turns out to be bust, it doesn't follow that Donald would fake a robbery. If he needed money he could simply have sold the stuff."

"Maybe he had." I took a slow breath and said nothing. "That wine, sir. As you said yourself, it would have taken a long time to move."

"My cousin Donald is an honourable man," I said mildly.

"That's an out-of-date word."

"There's quite a lot of it about."

He looked wholly disbelieving. He saw far too much in the way of corruption, day in, day out, all his working life.

Up in the kitchen again Frost wanted another private session with Don. While they talked I wandered aimlessly round the house, ending up in the big sunroom among sprawling potted plants looking out into the windy garden. Dead leaves blew in scattered showers from the trees and a few late roses clung hardily to thorny stems. I hated autumn. The time of melancholy, the time of death.

I went upstairs, fetched my suitcase and brought it down. Over years of wandering journeys I had reversed the painter's traditional luggage: my suitcase now contained the tools of my trade, and my satchel, clothes. The suitcase was a sort of portable studio, containing paints and brushes, a light collapsible metal easel, unbreakable containers of linseed oil and turpentine, and a rack which would hold four wet paintings safely apart. There were also a dust sheet, a large box of tissues, and generous amounts of white spirit, all designed for preventing mess and keeping things clean.

I untelescoped the easel and set out my palette, and on a middling-sized canvas laid in the beginnings of a melancholy landscape, Donald's garden against a sweep of bare fields and gloomy woods. Not my usual sort of picture, and not, to be honest, the sort to make headline news a century hence; but it gave me at least something to do until Frost chose to depart.

He went without seeing me again, leaving Donald in the kitchen, sitting with his arms folded on the table and his head on his arms, a picture of absolute despair. When he heard me he sat up wearily. "Do you know what he thinks?" he said.

19

"More or less."

He stared at me sombrely. "I couldn't convince him. He kept on and on. They would have to have had proper wine boxes, you see. That means they had to know in advance that the wine was there, and didn't just chance on it. And that means . . . Frost says . . . that I sold it myself some time ago and am now saying it is stolen so I can claim fraudulent insurance, or, if it was stolen on Friday, that I told the thieves they'd need proper boxes, which means that I set up the whole frightful mess myself."

We thought it over in depressed silence. Eventually I said, "Who *did* know you had the wine there? And who knew the house was always empty on Fridays? And was the prime target the wine, the antiques, or the paintings?"

"God, Charles, you sound like Frost."

"Sorry." I sucked my teeth. "I suppose he asked if the stolen things were insured for more than their worth?"

"Yes, he did. Several times. They weren't, though." He sighed. "Underinsured, if anything. God knows if they'll pay up for the Munnings. I'd only arranged the insurance by telephone. I hadn't actually sent the premium."

"It should be all right, if you can give them proof of purchase, and so on."

He shook his head listlessly. "All the papers to do with it were in the desk in the hall. The receipt from the gallery where I bought it, the letter of provenance, and the customs and excise receipt. All stolen."

"Well . . . I hope you pointed out to Frost that you would hardly be buying expensive pictures and going on world trips if you were down to your last farthing."

"He said it might be *because* of buying expensive pictures and going on world trips that I might be down to my last farthing. I'm not, but still he wants to meet me in my office tomorrow—to see the books."

THE POLICE sent a car the following morning to take him to the office. He was gone all day. I spent it painting.

Not the sad landscape. The sunroom seemed even greyer and

20

colder that morning, and I had no mind any more to sink into melancholy. I removed myself and trappings into the kitchen— maybe the light wasn't so good in there, but it was the only room in the house with the pulse of life.

I painted Regina standing beside her cooker. I painted the way she held her head back to smile, and I painted the smile, guileless and unmistakably happy. I painted her from the clearest of inner visions. And I painted the kitchen behind her.

I seldom worked for more than four hours at a stretch because for one thing the actual muscular control required was tiring, and for another the concentration always made me hungry; so I knocked off at around lunchtime and dug out a tin of corned beef to eat with pickles on toast.

The afternoon session was much shorter because of the light, and I frustratingly could not catch the right mix of colours for the tops of the kitchen fitments. Even after years of experience, what looked right on the palette looked wrong on the painting. I got it wrong three times and decided to stop.

I was cleaning the brushes when Donald came back. I heard the scrunch of the car, the slam of the doors, and, to my surprise, the ring of the front door bell. Donald had taken his keys.

I went through and opened the door. A uniformed policeman stood there, holding Don's arm. Behind, a row of faces watched hungrily. My cousin, who had looked pale before, now seemed as white as death.

"Don!" I said, and no doubt looked as appalled as I felt.

He didn't speak. The policeman leant forward, said, "There we are, sir," and transferred the support of my cousin from himself to me. I helped Donald inside and shut the door. I had never seen anyone in such a frightening state of disintegration.

"I asked," he said, "about the funeral. They said . . ." He stopped, dragged in air, tried again. "They said . . . no funeral."

"Donald . . ."

"They said . . . she couldn't be buried until they had finished their inquiries. They said it might be months. They said they will keep her refrigerated."

The distress was fearful.

"They said . . ." He swayed slightly. "They said . . . the body of a murdered person belongs to the State."

I couldn't hold him. He collapsed at my feet in a faint.

CHAPTER THREE

For two days Donald lay in bed heavily sedated, his doctor calling morning and evening with pills and injections. No matter that I was a hopeless nurse and a worse cook, I was appointed to look after him.

In fact, he turned down several offers of refuge with local friends. "I want Charles," he told the doctor. "He doesn't *fuss*."

I sat with him a good deal when he was awake, seeing him struggle to come to terms with the horrors in his mind. In between times, while he slept, I made progress with both the paintings. The sad landscape was no longer sad but merely autumnal, with three horses standing around in a field. Pictures of this sort, easy to live with and passably expert, sold quite well, and were my bread and butter.

The portrait of Regina, though, was the best work I'd done for months. She laughed out of the canvas, alive and glowing. Pictures often changed as one worked on them, and as the emphasis in my mind shifted, the kitchen background was growing less distinct and Regina herself more luminous. I hid her picture in my suitcase whenever I wasn't working on it. I didn't want Donald to come face to face with it unawares.

Early Wednesday evening he came shakily down to the kitchen in his dressing-gown, trying to pick up the pieces. He sat at the table, drinking the Scotch I had that day imported, and watching while I cleaned my brushes and tidied the palette.

"You're always so neat," he said.

"Paint's expensive."

He waved a limp hand at the horse picture which stood drying on the easel. "How much does it cost, to paint that?"

"In raw materials, about ten quid. In heat, light, rent, food, Scotch and general wear and tear on the nervous system, about the amount I'd earn in a week if I went back to selling houses."

"You don't regret it, then," he said seriously.

"No." I washed my brushes, pinched them into shape, and stood them upright in a jar to dry. Good brushes were expensive.

"They said I'd killed her," Donald said abruptly, shockingly.

"For God's sake!"

"After the digging into the company accounts, they took me along to the police station. They'd worked out that I could have got home at lunchtime and killed her because she'd come back and found me supervising the burglary."

"They must be crazy," I said. "She didn't leave the shop until half past two."

"The girl in the flower shop now says she doesn't know to the minute when Regina left. Only that it was soon after lunch. And I didn't get back from the pub until nearly three. I went to lunch late. I was hung up with a client all morning . . ." He stopped. "They let me come home, but I don't think . . ." His voice shook. He swallowed, trying to keep control on his hard-won calm. "I don't think they've finished."

It was five days since he'd walked in and found Regina dead. When I thought of the hammering he'd taken since it seemed marvellous that he had remained as sane as he had. "Have they got anywhere with catching the thieves?" I said.

He smiled wanly. "They haven't said. . . . It's ironic, you know. I've always had a great regard for the police. I didn't know they could be . . . the way they are."

A quandary, I thought. Either they leaned on a suspect in the hope of breaking him down, or they asked a few polite questions and got nowhere. Only the first system was effective, and under it the innocent suffered more than the guilty.

"I see no end to it," Donald said. "No end at all."

BY MIDDAY FRIDAY the police had called twice more at the house, but for my cousin the escalation of agony seemed to have slowed. He was still exhausted, but it was as if he were saturated with suffering and could absorb little more. Whatever Frost said to Donald rolled off without destroying him further.

"You're supposed to be painting someone's horse, aren't you?" Donald said suddenly, as we shaped up to lunch. "I remember you saying, when I asked you to stay, that it would fit in fine before your next commission."

"I telephoned and explained. Said I'd come later."

"All the same, you'd better go."

He insisted I look up the times of trains. He said he would be all right alone, now, and thanks for everything. I could see in the end that the time had indeed come for him to be by himself, so I packed up my things.

"I suppose," he said diffidently, as we waited for the taxi to fetch me, "that you never paint portraits? People, that is, not horses."

"Sometimes," I said.

"I just wondered . . . Could you, one day . . . I mean, I've got quite a good photograph of Regina. . . ."

I looked searchingly at his face. As far as I could see, it could do no harm. I unclipped the suitcase and took out the picture. "It's still wet," I warned.

He stared at the canvas but said nothing at all. The taxi drove up to the front door. "See you," I said, propping Regina against a wall.

He nodded and sketched a farewell wave. Speechlessly, because his eyes were full of tears.

I SPENT NEARLY a week in Yorkshire doing my best to immortalize a patient old steeplechaser, and then went home to my flat near Heathrow airport, taking the picture with me to finish.

Saturday I downed tools and went to the races, fed up with too much nose-to-the-grindstone. Jump racing at Plumpton, and the familiar excitement at the liquid movement of racehorses. Paintings could never do justice to them, never. The moment caught on canvas was always second best.

I would love to have ridden in races, but hadn't had enough practice or skill; nor, I dare say, nerve. Like Donald, my childhood background was of middle-sized private enterprise, my father an auctioneer in business on his own account in Sussex. I

24

had spent countless hours in my growing years watching the horses train on the Downs round Findon, and had drawn and painted them from about the age of six. Art school later had been fine, but at twenty-two, alone in the world with both parents newly dead, I'd had to face the need to eat. It had been a short step to the estate agents across the street, but I'd liked it well enough to stay a while. Now I was back to painting again.

"Todd!" said a voice in my ear. "You owe me fifteen smackers."

"I bloody don't," I said.

"You said Seesaw was a certainty for Ascot."

"Never take sweets from a stranger."

Billy Pyle laughed extravagantly and patted me heavily on the shoulder. Billy Pyle was one of those people you met on race-courses who greeted you as a bosom pal, plied you with drinks and bonhomie, and bored you to death. On and off I'd met Billy Pyle at the races for years, and had never yet worked out how to duck him without positive rudeness.

I waited for him to say "How about a beverage?" as he always did.

"How about a beverage?" he said.

"Er . . . sure," I agreed, resignedly. Billy pushed in through the door of the bar. "Know anything for the one-thirty?" he demanded.

"'Fraid not."

"Huh." He peered into the form book. "Treetops is well in at the weights, but can you trust his leg?" He looked up suddenly. "Why, there's Mrs. Matthews."

He turned to a large woman who had been standing in the shadows.

"Maisie! What do you want, love?"

"Oh . . . gin and tonic, thanks dear."

Maisie Matthews's clothes were noticeably new and expensive, and from laquered hair via crocodile handbag to gold-trimmed shoes she shouted money without saying a word. She was middle-aged—fifty-something, I thought—her appearance on the knife-edge between vulgarity and elegance.

"How do you do?" I said politely.

Billy returned with the drinks. "Maisie, this is Charles Todd."

"Cheers," Maisie Matthews said, looking cheerless.

"Down the hatch," said Billy, raising his glass. "Maisie's had a bit of bad luck. Her house burned down."

As a light conversation-stopper, it was a daisy.

"Hard luck," I said uncomfortably.

"Lost everything, didn't you, Maisie?"

"All but what I stand up in, dear," she agreed gloomily. "I wasn't there, of course, I was staying with my sister Betty up in Birmingham, and there was this policeman on the doorstep telling me what a job they'd had finding me. But by that time it was all over, of course. When I got back to Worthing there was just a heap of cinders with the chimney-breast sticking up in the middle. Anyway they finally said it was a flash fire, whatever that is, but they didn't know what started it, because there'd been no one in the house of course for days."

"Have another gin," I suggested.

"Thanks, dear."

When I returned with the refills she accepted the gin and returned to her story.

"Well, I was spitting mad, I'll tell you, losing everything like that, all the treasures Archie and I'd been collecting since heaven knows when."

"I think I'll have a bit on Treetops," Billy said. He had heard enough of disaster, clapped me on the shoulder, and said it was time to see the next contest.

Duty done, I thought with a sigh, and took myself off to watch the race from the top of the stands, out of sight and earshot. Treetops broke down and finished last, limping. Too bad for its owner, trainer, and Billy.

The afternoon went quickly, as usual. I won a little, lost a little, and filled my eyes with something better than money. On the stands for the last race, I found myself approached by Maisie Matthews. No mistaking the bright red coat, the air of gloss, and the big, kind-looking, worldly face. She drew to a halt on the step below me, looking up. Entirely self-confident, though registering doubt.

26

"Aren't you," she said, "the young man I had a drink with, with Billy?"

"Yes, that's right."

"He said you were an artist."

"Mm," I said, watching the runners canter past on the way to the post.

"Not very well paid, is it, dear?"

I grinned at her, liking her directness. "It depends who you are. Picasso didn't grumble."

"How much would you charge to paint a picture for me?"

"What sort of picture?"

"Well, dear, you may say it sounds morbid and I dare say it is, but I was just thinking this morning when I went over there, and really it makes me that mad every time I see it, well, I was thinking actually that it makes a crazy picture, that ruin with the chimney sticking up, and the burnt hedge and the sea, and when it's all cleared away and rebuilt no one will believe how awful it was, and I want to hang it in the new house, just to show them."

"But . . ."

"So how much would you charge? Because I dare say you can see I'm not short of the next quid but if it would be hundreds I might as well get a photographer instead."

"Of course," I agreed gravely. "How about if I came to see the house, or what's left of it, and gave you an estimate?"

She saw nothing odd in that. "All right, dear. That sounds very businesslike. Of course, it will have to be soon. Once the insurance people have been I'm having the rubble cleared up."

"How soon?"

"Well, dear, as you're halfway there, could you come today?"

We discussed it. She said she would drive me in her Jaguar as I hadn't a car, and I could go home by train just as easily from Worthing as from Plumpton. So I agreed.

One takes the most momentous steps unawares.

THE RUIN WAS definitely paintagenic, if there is such a word. On the way there, more or less non-stop, Maisie had talked about her late husband, Archie, who had looked after her well, dear.

"Well, that's to say, I looked after him, too, dear, because I was a nurse. Private, of course. I nursed his first wife all through her illness, and then I stayed on for a bit to look after him, and, well, he asked me to stay on for life, dear, and I did. Of course he was much older, he's been gone more than ten years now. He looked after me very well, Archie did."

She glanced fondly at her huge opal ring set in diamonds. Many a man would have liked to have been remembered as kindly.

"Since he went, and left me so well off, dear, it seemed a shame not to get some fun out of it, so I carried on with what we were doing when we were together, which was going round to auction sales in big houses, dear, because you pick up such nice things there." She changed gear with a jerk and aggressively passed an inoffensive little van. "And now all those things are burnt to cinders, and all the memories of Archie and the places we went together, and I'll tell you, dear, it makes me mad."

"It's really horrid for you."

"Yes, dear, it is."

I reflected that it was the second time in a fortnight that I'd been cast in the role of comforter, and I felt as inadequate for her as I had for Donald.

She stamped on the brakes outside the remains of her house and rocked us to a standstill. As she'd said, all that was left of what had obviously been a minor mansion was an extensive sprawling black heap, with the thick brick chimney pointing sturdily skyward from the centre.

Even before we climbed out of her big pale blue car, I could smell the ash.

"How long ago?" I asked.

"Last weekend, dear. Sunday."

While we surveyed the mess in silence a man walked slowly into view from behind the chimney. He was looking down, taking a step at a time and then bending to poke into the rubble.

"Hey," Maisie called, "What do you think you're doing?"

The man straightened up, looking startled. About forty, I judged, with a fawn raincoat, a crisp-looking trilby and a down-

28

turning moustache. He raised his hat politely. "Insurance, madam."

"I thought you were coming on Wednesday."

"I happened to be in the district. No time like the present, don't you think?"

"Well, I suppose not," Maisie said. "Have you found out what started it?"

"No, madam."

"Well, how soon can I get all this cleared away?"

"Any time you like, madam." He stepped carefully towards us, picking his way round clumps of blackened debris.

"What's your name?" Maisie asked.

"Greene, madam." He paused, and added, "With an 'e'."

"Well, Mr. Greene with an 'e'," Maisie said good-humouredly, "I'll be glad to have all that in writing."

He inclined his head. "As soon as I report back."

Maisie said, "Good," and Greene, lifting his hat again, wished her good afternoon and walked along to a white Ford parked a short way along the road.

"That's all right, then," Maisie said with satisfaction, watching him go. "Now, how much for that picture?"

"Two hundred plus two nights expenses in a local hotel."

"That's a bit steep, dear. *One* hundred, and two nights, and I've got to like the results, or I don't pay."

We settled on one-fifty if she liked the picture, and fifty if she didn't. I was to start on Wednesday unless it was raining.

CHAPTER FOUR

Wednesday came up with a bright breezy day and an echo of summer's warmth. I went to Worthing by train and to the house by taxi, and to the interest of the neighbours set up my easel at about the place where the front gates would have been, had they not been unhinged and transplanted by the firemen.

I worked over the whole canvas with an unobtrusive coffee-coloured underpainting, and while it was still wet drew in, with a darker shade of the same colour, the shape of the ruined house

against the horizontals of hedges, sea and sky. It was easy with a
tissue to wipe out mistakes at that stage, to get the proportions
right, and the perspective.

That done and drying, I strolled right round the whole garden,
looking at the house from different angles. The wind chilled my
ears, and I turned to get back to my task. Two men in overcoats
were standing by my easel appraising my handiwork. One, heavy
and fiftyish. One lean, in his twenties. Both with firm self-
confident faces and an air of purpose.

The elder raised his eyes as I approached. "Do you have
permission to be here?" he asked.

"The owner wants her house painted," I said.

"I see." His lips twitched a fraction.

"And you?" I inquired.

"Insurance," he said, as if surprised that anyone should ask.

"Same company as Mr. Greene with an 'e'?" I said.

"I don't know who you mean. We are here by arrangement with
Mrs. Matthews to inspect the damage to her house, which is
insured with us."

"No Greene?" I repeated.

"Neither with nor without an 'e'."

I warmed to him. Half an ounce of a sense of humour, as far as
I was concerned, achieved results where thumbscrews wouldn't.

"Well . . . Mrs. Matthews is no longer expecting you because
the aforesaid Mr. Greene, who said he was in insurance, told her
she could roll in the demolition squad."

His attention sharpened. "Are you serious?"

"I was here, with her. I saw him and heard him."

"Did he show you a card?"

"No, he didn't." I paused. "And . . . er . . . nor have you."

He reached into an inner pocket and did so, with the speed of
a conjurer. *Foundation Life and Surety. D.J. Lagland. Area
Manager.* "Gary," he said to his sidekick, "go and find a telephone and ring the Beach Hotel. Tell Mrs. Matthews we're here."

While Gary was away on the errand, D.J. Lagland turned his
attention to the ruin, and I, as he seemed not to object, tagged
along at his side. He was lifting small solid pieces of debris,

inspecting them closely, and carefully returning them to their former positions.

"What do you look for?" I asked.

He shot me a sideways look. "Evidence of arson. Evidence of the presence of the goods reported destroyed."

"Mr. Greene was doing much what you are, though in the area behind the chimney."

"Did he take anything?" he said.

"Not while we were watching."

Gary rolled back, and soon after him, Maisie. In her Jaguar. In her scarlet coat. In a temper.

"Don't tell me you're trying to wriggle out of paying my cheque, now," she said, advancing upon D.J. with eyes flashing. "Your man on Saturday said that everything was all right and I could start clearing away and rebuilding. And even if the question of arson hasn't been settled, you would still have to pay up because the insurance covered arson of course."

D.J. found his voice. "Didn't our Mr. Robinson tell you that the man you saw here on Saturday wasn't from us?"

Our Mr. Robinson, in the shape of Gary, nodded vigorously.

"Mr. Greene distinctly said he *was*," Maisie insisted.

"Well . . . what did he look like?"

"Smarmy," said Maisie. She thought, then shrugged. "He looked like an insurance man, that's all."

D.J. swallowed the implied insult manfully.

"About five feet ten," I said. "Suntanned skin with a sallow tinge, grey eyes with deep upper lids, widish nose, mouth straight under heavy drooping dark moustache, straight brown hair brushed back and retreating from the top corners of his forehead, ordinary eyebrows, gold signet ring on little finger of right hand, suntanned hands."

I could see him in memory as clearly as if he still stood there in the ashes before me.

"Good God," D.J. said.

"An artist's eye, dear," said Maisie admiringly. "Well I never."

D.J. said he was certain they had no one like that in their claims department, and Gary agreed.

D.J. AND GARY inched over the ruin all afternoon. I painted. At five o'clock, on the dot, we all knocked off.

Back at the Beach Hotel I cleaned my brushes, thought a bit, and at seven met Maisie downstairs in the bar, as arranged.

"Well, dear," she said, as her first gin and tonic gravitated comfortably. "Did they find anything?"

"Nothing at all, as far as I could see."

"Well, that's good, dear."

I tackled my pint of draught. Put the glass down carefully.

"Not altogether, Maisie."

"Why not?"

"What exactly were your treasures which were burned?"

"I dare say you wouldn't think so much of them, but we had ever such fun buying them, things like an antique spear collection that used to belong to old Lord Stequers, and six warming-pans from a castle in Ireland, and two tall vases with eagles on the lids signed by Angelica Kaufmann, which once belonged to a cousin of Mata Hari, they really did, dear, and a marble table from Greece, and a silver tea urn which was once used by Queen Victoria, and really, dear, if I tell you them all I'll go on all night."

"Did the insurance company have a full list?"

"Yes, they did, dear, and why do you want to know?"

"Because," I said regretfully, "I don't think many of those things were inside the house when it burned down."

"*What?*" Maisie, as far as I could tell, was genuinely astounded. "But they must have been."

"Mr. Lagland, the elder one, as good as told me they were looking for traces of them, and I don't think they found any."

Alternate disbelief and anger. Disbelief won. "You got it wrong dear," she said finally. "Everything was in its place last Friday week when I went off to stay with Betty, and I only went to Betty's with not having seen her for so long while I had been away in Australia, which is ironic when you come to think of it."

She paused for breath. Coincidence, I thought. "Australia?" I said.

"Well, yes, dear, wasn't that nice? I went out there for a visit to Archie's sister who's lived there since Heaven knows when. I was out there for six weeks—and we got on together like a house on fire . . . oh dear, I didn't mean that exactly. . . ."

I said idly, "I don't suppose you bought a Munnings there."

I didn't know why I'd said it, apart from thinking of Donald in Australia. I was totally unprepared for her reaction.

Incredulous and angry she had been before: this time, pole-axed. She knocked over her gin, slid off her bar stool, and covered her open mouth with four trembling red-nailed fingers.

"You didn't!" I said disbelievingly.

"How do you know? Are you from customs and excise?"

"Of course not."

"Oh dear. Oh dear. . . ."

I took her arm and led her over to an armchair beside a small bar table. "Sit down," I said coaxingly, "and tell me."

It took ten minutes and a refill double gin.

"Well, dear, I'm not an art expert, as you can probably guess, but there was this picture by Sir Alfred Munnings, signed and everything, dear, and it was such a bargain really, and I thought how tickled Archie would have been to have a real Munnings on the wall, what with us both liking the races, of course, and, well, Archie's sister egged me on a bit, so I bought it."

She stopped.

"And you brought it into this country without declaring it?"

She sighed. "Yes, dear, I did. Of course it was silly of me but I never gave customs duty a thought when I bought the painting, not until just before I came home, and Archie's sister asked if I was going to declare it, and well, dear, I really *resent* having to pay duty on things, don't you? So anyway I thought I'd better find out just how much the duty would be, and I found it wasn't duty at all in the ordinary way, dear, but a sort of Value Added Tax on buying things, eight per cent on whatever I had bought the picture for. Well, I ask you! I was that mad, dear, I can tell you so I just camouflaged it a bit with my best nightie and popped it in my suitcase, and pushed it through the 'Nothing to Declare' lane at Heathrow."

"How much would you have had to pay?" I said.

"Well, dear, to be precise, just over seven hundred pounds. And

I know that's not a fortune, dear, but it made me so mad to have to pay tax here for something I'd bought in Australia."

I did some mental arithmetic. "So the painting cost about nine thousand?"

"That's right, dear." She looked anxious. "I wasn't done, was I? Lots of Munningses cost more, don't they?"

"So they do," I said absently. And some, I dared say, could be got for less.

"Well, anyway, dear, it was only when I began to think about insurance that I wondered if the insurance people would want a *receipt* or anything, so I didn't do anything about it. And now the nine thousand's gone up in smoke and I won't see a penny of it back, and I dare say you'll think it serves me right."

She finished the gin and I bought her another.

"I know it's not my business, Maisie, but how did you happen to have nine thousand handy in Australia? Aren't there rules about exporting that much cash?"

She giggled. "You don't know much about the world, do you, dear? I had taken my jewellery with me on the trip, and I just toddled along with Archie's sister to a jewellers and sold him a brooch I⁻ had, a nasty sort of *toad*, dear, with a socking big diamond in its forehead. . . . You won't *tell* anyone, will you, dear, about the picture?"

"Of course not, Maisie."

"I could get into such trouble, dear. People can be so beastly about a perfectly innocent little bit of smuggling."

"No one will find out." A thought struck me. "Unless, that is, you've told anyone already that you'd bought it?"

"No, dear, I hadn't even hung it on the wall yet. I expect you'll think me silly, dear, but I suppose I was feeling a bit scared of being found out, not guilty exactly because I really don't see why we *should* pay that irritating tax but anyway I didn't not only not hang it up, I hid it."

I was fascinated. "Where did you hide it?"

She laughed. "I slipped it behind one of the radiators in the lounge, and don't look so horrified, dear, the central heating was turned off."

I PAINTED at the house all the next day. Neither D.J. nor anyone else turned up. In between stints at the easel I poked around a good deal on my own account, searching for Maisie's treasures. I found a good many recognizable remains, metal bed-frames, kitchen machines and radiators, all of them twisted and buckled. But of all the things Maisie had described, nothing.

No copper warming-pans, which after all had been designed to withstand red-hot coals. No marble table. No antique spears. And naturally, no Munnings.

When I took my paint-stained fingers back to the Beach Hotel I found Maisie waiting for me in the hall. Not the kindly, basically cheerful Maisie I had come to know, but a woman in a full-blown state of rage.

"I'm so *mad* I think I'll *burst*," she said. "The bar's shut, so come upstairs to my room. I've had the police here half the day, and those insurance men here the other half, and *do you know what they're saying?*"

I sighed inwardly. It had been inevitable.

"There they were," she said, "having the nerve to suggest I'd sold all my treasures and over-insured my house, and was trying to take the insurance people for a ride. That Mr. Lagland says they won't be paying out until they have investigated further and he was proper sniffy about it, and no sympathy at all for me having lost everything."

We entered the lift and she paused to re-gather momentum, vibrating visibly with the strength of her feelings. "It turns out that Lagland couldn't find any trace of my treasures in the ashes, and they said even if I hadn't sold the things first I had arranged for them to be stolen and the house burnt to cinders while I was away at Betty's!"

She threw open the door of her room and stalked in. I followed, closing it after me. "I don't suppose you told them about the Munnings," I said.

It looked for a moment as if I'd just elected myself as the new target for hatred. "I'm not *crazy*," she said bitingly. "If they found out about that, there would have been a fat chance of convincing them I'm telling the truth about the rest."

"I've heard," I said tentatively, "that nothing infuriates a crook more than being had up for the one job he didn't do." Suddenly, as she glared at me, her sense of humour reared its battered head. The stiffness round her mouth relaxed, her eyes softened and after a second or two, she ruefully smiled. "I dare say you're right, dear, when I come to think of it."

Little eruptions continued all evening through drink and dinner, but the volcano had subsided to manageable heat.

"I think," I said over coffee, "that if you will come, and he agrees, I'd like to take you to meet my cousin. You see, something very much the same has just happened to him. Too much the same, in too many ways."

And I told her how.

CHAPTER FIVE

Donald on the telephone had sounded unenthusiastic at my suggested return, but also too lethargic to raise objections. We went to Shropshire in Maisie's Jaguar, sharing the driving.

When Donald opened his front door to us, I was shocked. It was two weeks since I'd left him to go to Yorkshire. In that time he had shed at least fourteen pounds and aged ten years. His skin was tinged with blueish shadows, the bones in his face showed starkly, and even his hair seemed speckled with grey.

The ghost of the old Donald put an effort into receiving us with good manners. "Come in," he said. "I'm in the dining room now. I expect you'd like a drink."

"That would be very nice, dear," Maisie said.

The dining room had been roughly refurnished, containing now a large rug, all the sunroom armchairs, and a couple of small tables from the bedrooms. We sat in a fairly close group round one of the tables, because I had come to ask questions and wanted to write down the answers.

"Don," I said, "I want you to listen to a story."

"All right."

Maisie, for once, kept it short. When she came to the bit about buying a Munnings in Australia, Donald's head lifted a couple of inches and he looked from her to me with the first stirrings of attention. When she stopped, there was a small silence.

"So," I said finally, "You both went to Australia, you both bought a Munnings, and soon after your return you both had your houses burgled."

"Extraordinary coincidence," Donald said, but he meant simply that.

"Where did you buy your picture, Don? Where exactly, I mean."

"I suppose . . . Melbourne. In a gallery." He made a slight attempt to remember. "Might have been called something like Fine Arts."

"Would you have it on a cheque stub, or anything?"

He shook his head. "The wine firm I was dealing with paid for it, and I sent a cheque to their British office when I got back."

"Which wine firm?"

"Monga Vineyards Proprietary Limited of Adelaide and Melbourne."

I wrote it all down. "Could you tell us how you came to buy your picture. Did you, for example, deliberately go looking for a Munnings?"

Donald passed a weary hand over his face. "No. I wasn't especially wanting to buy anything at all. We just went into the Melbourne Art Gallery for a stroll round. We came to the Munnings they have there . . . and while we were looking at it we just drifted into conversation with a woman near us, as one does in art galleries. She said there was another Munnings, not far away, for sale in a small commercial gallery, and it was worth seeing even if one didn't intend to buy it. We had time to spare, so we went."

Maisie's mouth had fallen open. "But, dear," she said, recovering, "That was *just* the same as us, my sister-in-law and me, though it was Sydney Art Gallery, not Melbourne. They have this marvellous picture there, *The Coming Storm*, and we were admiring it when this man sort of drifted up to us and joined in. . . ."

Donald suddenly looked a great deal more exhausted, like a

sick person over-tired by healthy visitors. "Look Charles . . . you aren't going to the police with all this? Because I don't think I could stand . . . a whole new lot of questions."

"No, I'm not," I said. "But what was your picture like, Don? I mean, could you describe it?"

"One of those 'Going-Down-to-the-Start' things. Typical Munnings."

"So was mine," said Maisie, surprised. "And the nearest jockey in my picture had a purple shirt and green cap. I expect you'll think I was silly but that was one of the reasons I bought it, because when Archie and I were thinking what fun it would be to buy a horse and go to the races as owners, we decided we'd like purple with a green cap for our colours."

"Don?" I said.

"Mm? Oh . . . three bay horses cantering . . . one in front, two slightly overlapping behind. Bright colours on the jockeys. I don't remember exactly. White racetrack rails and a lot of sunny sky."

"What size?"

He frowned slightly. "Not very big. About twenty-four inches by eighteen, inside the frame."

"And yours, Maisie?"

"A bit smaller, dear, I should think." She finished her gin and tonic and smiled. "Which way to the little girls' room, dear?" she asked, and disappeared to the cloakroom.

Donald said faintly, "I can't concentrate . . . I'm sorry, Charles, but I can't seem to do anything while they still have Regina . . . unburied . . . just *stored*. . . ."

It seemed as if the keeping of Regina in a refrigerated drawer had stopped time from dulling his agony. He stood up suddenly and walked out of the door. I followed. He crossed the hall, opened the door of the sitting room, and went in.

Hesitantly, I went after him. The floor where Regina had lain was clean and polished. The air was cold. Donald stood in front of the empty fireplace looking at my picture of her, which was propped on the mantelpiece.

"I stay in here with her, most of the time," he said. "It's the only place I can bear to be."

He walked to one of the armchairs and sat down, directly facing the portrait. "You wouldn't mind seeing yourself out, would you, Charles?" he said. "I'm really awfully tired."

"Take care of yourself." Useless advice.

"I'm all right," he said. "Quite all right. Don't you worry."

I looked back from the door. He was sitting immobile, looking at Regina. I didn't know whether it would have been better or worse if I hadn't painted her.

MAISIE DROVE soberly, silently, mile after mile. Eventually she said, "We shouldn't have bothered him. Not so soon after . . ."

Three weeks, I thought. Only three weeks. You could live a lifetime in three weeks' pain.

"I'm going to Australia," I said.

If I could bring home enough to show beyond doubt that the plundering of Donald's house had its roots in the sale of a painting in Australia, it should get the police off his neck, the life back to his spirit, and Regina into a decent grave.

"You're very fond of him, dear, aren't you?" Maisie said.

Fond? I wouldn't have used that word, I thought, but perhaps after all it was accurate.

She drove another ten miles in silence. Then she said, "Are you sure it wouldn't be better to tell the police? About the paintings, I mean? Because you do think they had something to do with the burglaries, don't you, dear, and the police might find out things more easily than you."

I agreed. "I'm sure they would, Maisie. But how can I tell them? You heard what Donald said, that he couldn't stand a new lot of questions. Seeing him today, do you think he could? And what about you, having to confess to smuggling?"

"I didn't know you cared, dear." She tried a giggle, but it didn't sound right.

We stopped after a while to exchange places. The power purred elegantly under the pale blue bonnet and ate up the miles.

"Can you afford the fare, dear?" Maisie said. "And hotels, and things?"

"I've a friend out there. Another painter. I'll stay with him."

"Yes, well, dear, I dare say you will, but all the same, and I don't want any silly arguments, I've got a great deal of this world's goods thanks to Archie, and you haven't, and as because it's partly because of me having gone in for smuggling that you're going yourself at all, I am insisting that you let me buy your ticket."

"No, Maisie."

"Yes, dear. Now be a good boy, dear, and do as I say."

You could see why she'd been a good nurse. Swallow the medicine, dear, there's a good boy. I didn't like accepting her offer but the truth was that I would have had to borrow anyway.

She wrote out a cheque which was far more than enough for my journey.

"If you're so fussed, dear," she said across my protests, "you can give me back what you don't spend." She gazed at me earnestly. "You will be careful, dear, won't you?"

"Yes, Maisie."

"Because of course, dear, you might turn out to be a nuisance to some really *nasty* people."

I LANDED IN SYDNEY at noon five days later. Jik met me on the other side of customs with a huge grin and a waving bottle of champagne.

"Todd the sod," he said. "Who'd have thought it?" He slapped me on the back with an enthusiastic horny hand. Jik Cassavetes, long-time friend, my opposite in almost everything.

Bearded, which I was not. Exuberant, noisy, extravagant, unpredictable; qualities I envied. Blue eyes and sun-blond hair. Muscles which left mine gasping. An outrageous way with girls. And a wholehearted contempt for the things I painted.

We had met at art school, drawn together by mutual truancy on racetrains. Jik went racing to gamble, never to admire the contestants, and certainly not to paint them. No *serious* artist, he frequently said, would be seen dead painting horses.

Jik's paintings, mostly abstract, were dark, fruits of depression at the hatred and pollution destroying the fair world.

Living with Jik was like a toboggan run, dangerous and

41

exhilarating. We'd spent the last two years at art school sharing a studio flat. They would have chucked him out of school except for his prodigious talent, because he'd missed weeks in the summer for his other love, which was sailing.

I'd been out with him, deep sea, several times in the years afterwards. I reckoned he'd taken us on several occasions a bit nearer death than was strictly necessary, but it had been a nice change from the office. I had been sorry when one day he had said he was setting off single-handed back home to Australia. We'd had a paralytic farewell party on his last night ashore, and the next day, when he'd gone, I'd given the estate agent my notice.

He had brought a car to fetch me: his car, it turned out. A British M.G. sports, dark blue.

"Welcome to sunny Australia." He switched on the windscreen wiper against a starting shower. "It rains all the time here. Puts Manchester in the sun."

"But you like it?"

"Love it, mate. Sydney's like rugger, all guts and go."

"And how's business?"

"There are thousands of painters in Australia." He glanced at me sideways. "A hell of a lot of competition."

"I haven't come to seek fame and fortune."

"But I scent a purpose," he said.

"How would you feel about harnessing your brawn?"

"To your brain? As in the old days? What are the risks?"

"Arson and murder, to date."

"Jesus!"

The blue car swept gracefully into the centre of the city, nosed onto the expressway, pointing towards the bridge.

"If you look over your right shoulder," Jik said, "You'll see the triumph of imagination over economics. Like the Concorde. Long live madness, it's the only thing that gets us anywhere." I looked. It was the opera house. "The shape of the twenty-first century. Imagination and courage. I love this country."

The road went up and down out of the city through close-packed rows of one-storey houses.

42

"There's one snag," Jik said. "Three weeks ago, I got married."

His wife was living with him aboard his boat, which was moored among a colony of others near a headland called The Spit.

Sarah was not plain, but not beautiful. Oval-shaped face, mid-brown hair, so-so figure and a practical line in clothes. None of the style or instant vital quality of Regina. I found myself the target of bright brown eyes which looked out with impact-making intelligence.

We said hi and did I have a good flight and yes I did. I gathered she would have preferred me to stay at home.

Jik's thirty-foot ketch, which had set out from England as a cross between a studio and a chandler's warehouse, now sported curtains, cushions, and a flowering plant. When Jik opened the champagne he poured it into shining tulip glasses, not plastic mugs. I apologized for gatecrashing the honeymoon.

"Nuts to that," Jik said, obviously meaning it. "Too much domestic bliss is bad for the soul."

"It depends," said Sarah neutrally, "on whether you need love or loneliness to get you going."

For Jik, before, it had always been loneliness. I wondered what he had painted recently: but there was no sign, in the now comfortable cabin, of so much as a brush.

We ate a feast round the cabin table—crayfish, grilled with cheese and mustard, crisp lettuce and crusty bread and butter—the rain pattering on the portholes and roof and the sea water slapping against the sides in the freshening wind. Over coffee, at Jik's insistence, I told them why I had come to Australia.

Jik muttered darkly about "pigs". Sarah looked nakedly apprehensive. "Don't worry," I told her. "I'm not asking for Jik's help, now that I know he's married."

"You have it. You have it," he said explosively.

I shook my head. "No."

Sarah said, "What precisely do you plan to do first?"

"Find out where the two Munnings came from."

"Melbourne," Jik said. "You said one of the pictures came from Melbourne. Well, that settles it. Of course we'll help. It couldn't be better. Do you know what next Tuesday is?"

"No," I said. "What is it?"

"The day of the Melbourne Cup! We'll go there at once—for the whole meeting."

His voice was triumphant. Sarah stared at me darkly across the table. "I wish you hadn't come," she said.

CHAPTER SIX

I slept that night in the converted boathouse which constituted Jik's postal address. Apart from a bed alcove, new-looking bathroom, and rudimentary kitchen, he was using the whole space as studio. A huge old easel stood in the centre, with a table holding painting paraphernalia, the tubes of paint characteristically squeezed flat in the middles.

No work in progress, but along one wall a two-tiered rack held rows of canvases, which I pulled out one by one. Dark, strong, dramatic colours, leaping to the eye. Still the troubled vision, decay and crucifixions, obscurely horrific landscapes, flowers wilting, everything to be guessed, nothing explicit.

Jik hated to sell his paintings and seldom did, which I thought was just as well, as they made uncomfortable roommates. They had a vigour, though, that couldn't be denied. He was a major artist in a way I would never be, and he would have looked upon easy popular acclaim as personal failure.

In the morning I walked down to the boat and found Sarah there alone.

"Jik's gone for milk and newspapers," she said. "I'll get you some breakfast."

"I came to say goodbye."

She looked at me levelly. "The damage is done."

"Not if I go."

"Back to England?"

I shook my head.

"I thought not." A dim smile appeared briefly in her eyes. She turned away. "*Men*," she said. "Never happy unless they're risking their necks."

44

She was right, to some extent. A little healthy danger wasn't a bad feeling, especially in retrospect. "Some women, too," I said.

"Not me." Her back was still turned. "You'll get him killed."

NOTHING LOOKED less dangerous than the small Sydney gallery from which Maisie had bought her picture. It was shut for good. The bare premises could be seen nakedly through the shop-front window. "Where now?" Jik asked me.

"The city art gallery?" I suggested.

"In the Domain," Jik said, which turned out to be a chunk of park in the city centre. The Gallery of Art had a suitable façade of pillars outside and the Munnings, when we ran it to earth, inside.

No one else was looking at it. No one approached to fall into chat and advise us we could buy another one cheap in a little gallery in an outer suburb.

We drove back to the boat and lunch was an anti-climax. Jik's session telephoning round the Melbourne hotels, however, proved more rewarding. The city, it seemed, was crammed to the rooftops for the richest race meeting of the year, but he had been offered last-minute cancellations.

"Where?" I asked suspiciously.

"In the Hilton," he said.

I COULDN'T afford it, but we went anyway. Jik in his student days had lived on hand-outs from a family trust, and it appeared that the source was still flowing. The boat, the boathouse, the M.G. and the wife were none of them supported by paint.

We flew south to Melbourne the following morning. Sarah's disapproval from the seat behind froze the back of my head, but she had refused to stay in Sydney. I looked down on the Snowy Mountains en route and thought my own chilly thoughts. The Sydney trail was dead, and maybe Melbourne too would yield an un-looked-at public Munnings and a gone-away private gallery. And if it did, what then? For Donald the outlook would be bleaker than the strange puckered ranges sliding away underneath.

MELBOURNE WAS cold and wet and blowing a gale. We checked gratefully into the warm plush of the Hilton. I unpacked, which is to say, hung up my one suit, slightly crumpled from my squashy satchel, and then went to work again on the telephone.

The Melbourne office of the Monga Vineyards Proprietary Limited cheerfully told me that the person who had dealt with Mr. Donald Stuart from England was the managing director, Mr. Hudson Taylor, and he was just now in Melbourne for the races. He had a runner in the Cup. Reverence, the voice implied, was due.

Could I reach him anywhere, then?

Sure, if it was important. He was staying with friends. Number supplied. Ring in the evening.

Sighing a little I went two floors down and found Jik and Sarah bouncing around their room with gleeful satisfaction.

"We've got tickets for the races tomorrow and Tuesday," he said, "And a car pass, and a car."

"Miracles courtesy of the Hilton," Sarah said, looking much happier at this programme. "The whole package was on offer with the cancelled rooms."

"So what do you want us to do this afternoon?" finished Jik expansively.

"Could you bear the Arts Centre?"

It appeared they could. Even Sarah came without forecasting universal doom, my lack of success so far having cheered her.

The Victoria Arts Centre was huge, modern, and endowed with the largest stained-glass roof in the world. We ran the Munnings to earth, eventually, deep in the labyrinth of galleries: the *Departure of the Hop Pickers*, with its great wide sky and dignified gypsies with their ponies, caravans and children.

A young man was sitting at an easel slightly to one side, painstakingly working on a copy. He had light-brown hair and a bad case of acne. Two or three people stood about, watching him and pretending not to, in the manner of gallery-goers the world over.

Jik and I went round behind him to take a look. The young man glanced at Jik's face, but saw nothing there except raised eyebrows and blandness. On the easel stood his study, barely started. The

46

outlines were there, as precise as tracings, and a small amount of blue had been laid on the sky. We watched him squeeze flake white and cadmium yellow from tubes onto his palette and mix them together into a nice pale colour with a hogshair brush.

"Hey," Jik said suddenly, shattering the reverent gallery hush. "What you're doing is *criminal*. If you're an artist I'm a gas-fitter's mate."

Hardly polite, but not a hanging matter. On the young man, though, the effect was galvanic. He leapt to his feet, overturning the easel, snatching up his pots of linseed and turps and flinging the liquids at Jik's eyes.

I grabbed his arm. He swung round fiercely, aiming at my face. I ducked instinctively. Jik had his hands to his eyes and was yelling. Sarah rushed towards him, knocking into me and loosening my grip on the young man. He tore his arm free, ran for the exit, dodged round behind two open-mouthed middle-aged spectators and pushed them violently into my path. By the time I'd disentangled myself, he had vanished from sight. He knew his way through the passages, and I did not: and it took me long enough, when I finally gave up the hunt, to work out the route back to Jik.

A fair-sized crowd had surrounded him, and Sarah was in a fury based on fear, which she unleashed on me as soon as she saw me.

"Do something," she screamed. "Do something, he's going blind. . . . He's going *blind*. . . . I knew we should never have listened to you."

I caught her wrists. "Sarah," I said fiercely. "The linseed oil will do no harm. The turps is painful, but that's all. Jik is *not* going blind."

She glared at me, pulled her wrists out of my grasp, and turned to Jik, who was cupping his fingers in agony over his eyes.

"You know damn well you're not going blind," I said, "so stop hamming it up."

"They're not your eyes, you sod."

"And you're frightening Sarah," I said.

That message got through. He took his hands away. "Sorry, love," he said, blinking painfully. "The bastard's right. Turps never blinded anybody."

"Not permanently," I said, because to do him justice he obviously couldn't see anything but tears at the moment. "What he needs is water."

Jik produced a handkerchief and gently mopped his streaming eyes.

"He's right, love. Lots of water, as the man said. Washes the sting away. Lead me to the nearest gents." With Sarah holding one arm, and a sympathetic male spectator the other, he was solicitously helped away.

I looked at the overturned mess of paints and easel which the young man had left. None of it was marked with its owner's name. All regulation kit, obtainable from art shops. None of it new, but not old, either.

"I suppose," I said slowly, "that no one here was talking to the young artist before any of this happened?"

"We were," said one woman, surprised at the question.

"About his own work?" I said, bending down to pick it up.

The lady and her accompanying husband shook their heads and said they had talked with him about the pleasure of hanging a Munnings on their own walls, back home.

I smiled slowly. "I suppose," I said, "that he didn't happen to know where you could get one?"

"Well, yeah," the lady said. "As a matter of fact—"

"Now, look here, young fellow. . . ." Her husband, a seventyish American with the unmistakable stamp of wealth, shushed her with a practised damping movement of his right hand. "You're asking a lot of questions."

"I'll explain," I said. "Would you like some coffee?"

He looked doubtfully at his watch. "There's a coffee shop just down the hall," I said. "I saw it when I was trying to catch that young man . . . to make him tell why he flung turps in my friend's eyes."

Curiosity sharpened in his face. He was hooked.

THEY WERE Mr. and Mrs. Wyatt L. Minchless from Carter, Illinois, rich, retired, and fond of racing.

Wyatt Minchless was a white-haired man, with black-framed

48

specs, pale indoor complexion, pompous manner. "Now, young fellow, let's hear it from the top."

"Um," I said. Where exactly was the top? "The artist boy attacked my friend Jik because Jik called him a criminal."

"Now why would he do that?" Mrs. Minchless said. "It isn't criminal to copy good painting. In the Louvre in Paris, France, you can't get near the Mona Lisa for those irritating students." She had blue-rinsed puffed-up hair, uncreasable navy and green clothes, and enough diamonds to attract a top-rank thief.

"It depends what you are copying *for*," I said. "If you're going to try to pass your copy off as an original, then that definitely is a fraud."

"Are you saying," Wyatt Minchless demanded, "that this artist boy was painting a Munnings he later intended to sell as the real thing? Are you saying that the Munnings picture he told us we might be able to buy is itself a forgery?"

His wife looked both horrified at the possibility and admiring of Wyatt for his perspicacity.

"I don't know," I said. "I just thought I'd like to see it."

"You don't want to buy a Munnings yourself? You are not acting as an agent for anyone else?"

"Absolutely not," I said.

"Well, then." He fished into his outer breast pocket. "He told Ruthie and me there was a good Munnings racing picture at a very reasonable price in a little gallery not far away . . . Yes, here we are. Yarra River Fine Arts. Third turning off Swanston Street, about twenty yards along."

"He seemed such a nice young man," Ruthie added sadly. "He asked where we would be going after Melbourne. We told him Adelaide and Alice Springs, and he said Alice Springs was a mecca for artists and to be sure to visit the Yarra River gallery there. The same firm he said. Always had good pictures."

I concentrated on my coffee and kept my excitement to myself.

"You didn't tell us," Wyatt said, "why your friend called the young man a criminal."

"My friend," I said, "is an artist himself. He didn't think much of the young man's effort. He called *it* criminal. He might just as well have said lousy. The young man was painting with paints which won't really mix."

"What do you mean, won't mix?"

"Paints are chemicals," I said. "If you mix flake white, which is lead, with cadmium yellow, which contains sulphur, like the young man was doing, you get a nice pale colour to start with but the two minerals react against each other and in time darken and alter the picture." The permanence of colours had always been an obsession with Jik, and he'd dragged me along once to a course on their chemistry.

Wyatt Minchless looked at his watch, then got up to go. "All very interesting," he said with a dismissive smile. "I guess I'll keep my money in regular stocks."

CHAPTER SEVEN

Jik had gone from the gents, gone from the whole Arts Centre. I found him back with Sarah in their hotel room, being attended by the Hilton's attractive resident nurse. The door to the corridor stood open, ready for her to leave.

"Try not to rub them, Mr. Cassavetes," she was saying. "If you have any trouble, call the reception desk, and I'll come back."

She gave me a professional half-smile in the open doorway and walked briskly away.

"How are the eyes?" I said, advancing tentatively.

"Ruddy awful." They were bright pink, but dry. Getting better.

Sarah said with tight lips, "This has all gone far enough. I know that this time Jik will be all right again in a day or two, but we're not taking any more risks."

Jik said nothing and didn't look at me. It wasn't exactly unexpected. I said, "O.K. . . . Well, have a nice weekend, and thanks anyway."

"Todd. . . ." Jik said.

Sarah leapt in fast. "No, Jik. It's not our responsibility. I've been against all this silly poking around all along, and this is where it stops."

A blank pause.

"Well," I said, raising a smile. "Have fun at the races. I might go too, you never know." Neither of them said a word. I eased myself out and took the lift up to my own room.

A pity about Sarah, I thought. She would have Jik in cotton wool if he didn't look out; and he'd never paint those magnificent brooding pictures any more, because they sprang from a torment he would no longer be allowed.

I looked at my watch and decided the Yarra River Fine Arts set-up might still have its doors open. Worth trying.

I wondered, as I walked up Swanston Street, whether the young turps-flinger would be there, and if he was, whether he would know me. Mostly I'd been standing behind him.

The gallery was open, brightly lit, with a horse painting, not a Munnings, in the centre of the window, and beside it a notice announcing a special display of distinguished equine art.

The gallery looked typical of hundreds of others round the world; narrow frontage, with premises stretching back a good way from the street. Two or three people were wandering about inside, looking at the merchandise on the well-lit neutral grey walls.

I had gone there intending to go in. But I hesitated outside feeling as if I were at the top of a ski jump. Stupid, I thought. Nothing venture, nothing gain, and all that. I took a deep breath and stepped over the threshold.

An antique desk near the door, with a youngish woman handing out small catalogues and large smiles. "Feel free to look around," she said. "More pictures downstairs." She handed me a catalogue. I thanked her. "Just passing by," I said.

She nodded and smiled professionally summing up my denim clothes and general air of not belonging to the jet set. "You're welcome anyway," she said.

I walked slowly down the long room, checking the pictures against their notes. Most were by Australian artists, and I could see what Jik had meant about the hot competition. As usual when faced with other people's flourishing talents I began to have doubts of my own.

At the far end of the ground floor display there was a staircase.

I went down. Same carpet, same lighting. But below stairs, the gallery was not one straight room but a series of small rooms off a long corridor. This late they were all deserted. To the rear of the stairs was an office. Heavily framed pictures adorned the walls, and an equally substantial man was writing in a ledger at the desk.

He, like the whole place, had an air of permanence and respectability quite unlike the fly-by-night suburban affair in Sydney. I had got the whole thing wrong. This respectable business, I thought, could not be what I was looking for.

Sighing, I continued down the line of rooms, thinking I might as well finish taking stock of the opposition. And in the end room, which was larger than the others, I came across the Munningses. Three of them. They were not in the catalogue.

They hung without ballyhoo in a row of similar subjects, and to my eyes stuck out like thoroughbreds among hacks.

Prickles began up my spine. It wasn't just the workmanship, but one of the pictures itself. Horses going down to the start. A long line of jockeys, the silks of the nearest rider purple, with a green cap. . . . The picture, size, subject, and colouring was exactly like Maisie's, which had been hidden behind a radiator, and, presumably, burned.

The picture in front of me looked authentic. The right sort of patina for the time since Munnings's death, the right excellence of draughtsmanship, the right indefinable something which separated the great from the good. I put out a gentle finger to feel the surface of canvas and paint. Nothing there that shouldn't be.

An English voice from behind me said, "Can I help you?"

"Isn't that a Munnings?" I said casually, turning round. He was standing in the doorway, looking in, his expression full of guarded helpfulness.

I knew him instantly. Mr. Greene. With an "e". Last on view thirteen days ago beside the sea in Sussex, England, prodding around in a smokey ruin.

It took him only a fraction longer, the realization of where he'd last seen me. He took a sharp step backwards and raised his hand to the wall outside.

I was on my way to the door, but I wasn't quick enough. A steel mesh gate slid down very fast in the doorway and clicked into some sort of bolt in the floor. Mr. Greene stood on the outside, disbelief still stamped on every feature.

"What's the matter?" called a deeper voice from up the corridor. The man from the office appeared and looked at me through the imprisoning steel. "A thief?" he asked with irritation.

Mr. Greene shook his head. A third person arrived, his young face bright with curiosity, and his acne showing like measles.

"Hey," he said in loud Australian surprise. "He was the one at the Arts Centre. The one who chased me. I swear he didn't follow me. I swear it."

"Shut up," said the man from the office briefly. He stared at me steadily. I stared back.

I revised all my early theories about danger being good for the soul. I was standing in the centre of a bright, windowless room about fifteen feet square. No way out, nowhere to hide, no weapons to hand. A long way down the ski jump and no promise of a soft landing.

"I say," I said plaintively. "Just what is all this about?" I walked up to the steel gate and tapped on it. An innocent-at-large, and a bit dim. "Open this up, I want to get out."

"What are you doing here?" the office man said. He was bigger than Greene and obviously more senior in the gallery. Heavy dark spectacle frames over unfriendly eyes, hair thinning, and a blue bow tie with polka dots under a double chin.

"Looking," I said, trying to sound bewildered. "Just looking at pictures."

"He chased me in the Arts Centre," the boy repeated.

"You threw some stuff in that man's eyes," I said indignantly. "You might have blinded him."

"Friend of yours, was he?" the office man said.

"No," I said. "I was just there, that was all. Same as I'm here. Just looking at pictures. There's nothing wrong in that, is there?"

Mr. Greene got his voice back. "I saw him in England," he said.

"Who *are* you?" said the office man.

"Charles Neil." Charles Neil Todd. "I'm just here for the racing."

"What were you doing in England?"

"I live there!" I said. "Look," I went on, as if trying to be reasonable under great provocation. "I saw this man here," I nodded to Greene, "at the home of a woman I know slightly in Sussex. He said his name was Greene and that he was from an insurance company, and that's all I know about him. So what's going on?"

"It is a coincidence that you should meet here again, so soon."

"It certainly is," I agreed fervently. "But that's no bloody reason to lock me up."

I read indecision on all their faces. I hoped the sweat wasn't running visibly down my own. "Fetch the police or something," I said. "If you think I've done anything wrong."

The man from the office put his hand to the switch on the outside wall, and the steel gate slid up out of sight, a good deal more slowly than it had come down. "Sorry," he said perfunctorily. "But we have to be careful, with so many valuable paintings on the premises."

"Well, I see that," I said, stepping forward and resisting a strong impulse to make a dash for it. "But all the same . . ." I managed an aggrieved tone.

They all walked behind me up the stairs and through the upper gallery, doing my nerves no slightest good. All the other visitors seemed to have left. The receptionist was locking the front door. "I thought everyone had gone," she said in surprise.

"Slight delay," I said, with a feeble laugh.

She gave me the professional smile and reversed the locks. Opened the door. Held it, waiting for me.

Six steps. The fresh air smelled good. I half turned. All four stood in the gallery watching me go. I nodded and trudged away, feeling as weak as a fieldmouse dropped by a hawk.

I caught a passing tram and travelled into unknown regions of the huge city, conscious only of an urgent desire to put a lot of distance between myself and that basement prison.

They would have second thoughts. They were bound to. They

54

would wish they had found out more about me before letting me go. If they wanted to find me, where would they look? Not at the Hilton, I thought. At the races: I had told them I would be there. On the whole I wished I hadn't.

I left the tram and began to walk back through the bright streets and dark parks, asking the way. Thinking of Donald and Maisie and Greene with an "e", and of paintings and burglaries and violent minds.

The overall plan seemed fairly simple: to sell pictures in Australia and steal them back in England, or America or anywhere that was worth the risk, together with everything else lying handy.

Suppose I were a villain, I thought, and I didn't want to waste weeks in foreign countries finding out exactly which houses were worth robbing. I could just stay quietly at home in Melbourne selling paintings to rich visitors who could afford an impulse-buy of ten thousand pounds or so, carefully steered my way by talkative accomplices who stood around in the States' Capitals' art galleries. When they bought my paintings, they would give me their addresses. Nice and easy. Just like that. I would chat away with them about their picture collections back home, and I could shift the conversation easily to their silver and china and *objets d'art*.

I wouldn't want the sort of customers who had Rembrandts or anything well known and unsaleable like that. Just the middling wealthy with Georgian silver and Chippendale chairs. And I would reckon that if I kept the victims reasonably well scattered, the fact that they had been to Australia within the past year or so would mean nothing to each regional police force or insurance company.

Supposing when I'd sold a picture to a man from England and robbed him, and got my picture back again, I then sold it to someone from America. And then robbed him, and got it back, and so on round and round.

Suppose I sold a picture to Maisie in Sydney, and got it back, and started to sell it again in Melbourne. . . . My supposing stopped right there, because it didn't fit.

If Maisie had left her picture in full view it would have been stolen like her other things. Maybe it even had been, and was right now glowing in the Yarra River Fine Arts, but if so, why had the house been burnt, and why had Mr. Greene turned up to search the ruins?

It only made sense if Maisie's picture had been a copy, and if the thieves hadn't been able to find it. Rather than leave it around, they'd burned the house.

I sighed. To fool even Maisie you'd have to find an accomplished artist willing to copy instead of pressing on with his own work, and they weren't that thick on the ground. Certainly the acne'd young man wasn't up to the job. . . .

The huge bulk of the Hilton rose ahead of me across the last stretch of park. Upstairs, I telephoned Hudson Taylor at the number I'd been given. He sounded courteous, his voice strong and vibrantly Australian.

"Donald Stuart's cousin? It's a real tragedy little Regina being killed. A real nice lass, that Regina."

"Yes."

"Lookee here, then, what can I do for you? Is it tickets for the races?"

"Er, no," I said. "It was just that since the receipt and provenance letter of the Munnings have been stolen along with the picture, Donald would like to get in touch with the people who sold it to him, for insurance purposes, but he forgot their name. And as I was coming to Melbourne for the Cup. . . ."

"That's easy enough," Hudson Taylor said pleasantly. "I remember the place well. I went with Donald to see the picture there. Now let's see . . ." There was a pause for thought. "I can't remember the name of the place just now. It was some months ago, do you see? But I've got it on record here in the Melbourne office, and I'm calling in there anyway in the morning, so I'll look them up. You'll be at the races tomorrow?"

"Yes," I said.

"How about meeting for a drink, then? You can tell me all about poor Donald and Regina, and I'll have the information he wants."

I said that would be fine, and he gave me detailed instructions as to where I would find him, and when. The spot he had described sounded public and exposed. I hoped that it would only be he who found me on it.

"I'll be there," I said.

CHAPTER EIGHT

Jik called through on the telephone at eight next morning. "Come down to the coffee shop and have breakfast."

I went down in the lift and along to the hotel's informal restaurant. He was sitting at a table alone, wearing dark glasses and making inroads into a mountain of scrambled eggs.

"They bring you coffee," he said, "but you have to fetch everything else from that buffet." He nodded towards a well-laden table in the centre of the breezy blue and sharp green decor.

"How are the eyes?"

He whipped off the glasses and leaned forward to give me a good look. Still pink, they were, but on the definite mend.

"Where did you get to yesterday?" he said.

"Aladdin's cave," I said. "Treasures galore and damned lucky to escape the boiling oil."

I told him about the gallery, the Munnings, and my brief moment of captivity. I told him what I thought of the burglaries. It pleased him. "How are we going to prove it?" he said.

He heard the "we" as soon as he said it. He laughed ruefully, the fizz dying away. "I'd like to help," he said. "But . . ."

"Sarah hasn't relented?" I asked.

He slid me a glance. "She says she's got nothing against you personally."

"But," I said.

He nodded. "The mother hen syndrome."

"Wouldn't have cast you as a chick."

He put down his knife and fork. "Nor would I. Anyway, there's this car we've got. Damned silly if you didn't come with us to the races."

"Would Sarah . . ." I asked carefully, ". . . scowl?"

"She says not."

I accepted this offer and we finished breakfast amicably trying to build a suitable new relationship on the ruins of the old, both knowing well what we were about.

When I met them later in the hall at setting-off time it was clear that Sarah too had made a reassessment and put her mind to work on her emotions. She greeted me with a smile and an outstretched hand. I shook the hand lightly and also gave her a token kiss on the cheek. She took it as it was meant.

Truce made, terms agreed, pact signed.

We found the car park at Flemington racecourse looking like a giant picnic ground, with hundreds of full-scale lunch parties going on between the cars. Tables, chairs, cloths, china, silver, glass. Sunshades optimistically raised in defiance of the rain-clouds threatening above.

To my mild astonishment Jik and Sarah had come prepared. They whipped out table, chairs, drinks and food from the rented car's boot and said it was easy when you knew how, you just ordered the whole works. Champagne. Steak and oyster pie.

"I have an uncle," Sarah said, "who holds the title of Fastest Bar in the West. It takes him roughly ten seconds from putting the brakes on to pouring the first drink."

She was really trying, I thought. Not just putting up with an arrangement for Jik's sake, but actually trying to make it work. If it was an effort, it didn't show. She was wearing an interesting olive green linen coat, with a broad brimmed hat of the same colour, which she held on from time to time against little gusts of wind. Overall, a new Sarah, prettier, more relaxed, less afraid.

We demolished the goodies, repacked the boot, and with a sense of taking part in some vast semi-religious ritual, squeezed along with the crowd through the gate to the Holy of Holies.

"It'll be much worse than this on Melbourne Cup day," observed Sarah. "It's a public holiday. The city has three million inhabitants and all of them will try to get here."

"If they've got any sense they'll stay home and watch it on the box," I said breathlessly, receiving a hefty kidney punch from the elbow of a man fighting his way into a can of beer.

"It won't be on the television in Melbourne, only on the radio."

"Good grief. Why ever not?"

"Because they want everyone to come. It's televised all over the rest of Australia, but not on its own doorstep."

We went through the bottleneck and, by virtue of the badges inherited with the cancelled Hilton bookings, through a second gate and round into the calmer waters of the green oblong of the Members' lawn. Much like a Derby Day at home, I thought. Same triumph of will over weather. Bright faces under grey skies. Warm coats over the pretty silks, umbrellas at the ready.

My friends were deep in a cross-talking assessment of the form of the first race. Sarah, it appeared, had a betting pedigree as long as her husband's, and didn't agree with him.

"Want to bet?" Jik asked me.

"Don't know the horses."

"As if that mattered."

"Right." I consulted the racecard. "Two dollars on Generator."

They both looked him up, and they both said, "Why?"

"If in doubt, back number eleven."

They told me I might as well make a gift of my two dollars to the bookies. Generator, however, won at twenty-fives.

"Beginner's luck," Sarah said.

Jik laughed. "He's no beginner. He got kicked out of playschool for running a book."

They tore up their tickets, set their minds to race two. I settled for four dollars on number one.

"Why?"

"Double my stake on half of eleven."

"Oh God," said Sarah. "You're something else." She and Jik screamed encouragement to their fancies but Number One finished in front by two lengths, at eight to one.

"It's disgusting," said Sarah, tearing up more tickets. "What number do you fancy for the third?"

"I won't be with you for the third. I've got an appointment to have a drink with someone who knows Donald."

The lightness went out of her manner. "More . . . investigating?"

"I have to."

"Yes." She swallowed. "Well, good luck."

It was at the corner of the Members' lawn where the horses' path from the saddling boxes reached the parade ring that I was to meet Hudson Taylor. I reached the appointed spot and stood there waiting, admiring the brilliant scarlet of the long bedful of flowers which lined the railing between horse-walk and lawn. Cadmium red mixtures with highlights of orange and white and maybe a streak or two of expensive vermilion . . .

"Charles Todd?"

"Yes . . . Mr. Taylor?"

"Hudson. Glad to know you." He shook hands, his grip dry and firm. Late forties, medium height, comfortable build, with affable slightly sad eyes sloping downwards at the outer corners. He was one of the minority of men in morning suits, and he wore his as comfortably as a sweater.

He led me in through a door, past a uniformed guard and a notice saying "Committee Only", and into a large square comfortable room fitted out as a small-scale bar. Men stood chatting with half-filled glasses held close to their chests, and two women in furs were complaining loudly of the cold.

"They love to bring out the sables," Hudson Taylor chuckled, fetching two glasses of Scotch and gesturing to me to sit by a small table. "Spoils their fun, the years it's hot."

"Is it usually hot?"

"Melbourne's weather can change twenty degrees in an hour." He sounded proud of it. "Now then, this business of yours." He delved into an inner breast pocket and surfaced with a folded paper. "Here you are, typed out for Donald. The gallery was called Yarra River Fine Arts."

I would have been astounded if it hadn't been.

"And the man we dealt with was someone called Ivor Wexford."

"What did he look like?" I asked.

"I don't remember clearly. It was back in April, do you see?"

I thought briefly and pulled a small sketchbook out of my pocket. "If I draw him, might you know him?"

He looked amused. "You never know."

I drew quickly in soft pencil a reasonable likeness of Greene.

Hudson Taylor shook his head decisively. "No, that wasn't him."

"How about this?" I flipped over the page and started again, doing my best with the man from the basement office.

"That's him," said Hudson in surprise. "I remember the bow tie, anyway. You don't see many of those these days. How did you know? You must have met him."

"I walked round a couple of galleries yesterday afternoon."

"That's quite a gift you have there," he said with interest, watching me put the notebook away.

"Practice, that's all." Years of seeing people's faces as matters of shapes and proportions and planes, and remembering which way the lines slanted. I could already have drawn Hudson's eyes from memory. It was a knack I'd had from childhood.

"Sketching is your hobby?" Hudson asked.

"And my work. I mostly paint horses."

We talked a little about painting for a living. "Maybe I can give you a commission, if my horse runs well in the Cup." He smiled, the outer edges of his eyes crinkling finely. "If he's down the field, I'll feel more like shooting him." He shook my hand, told me to remember him to Donald, and asked if I could find my way out.

"Thank you for your help," I said.

He smiled. "Any time. Any time."

Jik and Sarah, when I rejoined them, were arguing about their fancies for the Victoria Derby, the next race on the card.

"Ivory Ball has as much chance as a blind man in a blizzard," said Jik. Sarah ignored him.

"Hello Todd," she said, "Pick a number, for God's sake."

"Ten."

"Why ten?"

"Eleven minus one."

"You used to have more sense," Jik said.

Sarah looked it up. "Royal Road. Compared with Royal Road, Ivory Ball's a certainty."

We bought our tickets. Sarah disgustedly yelled at Ivory Ball who at least managed fifth, but Royal Road fell entirely by the wayside. The winner was number twelve.

"You should have *added* eleven and one," Sarah said. "You make such silly mistakes."

"What are you staring at?" Jik said.

I was looking attentively at the crowd on the Members' lawn. "Lend me your race-glasses. . . ."

Jik handed them over. I raised them, took a long look, and slowly put them down.

"What is it?" Sarah said anxiously. "What's the matter?"

"That," I said, "has not only torn it, but ripped the bloody works apart."

"What has?"

"Do you see those two men . . . about twenty yards along from the parade ring railing. The man in the morning suit is Hudson Taylor, the man I just had a drink with. He's the managing director of a wine-making firm, and he saw a lot of my cousin Donald when he was over here. And the other man is called Ivor Wexford, and he's the manager of the Yarra River Fine Arts gallery."

"So what?" Sarah said.

"So I can just about imagine the conversation that's going on down there," I said. "Something like, 'Excuse me, sir, but didn't I sell a picture to you recently?' 'Not to me, Mr. Wexford, but to my friend Donald Stuart.' 'And who was that young man I saw you talking to just now?' 'That was Donald Stuart's cousin, Mr. Wexford.' 'And what do you know about him?' 'That he's a painter by trade and drew a picture of you, Mr. Wexford, and asked me for your name.'"

I stopped. "Go on," Jik said.

I watched Wexford and Hudson Taylor stop talking, nod casually to each other, and walk their separate ways. "Ivor Wexford now knows he made a horrible mistake in letting me out of his gallery last night."

Sarah looked searchingly at my face. "You really do think that's very serious."

"Yes, I really do." I loosened a few tightened muscles and tried a smile. "At the least, he'll be on his guard."

"And at the most," Jik said, "He'll come looking for you."

"Er . . ." I said thoughtfully. "What do either of you feel about a spot of instant travel?"

"Where to?"

"Alice Springs?" I said.

CHAPTER NINE

Jik complained all the way to the airport. His Derby clothes would be too hot in Alice. And anyway, he wasn't missing the Melbourne Cup for any little ponce with a bow tie. . . . None of the gripes touched on the fact that he was paying for all our fares with his credit card, as I had left my travellers' cheques in the hotel.

It had been Sarah's idea not to go back there.

"If we're going to vanish, let's get on with it," she said. "It's running back into fires for handbags that gets people burnt."

"You don't have to come," I said tentatively.

"We've been through all that. What do you think the rest of my life would be like if I stopped Jik helping you, and you came to grief?"

"You'd never forgive me."

She smiled ruefully. "You're dead right."

As far as I could tell we had left the racecourse unobserved, and certainly no one car had followed us to the airport. We travelled uneventfully on a half-full aircraft on the first leg to Adelaide, and an even emptier one from there to Alice Springs.

The night air in Alice was hot, as if someone had forgotten to switch off the oven. The luck which had presented us with an available flight as soon as we reached Melbourne airport seemed still to be functioning: a taciturn taxi driver took us straight to a new-looking motel which proved to have room for us.

"The season is over," he grunted, when we congratulated and thanked him. "It will soon be too hot for tourists."

Our rooms were air-conditioned, however. Jik and Sarah's was down on the ground floor, their door opening directly onto a shady covered walk which bordered a small garden with a pool.

Mine, in an adjacent wing across the car park, was two tall floors up, reached by an outside tree-shaded staircase and a long open gallery. The whole place looked greenly peaceful in the scattered spotlights which shone unobtrusively from palms and gums.

At breakfast next morning Sarah said, "You'll never guess. The main street here is Todd Street. So is the river. Todd River."

"Such is fame," I said modestly.

"And there are eleven art galleries."

"She's been reading the Alice Springs Tourist Promotion Association's handout," Jik explained.

"There's also a Chinese Takeaway."

The radio was cheerfully forecasting a noon temperature of thirty-nine, which was a hundred and two in the old Fahrenheit scale. Our walk to the Yarra River gallery, though less than half a mile, was exhausting.

"I suppose one would get used to it, if one lived here," Jik said. "Thank God Sarah's got her hat."

We dodged in and out of the shadows of overhanging trees and the local inhabitants marched around bare-headed as if the branding-iron in the sky was pointing another way. Mercifully, the Yarra River gallery was open, even on a Sunday. Quiet and air-conditioned, it provided chairs near the entrance for flaked-out visitors.

All visible wall space was deep in watercolour paintings typical of the disciples of the Aboriginal painter Namatjira. I vaguely remembered reading somewhere that he'd produced more than two thousand paintings, and certainly his influence on the town where he'd been born had been extraordinary. Eleven art galleries. Mecca for artists. Tourists buying pictures by the ton. He had died, a plaque on the wall said, in Alice Springs hospital on August 8th 1959.

We had been wandering around for a good five minutes before anyone came. Then the plastic strip curtain over a recessed door-way parted, and the gallery keeper came gently through.

"See anything you fancy?" he said.

His voice managed to convey an utter boredom with tourists and a feeling that we should pay up quickly and go away. He was small, languid, long-haired and pale, and had large dark eyes with drooping tired-looking lids. About the same age as Jik and myself, though a lot less robust.

"Do you have any pictures of horses?" I asked.

He glanced at our clothes. Jik and I wore the trousers and shirts in which we'd gone to the races: we had discarded our ties and jackets, but still looked more promising to picture-sellers than if we'd been dressed in denims. "Yes we do, but this month we are displaying works by native Australians." Without discernible enthusiasm he held back half of the strip curtain. "If you wish to see horse paintings, they are in racks through there."

The inner room was bright from skylights. Half of it, as promised, was occupied by well-filled double tiers of racks. The other half was the office and packing and framing department. Directly ahead a glass door led out to a dusty parched-looking garden. Beside the door stood an easel bearing a small canvas with its back towards us. Various signs showed work in progress and recently interrupted.

"Your own?" asked Jik inquisitively, walking over for a look.

The pale gallery keeper made a fluttering movement with his hand as if he would have stopped Jik if he could, and something in Jik's expression attracted me to his side like a magnet.

A chestnut horse, three-quarters view, its elegant head raised as if listening. In the background, the noble lines of a mansion. The rest, a harmonious composition of trees and meadow. The painting, as far as I could judge, was more or less finished.

"That's great," I said with enthusiasm. "Is that for sale? I'd like to buy that."

After the briefest hesitation he said, "Sorry. That's commissioned."

"What a pity! Do tell me your name," I said earnestly.

He was unwillingly flattered. "Harley Renbo."

"Is there anything else of yours here?"

He gestured towards the racks. "One or two. The horse paintings are all in the bottom row, against the wall."

We all three of us pulled out the paintings one by one, making amateur-type comments.

"That's nice," said Sarah, holding a small picture of a fat grey pony with two old-fashioned country boys. "Do you like that?" She showed it to Jik and me.

"Very nice," I said kindly.

Jik turned away as if uninterested. Harley Renbo stood motionless.

"Oh well," Sarah said, shrugging. "I just thought it looked nice." She put it back in the rack and pulled out the next one, which had a flourishing signature: Harley Renbo. Large canvas, varnished, unframed.

"Ah," I said appreciatively. "Yours."

Harley Renbo inclined his head. Jik, Sarah and I gazed at his acknowledged work. Elongated horses set in a Capability Brown landscape. Composition fair, anatomy poor, execution good, originality nil.

At our urging, Harley Renbo brought out two more examples of his work. Neither was better than the first, but one was a great deal smaller. "How much is this?" I asked.

Jik glanced at me sharply, but kept quiet.

Harley Renbo mentioned a sum. "Awfully sorry," I said. "I like your work, but . . ."

The haggling continued politely and we came to the usual conclusion, higher than the buyer wanted, lower than the painter hoped. Jik resignedly lent his credit card and we bore our trophy away.

"You could paint better than that when you were in your cradle," Jik exploded when we were safely out of earshot. "Why the hell did you want to buy that rubbish?"

"Because," I said contentedly, "Harley Renbo is the copier."

"But this," Jik pointed to the parcel under my arm, "Is his own abysmal original work."

"Like fingerprints?" Sarah said. "You can check other things he paints against this"

"Got brains, my wife," Jik said. "But that picture he wouldn't sell was nothing like any Munnings I've ever seen."

"How about Raoul Millais?" I said.

"Jesus."

67

We walked along the scorching street almost without feeling it.

"I don't know about you two," Sarah said, "but I'm going to buy a bikini and spend the rest of the day in the pool."

We all bought swimming things, changed into them, splashed around, and laid ourselves out on towels to dry. It was peaceful in the shady little garden. We were the only people there.

"That picture of a pony and two boys, that you thought was nice," I said to Sarah. "It was a Munnings. A real one."

She sat up abruptly on her towel. "Why ever didn't you say so?"

"I was waiting for our friend Renbo to tell us, but he didn't."

"Munnings had that grey pony for years when he was young," Jik said, "and painted it dozens of times."

"You two do know a lot," Sarah said, lying down again.

"Engineers know all about nuts and bolts," Jik said. "Do we get lunch in this place?"

I looked at my watch. Nearly two o'clock. "I'll go and get it," I said. "What do you want?"

Anything, they said.

"And drink?"

"Cinzano," Sarah said, and Jik nodded. "Dry white."

I put shirt and trousers on over my sun-dried trunks, picked up my room key from the grass, and set off to collect some cash. Walked along to the tree-shaded outside staircase, went up two storeys, and turned onto the blazing hot balcony.

There was a man walking along it towards me, about my own height, build and age; and I heard someone else coming up the stairs at my back. Thought nothing of it. Guests like me. What else?

I was totally unprepared for the attack, and for its ferocity.

CHAPTER TEN

They simply walked up to me, one from in front, one from behind.

They reached me together. They sprang into action like cats. They snatched the dangling room key out of my hand.

68

The struggle, if you could call it that, lasted less than five seconds. They simply picked me up by my legs and armpits and threw me over the balcony.

It probably takes a very short time to fall two storeys. I found it long enough for thinking that my body, which was still whole, was going to be smashed. That disaster, not yet reached, was inevitable. Very odd, and very nasty.

What I actually hit first was one of the young trees growing round the staircase. Its boughs bent and broke and I crashed on through them to the hard driveway beneath.

The monstrous impact was like being wiped out. I felt like pulp.

It was ten minutes, Jik told me later, before he came looking for me: and he came only because he wanted a lemon to go with the Cinzano.

"Jesus Christ Almighty," Jik's voice, low and horrified, near my ear.

I heard him clearly. I'm alive, I thought. Eventually, I opened my eyes. There was no one where Jik's voice had been. Perhaps I'd imagined it. No I hadn't. The world began coming back fast, very sharp and clear. I knew, with increasing insistence, that I hadn't broken my neck and hadn't broken my back. It wasn't so much a matter of which bits of me hurt, as of finding out which didn't.

After a while I heard Jik's voice returning. "He's alive," he said, "and that's about all."

"It's impossible for anyone to fall off our balcony. It's more than waist high." The voice of the reception desk, sharp with anger and anxiety. A bad business for motels, people falling off their balconies.

"Don't . . . panic," I said. It sounded a bit croaky.

"Todd!" Sarah appeared, kneeling on the ground and looking pale.

"You sod," Jik said, standing at my feet and staring down. "You gave us a shock." He was holding a broken-off branch of tree.

"Shall I cancel the ambulance?" said the reception desk hopefully.

"No," I said.

ALICE SPRINGS hospital, even on a Sunday, was as efficient as one would expect from a Flying Doctor base. They investigated and X-rayed and stitched, and presented me with a list.

One broken shoulder blade. (Left.)

Two broken ribs. (Left side. No lung puncture.)

Large contusion, left side of head. (No skull fracture.)

Four jagged tears in skin of trunk, thigh, and left leg. (Stitched.)

Grazes, cuts and contusions on practically all of left side of body.

"Thanks," I said, sighing.

"Thank the tree. You'd've been in a right mess if you'd missed it."

They suggested I stop there for the rest of the day and also all night. "O.K." I said resignedly. "Are my friends still here?"

They were. In the waiting room. Arguing about the favourite for the Melbourne Cup. "Fantastic," Jik said, as I shuffled stiffly in. "He's on his feet."

"Yeah." I perched gingerly on the arm of a chair, feeling like a mummy, wrapped in bandages from neck to waist with my left arm anchored firmly inside.

"Don't damn well laugh," I said.

"No one but a lunatic would fall off that balcony," Jik said.

"Mm," I agreed. "I was pushed."

Their mouths opened like landed fish. I told them exactly what had happened.

"Who were they?" Jik said.

"I don't know. They didn't introduce themselves."

Sarah said, definitely, "You must tell the police."

"Yes," I said. "But first would you see if they've pinched my wallet. Or that picture? They took my room key."

They stared at me in awakening unwelcome awareness.

TWO POLICEMEN came, took notes, and departed. Very non-committal. The locals wouldn't have done it. The town had a constant stream of visitors so, by the law of averages, some would be muggers. Their downbeat attitude suited me fine.

By the time Jik and Sarah came back I'd been given a bed. I felt absolutely rotten, shivering, gripped by shock.

"The police've been to the motel," Jik said. "The picture is missing, and your wallet. We told the police about them, but I don't think they'll do much more about it unless you tell them the whole story."

"I'll think about it," I said.

"So what do we do now?" Sarah asked.

"Well . . . there's no point in staying here any more. Tomorrow we'll go back to Melbourne."

"Thank God," she said, smiling widely. "I thought you were going to want us to miss the Cup."

IN SPITE OF a battery of pills I spent a viciously uncomfortable and wideawake night. Unable to lie flat. Feverishly hot. Throbbing in fifteen places. Every little movement screeched like an engine without oil. I counted my blessings until daybreak. It could have been so very much worse.

When Jik and Sarah turned up at eleven I was still in bed. Sitting up, but not exactly perky.

"God," Sarah said. "You look much worse than yesterday."

"So kind."

"You're never going to make it to Melbourne." She sounded despondent. "So goodbye Cup."

"Nothing to stop you going," I said.

"Don't be so bloody stupid."

Jik sprawled in a visitor's chair. "We went round to the gallery," he said. "It's shut. We also found our way round into the back garden, and looked in through the glass door, and you can guess what we saw."

"Nothing."

"Dead right. No easel with imitation Millais. I'll bet everything the least bit incriminating disappeared yesterday afternoon."

Sarah said, "We asked the girl in the reception desk at the motel if anyone had been asking for us yesterday."

"And they had?"

She nodded. "A man telephoned. She thought it was about midday. He asked if a Mr. Charles Todd was staying there with two friends, and when she said yes, he asked for your room number. He said he had something to deliver."

Some delivery. "Express. Downwards."

"There aren't all that many motels in Alice," Jik said. "It wouldn't have taken long to find us, once they knew we were in the town. I suppose the Melbourne lot telephoned Renbo, and that set the bomb ticking. They must have been apoplectic when they heard you'd bought that picture."

I'd known ever since I'd seen Regina's head that the directing mind was ruthlessly violent. The acts of the team always reflected the nature of the boss. A less savage attitude would have left Regina gagged and bound, not brutally dead.

I had to conclude that it was chiefly this pervading callousness which had led to my being thrown over the balcony. As a positive means of murder, it was too chancy. After all, the two men had not come along to finish the job while I lay unconscious. No, it had been simply a shattering way of getting rid of me while they robbed my room, possibly with the intention of injuring me so badly that I would have to stop poking my nose into their affairs.

Sarah sighed. "Well . . . what are we going to do?"

"Last chance to go home," I said.

"Are you going?" she demanded.

I listened briefly to the fierce plea from my battered shell, and I thought too of Donald in his cold house.

My attackers could reasonably believe they had done a good job of putting me out of action. Presumably they wanted time to tighten up their security, and cover their tracks, so that any investigation I might persuade the police to make would come up against the most respectable of brick walls.

Even if they knew I'd survived, they would not expect any action from me in the immediate future: therefore the immediate future was the best time to act.

Right. Easy enough to convince my brain. From the neck down, a different story.

Sarah listened to my silence. "Quite," she said. "So what do we do next?"

"Well . . ." I said. "First of all, tell the girl in the reception desk at the motel that I'm in a pretty poor state and likely to be in hospital for at least a week."

"No exaggeration," Jik murmured.

"Tell her it's O.K. to pass on that news, if anyone inquires. Tell her you're leaving for Melbourne, pay all our bills, confirm your bookings on the afternoon flight, and cancel mine, and make a normal exit to the airport on the airport bus."

"But what about you?" Sarah said. "When will you be fit to go?"

"With you," I said. "If between you you can think of some unobtrusive way of getting a bandaged mummy onto an aeroplane without anyone noticing."

Jik looked delighted. "I'll do that," he said.

"Telephone the airport and book a seat for me under a different name."

"Right."

"Buy me a shirt and trousers. Mine are in the dustbin."

"And after we get to Melbourne, what then?" Sarah said.

I chewed my lip. "I think we'll have to go back to the Hilton. All our clothes are there, not to mention my passport and travellers' cheques. We don't know if Wexford and Greene ever knew we were staying there, so it may well be a hundred per cent safe. And anyway, where else in Melbourne are we likely to get beds on the night before the Melbourne Cup?"

"And tomorrow," Sarah said. "What about tomorrow?"

Hesitantly I outlined what I had in mind for Cup day. When I had finished, they were both silent.

"So now," I said. "Do you want to go home?"

Sarah stood up. "We'll talk it over," she said soberly. "We'll come back and let you know."

Jik stood also, but I knew from the jut of his beard which way he'd vote. At heart he was more reckless than I.

THEY CAME BACK at two o'clock lugging a large fruit-shop carrier with a bottle of Scotch and a pineapple sticking out of the top.

"Provisions for hospitalized friend," said Jik, whisking them out and putting them on the end of the bed. "Well, Sarah says we go ahead."

I looked searchingly at her face. Her dark eyes stared steadily back, giving assent without joy. She was committed, but from determination, not excitement.

"O.K." I said.

Jik was busy with the carrier. "One pair of medium grey trousers. One light blue cotton shirt."

"Great."

"For leaving Alice Springs, though, we bought something else."

I saw the amusement in both their faces. I said with misgiving, "What else?"

With rising glee they laid out what they had bought for my unobtrusive exit from Alice Springs.

A brilliant orange, red and magenta poncho-type garment which hung loosely over both arms like a cape from shoulders to crutch. Faded jeans cut off and busily frayed at mid-calf. Flip-flop rope-soled sandals. A large pair of sunglasses. Artificial suntan for every visible bit of skin. And to top it all, a large straw sunhat with a two inch raffia fringe round the brim, the sort of hat in favour out in the bush for keeping flies away.

"No one," Jik said with satisfaction, laying out my wardrobe, "will guess you're a walking stretcher case, if you're wearing these."

"More like a walking nut case."

"Not far out," Sarah said dryly.

My exit from hospital was the gift of one of the doctors, who had said he couldn't stop me if I chose to go, but another day's rest would be better.

"I'd miss the Cup," I said, protesting.

"You're crazy."

"Yeah. . . . Would it be possible for you to arrange that the hospital said I was 'satisfactory', and 'progressing' if anyone telephoned to ask, and not on any account to say that I'd left?"

"Whatever for?"

"I'd just like those muggers to think I'm still flat out. For several days, if you don't mind. Until I'm long gone."

74

"You mean you're nervous?"

"You could say so."

"All right. For a couple of days, anyway. I don't see any harm in it, if it will set your mind at rest."

"It would indeed," I said gratefully.

He returned an hour later with a paper for me to sign before I left, Jik's credit card having again come up trumps, and at the sight of me, nearly choked. I had struggled slowly into the clothes and was trying on the hat.

"Are you going to the airport dressed like that?" he said incredulously.

"My friend's idea of suitable travelling gear."

"You're having me on?"

"He's an artist," I said, as if that explained any excesses.

"You'd better let me drive you," he said, sighing. "Then if you feel too rotten I can bring you back."

He drove carefully, his lips twitching. "Anyone who has the courage to go around like that shouldn't worry about a couple of thugs." He dropped me solicitously at the airport door, and departed laughing.

Jik and Sarah were both at the airport when I arrived. They gave me a flickering glance and gazed thereafter at the floor, both of them, they told me later, fighting off terrible fits of giggles at seeing all that finery on the march.

I walked composedly down to the postcard stand and waited there on my feet, for truth to tell it was more comfortable than sitting. Alternately with inspecting the merchandise I took stock of the room. About fifty prospective passengers, highly assorted. Some airline ground-staff, calm and unhurried. A couple of Aborigines with shadowed eyes and patient black faces. No one remotely threatening.

The flight was called. The assorted passengers, including Jik and Sarah, straggled out to the tarmac. Sarah carried the Trans-Australia airline bag she had bought on the way up, containing my new shirt and trousers, and the jacket I'd worn up to Alice.

It was only then that I saw him. The man who had come towards me on the balcony to throw me over.

He had been sitting among the waiting passengers, reading a newspaper which he was now folding up. He stood still, watching Jik and Sarah present their boarding passes at the door and go across the tarmac to the aircraft. When they'd filed up the steps and vanished, he peeled off and made a bee-line in my direction.

My heart lurched painfully. I absolutely could not run.

He looked just the same. Young, strong, purposeful, as well-coordinated as a cat. Coming towards me.

He didn't even give me a glance. Three yards before he reached me he came to a stop beside a wall telephone. I was still sure he would see me, recognize me . . . and do something I would regret. I could feel sweat prickling under the bandages.

"Last call for flight to Adelaide and Melbourne."

I would have to walk past him to get to the door. I unstuck my feet. Walked. Waiting with every awful step for his heavy hand. I got to the door, presented the boarding pass, made it out onto the tarmac.

Couldn't resist glancing back. I could see him through the glass, earnestly telephoning, and not even looking my way.

The walk to the aircraft was all the same quite far enough. God help us all, I thought, if the slightest fright is going to leave me so weak.

CHAPTER ELEVEN

I had a window seat near the rear of the aircraft. After a while I took off the exaggerated hat, laid it on the empty seat beside me, and tried to find a comfortable way to sit, my main frustration being that if I leaned back in the ordinary way my broken shoulder blade didn't care for it. You wouldn't think that one *could* break a shoulder blade.

Oh well . . . I shut my eyes for a bit and wished I didn't still feel so shaky.

"Todd?" Sarah's voice.

I opened my eyes. She had walked towards the back of the aeroplane and was standing in the aisle beside my seat.

"Are you all right?"

"Mm."

She gave me a worried look and went on into the toilet compartment. By the time she came out, I'd assembled a few more wits, and stopped her with the flap of a hand.

"Sarah . . . you were followed to the airport: I think you'll very likely be followed from Melbourne. Tell Jik . . ."

"Is this tail on the aeroplane?" She looked alarmed at the thought.

"No. He telephoned . . . from Alice."

She went away up front to her seat. The aeroplane landed at Adelaide, people got off, people got on, and we took off again for the hour's flight to Melbourne. Halfway there, Jik himself came back to make use of the facilities.

He too paused briefly beside me on the way back.

"Here are the car keys," he said. "Sit in the car, and wait for us. You can't go into the Hilton like that and you're not fit enough to change on your own."

"Of course I am."

"Don't argue. I'll lose any tail, and come back. You wait."

He went without looking back. I picked up the keys and put them in my jeans pocket, and thought grateful thoughts to pass the time.

At disembarkation I dawdled a long way behind Jik and Sarah. My gear attracted more scandalized attention in this solemn financial city, but I didn't care in the least. Nothing like fatigue and anxiety for killing off embarrassment.

Jik and Sarah, with only hand-baggage, walked straight out towards the waiting queue of taxis. The whole airport was bustling with Cup eve arrivals, but only one person, that I could see, was bustling exclusively after my fast-departing friends. Young and eel-like, he slithered through the throng, pushing a young woman with a baby out of the way to grab the next taxi behind Jik's. They'd sent him, I supposed, because he knew Jik by sight. He'd flung turps in his eyes at the Arts Centre.

I wandered around for a bit looking gormless, but as there was no one else who seemed the remotest threat, I eased out to the car park. The night was chilly after Alice Springs. I unlocked the car, climbed into the back, took off the successful hat, and settled to wait for Jik's return.

They were gone nearly two hours, during which time I grew stiffer and ever more uncomfortable and started swearing.

"Sorry," Sarah said breathlessly, pulling open the car door and tumbling into the front seat.

"We had the devil's own job losing the little swine," Jik said, getting in beside me in the back. "Are you all right?"

"Cold, hungry, and cross."

"That's all right, then," he said cheerfully. "He stuck like a bloody little leech. That boy from the Arts Centre."

"Yes, I saw him."

"We thought it would be better not to let him know we'd spotted him," Sarah said. "So we set off to the Naughty Ninety, which is about the only noisy big dine and dance place in Melbourne."

"It was absolutely packed," Jik said. "It cost me ten dollars to get a table. Marvellous for us, though. All dark corners and psychedelic coloured lights. We ordered and paid for some drinks, and read the menu, and then got up and danced."

"He was still there, when we saw him last, standing in the queue for tables just inside the entrance door. We got out through an emergency exit down a passage past some cloakrooms. We'd dumped our bag there when we arrived, and simply collected it again on the way out."

"I don't think he'll know we ducked him on purpose," Jik said. "It's a proper scrum there tonight."

"Great."

With Jik's efficient help I exchanged Tourist, Alice style, for Racing Man, Melbourne Cup, my bandages hidden. Jik drove us back to the Hilton, parked in its car park, and we walked into the front hall as if we'd never been away.

No one took much notice of us. The place was alive with excitement, everyone discussing the chances of the next day's race.

Jik collected our room keys. "No messages," he said.

"Todd," Sarah said. "Jik and I are going to have some food sent up. You'll come as well?"

I nodded. We went up in the lift and along to their room, and ate a subdued supper out of collective tiredness.

"'Night," I said eventually, getting up to go. "And thanks for everything."

"Thank us tomorrow," Sarah said.

THE NIGHT passed. Well, it passed.

In the morning I did a spot of one-handed shaving and some washing, and Jik came up, as he'd insisted, to help with my tie. I opened the door to him in underpants and dressing-gown and endured his comments when I took the latter off.

"God Almighty, is there any bit of you neither blue nor patched?"

"I could have landed face first," I said. "Now, help me rearrange these bandages."

"I'm not touching that lot."

"Oh come on, Jik. Unwrap the swaddling bands. I'm itching like hell underneath and I've forgotten what my left hand looks like."

With a variety of oaths he undid the expert handiwork of the Alice hospital. Under the top layer there was a system of crepe bandages tying my arm in one position, with my hand across my chest and pointing up towards my right shoulder. Also a sort of tight cummerbund of adhesive strapping, presumably to deal with the broken ribs. Also, just below my shoulder blade, a large padded wound dressing, which, Jik kindly told me after a delicate inspection from one corner, covered a mucky looking bit of darning.

"Fasten it up again."

"I have, mate, don't you worry."

There were three similar dressings, two on my left thigh and one, a bit smaller, just below my knee: all fastened both with adhesive strips and tapes with clips. We left them all untouched.

"What the eye doesn't see doesn't scare the patient," Jik said. "What else do you want done?"

"Untie my arm."

"You'll fall apart."

"Risk it."

He laughed and undid another series of clips and knots. I tentatively straightened my elbow. Nothing much happened except that the hovering ache and soreness stopped hovering and came down to earth.

From the bits and pieces we designed a new and simpler sling which gave my elbow good support but was less of a strait-jacket. I could get my hand out easily, and also my whole arm, if I wanted.

"That's fine," I said.

WE ALL MET downstairs in the hall at ten thirty.

Around us a buzzing atmosphere of anticipation pervaded the chattering throng of would-be winners who were filling the morning with celebratory drinks. The hotel, I saw, had raised a fountain of real champagne at the entrance to the bar-lounge.

"Free booze," Jik said reverently, picking up a glass and holding it under the prodigal bubbly. "Not bad," he added, tasting.

Sarah was wearing a cream dress with gold buttons; neat, tailored, a touch severe. An impression of the military for a day in the front line.

"Don't forget," I said. "If you think you see Wexford or Greene, make sure they see you."

"Give me another look at their faces," she said.

I pulled the small sketch book out of my pocket and handed it to her again, though she'd studied it on and off all the previous evening through supper. "As long as they look like this, maybe I'll know them," she said, sighing.

I glanced at the clock. We all finished the champagne and put down the glasses. "Back a winner for me," I said to Sarah, kissing her cheek.

"Your luck might run out."

I grinned. "Back number eleven. See you later."

I watched them through the door and wished strongly that we

were all three going for a simple day out to the Melbourne Cup. The effort ahead was something I would have been pleased to avoid. The beginning, I supposed, was the worst. Once you were in, you were committed. Sighing, I went to the cashier's end of the reception desk and changed a good many travellers' cheques into cash. Maisie's generosity had been far-sighted. There would be little enough left by the time I got home.

Four hours to wait. I spent them upstairs in my room calming my nerves by drawing the view from the window. Half an hour before the Cup was due to be run I left the Hilton on foot, walking along towards Swanston Street and the main area of shops. They were all shut, of course. Melbourne Cup day was a national public holiday. Everything stopped for the Cup.

I had taken my left arm out of its sling and threaded it gingerly through the sleeves of my shirt and jacket. A man with his jacket hunched over one shoulder was too memorable. I found that by hooking my thumb into the waistband of my trousers I got quite good support.

Jik arrived exactly on time, fifteen minutes before the race which annually stopped Australia in its tracks, driving up Swanston Street in the hired car and turning smoothly round the corner to where I stood waiting. He stopped outside the Yarra River Fine Arts gallery. He got out, opened the boot, and put on a brown coat-overall, of the sort worn by storemen.

I walked quietly along towards him. He brought out a small radio, switched it on, and stood it on top of the car. The commentator's voice emerged tinnily, giving details of the runners currently walking round the parade ring at Flemington races.

"Hello," he said unemotionally, when I reached him. I nodded, and walked to the door of the gallery. It was solidly shut. Jik dived again into the boot, which held further fruits of his shopping expedition in Alice Springs.

"Gloves," he said, handing me one pair and putting the others on himself. They were of white cotton, and looked a lot too clean. I wiped the backs of mine along the wings of Jik's car, and he gave me a glance and did the same with his.

"Handles and impact adhesive."

81

One or two people passed, paying no attention. We were not supposed to park there, but no one told us to move. He gave me the two handles to hold. They were sturdy, chromium plated, big enough for gripping with the whole hand. I held them bottom side up while Jik covered the screw-plate areas at each end with adhesive. We couldn't screw these handles where we wanted them. They had to be stuck.

We walked across the pavement to the gallery. Its doorway was recessed at the right-hand end of the front with a window joining it to the front display window at right angles to the street. To this sheet of glass Jik stuck the handles, at just above waist height. He tested them after a minute, and he couldn't pull them off. We returned to the car.

One or two more people passed, turning their heads to listen to the radio on the car roof, smiling in brotherhood at the universal national interest. The street was noticeably emptying as the crucial time drew near.

". . . *Vinery carries the colours of Mr. Hudson Taylor of Adelaide and must be in with a good outside chance . . .*"

"Stop listening to the damn race!" Jik said sharply.

"Sorry."

We walked back to the entrance to the gallery, Jik carrying the sort of diamond glass cutter used in picture framing. Without casting a glance around for possible onlookers, he applied the cutting edge, using considerable strength as he pushed the professional tool round the outside of the window pane. I stood behind him to block any passing curious glances.

"Hold the right-hand handle," he said, as he started on the last of the four sides, the left-hand vertical.

I stepped past him and slotted my hand through the grip. None of the few people left in the street paid the slightest attention.

"Put your knee against the glass. Gently, for God's sake."

I did what he said. He finished the fourth cut. "Press smoothly."

I did that. Jik's knee, too, was firmly against the glass. With his left hand he gripped the chromium handle, and with the palm of his right he began jolting the top perimeter of the heavy pane.

Jik had cut a lot of glass in his time, even if not in exactly these

82

circumstances. The sheet cracked away evenly all round under our pressure and parted with hardly a splinter. The weight fell suddenly onto the handle I held in my right hand, and Jik steadied the now free sheet of glass with hands and knees and blasphemy.

"Don't let go!"

"No."

Jik took over the right-hand handle from me. Without any seeming inconvenience he pivoted the sheet of glass so that it opened like a door. He stepped through the hole, carried the glass in, and propped it against the wall to the right of the more conventional way in.

He came out, and we went over to the car. From there, barely ten feet away, one could not see that the gallery was not still securely shut. There were by now in any case very few to look.

I picked up the radio. ". . . *Most jockeys have now mounted and the horses will soon be going out onto the course . . .*" Jik exchanged the glass cutter for a metal saw, a hammer and a chisel, and shut the boot, and we walked through the unorthodox entrance as if it was all in the day's work. Often only the furtive manner gave away the crook.

"The stairs are at the back," I said.

"Lead on."

We walked the length of the plushy green carpet and down the beckoning stairs. There was a bank of electric switches at the top: we pressed those lighting the basement and left the upstairs lot off.

Heart-thumping time, I thought. It would take only a policeman to walk along and start fussing about a car parked in the wrong place to set Cassavetes and Todd on the road to jail.

". . . *cantering down to the start, and the excitement is mounting here now . . .*"

I put the radio on Wexford's desk, where it sat like an hourglass, ticking away the minutes as the sands ran out.

Jik turned his attention to the desk drawers, but they were all unlocked. One of the waist-high line of filing cabinets, however, proved to be secure. Jik's strength and chisel soon ensured that it didn't remain that way.

In his wake I looked through the drawers. Nothing much in

84

them except catalogues and stationery. In the broken-open filing cabinet, a gold mine.

Not that I realized it at first. The contents looked merely like ordinary files with ordinary headings. Letters, insurance policies . . . I didn't really know what I was looking for, which made it all a bit difficult.

"*. . . handlers are beginning to load the runners into the starting stalls, and I see Vinery playing up . . .*"

There were a good many framed pictures in the office, some on the walls but even more standing in a row on the floor. Jik began looking through them at high speed, like flicking through a rack of record albums.

"Look at this," he said suddenly.

He had reached the end of the row and was looking at the first of three unframed canvases. It had Alfred Munnings written large and clear in the right-hand bottom corner. It was a picture of four horses with jockeys cantering on a racecourse: and the paint wasn't dry. The two other pictures were exactly the same.

"God Almighty," Jik said in awe.

"*. . . Vinery carries only fifty-one kilograms and has a good barrier position so it's not impossible . . .*"

"Keep looking," I said. We needed more than those Munnings copies and I still hadn't found a thing. I went back to the files. One marked Overseas Customers. My eyes flicked over the heading and then went back. Overseas Customers. I opened the file. Lists of people, sorted into countries. Pages of them. Names and addresses.

"*. . . only Derriby now to enter the stalls . . .*"

England. A long list. Not alphabetical. Too many to read through in a short time. A good many of the names had been crossed out.

"*. . . They're running! This is the moment you've all been waiting for, and Special Bet is out in front . . .*"

Donald Stuart. Donald Stuart, crossed out. Wrenstone House, Shropshire, England. Crossed out. I practically stopped breathing.

I showed Jik. "We've got less than three minutes before the race ends and Melbourne comes back to life," I said, shoving the filing drawer shut. "Take this file and the paintings and let's go."

". . . *down the backstretch by the Maribyrnong River it's still Special Bet with Vinery second now . . .*"

I picked up the radio and Jik's tools, and we went up the stairs. Switched off the lights. Eased round into a view of the car. It stood there, quiet and unattended, just as we'd left it. No policemen. Everyone elsewhere, listening to the race.

We walked steadily down the gallery. The commentator's voice rose in excitement.

". . . *Vinery in third with Wonderbug, and here comes Ringwood very fast on the stands side . . .*"

Nothing stirred out on the street. I went first through our hole in the glass. Jik carried out the plunder and stacked it in the boot. He took the tools from my hands and stored them also. We climbed into the car.

". . . *Coming to the line it's Ringwood by a length from Wonderbug, with Newshound third, then Derriby, then . . .*"

Jik started the engine and drove away.

". . . *Might be a record time. Just listen to the cheers. The result again. The result of the Melbourne Cup. In the frame . . . first Ringwood, owned by Mr. Robert Khami . . . second, Wonderbug . . .*"

"Phew," Jik said, his beard jaunty. "That wasn't a bad effort. We might hire ourselves out sometime for stealing politicians' papers." He chuckled fiercely.

"It's an overcrowded field," I said.

We were both feeling the euphoria which follows the safe deliverance from danger. "Take it easy," I said. "We've a long way to go."

He drove to the Hilton, parked, and carried the file and pictures up to my room. He moved economically and fast, losing as little time as possible before returning to Sarah on the racecourse and acting as if he'd never been away.

"We'll be back here as soon as we can," he promised.

Two seconds after he'd shut my door there was a knock on it. I opened it. Jik stood there. "I'd better know," he said. "What won the Cup?"

CHAPTER TWELVE

When he'd gone I looked closely at the spoils.

The more I saw, the more certain it became that we had hit the absolute jackpot. I began to wish we hadn't wasted time in establishing that Jik and Sarah were at the races. It made me nervous, waiting for them in the Hilton. Instinct urged immediate departure.

The list of Overseas Customers would to any other eyes have seemed the most harmless of documents. Each page had three columns, a narrow left-hand column for dates, the broad centre one for names and addresses, and the right-hand column for the name of the painting and of the gallery in Australia or New Zealand where the picture had been purchased. I searched rapidly down all the other crossed-out names in the England sector. Maisie Matthews's name was not among them.

Damn, I thought. Why wasn't it? I turned all the papers over rapidly. As far as I could see all the overseas customers came from English-speaking countries, and the proportion of crossed-out names was about one in three. If every crossing out represented a robbery, there had been literally hundreds since the scheme began.

At the back of the file I found there was a second and separate section, again divided into pages for each country. The lists in this section were much shorter.

England. Halfway down. Mrs. M. Matthews, Treasure Holme, Worthing, Sussex. Crossed out. And the date in the left-hand column looked like the date on which Maisie had bought her picture. It seemed that this second section might concern the sale of copies rather than of originals.

I put down the file and sat for five minutes staring at the wall, thinking. My conclusions were that I had a great deal to do before Jik and Sarah came back from the races.

I looked again at the three identical finished paintings which we had also brought away. The technical standard of the work couldn't be faulted. The paintings did look very much like Munnings's own, and would do much more so after they had dried thoroughly and been varnished. The brushwork throughout was painstaking and controlled. Nothing slapdash. No time skimped. The quality of care was the same as in the Raoul Millais copy at Alice.

I was looking, I knew, at the true worth of Harley Renbo.

All three paintings were perfectly legal. It was never illegal to copy: only to attempt to sell the copy as real.

I thought it all over for a bit longer, and then set rapidly to work.

The Hilton, when I went downstairs an hour later was most amiable and helpful. Certainly, they could do what I asked. Certainly, I could use the photo-copying machine, come this way. Certainly, I could pay my bill now, and leave later.

I thanked them for their many excellent services.

"Our pleasure," they said.

UPSTAIRS AGAIN, waiting for Jik and Sarah, I packed all my things, then did my best at rigging the bandages back into something like the Alice shape, with my hand inside across my chest. No use pretending that it wasn't a good deal more comfortable that way than the dragging soreness of letting it all swing free.

As I buttoned my shirt over the top, the telephone rang. Jik's voice, sounding hard and dictatorial. "Charles, will you please come down to our room at once."

"Well . . ." I said hesitantly. "Is it important?"

"Bloody chromic oxide!" he said explosively. "Can't you do anything without arguing?"

Christ, I thought. A lot of Jik's great oaths galloped across my mind, wasting precious time.

I took a breath. "Give me ten minutes," I said. "I need ten minutes. I'm . . . er . . . in my underpants."

"Thank you, Charles," he said. The telephone clicked as he disconnected.

Stifling my fear I picked up the telephone and made a series of internal calls.

"Please could you send a porter up right away to room seventeen eighteen to collect Mr. Cassavetes's bags?"

"Housekeeper . . . ? Please will you send someone along urgently to seventeen eighteen to clean the room as Mr. Cassavetes has been sick. . . ."

"Please will you send the nurse along to seventeen eighteen at once as Mr. Cassavetes has a severe pain. . . ."

"Please will you send four bottles of your best champagne and ten glasses up to seventeen eighteen immediately. . . ."

"Please bring coffee for three to seventeen eighteen at once. . . ."

"Electrician? All the electrics have fused in room seventeen eighteen, please come at once."

"The water is overflowing in the bathroom, please send the plumber urgently."

Who else was there? I ran my eye down the list of possible services. Television, why not? "Please would you see to the television in room seventeen eighteen. There is smoke coming from the back and it smells like burning. . . ."

That should do it, I thought. I made one final call for myself, asking for a porter to collect my bags. Right on, they said. Ten dollar tip, I said, if the bags could be down in the hall within five minutes. No sweat, an Australian voice assured me happily. Coming right that second.

I left my door ajar for the porter and rode down in the lift to the corridor outside Jik and Sarah's room. My ten minutes had gone, and it was still a broad empty expanse.

I fretted.

The first to arrive was the waiter with the champagne, and he came not with a tray but a trolley, complete with ice buckets and spotless white cloths. It couldn't possibly have been better.

As he stopped outside Jik's door, two other figures turned into the corridor, hurrying, and behind them came a cleaner slowly pushing another trolley of linen and buckets and brooms.

I said to the waiter, "Thank you so much for coming so quickly." I gave him a ten dollar note. "Please go and serve the champagne straight away."

He grinned, and knocked on Jik's door. After a pause, Jik opened it. He looked tense.

"Your champagne, sir," said the waiter.

89

"But I didn't . . ." Jik began. He caught sight of me suddenly, where I stood a little back from his door. I made waving-in motions with my hand, and a faint grin appeared to lighten his anxiety. He retreated into the room, followed by trolley and waiter.

At a rush, after that, came the electrician, the plumber and the television man. I gave them each ten dollars and thanked them for coming so promptly. "I had a winner," I said. They took the money with more grins and Jik opened the door to their knock.

He looked across to me in rising comprehension, flung wide his door and invited them in with all his heart.

"Give them some champagne," I said.

After that, in quick succession, came the porter, the man with the coffee, and the nurse. I gave them all ten dollars from my mythical winnings and invited them to join the party. Finally came the cleaner, pushing her top-heavy load. She took the ten dollars, congratulated me on my good fortune, and entered the crowded and noisy fray.

It was up to Jik, I thought. I couldn't do any more.

He and Sarah suddenly popped out like the corks from the gold-topped bottles. I gripped Sarah's wrist and tugged her towards me. "Push the cleaning trolley through the door and turn it over," I said to Jik.

He wasted no time. The brooms crashed to the carpet inside the room and Jik pulled the door shut after him.

Sarah and I were already running on our way to the lifts. She looked extremely pale and I knew that whatever had happened in their room had been almost too much for her. Jik sprinted along after us. There were six lifts and one never had to wait more than a few seconds for one to arrive. The seconds this time seemed like hours. The doors slid open, and we leapt inside. The doors closed.

The lift descended, smooth and fast. "Where's the car?" I said.

"Car park."

"Get it and come round to the side door. And Sarah—my satchel will be in the hall. Will you carry it for me?"

She looked vaguely at my one-armed state, my jacket swinging loosely over my left shoulder. "Yes . . . all right."

90

The foyer had filled with people returning from the Cup. All to the good, I thought.

My suitcase and satchel stood waiting near the front entrance, guarded by a young porter. I parted with another ten dollars. "Thank you very much," I said.

"No sweat," he said cheerfully. "Can I get you a taxi?"

I shook my head. I picked up the suitcase and Sarah the satchel and we headed out of the door. Turned right, hurried, turned right again, round to the side where I'd told Jik we'd meet him.

"He's not here," Sarah said with rising panic.

"He'll come," I said encouragingly. "We'll just go on walking to meet him."

We walked. I kept looking back nervously for signs of pursuit, but there was none. Jik came round the corner on two wheels and stopped beside us. Sarah scrambled into the front, I and my suitcase in the back. Jik made a hair-raising U turn and took us away from the Hilton at an illegal speed.

"Wowee," he said, laughing with released tension. "Whatever gave you that idea?"

"The Marx Brothers."

"Where are we going?" Sarah said.

"Have you noticed," Jik said, "how my wife always brings us back to basics?"

We drove randomly north and east through seemingly endless suburban developments.

"You do realize we skipped out of the Hilton without paying," Sarah said.

"No we didn't," Jik said. "According to our clothes, we are still resident. I'll ring them up later."

"But Todd . . ."

"I did pay," I said. "Before you got back."

She looked slightly happier. "How did you know there was anyone in our room besides Jik and me?" she said. "He couldn't risk warning you." Her voice quivered. The tears weren't far from the surface.

"Jik told me," I said. "First, he called me Charles, which he never does, so I knew something was wrong. Second, he told me it was Mr. Greene putting pressure on you both. Chromic oxide is the pigment in green paint."

"Green paint!" The tearful moment passed. "You really are both extraordinary," Sarah said.

"Long practice," Jik said cheerfully.

"Tell me what happened," I said.

"We left before the last race, to avoid the traffic, and we just drove back normally to the Hilton. We'd only been in our room about a minute when there was this knock on the door, and when I opened it they just pushed in. . . ."

"They?"

"Three of them. One was Greene. We both knew him straight away, from your drawing. Another was the boy from the Arts Centre. The third was all biceps and beetle brows, with his brains in his fists." As he drove Jik absentmindedly rubbed an area south of his heart.

"It was all so quick . . ." he said apologetically. "They just crammed in . . . the next thing I knew they'd got hold of Sarah and were twisting her arm and the boy had this ruddy great cigarette lighter with a flame like a blow torch just a couple of inches from her cheek . . . and I was a bit groggy . . . and Greene said they'd burn her if I didn't get you . . . and I couldn't fight them all at once."

"Stop apologizing," I said.

"Yeah . . . well, so I rang you. I told Greene you'd be ten minutes because you were in your underpants, but I think he heard you anyway because he was standing right beside me. I didn't know really whether you'd cottoned on, but I hoped to God . . . and you should have seen their faces when the waiter pushed the trolley in. Beetle-brows let go of Sarah and the boy just stood there with his mouth open and the cigarette lighter flaring like an oil refinery . . ."

"Greene said we didn't want the champagne and to take it away," Sarah said. "But Jik and I said yes we did, and Jik asked the waiter to open it at once."

"Before he got the first cork out the others all began coming . . .

and then they were all picking up glasses . . . and the room was filling up . . . and Greene and the boy and Beetle-brows were all on the window side of the room, sort of pinned in by the trolley and all those people . . . and I just grabbed Sarah and we ducked round the edge. The last I saw, Greene and the others were trying to push through, but our guests were pretty thick on the ground by then . . . and I should think the cleaning trolley was just enough to give us that start to the lift."

"They must all have thought you mad," Sarah said.

"Anything goes on Cup day," I said. "And the staff of the Hilton would be used to eccentric guests."

"What if Greene had had a gun?" Sarah said.

I smiled at her twistedly. "He would have had to wave it around in front of a hell of a lot of witnesses. And he was a long way from the front door." I bit my thumbnail. "Er . . . how did he know I was in the Hilton?"

There was a tangible silence.

"Greene said they'd burn my face if Jik didn't tell them where you were," Sarah said finally. "He didn't want to . . . but he had to . . . so I told them, so that it wouldn't be him . . . I suppose that sounds stupid."

I thought it sounded extraordinarily moving. I smiled at her. "So they didn't know I was there, to begin with?"

Jik shook his head. "I think all they knew was that you weren't still in hospital in Alice Springs."

"Did they know about our robbery?"

"I'm sure they didn't."

I grinned. "They'll be schizophrenic when they find out."

We stopped at a modern motel which had bright coloured strings of triangular flags fluttering across the forecourt. A far cry from the Hilton, but at least the rooms we took were clean.

We ate in a small restaurant nearby, with people at tables all around us talking about what they'd backed in the Cup.

"Good heavens," Sarah exclaimed. "I'd forgotten about your winnings on Ringwood."

"But . . ." I began.

"It was number eleven!"

"I don't believe it."

She opened her handbag and produced a fat wad of notes. Somehow, in all the mêlée in the Hilton, she had managed to emerge with the cream leather pouch still swinging from her arm. The strength of the instinct which kept women attached to their handbags had often astounded me, but never more than that day.

"It was forty to one," she said "I put twenty dollars on for you, so you've got eight hundred dollars, and I think it's disgusting."

"Share it," I said laughing. "I owe most of it to Jik, anyway."

"Keep it," he said. "We'll add and subtract later. Do you want me to cut your steak?"

"Please." He sliced away neatly at my plate, and pushed it back, with the fork placed ready.

"What else happened at the races?" I said. "Who did you see?" The steak tasted good, and I realized that in spite of all the sore patches I had at last lost the overall feeling of sickness. Things were on the mend, it seemed.

"We didn't see Greene," Jik said. "Or Wexford, or the boy, or Beetle-brows."

"I'd guess they saw you and simply followed you back to the Hilton."

"We never spotted them," Jik groaned. "There was a whole mass of traffic."

"We saw a girl I know in Sydney," Sarah said. "We watched the first two races with her. And Jik and I were talking to a photographer we both knew just after he got back . . . so it would be pretty easy to prove Jik was at the races all afternoon, like you wanted."

"We even talked to that man you met on Saturday," Jik said. "Hudson Taylor. The one you saw talking to Wexford."

"He asked if you were at the Cup," Sarah said. "He said he'd been going to ask you along for another drink. We said we'd tell you he'd asked."

"Another commission down the drain," I said. "He would have had Vinery painted if he'd won."

"Anyway," Sarah said cheerfully, "you won more on Ringwood than you'd've got for the painting."

94

I looked pained, and Jik laughed.

We drank coffee, went back to the motel, and divided to our separate rooms. Five minutes later Jik knocked on my door.

"Thought you might come," I said.

He sat in the armchair, his gaze falling on my suitcase, which lay flat on one of the divans. "What did you do with the stuff we took from the gallery?"

I told him.

"You don't mess about, do you?" he said.

"A few days from now," I said, "I'm going home."

"And until then?"

"Um . . . until then, I aim to stay one jump ahead of everyone. New Zealand, I thought."

"That should be far enough," Jik said dryly.

"Not you. Not from here on. This is where you take Sarah home."

He slowly shook his head. "I don't reckon it would be any safer than staying with you. We're too easy to find. What's to stop Wexford from marching onto the boat with a bigger threat than a cigarette lighter? And anyway . . ." the old fire gleamed in his eye ". . . it will be a great game. Cat and mouse."

More like a bullfight, I thought, with myself waving the cape to invite the charge. Or a conjurer, attracting attention to one hand while he did the trick with the other. On the whole I preferred the notion of the conjurer. There seemed less likelihood of being gored.

CHAPTER THIRTEEN

After Jik had gone back to Sarah I made a telephone call. It was harder to arrange from the motel than it would have been from the Hilton, but the line was loud and clear.

"You got my cable?" I said.

"I've been waiting for your call for half an hour."

"Sorry."

"What do you want?"

"I've sent you a letter," I said. "I want to tell you what's in it."

"But . . ."

"Just listen," I said. "And talk after." I spoke for quite a long time to a response of grunts from the far end.

"Are you sure of all this?"

"Positive about most," I said. "Some of it's a guess. Er . . . there's one other thing. Can I reach you by telex if I want to get a message to you in a hurry?"

"Telex? Wait a minute."

I waited.

"Yes, here you are." A number followed. I wrote it down. "Address any message to me personally and head it urgent."

"Right," I said. "And could you get an answer to a couple of questions for me?" He listened, and said he could. "Thank you very much," I said, "And goodnight."

I spent a good deal of the night studying the two lists of "Overseas Customers", mostly because I still found it difficult to lie comfortably to sleep, and partly because I had nothing else to read.

All the pictures in the shorter section had been sold within the past three years. The first dates in the long first section were five and a half years old.

I wondered which had come first, five and a half years ago: the gallery or the idea. Had Wexford originally been a full-time crook deliberately setting up an imposing front, or a formerly honest art dealer struck by criminal possibilities? Judging from the respectable air of the gallery and what little I'd seen of Wexford himself, I would have guessed the latter. But the violence lying just below the surface didn't match.

I sighed, put down the lists, and switched off the light.

ON WEDNESDAY MORNING we checked out of the motel, packed my baggage into the boot of the car, and sat in the passenger seats to plan the day.

"Can't we please get our clothes from the Hilton?" Sarah said, sounding depressed.

Jik and I said "no" together.

"I'll ring them now," Jik said. "I'll get them to pack all our things and keep them safe for us, and I'll tell them I'll send a cheque for the bill." He levered himself out of the car again and went off.

"Buy what clothes you need out of my winnings from the race," I said.

She shook her head. "I've got some money. It's not that. It's just . . . I wish all this was over."

"It will be, soon," I said neutrally.

She sighed. "You may think, Todd, that I don't know Jik is a complicated character, but you've only got to look at his paintings . . . I'm no fool, I know that in the end whatever it is that drives him to paint like that will come back again. . . . But I think these first few months together are precious. I have the feeling that I've lost the rest of that golden time."

I looked away from her, out of the window.

Jik came back with a satisfied air. "That's all fixed. They said there's a letter for you, Todd, delivered by hand a few minutes ago. They asked me for a forwarding address."

"What did you say?"

"I said you'd call them yourself."

"Right. . . . Well, let's get going."

"Where to?"

"New Zealand, don't you think?"

"New Zealand?" Sarah said. "I don't see why we have to go so far. Jik said you found enough in the gallery to blow the whole thing wide open."

"Um . . ." I said. "Because we don't want to blow it wide open yet. We want to hand it to the police in full working order. I want Wexford and Greene to spend all their energies looking for us in New Zealand and not clearing away every vestige of evidence here in Melbourne. So that when the police start moving, there'll be plenty left for them to find."

Jik nodded. "Todd's got that list, and the pictures we took. And they'll want them back. Todd wants them to concentrate exclusively on that, because if they think they can get them back and shut us up . . ."

Sarah looked from me to him and back again. A sort of hopeless calm took over. "If they think they can get everything back and shut us up," she said, "they will be actively searching for us in order to kill us. And they will surely be watching here at the airport."

If they weren't, I thought, we'd have to lay a trail. "They can't do much in public," I said comfortingly.

We bought tickets to Auckland, leaving at lunchtime.

Till then we wandered around the airport shops, buying yet more toothbrushes and so on for Jik and Sarah, and another airline bag. There was no sign of Wexford or Greene or the boy or Beetle-brows or Renbo, or even the tough who'd been on watch at Alice Springs. If they'd seen us without us seeing them, we couldn't tell.

"I think I'll ring the Hilton," I said.

Jik nodded. I put the call through with him and Sarah sitting near, within sound and sight.

"I called about a forwarding address . . ." I told the reception desk. "I can't really give you one. I'll be in New Zealand. I'm flying to Auckland in an hour or two."

They asked for instructions about the hand-delivered letter.

"Er . . . Would you mind opening it, and reading it to me?"

Certainly, they said. Their pleasure. The letter was from Hudson Taylor, saying he was sorry to have missed me at the races, and that if while I was in Australia I would like to see round a vineyard, he would be pleased to show me his.

Thanks, I said. Our pleasure, sir, they said. If anyone asked for me, I said, would they please mention where I'd gone. They would. Certainly. Their pleasure.

During the next hour Jik called the car-hire firm about settling their account and leaving the car in the airport car park, and I checked my suitcase through with Air New Zealand. Passports were no problem: I had mine with me, and for Jik and Sarah they were unnecessary, as passage between New Zealand and Australia was as unrestricted as between England and Ireland.

It was again only when our flight was called that I spotted the spotter. A neat day dress, neat hair, unremarkable handbag and shoes. A calm concentrated face. I saw her because she was staring at Sarah. She was standing outside the departure bay, looking in. The woman who had welcomed me into the Yarra River Fine Arts, and given me a catalogue, and let me out again afterwards.

I looked away instantly, hoping she wouldn't know I'd seen her, or wouldn't know at least that I'd recognized her. Jik, Sarah and I stood up and drifted with everyone else towards the departure doors. In their glass I could see the woman's reflection: standing still, watching us go. I walked out towards the aircraft and didn't look back.

THE SHOPS IN AUCKLAND, it appeared, were in Queen Street, and still open for another hour. Sarah was adamant. "I must have some clothes," she said.

Jik and I sat in the rented car, waiting and watching the world go by. "The dolly-birds fly out of their office cages about now," Jik said happily.

"What of it?"

"I sit and count the ones with no bras."

"And you a married man."

"Old habits die hard."

We had counted eight definites and one doubtful by the time Sarah returned. She was wearing a light olive skirt with a pink shirt, and reminded me of pistachio ice cream.

"That's better," she said, tossing two well-filled carriers onto the back seat. "Off we go, then."

The therapeutic value of the new clothes totally amazed me. Sarah seemed to feel safer if she looked fresh and clean, her spirits rising accordingly.

Jik drove us from Auckland to Wellington; eight hours in the car.

We stopped overnight in a motel in the town of Hamilton, south of Auckland, and went on in the morning. No one followed us, molested us or spied on us. As far as I could be, I was sure no one had picked us up in the northern city.

Wexford must know, all the same, that I had the Overseas Customers list, showing the galleries he operated in New Zealand.

He couldn't guess which one I'd pick to visit, but he could and would make his plans accordingly. So in the gallery in Wellington, he'd be ready. . . .

There were so many of them, I thought. Wexford and Greene. The boy. Harley Renbo. Two toughs at Alice Springs, one of whom I knew by sight, and one (the one who'd been behind me), whom I didn't. The one I didn't know might, or might not, be Beetle-brows. If he wasn't, Beetle-brows was extra.

And now the woman. And perhaps another one, somewhere.

Nine at least. Maybe ten. How could I possibly tangle all that lot up without getting crunched? Or worse, getting Sarah crunched, or Jik. Every time I moved, the serpent grew another head.

I wondered who did the actual robberies. Did they send their own two (or three) toughs overseas, or did they contract out to local labour, so to speak. If they sent their own toughs, was it one of them who had killed Regina?

Had I already met Regina's killer? Had he thrown me over the balcony at Alice? I pondered uselessly, and added one more twist . . . Was he waiting ahead in Wellington?

We passed the turning to Rotorua and the land of hot springs. Anyone for a boiling mud pack, Jik asked. There was a power station farther on run by steam jets from underground, Sarah said, and horrid black craters stinking of sulphur, and the earth's crust was so thin in places that it vibrated and sounded hollow. She had been taken round a place called Waiotapu when she was a child, she said, and had had terrible nightmares afterwards, and she didn't want to go back.

"Pooh," Jik said dismissively. "They only have earthquakes every other Thursday."

We reached the capital in the afternoon and booked into the Townhouse Hotel because of its splendid view over the harbour. With such marvellous coastal scenery, I thought, it would have been a disgrace if the cities of New Zealand had been ugly. Wellington, new and cared for, had life and character to spare.

We looked up Wexford's Wellington gallery, the Ruapehu Fine Arts, in the telephone directory.

100

"We can easily find it," Jik said. "But what do we do when we get there?"

"Make faces at them through the window?"

"You'd be crazy enough for that, too," Sarah said.

"And after all," Jik said, "we do want them to know we're here in Wellington."

"So how do we do it?"

I grinned at her. "We address ourselves to the telephone."

In the end Sarah herself made the call.

"Is that the Ruapehu Fine Arts gallery? It is? I wonder if you can help me. . . ." she said. "I would like to speak to whoever is in charge. Yes, I know, but it is important. Yes, I'll wait." She rolled her eyes and put her hand over the mouthpiece. "She sounded like a secretary. New Zealand, anyway."

"You're doing great," I said.

"Oh . . . Hello? Yes. Could you tell me your name, please?" Her eyes suddenly opened wide. "*Wexford*. Oh, er . . . Mr. Wexford, I've just had a visit from three extraordinary people who wanted to see a painting I bought from you some time ago. Quite extraordinary people. They said you'd sent them. I didn't believe them. I wouldn't let them in. But I thought perhaps I'd better check with you. Did you send them to see my painting?"

There was some agitated squawking from the receiver.

"Describe them? A young man with fair hair and a beard, and another young man with an injured arm, and a bedraggled looking girl. I sent them away. I didn't like the look of them."

She grimaced over the phone and listened to more squawks.

"No, of course I didn't give them any information. I told you I didn't like the look of them. Where do I live? Why, right here in Wellington. Well, thank you so much Mr. Wexford, I am so pleased I called you."

She put the receiver down while it was still squawking.

"He was asking me for my name," she said.

"What a girl," Jik said. "What an actress, my wife."

Wexford. Wexford himself. It had *worked*.

"So now that they know we're here," I said, "would you like to go off somewhere else until I can fix the Melbourne police?"

101

"Oh no," Sarah said instinctively. She looked out of the window across the busy harbour. "It's lovely here, and we've been travelling all day already."

"And they won't find us just by checking the hotels by telephone," Jik pointed out. "Even if it occurred to them to try the Townhouse, they'd be asking for Cassavetes and Todd, not Andrews and Peel."

"Are we Andrews and Peel?" Sarah asked.

"We're Andrews. Todd's Peel."

"So nice to know," she said.

Mr. and Mrs. Andrews and Mr. Peel took dinner in the hotel restaurant without mishap, Mr. Peel having discarded his sling for the evening on the grounds that it was a bit too easy to notice. Mr. Andrews had declined, on the same consideration, to remove his beard.

We went in time to our separate rooms, and so to bed. I spent a jolly hour unsticking the Alice bandages from my leg and admiring the hemstitching. The tree had made tears that were far from the orderly cuts of operations, and as I inspected the long curving lines I reckoned that those doctors had done an expert job. It was four days since the fall, during which time I hadn't exactly led an inactive life, but none of their handiwork had come adrift. I realized I had progressed from feeling terrible all the time to scarcely feeling anything worth mentioning. It was astonishing, I thought, how quickly the human body repaired itself, given the chance.

I covered the mementoes with fresh adhesive plaster bought that morning in Hamilton for the purpose, and even found a way of lying in bed that drew no strike action from mending bones. Things, I thought complacently as I drifted to sleep, were altogether looking up.

In the morning I woke late to a Friday of warm windy spring sunshine and made coffee from the fixings provided by the hotel in each room; and Jik rang through on the telephone.

"Sarah says she *must* wash her hair today. Apparently it's sticking together."

"It looks all right to me."

His grin came down the wire. "Marriage opens vast new feminine horizons. Anyway, she's waiting down in the hall for me to drive her to the shops to buy some shampoo, but I thought I'd better let you know we were going."

I said uneasily, "You will be careful . . ."

"Oh sure," he said. "We won't go anywhere near the gallery. We won't go far. I'll call you as soon as we get back."

He disconnected cheerfully, and five minutes later the bell rang again. I lifted the receiver.

It was the girl from the reception desk. "Your friends say would you join them downstairs in the car."

"O.K." I said. I went jacketless down in the lift, left my room key at the desk, and walked out to the windy car park. I looked around for Jik and Sarah; but they were not, as it happened, the friends who were waiting.

It might have been fractionally better if I hadn't had my left arm slung up inside my shirt. As it was they simply clutched my clothes, lifted me off my feet, and ignominiously bundled me into the back of their car.

Wexford was sitting inside it; and there was no indecision this time in his manner. This time he as good as had me again behind his steel mesh door, and this time he was intent on not making mistakes.

He still wore a bow tie. The jaunty polka-dots went oddly with the unfunny matter in hand.

The muscles propelling me towards him turned out to belong to Greene with an "e", and to a thug I'd never met but who answered the general description of Beetle-brows.

My spirits descended faster than the Hilton lifts. I ended up sitting between Beetle-brows and Wexford, with Greene climbing into the driving seat.

"How did you find me?" I said.

Greene, with a wolfish smile, took a polaroid photograph from his pocket and held it for me to see. It was a picture of Jik, Sarah and me standing by the shops in Melbourne Airport. The woman from the gallery, I guessed, had not been wasting the time she spent watching us depart.

103

"We went round asking the hotels," Greene said. "It was easy."

There didn't seem to be much else to say, so I didn't say anything. A slight shortage of breath might have had something to do with it.

None of the others, either, seemed over-talkative. Greene started the car and drove out into the city, and Beetle-brows began twisting my free right arm behind my back until my head went practically down to my knees. It was all most undignified and excruciating.

Wexford said finally, "We want our lists back."

He wasn't making light conversation. His rage had no trouble at all in communicating itself to me. Oh Christ, I thought, I'd been such a bloody fool, just walking into it, like that.

I didn't answer. Too busy suffering.

Nothing else was said on the journey. My thoughts about what very likely lay at the end of it were so unwelcome that I did my best not to allow them houseroom. I could give Wexford his list back, but what then? What then, indeed.

From external sounds I guessed we were travelling through busy workaday Friday morning city streets, but as my head was below window level, I couldn't actually see.

The car turned sharply left and ground uphill for what seemed like miles. Then the road began to descend. After a long time the car halted briefly and then turned to the right. We had exchanged city sounds for those of the sea. There were also no more cars passing us from the opposite direction. I came to the sad conclusion that we had turned off the highway and were on our way along an infrequently used side road.

The car stopped eventually, and Beetle-brows removed his hands. I sat up stiffly, wrenched and unenthusiastic.

They could hardly have picked a lonelier place. The road ran along beside the sea so closely that it was more or less part of the shore, and the shore was a jungle of sharply pointed rough black rocks, with frothy white waves slapping among them.

On the right rose jagged cliffs, steeply towering. Ahead, the road ended blindly in some workings which looked like a sort of quarry. Slabs had been cut from the cliffs, and there were dusty clearings, and huge heaps of small jagged rocks, and graded stones, and sifted chips. All raw and harsh and blackly volcanic.

No people. No machinery. No sign of occupation.

"Where's the list?" Wexford said. "And the pictures you took."

Greene twisted round in the driving seat and looked seriously at my face. "You'll tell us," he said. "With or without a beating."

"What if I do tell you?" I said.

There was a furtiveness in their expressions. I looked at the cliffs, the quarry, the sea. No easy exit. And behind us, the road. If I ran that way, they would drive after me, and mow me down. If I could run. And even that was problematical. Regina, I thought. Regina, with her head bashed in.

I swallowed and looked dejected, which wasn't awfully difficult.

"I'll tell you. . . ." I said. "Out of the car."

There was a small silence while they considered it; but as they weren't anyway going to have room to beat me up in that crowded interior, they weren't entirely against.

"Get out, then," Wexford said.

We all got out, and I made sure that I ended up on the side by the sea. The wind was much stronger on this exposed coast.

"All right then," Wexford said roughly, shouting a little to bring his voice above the din of sea and wind. "Where's the list?"

Thrusting my right hand inside my shirt and tugging at the sling-forming bandages, I whirled away from them and did my best to sprint for the sea.

Wexford, Greene and Beetle-brows shouted furiously and almost trampled on my heels.

I pulled the lists of Overseas Customers out of the sling, and flung them with a bowling action as far out to sea as I could manage. The pages fluttered apart in mid-air, but the offshore winds caught most of them beautifully and blew them like great leaves out to sea.

I didn't stop at the water's edge. I went straight on into the cold inhospitable battlefield of shark-teeth rocks and green water and white foaming waves. Slipping, falling, getting up, staggering on, finding that the current was much stronger than I'd expected, and the rocks more abrasive, and the footing more treacherous.

105

Finding I'd fled from one deadly danger to embrace another.

For one second, I looked back.

Wexford had followed me a step or two into the sea, but only, it seemed, to reach one of the pages which had fallen shorter than the others. He was standing there with the frothy water swirling round his trouser legs, peering at the sodden paper.

Greene was beside the car, reaching in to the glove compartment by the front passenger seat.

Beetle-brows had his mouth open.

I reapplied myself to the problem of survival.

The shore shelved, as most shores do. Every forward step led into a stronger current. Hip-deep between waves, I found it difficult to stay on my feet, and every time I didn't I was in dire trouble, because of the black needle-sharp rocks waiting to scratch and tear. They were the raw stuff of volcanoes, as scratchy as pumice. One's groping hand didn't slide over them: one's skin stuck to them, and tore off. Clothes fared no better. Before I'd gone thirty yards I was running with blood from a dozen superficial grazes.

My left arm was still tangled inside the sling, which had housed the Overseas Customers since Cup day as an insurance against having my room robbed, as at Alice. Soaking wet, the bandages now clung like leeches, and my shirt also. Muscles weakened by a fracture and inactivity couldn't deal with them. My foot stepped awkwardly on the side of a submerged rock and I lost my balance, fell forward, crashed chest against a small jagged peak dead ahead.

The rock beside me splintered suddenly as if exploding. For a flicker of time I couldn't understand it, and then I struggled round and looked back to the shore.

Greene was standing there, aiming a pistol, shooting to kill.

CHAPTER FOURTEEN

Thirty to thirty-five yards is a long way for a pistol; but Greene seemed so close. He was standing with his legs straddled and his arms out straight ahead, aiming the gun with both hands.

I couldn't hear the shots above the crash of the waves on the rocks. But I did see the upward jerk of the arms at the recoil, and I reckoned it would be just plain silly to give him a stationary target. So I turned and stumbled a yard or two onwards, fell on a jagged edge, and gashed the inside of my right forearm, and out poured more good red life. Christ, I thought, I must be scarlet all over, leaking from a hundred tiny nicks.

It gave me at least an idea.

I was waist-deep in dangerous green water. Close to one side a row of bigger rock-teeth ran out from the shore like a nightmarish breakwater, and I'd shied away from it, because of the even fiercer waves crashing against it. But it represented the only cover in sight. Three stumbling efforts took me nearer; and the current helped.

I looked back at Greene. He was reloading. Wexford was practically dancing up and down beside him, urging him on; and Beetle-brows, from his disinclination to chase me, probably couldn't swim. Greene slapped the gun shut and raised it again.

I took a frightful chance, held my fast-bleeding forearm close across my chest—and stood up, swaying in the current. I watched him aim. It would take a marksman, I believed, to hit me with that pistol from that distance, in that wind. A marksman whose arms didn't jerk upward when he fired.

All the same, I felt sick.

The gun was pointing straight at me. I saw the jerk as he squeezed the trigger.

For a second I was convinced he had shot accurately; but I didn't even hear the passing of the flying death. I flung my right arm wide and high, and paused there facing him for a frozen second; letting him see that most of the front of my shirt was scarlet with blood.

Then I twisted artistically and fell flat, face downwards, into the water; and hoped to God he would think he had killed me.

THE SEA WASN'T much better than bullets. Nothing less than extreme fear of the alternative would have kept me down in it, tumbling like a piece of cheese in a grater.

I tried to get a grip on the submerged edges, to avoid being alternately sucked off and flung back. As much by luck as trying I found the sea shoving me into a crevice between the rocks, from where I was unable to see the shore. I clutched for a handhold, and then with bent knees found a good foothold, and clung there precariously while the sea tried to drag me out again.

I could hear nothing except the waves on the rocks. The water was cold, and the grazes gradually stopped bleeding. I wondered how long Wexford and Greene would stay there, staring out to sea for signs of life. I didn't dare to look, in case they spotted my moving head.

Fatigue, in the end, made me look. It was either that or cling like a limpet until I fell off, too weak to struggle back to life.

I caught a glimpse of the shore, the road, the cliffs, the quarry. Also the car. Also people.

Bloody damn, I thought. It was a measure of my tiredness that it took the space of three in and out waves for me to realize that it wasn't Wexford's car, and it wasn't Wexford standing on the road.

If it wasn't Wexford, it didn't matter who it was. I stood up gingerly. A grey-white car. A couple beside it, standing close, the man with his arms round the girl. A nice quiet spot for it, I thought sardonically.

They moved apart and stared out to sea. I stared back. For an instant it seemed impossible. Then they started waving their arms furiously and ran towards the water; and it was Sarah and Jik.

Throwing off his jacket, Jik ploughed into the waves with enthusiasm, and came to a smart halt as the realities of the situation scraped his legs. All the same, he came on after a pause towards me, taking care.

I made my slow way back. Jik put his arm round my waist and I held on to his shoulders, and together we stumbled slowly to land. We fell now and then. Got up gasping. Reclutched, and went on.

He let go when we reached the road. I sat down on the edge of it.

"Todd," Sarah said anxiously. She came nearer. "*Todd.*" Her voice was incredulous. "Are you *laughing?*"

"Sure." I looked up at her, grinning. "Why ever not?"

109

Jik's shirt was torn, and mine was in tatters. We took them off and used them to mop up the grazes.

"What a damn silly place to bathe," Jik said. He glanced at my back. "Your Alice Springs dressing has come off."

"How're the stitches?"

"Intact."

"You'll both get pneumonia, sitting there," Sarah said.

I took off the remnants of sling. All in all, I thought, it had served me pretty well. The adhesive rib-supporting cummerbund was still more or less in place. "We need a telephone," I said, pouring water out of my shoes.

"Give me strength," Sarah said. "What you need is hot baths, warm clothes, and half a dozen psychiatrists."

"How did you get here?" I asked.

"How come you aren't dead?" Jik said.

"You first."

"I came out of the shop where I'd bought the shampoo," Sarah said, "and I saw Greene drive past. I nearly died on the spot. I just stood still hoping he wouldn't look my way, and he didn't. . . . The car turned to the left just past where I was . . . and I could see there were other people in the back . . . and I went back to our car and told Jik."

"We thought it damn lucky he hadn't spotted her," Jik said, dabbing at persistent scarlet trickles. "We went back to the hotel, and you weren't there, so we asked the girl at the desk if you'd left a message, and she said you'd gone off in a car with some friends. . . . With a man with a droopy moustache."

"Friends!" Sarah said.

"Anyway," Jik continued, "choking down our rage, sorrow, indignation and what not, we thought we'd better look for your body."

"Jik!" Sarah protested.

"And who was crying?"

"Shut up."

He grinned. "So we set off in pursuit. Turned left where Greene had gone, and found ourselves climbing a ruddy mountain."

110

I could hear his teeth chattering even above the din of my own.
"Let's get out of this wind," I said. "And bleed in the car."

We crawled stiffly into the seats. Sarah said it was lucky the
upholstery was plastic. Jik automatically took his place behind
the wheel.

"We drove for miles," he said. "Growing, I may say, a little
frantic. Over the top of the mountain and down this side. At the
bottom of the hill the road swings round to the left and we could
see from the map that it follows the coastline. round a whole lot of
bays and eventually ends up right back in Wellington."

"We went that way," Sarah said. "There was nothing but miles
of craggy rocks and sea."

"I'll paint those rocks," Jik said. He started the car, turned it,
and rolled gently ahead.

Sarah glanced at his face, and then at me. She'd heard the
fervour in that statement of intent. The honeymoon was almost
over.

"After a bit we turned back," Jik said. "There was this bit of
road saying 'no through road', so we came down it. No you, of
course. We stopped here on this spot and Sarah got out of the car
and started bawling her eyes out."

"You weren't exactly cheering yourself," she said.

"Huh," he smiled. "Anyway, I kicked a few stones about,
wondering what to do next, and there were these cartridges on the
edge of the road. All close together. Maybe dropped out of one of
those spider-ejection revolvers, or something like that."

"They really did shoot at you?" Sarah said.

"Greene. He missed."

"Inefficient." Jik shifted in his seat, wincing. "They must have
gone back over the hill while we were looking for you round the
bays. Did they take the list?"

"I threw it in the sea." I smiled lopsidedly. "It seemed too
tame just to hand it over . . . and it made a handy diversion. They
salvaged enough to see that they'd got what they wanted."

"What now?" Sarah said.

"Telephone," I said.

Over the hill there was a village with the sort of store which

111

sold everything from hammers to hairpins. Also clothes. Sarah vanished inside.

I pulled on the resulting jeans and T-shirt, and made wobbly tracks for the telephone, clutching Sarah's purse.

I called the Townhouse. Remembered, with an effort, that my name was Peel.

"But, Mr. Peel . . ." the girl sounded bewildered. "Your friend . . . the one with the moustache, not the one with the beard . . . he paid your account not half an hour ago and collected all your things . . . Yes, I suppose it is irregular, but he brought your note, asking us to let him have your room key. . . . I'm sorry but I didn't know you hadn't written it. . . . Yes, he took all your things, the room's being cleaned at this minute. . . . I'm sorry. . . ."

I called the international exchange and gave them a number. The call would be through in ten minutes. They would ring back.

The telephone was on the wall of a booth inside the general store. There was nothing to sit on. I wished to God there was.

The bell rang, and I picked up the receiver. "Your call to England. . . ."

The modern miracle. Halfway round the world, and I was talking to Inspector Frost as if he were in the next room. Eleven thirty in the morning at Wellington: eleven thirty at night in Shropshire.

"Your letter arrived today, sir," he said. "And action has already been started."

"Stop calling me sir. I'm used to Todd."

"All right. Well, we telexed Melbourne to alert them and we've started checking on all the people on the England list. The results are already incredible. All the crossed-out names we've checked so far have been the victims of break-ins. We're alerting the police in all the other countries concerned. The only thing is, we see the list you sent us is a photo-copy. Do you have the original?"

"No . . . Most of it got destroyed. Does it matter?"

"Not really. Can you tell us how it came into your possession?"

"Er . . . I think we'd better say it just did."

A dry laugh travelled twelve thousand miles. "All right. Now what's so urgent that you're keeping me from my bed?"

112

I told him about Wexford and Greene being in Wellington, and about them stealing my things. "They've got my passport and travellers' cheques, and my suitcase. I think they may also have a page or two of the list . . ."

"Say that again."

I said it again. "Most of it got thrown into the sea, but I know Wexford regained at least one page. Well . . . I thought . . . they'd be going back to Melbourne, probably today, any minute really, and when they land there, there's a good chance they'll have at least some of those things with them . . ."

"I can fix a customs search," he said. "But why should they risk stealing?"

"They think I'm dead."

"Good God. Why?"

"They took a pot shot at me."

"I see . . ." He sounded faint. "Unfortunately the Melbourne police believe that the disappearance of the list from the gallery there will have already led to the immediate destruction of anything else incriminating."

"They may be wrong. Wexford and Greene don't know I photo-copied the list and sent it to you. They think the list is floating safely out to sea, and me with it."

"I'll pass your message to Melbourne."

"Did you get any answers from Donald to my questions?" I asked.

"Rest assured," he said dryly. "We carried out your wishes to the letter. Mr. Stuart's answers were 'Yes of course' to the first question, and 'Yes' to the second."

"Was he absolutely certain?"

"Absolutely." He cleared his throat. "He seems distant and withdrawn. Uninterested. But quite definite."

"How is he?" I asked.

"He spends all his time looking at a picture of his wife. Every time we call at his house, we can see him through the front window, just sitting there."

"You could at least let him know that he's no longer suspected of engineering the robbery and killing Regina."

113

"That's a decision for my superiors," he said.

"Well, kick them into it," I said.

He paused. "Where are you going next? When I've telexed Melbourne, I may need to talk to you again."

"I'm in a phone booth in a country store in a village on the hills above Wellington, and I'm staying right here. Wexford and Greene will be still around in the city and I don't want to risk the outside chance of their seeing me."

"Give me the number, then."

I read it off the telephone. "I want to come home as soon as possible," I said. "Can you do anything about my passport?"

"You'll have to find a consul."

Oh ta, I thought tiredly. I hung up the receiver and wobbled back to the car.

We sat there for two hours.

The store didn't sell liquor or hot food. Sarah bought a packet of biscuits. We ate them.

"We can't stay here all day," she said explosively, after a lengthy glum silence.

"We're safer here," I said. I couldn't be sure that Wexford wasn't out searching for her and Jik with murderous intent.

A delivery van struggled up the hill and stopped outside the shop. A man in an overall opened the back, took out a large bakery tray, and carried it in.

"Food," I said hopefully.

Sarah went in to investigate, came back with fresh doughnuts and cans of Coke. We made inroads, and I at least felt healthier.

After another half hour, the storekeeper appeared in the doorway, shouting and beckoning. "A call for you . . . ."

I went stiffly to the telephone. It was Frost, clear as a bell.

"Wexford, Greene and Snell have booked a flight to Melbourne. They will be met at Melbourne airport. . . ."

"Who's Snell?" I said.

"How do I know? He was travelling with the other two."

Beetle-brows, I thought.

"Now listen," Frost said. "The telex has been red-hot between here and Melbourne, and the police there want your co-operation, just to clinch things . . ." He went on talking for a long time. At the end he said, "Will you do that?"

I'm tired, I thought. I'm battered, and I hurt. I've done just about enough. "All right."

"The Melbourne police want to know for sure that the three Munnings copies you . . . er . . . acquired from the gallery are still where you told me."

"Yes, they are."

"Right. Well . . . good luck."

CHAPTER FIFTEEN

We flew Air New Zealand that afternoon, back to Melbourne, tended by angels in sea-green, our passage oiled by telexes from above. We'd collected Sarah's belongings from the Townhouse, and when we arrived at the airport we found ourselves whisked into a private room, plied with strong drink, and subsequently taken by car straight out across the tarmac to the aeroplane.

A thousand miles across the Tasman Sea and an afternoon tea later, we were driven straight from the aircraft's steps to another small airport room, which contained no strong drink but only a large hard Australian plainclothes policeman.

"Porter," he said, introducing himself and squeezing our bones in a blacksmith's grip. "Which of you is Charles Todd?"

"I am."

"Right on, Mr. Todd." He looked at me without favour. "Are you ill, or something?"

"No," I said, sighing slightly. Time and airline schedules waited for no man. If I'd spent time on first aid we'd have missed the only possible flight. "Did you manage what you planned?" I asked.

"We decided not to go ahead until you had arrived," he said. "There's a car waiting outside." He wheeled out of the door and marched briskly off.

The car had a chauffeur. Porter sat in front. "We got your things back, Todd," he said with satisfaction. "Wexford, Greene and Snell were turned over on entry, and they copped them with the lot. You can collect your bags in the morning."

"That's great," I said. "Did they still have any of the lists of customers?"

"Yeah. Damp but readable. Names of guys in Canada. We're turning over that Yarra gallery right this minute, and Wexford is there helping. We've let him overhear what we wanted him to. As soon as I give the go-ahead we'll let him take action. We'll give him the opportunity of using a telephone when he thinks no one's listening."

"Do you think he will?" I said.

"Look, mister, wouldn't you?"

I thought I might be wary of gifts from the Greeks, but then I wasn't Wexford, and I didn't have a jail sentence breathing down my neck.

"Where are we going?" Sarah said.

"To reunite you with your clothes," I said.

Her face lit up. "Are we really?"

"And what for?" Jik asked.

"To bring the mouse to the cheese."

We pulled up at the side door of the Hilton. Porter raised himself agilely to the pavement and stood like a solid pillar, watching with half-concealed impatience while Jik, Sarah and I eased ourselves slowly out. We all went across the familiar entrance hall, and from there through a gate in the reception desk into the hotel manager's office at the rear.

A member of the hotel staff offered us chairs, coffee, and sandwiches. Porter looked at his watch and offered us an indeterminate wait. It was six o'clock. After ten minutes a man in shirt and necktie brought a two-way personal radio for Porter, who slipped the ear-plug into place and began listening to disembodied voices.

We sat, and drank coffee, and waited. Porter ate three of the sandwiches simultaneously. Time passed.

Seven o'clock. Sarah was looking pale and tired. So was Jik. I sat and thought about life and death and polka dots.

At seven eleven Porter clutched his ear and concentrated

116

intently on the ceiling. When he relaxed, he passed me the galvanic message.

"Wexford did just what we reckoned he would. He's taken the bait."

"He's a fool," I said.

Porter came as near to a smile as he could. "All crooks are fools, one way or another."

Seven thirty came and went. I raised my eyebrows at Porter. He shook his head. "We can't say too much on the radio," he said. "Because you get all sorts of ears listening in."

We waited. The time dragged. Jik yawned and Sarah's eyes were dark with fatique. Outside, in the lobby, the busy rich life of the hotel chattered on unruffled.

Porter clutched his ear again, and stiffened. "He's here," he said. He disconnected himself from the radio, put it on the manager's desk, and went out into the foyer.

"What do we do?" Sarah said.

"Nothing much except listen."

We all three went over to the door and held it six inches open. We listened to people asking for their room keys, asking for letters and messages. Then suddenly, the familiar voice, sending electric fizzes to my finger tips. Confident: not expecting trouble. "I've come to collect a package left in your baggage room last Tuesday by a Mr. Charles Todd. I have a letter here from him, authorizing you to release it to me."

There was a crackle of paper as the letter was handed over. Sarah's eyes were startled. "Did you write it?" she whispered.

I shook my head. "No."

The desk clerk outside said, "Thank you, sir. If you'll just wait a moment I'll fetch the package."

There was a long pause. My heart made a lot of noise, but nothing much else happened.

The desk clerk came back. "Here you are, sir. Paintings, sir."

"That's right."

There were vague sounds of the bundle of paintings being carried along outside the door.

"Can you manage them, sir?" said the clerk.

117

"Yes. Yes. Thank you." There was haste in his voice, now that he'd got his hands on the goods. "Thank you. Goodbye."

Sarah had begun to say "Is that all?" in disappointment when Porter's loud voice chopped into the Hilton velvet like a hatchet.

"I guess we'll take care of those paintings, if you don't mind," he said. "Porter, Melbourne city police."

I opened the door a little, and looked out. Porter stood four square in the lobby, large and rough, holding out a demanding hand. At his elbows, two plainclothes policemen. At the front door, two more, in uniform. There would be others, I supposed, at the other exits. They weren't taking any chances.

"Why Inspector . . . I'm only on an errand for my young friend, Charles Todd."

"And these paintings?"

"I've no idea what they are. He asked me to fetch them for him."

I walked quietly out of the office and round to the front of the reception desk. He was only six feet away, in front of me to my right. I hoped Porter would think it near enough, as requested.

A certain amount of unease had pervaded the Hilton guests. They stood around in an uneven semicircle, eyeing the proceedings sideways.

"Mr. Charles Todd asked you to fetch them?" Porter said loudly.

"Yes, that's right."

Porter's gaze switched abruptly to my face. "Did you ask him?"

"No," I said.

The explosive effect was all that the Melbourne police could have asked, and a good deal more than I expected. There was no polite quiet identification followed by a polite quiet arrest. I should have remembered all my own theories about the basic brutality of the directing mind.

He realized that he'd been tricked. Had convicted himself out of his own mouth and by his own presence on such an errand. The fury rose in him like a geyser and his hands reached out to grab my neck. *"You're dead,"* he yelled. "You're bloody dead!"

His plunging weight took me off balance and down onto one knee, smothering under his choking grip. Heaven knows what he

118

intended, but Porter's men pulled him off before he did bloody murder on the plushy carpet. As I got creakily to my feet, I heard the handcuffs click.

He was standing there, quivering in the restraining hands, breathing heavily, dishevelled and bitter-eyed. Civilized exterior stripped away by one instant of ungovernable rage. The violent core plain to see.

"Hello, Hudson," I said.

"SORRY," Porter said perfunctorily. "Didn't reckon he'd turn wild."

"He always was wild," I said. "Underneath."

"You'd know," he said. "I never saw the guy before." He nodded to Jik and Sarah and finally to me, and hurried away after his departing prisoner.

It had taken nine days. It had been a long haul.

"TODD," said Sarah. "Start talking."

We were upstairs in a bedroom (mine) with me in Jik's dressing-gown, and he and I in a cloud of Dettol.

I yawned. "About Hudson?"

"Who else? And don't go to sleep before you've told us."

"Well . . . I was looking for him, or someone like him, before I ever met him."

"But why?"

"Because of the wine which was stolen from Donald's cellar. Whoever stole it not only knew it was there, but came prepared with proper cases to pack it in. Two thousand or more bottles stolen. In bulk alone it would have taken a lot of shifting. A lot of time, too, and time for housebreakers is risky. But it was special wine, worth a small fortune, so Donald said. The sort of wine that needed expert handling and marketing if it was to be worth the difficulty of stealing it in the first place . . . so I started looking right away for someone who knew Donald, knew he'd bought a Munnings, and knew about good wine and how to sell it. And there, straightaway, was Hudson Taylor, who matched like a glove. But he didn't *look* right."

119

"Too rich," Jik said, nodding.

"Probably a moneyholic," I said, sitting on the bed with my feet up, feeling less than fit. Sore from too many bruises, on fire from too many cuts. Jik too, I guessed. They had been wicked rocks.

"A what?" asked Sarah.

"Moneyholic. A word I've just made up to describe someone with an uncontrollable addiction to money."

"Moneyholism," Jik said, like a lecturer to a dimmish class, "is a widespread disease easily understood by everyone who has ever felt a twinge of greed, which is everyone."

"Go on about Hudson," Sarah said.

"Hudson had the organizing ability . . . but he convinced me I was wrong about him because he was so careful. He pretended he had to look up the name of the gallery where Donald bought his picture. He didn't even think of me as a threat then, of course, but just as Donald's cousin. Not until he talked to Wexford down on the lawn."

"I remember," Sarah said. "When you said it had ripped the whole works apart."

"Mm . . . I thought it was only that he had told Wexford I was Donald's cousin, but of course Wexford also told *him* that I'd met Greene in Maisie's ruins in Sussex and then turned up in the gallery looking at the original of Maisie's burnt painting."

"No wonder we beat it to Alice Springs," Jik said.

"Yes, but by then I didn't think it could be Hudson I was looking for. I was looking for someone brutal, who passed on his violence through his employees. Hudson didn't look or act brutal." I paused. "Then on the night of the Cup you said Hudson had made a point of asking you about me . . . and I wondered how he knew you."

"Do you know," Sarah said, "I did wonder too at the time, but it didn't seem important. I mean, *we'd* seen *him* from the stands, so it didn't seem impossible that somewhere he'd seen you with us."

"The boy knew you," I said. "And he was at the races, because he followed you, with Greene, to the Hilton. The boy must have pointed you out to Greene. And Greene to Wexford, and Wexford to Hudson."

120

"And by then," Jik said, "they all knew they wanted to silence you pretty badly, and they'd had a chance and muffed it. . . ."

"On the morning after," I said, "a letter from Hudson was delivered by hand to the Hilton. How did he know we were there?"

They stared. "Greene must have told him," Jik said. "We certainly didn't."

"Nor did I," I said. "That letter offered to show me round a vineyard. Well, if I hadn't been so doubtful of him, I might have gone. He was a friend of Donald's and a vineyard would be interesting. From his point of view, anyway, it was worth a try."

"Jesus!"

"On the night of the Cup, when we were in that motel, I telephoned the police in England and spoke to the man in charge of Donald's case. I asked him to ask Donald some questions . . . and this morning outside Wellington I got the answers."

"This morning seems several light years away," Sarah said.

"Mm . . ."

"What questions and what answers?" Jik said.

"The questions were, did Donald tell Hudson all about the wine in his cellar, and was it Hudson who had suggested to Donald that he should go and look at the Munnings in the Arts Centre. And the answers were 'Yes, of course', and 'Yes'."

They thought about it in silence. "So what then?" Sarah said.

"So the Melbourne police said it was too unsubstantial, but if they could tie Hudson in definitely with the gallery they might believe it. So they let Wexford accidentally overhear snippets from a fake report from several hotels about odd deposits in their baggage rooms, including the paintings at the Hilton. When he thought no one was listening he rang Hudson and told him. So Hudson wrote himself a letter to the Hilton from me and zoomed along to remove the incriminating evidence."

"He must have been crazy."

"Stupid. But he thought I was dead . . . and he'd no idea anyone suspected him. Still, he should have had the sense to know that Wexford's call to him would be bugged by the police. . . ."

121

"You'd never have thought Hudson would blaze up like that," Sarah said. She shivered. "You wouldn't think people could hide such really frightening violence under a friendly public face."

"What do you think I paint?" Jik said, standing up. "Vases of flowers?" He looked down at me. "Horses?"

WE PARTED the next morning at Melbourne airport, where we seemed to have spent a good deal of our lives.

"It seems strange, saying goodbye," Sarah said.

"I'll be coming back," I said.

They nodded. "Well . . ." We looked at watches.

It was like all partings. There wasn't much to say. I leaned forward and kissed Sarah, my oldest friend's wife.

"Hey," he said. "Find one of your own."

CHAPTER SIXTEEN

Maisie saw me before I saw her, and came sweeping down like a great scarlet bird, wings outstretched.

Monday lunchtime at Wolverhampton races, misty and cold.

"Hello, dear, I'm so glad you've come." She patted my arm and peered acutely at my face. "You don't look awfully well, dear, if you don't mind me saying so, and you don't seem to have collected any suntan."

She stopped to watch a row of jockeys canter past on their way to the start. Bright shirts against the thin grey mist. A subject for Munnings.

"Have you backed anything, dear? And are you sure you're warm enough? I never think jeans are good for people in the winter, they're only cotton, dear, don't forget, and how did you get on in Australia? I mean, dear, did you find out anything?"

"It's an awfully long story . . ."

"Best told in the bar, then, don't you think, dear?"

She bought us immense brandies with ginger ale and I told her about Hudson's organization, about the Melbourne gallery and about the list of robbable customers.

"Was I on it?"

I nodded. "Yes, you were."

"And you gave it to the police?" she said anxiously.

I grinned. "Don't look so worried, Maisie. Your name was crossed out already. I just crossed it out more thoroughly. By the time I'd finished, no one could ever disentangle it, particularly on a photo-copy."

She smiled broadly. "No one could call you a fool, dear."

I wasn't so sure about that.

"Anyway, dear, I've decided not to rebuild the house at Worthing because it wouldn't be the same without the things Archie and I bought together, so I'm selling that plot of seaside land for a fortune, dear, and I've chosen a nice place just down the road from Sandown Park racecourse."

"You're not going to live in Australia!"

"Oh no, dear, that would be too far away. From Archie, you see, dear."

I saw. I liked Maisie very much. "I'm afraid I spent all your money," I said.

She smiled at me with her well-kept head on one side and absentmindedly stroked her crocodile handbag. "Never mind, dear. You can paint me *more* pictures."

I LEFT AFTER the third race, took the train along the main line to Shrewsbury, and from there travelled by bus to Inspector Frost's official doorstep.

He was in an office, chin deep in papers. He offered me a chair. "You sure kicked open an ant-hill," he said, faintly smiling.

"What about Donald?" I asked. "He wants Regina buried."

Frost looked up with compassion. "The difficulty is," he said, "that in a murder case, one has to preserve the victim's body in case the defence wishes to call for its own post mortem. In this case, we have not been able to accuse anyone of her murder, let alone get as far as them arranging a defence." He cleared his throat. "We'll release Mrs. Stuart's body for burial as soon as official requirements have been met."

I looked at my fingers, interlacing them.

"Unofficially," Frost said, "I'll tell you that the Melbourne police found a list of names in the gallery which it turns out are of known housebreakers. Divided into countries, like the Overseas Customers. There were four names for England. There's a good chance Mrs. Stuart's killer may be one of them."

"Really? So the robberies were local labour?"

"It seems to have been their normal method."

Greene, I thought. With an "e". Greene could have recruited them. And checked afterwards, in burnt houses, on work done.

"Greene," I said, "was in England about the time Regina died."

Frost stared.

"Maybe Regina knew him," I said. "She had been in the gallery in Australia. Maybe she saw him helping to rob her house . . . supervising, perhaps . . . and maybe that's why she was killed, because it wouldn't have been enough just to tie her up and gag her . . . she could identify him for certain if she was alive."

He looked as if he was trying to draw breath. "That's all . . . guessing," he said.

"I know for certain that Greene was in England two weeks after Regina's death. I know for certain he was up to his neck in selling paintings and stealing them back. I know for certain that he would kill someone who could get him convicted. The rest . . . well . . . it's over to you."

"My God," Frost said. He shook his head. "What everyone wants to know," he said, "is what put you onto the organization in the first place."

I smiled. "A hot tip from an informer." A smuggler in a scarlet coat, glossy hair-do and crocodile handbag. "And you can't grass on informers," I said.

He sighed and pulled a piece of torn-off telex paper out of his jacket. "Did you meet an Australian policeman called Porter?"

"I sure did."

"He sent you a message." He handed me the paper. I read the neatly typed words. *Tell that Pommie painter Thanks.*

"Will you send a message back?"

He nodded. "What is it?"

"No sweat," I said.

124

I STOOD IN the dark outside my cousin's house, looking in.

Donald sat in his lighted drawing room, facing Regina, unframed on the mantelshelf. I sighed, and rang the bell.

Donald came slowly. Opened the door. "Charles!" He was mildly surprised. "I thought you were in Australia."

"Got back yesterday."

"Come in." We went into the kitchen, where at least it was warm, and sat one each side of the table. He looked gaunt and fifty, a shell of a man, retreating from life.

"How's business?" I said.

"I don't really care."

"You've got stuck," I said. "Like a needle in a record. Playing the same little bit of track over and over again."

He looked blank.

"The police know you didn't fix the robbery," I said.

He nodded slowly. "That man came and told me so. This morning. It doesn't seem to make much difference."

"You've got to stop it, Donald," I said. "Regina's dead. She's been dead five weeks and three days. Do you want to see her?"

He looked absolutely horrified. "No! Of course not."

"Then stop thinking about her body."

"Charles!" He stood up violently, knocking over his chair. He was somewhere between outrage and anger, and clearly shocked.

"She's in a cold drawer," I said, "and you want her in a box in the cold ground. So where's the difference?"

"Get out," he said loudly. "I don't want to hear you."

"That . . . that *shape* lying in storage isn't Regina," I said, not moving. "The real girl is in your head. In your memory. The only life you can give her is to remember her. That's her immortality, in your head."

He turned on his heel and walked out. I heard him go across the hall. Open the door. Go in.

He was sitting in his chair, in the usual place. "Go away," he said.

What did it profit a man, I thought, if he got flung over balconies and shot at and mangled by rocks, if he couldn't save his cousin's soul.

125

"I'm taking that picture with me to London," I said.

He was alarmed. He stood up. "You can't. You gave it to me."

"It needs a frame," I said. "Or it will warp."

"You can't take it."

"You can come as well."

"I can't leave here," he said.

"Why not?"

"Don't be stupid," he said explosively. "You know why not. Because of . . ." His voice died away.

"Regina isn't in this room," I said. "She's in your head. You can go out of here and take her with you."

Nothing.

"She was a great girl. It must be bloody without her. But she deserves the best you can do."

I went over to the fireplace and picked up the picture. Regina's face smiled out, vitally alive. I hadn't done her left nostril too well, I thought.

Donald didn't try to stop me. I put my hand on his arm. "Let's get your car out," I said, "and drive down to my flat. Right this minute."

A little silence.

"Come on," I said.

He began, with difficulty, to cry.

I took a long breath and waited. "O.K.," I said. "How are you off for petrol?"

"We can get some more . . ." he said, sniffing, ". . . on the motorway."

Dick Francis

Champion Steeplechase Jockey in 1954, and rider of innumerable winners for the Queen Mother, Dick Francis retired from racing in 1957 after a particularly bad fall. He then embarked on a new career as a writer, both as racing correspondent for the *Sunday Express*, and as a novelist with a remarkable series of fifteen winners to his credit, including *Nerve*, a past Condensed Books selection.

Winter is his time for writing books; he now produces a novel a year, and is at present also working on a collection of short stories and collaborating with Lester Piggott on the latter's life story. Dick's wife Mary ably assists her husband in research for his novels, and as she paints herself could give first-hand advice for *In the Frame*. A tour of Australia and New Zealand and Dick's friendship with two professional painters supplied the background.

He and his wife live at the foot of the Berkshire Downs in a house they built in 1954, close to the training stables where he was First Jockey for many years. Up to a short time ago Dick still rode out regularly with the string, and his interest in horses and racing remains as strong as ever. He goes to race meetings all over the world, and judges hunters at horse shows. He is himself the son and grandson of jockeys. One of his sons rode as an amateur and now has his own training stables. His two-year-old granddaughter is already in the saddle. The family tradition seems secure for some time to come.

Baker's Hawk

A condensation of the book by
JACK BICKHAM

WATERCOLOURS BY
NITA ENGLE

DRAWINGS BY STANLEY GALLI

Published by Robert Hale, London

On a mountain slope young Billy Baker watched, enthralled, as a red-tailed hawk rose in triumphant flight. Not so long ago the majestic bird had been a poor bedraggled thing; but Billy had nursed it back to health and now, in a strange sense, they were friends.

The hawk had helped him make another friend: a reclusive mountain man who understood Billy's loneliness as no one else ever had. They had happy times together, this unusual trio, until the prejudices of the townsfolk threatened them with disaster. Then, against his will, Billy was forced to confront some ugly realities and face for the first time shocking doubts about his father's wisdom and bravery. Out of the boy's agonized questioning comes a mature understanding of what courage really means.

ONE

NIGHT was coming to the Oregon sky. To the west, over jagged peaks, pink clouds drifted against a cobalt horizon; to the east, the Cascades stood sawtooth black in a wine-colored infinity. There was a little road, yellow-dusty, which was visible only here and there as it twisted between hills and upthrusting firs.

A buggy drawn by a single horse came along the road. There were two men in it: the driver, a bulky businessman of perhaps fifty, and a much younger man, whip thin, with long blond hair.

The older man flicked the reins to speed the horse. "Getting chilly," he observed.

The younger man smiled and took a deep breath of the sweet, cool air. "It's a lot like home."

"Well, we ought to make it back to town in another thirty minutes or so. I guess we won't freeze by then, anyhow."

The younger man, William R. Baker, attorney-at-law, did not reply. He felt good: relaxed, tired, and keen with anticipation. The trip to inspect the land had been tough but had borne out all his expectations. It was fine, virgin land, heavily timbered and in an ideal location. His report to the investors in Denver would be affirmative.

Chumley, the older man, drove on in silence. Baker knew what the rancher wanted to ask, and waited.

Finally Chumley came out with it directly. "Well, Mister Baker, you've seen the parcel of land. What's your opinion?"

"I like it," Baker told him forthrightly.

"Good."

"I also think the price is a shade too high."

"Too high!" Chumley growled. "With the way land speculation is going these days, the price we're asking is dirt cheap!"

"Two hundred is high. The Duggan land transaction in this area six months ago showed a price in the one-sixties."

Chumley glanced at him with new respect. "What do you know about the Duggan sale?"

Baker smiled at him. "Duggan, Brownson, and Plimmer, sale to Fredrickson, et al. Proposed January of 1894. Papers registered February 16, 1894. Legal description—"

"All right, all right! You've done some homework."

"The people I represent do not want to be unreasonable, Mister Chumley. But yes, we do our homework."

There was an impish admiration in Chumley's sidelong glance. "Well, sir, I'll admit it: when I saw you get off that train, and I saw how young you were, I thought, Burt, old boy, you've got you a fresh chicken for the plucking. I figured you wouldn't know a contract from a pinecone. *Now* I'd say your clients have got them a real lawyer."

It was a nice compliment, the kind that a man of Chumley's gruff character did not give unless it was meant. Baker paused, considering his reply, and that was when he saw the hawk.

He had seen a lot of hawks, and whether the sight of this particular one was affecting because it was unexpected, or because it was so beautiful, he had no way of knowing. It struck him instantly, however, and deep—this particular hawk, alone, a high shaft of sunlight touching rust-colored wings as it soared with infinite grace up beyond the mountain backdrop.

Chumley saw his look. "Lots of hawks around here. I suppose you got 'em in Colorado, too."

"Yes," Baker said. "I had a red-tailed hawk myself once. . . ."

"Is that a fact! You raise him, did you?"

132

"I—didn't quite finish."

"Well." Chumley was a little stumped. "They can be a nuisance. They like to kill, you know. They're loners, hawks are."

"That's just their nature," Baker said, and smiled because he realized he was quoting from very old memory. "You can never ask any being to change its nature."

"Well, now," Chumley muttered, and fell silent.

The hawk circled and vanished. The mood it had suddenly aroused in Baker, however, was not so easy to put away. The coincidence of this kind of night, this setting and this hawk had worked an alchemy in his memory. He was touched and saddened, and he said nothing.

Chumley, seeming to sense that the hawk had opened a door into something long ago, was quiet for the rest of the ride. At the hotel, there was talk about tomorrow's conference with the other landholders. With a handshake, Chumley left him. Baker had a light supper and went to his room.

Night lay over the country by this time, and the sky was alive with stars. He stood at the window, looking down the narrow, dusty street to the vast mountain wilderness beyond. You imagined old things were put away, he thought. But the past was never really behind a man; he carried it in his mind and in his gut.

It did no good to remember, he told himself. Now, in 1894, he was twenty-three years old; his law practice was growing with his reputation, ability and nerve. Only a fool would look back a dozen years to when a skinny kid had had his entire life changed.

But Baker was remembering. There was no help for it. He stood there and looked out on the Oregon night, and went back.

TWO

THE hawk had been born on April 15, 1882, on a mountain slope a few miles out from the small town of Springer, Colorado. There were three baby hawks hatched in the nest that day, but right from the start Billy Baker had his eye on just one of them.

The parent hawks had come back very early this year, while

there was still snow in the valley where Billy lived. Late in March, Billy had spotted them nesting high up in a juniper.

The tree they had chosen was one he knew. Owls had nested there the year before, and he had figured out a way to climb a cliff nearby, to watch them yet be hidden. The hawks had enlarged the owl's nest and lined it with boughs from soft conifers. Billy had to attend school in Springer every day, and then do chores, but nearly every afternoon, late, he hiked up to check on the hawks. He knew when the rust-speckled eggs appeared in the nest, and he knew about when the eggs would hatch.

The hawks were red-tails, big ones, with wings that spread almost as far as Billy could stretch out his arms. They were a dark brownish gray, with white breasts shading back to tan, and flared red tails. When they flew, shades of tan and white and red and rust caught in the thin sunlight. They were just about the most beautiful things in the world. Billy never tired of watching them.

"What have you been up to these last weeks?" his father asked him one night at supper. They were at the plank table in front of the fireplace in their single-room house, just the three of them.

"I'm not up to *anything*," Billy said, startled by the question.

His father gave him a stern look. He was a tall man, lank, with close-cropped hair and a blue-black stubble beard. He didn't smile much. Oh, Billy had seen him laugh—really laugh, like a boy. But these moments were few and far between.

"You're up to something," his father said. "Every day you race through your chores and then light out for the tall timber. What have you got up there? I won't have you dragging another coon in here."

"I don't have my eye on one, honest."

Billy's mother, a pretty blond woman, younger, murmured, "He's doing all his chores, Dan, and he's doing just fine in school."

"I know that, Ellen. I just don't like the way he always slips off by himself, just roaming around. He's almost twelve now. He's got to start growing up. We have to get the garden in. There's fence down. I need his help. As soon as school's out we *have* to get at the plowing."

135

Billy's mother sort of sighed. "Oh, Dan, he has time yet."

Dan Baker threw up his hands. "All right! But no more pets around here, boy! I mean it! We've got rabbits out there, we've got that coon, we've got those stupid mice in those boxes, we've got Rex—for all the good the useless hound ever does—we've got all these damned cats, and I'm not having any more!"

"Yes, sir."

The rest of the meal passed in silence. Paw went out to get the cow in while Billy was still spooning out the last of the pudding. His mother leaned over him. She smiled, and her gold hair hung down so that the firelight behind it was crimson.

"Billy, *do* you have some new pet out there in the woods?"

"No, ma'am." Which was *true*. So far.

She patted his head. "You're a good boy."

It sounded nice, but he knew better. He was a liar, if not in fact then in intent, and his plan was going to get him into a whole lot of trouble—unless he was awfully careful. He had figured he might—he only just *might*—get himself a hawk. After all, there were three eggs in that nest. . . .

But when the baby hawks appeared, he knew he was probably a goner. That was because, right from the start, this one hawk—the one he knew he wanted—was different from the other two. They all hatched pretty much alike, naked, awkward, slippery little things with stubs where their wings should have been and soft little beaks surmounting mouths that looked as big as doughnut holes. One of the three, though—Billy's—was slightly smaller.

The mother or father, a dark knife-slash against the evening sky, would come back to the nest and bring prey: a small bird, sometimes a field mouse or insects. *Plop.* The food went into the mouth that yelled the loudest and fought hardest to outreach its competitors. Baker's hawk—that was the way Billy was thinking of it already—was not quite as pushy as the other two. He moved around in the nest and got some food, but not as much as the other two, and they grew faster than he did because of it.

By the time school was let out for the summer, the baby hawks were covered with puffy soft down. They climbed up onto the lip of the nest often now and looked around and flapped their developing wings, making a great racket. Before long, they were going to fly.

That would be the turning point, Billy knew this. Once the young hawks were flying, it would probably be beyond his ability to catch one of them. He knew that he ought to try to climb the tree now and get one—*his* hawk—if he was going to do so.

It would not have been that difficult. The parents often were gone for long periods of time now, leaving the young on their own. There were enemies around who'd have liked a meal of hawk if they could have gotten to the nest. They couldn't. But Billy could. He could climb up there and grab the baby hawk and then—and then *what?* He was stuck. He didn't dare take a hawk home. And there was nowhere else. So each evening he tortured himself with visions of his hawk flying free today—and gone forever.

It was on a hot Saturday and Billy was behind the barn, hoeing weeds from around the corn hills, when he became aware of the other trouble. His father, who had been working on the plow, had walked to the front to meet someone coming up the road. Billy heard the voices, the first a little louder than it should have been.

"Everybody has to pitch in, Baker."

"No, not that way." His father's voice.

"Unless we're together on this, it's no good."

Curious, Billy went around the barn and along the shallow ditch that ran toward the road. He hunched down in the tall grass and got a look.

His father stood facing three men who had come up on horseback. They had not dismounted, and this made the visit appear unfriendly. And yet the men were familiar: Paul Carson, who operated the general store; Calvin White, a gaunt-faced rancher; and a massive older man, the blacksmith. They looked grim. So did Billy's father.

Carson's faced worked. "The law isn't getting the job done. We're talking about a vigilance committee."

"That's mob rule, Mister Carson."

"Not with good people running it. All of us together."

"It's still not legal. It's still not right."

This was so like his father, Billy had to smile. Dan Baker marched to the drum of a stern God and a law one did not bend.

"More and more riffraff," Carson said now. "More and more crime. It's time to do something."

Paw nodded. "I've heard the talk. But a vigilance committee is no answer. It just sets up one mob to fight another."

Carson said, "You've got a reputation for being independent, Dan. A man can admire that. But here we sit with just one deputy, and he's not very smart. The sheriff says he can't afford to send more help. Plotford is our deputy, and he's all we're going to get! That isn't good enough. We have to act."

"Volunteer as deputies," Paw suggested. "Unpaid."

"That's no good! There are things the regular law can't deal with. While the law is messing with its rules of evidence, these thieves are stealing us blind. Providing bad examples for our children, making them run crazy. It has to be stopped."

It seemed odd to Billy to hear Carson so excited about law and order. His son Morrie was running crazier than any boy in town.

Paw was saying, "There's an election in July. If Sweeney is doing a bad job as sheriff, we ought to look for a man to run against him. That's the way to deal with this; you just make matters worse when you start trying to set up your own law."

"We can't wait." Carson's face darkened as rage worked in him. "The break-in at Purvis's store. Jake Smith beaten up in the alley behind his office as he was closing up. Drunks on the streets, fighting, cussing—womenfolk aren't safe. Bad people are drifting in, Baker. Word's getting out that they can have a high old time in Springer. Somebody's got to stop it."

"How would you do it?" Dan Baker asked, his eyes narrowed.

"First, every decent man in the valley has to sign an oath to the vigilance committee. We've got to be together on this, all of us. Then we let the rowdies know we want them out of the area."

"And what if they don't go? You rough them up? Burn them out? Hang them?"

138

"That won't be necessary! Once they see we're *together,* they'll move out fast. If you're a thief, and you know *everybody in town* is a law enforcer, you'll think twice before you test the system!"

"People will test it," Paw said. "Members will have to test it, too. That's the way it works, Mister Carson. I *know.*"

Carson's bearded face showed that he could not understand resistance to his idea. "Join us," he said.

"I'm sorry. No."

The blacksmith spoke. "You could regret it. A man stands against his neighbors, they might think he was for the other side."

"Oh, I don't think so," Paw said. "That would be plumb stupid. All my neighbors are smarter than that."

"I want you to think about it," Carson said.

"I knew this was coming, Mister Carson. I already have." Pain was deep in Paw's eyes.

Without more words, Carson flicked reins to turn his horse. The other two men followed, heading north toward the Sled farm a mile distant. Dan Baker stood and watched them go.

As Billy scrambled out of the ditch, his mother appeared on the porch. Dan Baker turned to look at them and showed a slight smile. "Suddenly I seem to be mighty popular."

"Dan, if everyone else *does* join . . . can we stay out of it?"

"I don't know, Ellen."

Billy said, "If there are bad people around, Paw, wouldn't it be better to make 'em run, like Mister Carson said?"

His father looked at him. "*Would* it?"

"I dunno," Billy said, confused. "But it looks to me like, if the bad guys knew all the good people would really *bust* 'em if they tried anything, then they wouldn't try anything."

"Okay," his father said. "So if all of us get together and decide to gang up on a bad man, that's a good thing?"

"Right!"

"So what if we decide to go burn down the Sled place?"

Billy was horrified. "No! The Sleds are nice folks!"

"But what if all the rest of us decided we didn't think they were anymore? Why couldn't we just go burn them out?"

"That wouldn't be *right!*"

"If we *said* it was right, it would be, wouldn't it? If we can just decide on whether a man's good, without reference to anything but how we feel, can't we decide on any other man the same way?"

Billy began to see he had talked himself into a mousehole.

"It sounds good, Billy, people getting together and doing the 'right' thing. But if a mob can take after a bad man, it can take after a good man, too. That's why we have laws. They're so everybody knows what the rules are, and we all go by the same ones. We can't make them up as we go along. No one's bigger than the law. There are some bad men coming into Springer, I know that. But we can't ignore the law to fight them, for once people start doing that, nobody is safe."

Billy digested it for a moment. It made sense. But it wasn't quite enough. He wanted to be wholly convinced, and he wasn't. "But what if Deputy Plotford can't handle stuff?" he asked. "What if ole Sheriff Sweeney won't send in some more help? If there *is* trouble, what do folks do then? Just *set* here?"

"I don't know, boy," Paw said. "I just don't rightly know."

"You don't know?" Billy repeated. "You *acted* like you did!"

"Sometimes you have to make a decision whether you're sure of yourself or not. And I think I'm right about not signing that oath. It's the future I'm uncertain about . . . now."

"Will Mister Carson and those guys give you a tough time?"

"I don't know that either."

Billy had the feeling that something was slipping away from him. He groped for it. "But you told 'em off—you're really surer than you're letting on, Paw."

His father smiled glumly. "Sometimes all a man can do is take it one decision at a time—and hope."

This was a shock, this admission of Paw's that he might not *know*. It cast doubt on all his decisions, for if he was unsure *this* time, how many *other* times had he guessed? For the first time, Billy doubted his father.

He didn't like the feeling. He had always been sure that his father could do no wrong. Now Paw had *admitted* he sometimes

140

wasn't sure he was right. And his action on the vigilance oath made Billy doubt even his courage. Which was ridiculous, doubting Paw's courage. But there the doubt was, and it hurt.

Billy had seen evidence of the problem in town himself: the fist-fight on Main Street that no one dared break up; the window somebody had broken to get into Steeder's store; the dark spot on the post-office porch that had been made by the blood of the old man stabbed in the night. Weren't these things worthy of vigilante action? Was his father right in refusing to help?

Billy was shaken, and his father sensed it.

"Billy? You *do* understand . . . don't you, boy?"

Billy's throat was dusty. "We better—git to work, Paw."

He turned and walked to the garden. He had turned his back on his father, he realized, and he was so confused and upset he couldn't correct it.

They worked side by side at the planting, Paw silent, deeply hurt. But as the backbreaking work went on, he seemed to cheer. Paw was almost always cheerful when he worked hard.

For Billy it was like being closed in a small place. He could not shake his doubts. There was fear, too. He had seen a look in the eyes of the men who had come to call—a look he had seen when a wolf stalked a hurt rabbit. This cruelty in nature was obvious to him, but he hadn't seen it before in men. It seemed, somehow, that men ought to be better than that.

By the time the digging was done, it was almost suppertime. Billy knew it was late in the day to slip off to the hawks. But he had to. Today had been a day when they might fly.

He hurried down to the willow-lined creek, crossed it on a log and ran through the meadow. He skirted the woods and climbed the gully that led to the box canyon. Out of breath, he struggled up the steep shale slope of the hill and headed for the tree and the cliff. The sun gleamed gold on the face of the mountain high above him. Birds of all descriptions pinwheeled in the evening sky. Billy scrambled nimbly up to the shelf from which he could look down into the hawks' nest.

There was only one hawk there. His hawk.

141

Billy knew immediately what had happened. The two stronger babies, after days of flapping around on the edge of the nest, had at last taken the ultimate step—had sailed out beyond it.

His hawk had not taken that last step. It was crying and jumping around, beside itself with outrage at being left behind, but it couldn't quite get up the courage to take off. Possibly that first takeoff was always an accident; Billy didn't know. As he watched, torn between pity and amusement, he saw the little bird jump so high that it tumbled over backward into the deep center of the nest. It gleeped once, got itself in a sitting position, and settled down, trembling and worn out.

"You poor, dumb ole thing," Billy whispered. And the hawk, as if hearing his words, stared up straight at him.

Billy leaned back and studied the sky. Against high clouds, crimson in the setting sun, he spotted a tiny black speck—then another, and then two more. Billy felt sure that those specks were the rest of this family, soaring. What would it be like to *fly* like that? To feel the wind from the cloud, and know the gusty, thrusting power of wings as you turned and spun and soared free, swifter than anything else in the sky? Watching the hawks, Billy felt the chill bumps rise.

Below, the remaining hawk creeked in dismay.

"Aw," Billy called down to him, "you'll make it tomorrow, dummy. Don't worry about it." The prospect depressed him a little. His last chance to have the hawk was just about gone. But at least tomorrow was Sunday, and he might get to see the hawk's first flight.

Thinking about this as he headed for home, Billy did not notice the two young horsemen in the grove until they rode out in front of him. They were upon him so quickly that he jumped with fright before recognizing them and getting himself under control.

The taller one grinned. "Hey, Bobby, did you see him jump?"

"I sure did," the smaller youth said. "He scares easy!"

Looking up at Morrie Carson, oldest son of Paul Carson, and Bobby Robertson, whose father was the doctor, Billy felt a pang of resentment. It wasn't the first time they had scared him. The

142

fact that he had jumped in his surprise, and given them their satisfaction, irked him. "You guys want something?" he asked.

"We might," Morrie said. His lip curled. "Then again, we might
just be out to make rabbits like you jump."

"If you want something, say so. I've gotta git on home."

"We better let him go right away, then," Morrie Carson told
Robertson, "or he'll blubber all the way home."

Billy started past the horses. Morrie reached down and grabbed
him by the shirt collar. Morrie's horse moved several nervous
strides to the side, hauling Billy off his feet and dragging him.

"Let him go!" Bobby Robertson pleaded.

Morrie let go, and Billy fell to the ground with shocking impact. He staggered up, tasting dirt in his mouth.

"Don't try to walk off from me, Billy boy," Morrie warned.
"When I'm through talking to you, I'll say so. Got it?"

Billy hesitated. There was a wild, killing light behind Morrie
Carson's eyes, which looked a little pale and crazy under the best
of circumstances. Morrie wanted an argument, an excuse to beat
him, Billy knew. It had been that way for years. Morrie had a

coterie of friends whom he always led, and they had always terrorized younger boys. Now Morrie was grown, practically—and the game was still on. The possibilities gave Billy a chill.

"You going to stand there like I said?" Morrie's voice rose.

"Yes," Billy said.

"That's because you're yellow, then, Billy boy. *Yellow*."

Billy shuddered with the effort to remain quiet.

"Hey, Morrie, he's too scared for it to be any fun, even," Robertson said weakly. "Let's just go—all right?"

A long moment passed. Then Morrie turned his horse abruptly. "Yeah. Let's go. He's too gutless to try *any*thing."

The two young riders went off at a full gallop. Billy stood there in the dust, humiliation bitter in his throat. The day would come when a showdown with Morrie Carson would be forced upon him. Today had only been a postponement, so maybe he could grow a little more. Or get a little braver.

THREE

GOING to church on Sunday was not something Billy judged in any way; it was just something one did. Set on the edge of the town of Springer, their church was small, painted white, with a small steeple. There were not many windows, which was a blessing in the winter, but in the summer it became a bake oven inside. Going to church was a family thing. The building was usually crowded, babies wailed, little kids scuffled and got whapped for their nonsense, the singing was fairly good, and Preacher Wattle gave a long sermon. The sermon was the hardest part to get through, but Billy managed by thinking about other things.

This Sunday, anxious to get away to see if his hawk had flown, he was more impatient than usual. But Preacher Wattle had been talking maybe ten or fifteen minutes when Billy was alerted somehow to the fact that something was going on. His father, he realized, had stiffened in the pew. His mother was looking across at him—quick, nervous glances—and everybody was really paying attention to what the preacher was saying. Paw's jaw was set in

144

a hard line and his face was red. Billy perked up and listened.

Preacher Wattle was a short, fat man, and when he stood at the pulpit he balanced on tiptoes to lean over. If he got excited, he got a little wild-eyed. He was a little wild-eyed now. "And so, brothers and sisters," he said shrilly, "the good Lord told His people to subdue that land, to obey His laws, to work hard and to prosper. Man earns his way by the sweat of his brow, and if he is righteous, then God will stand beside him."

It sounded like the same old stuff. Billy didn't get it. His father looked tense, like an angry man backed into a corner.

Preacher Wattle waited a long, impressive moment. Then he raised his fist toward heaven.

"And note, brothers and sisters—note *carefully*—how the good Lord instructed His chosen people in the ways of law and righteousness. If a man causes a feud in the promised land, they are to root out the offender. 'You are,' He said, 'to show no mercy.' And if there was a false witness, he was to be banished in a way that others would hear of it, and know they should not do likewise. Again, God told them, 'You are to show no pity.'

"And then God told them that there might come times when they had to be stern, and take action against evil. He told them that dreadful rule of the just." Preacher Wattle paused dramatically, and the church was still. "Life for life," the preacher boomed. "An eye for an eye. A tooth for a tooth."

Billy saw his mother glance at his father again. But his father did not move a muscle. He was staring at the preacher. Billy thought he had begun to get it, and he felt this strange, vacant sensation in the pit of his stomach.

"A stern—yea, even a cruel code, brothers and sisters," Preacher Wattle went on. "And yet it is the word of God. What does it mean to us today?" He took a handkerchief out of the sleeve of his coat and mopped at his streaming face. The church remained very quiet—no one even coughed—and Billy understood.

Preacher Wattle resumed darkly, "The message of the word of God, I believe, is that there are occasions when just men must rise up—rise *up*, I say!—to stand against sin and corruption . . . to

145

take a position—the high ground, if you will—and fight." He took a deep breath and looked slowly around the crowd, his gaze pausing for what seemed an awfully long time on the pew Billy was sitting in. Then he continued in solemn tones.

"We have in our own fair community a growing lawless element. There has been talk of taking action against this element. Some speak of political action. Some of a vigilance committee.

"Pray over this question, brothers and sisters. Ask God's help, seek His grace in your minds and hearts. If a peaceful solution to problems can be found, it must be found. But if, after prayer and deliberation, you decide you must take stern action, then I say to you that in the face of the lesson I preached today, no just man can say that direct action against evil is immoral, or sinful, or without blessing by God himself; and now, let us pray."

Billy was stunned. He felt that Preacher Wattle's words had been directed exclusively at his father—and it seemed totally unfair. You couldn't argue back with a sermon.

He risked a glance at his father. The expression was stubbornly unreadable.

"Well, the handwriting is on the wall," Paw said bitterly.

He stood with his hands on his hips. Mom faced him. Billy stayed as inconspicuous as possible, because the fast, wagon-punishing ride home had told him how upset his father really was.

"Maybe Preacher Wattle wasn't talking about us," Mom said.

"Did you see that look he threw at me? In front of my own family. In front of my wife and *son*. And did you see the way people looked at us when we left?"

Mom tried a slight, unconvincing smile. "You did hurry us off fast, and you looked like a thundercloud. Maybe they—"

"No. I thought they'd just leave us alone. But it's clear now, that mob is going to exert all possible pressure to force everybody to go along with them. Using the preacher—that was a filthy thing to do. Of course Carson and his friends are the biggest givers in the collection—"

"Dan!" She was shocked. "He wouldn't *sell* a sermon!"

146

"I didn't mean that, Ellen. But it's human nature. Carson and his people put Wattle up to it." He ran a gnarled hand through his hair. "If they think I'll knuckle under, they're crazy. I'm a free man, Ellen! I intend to *stay* that way."

Mom put a hand on his arm. "You're upset now, dear. Maybe it won't be that bad."

Dan Baker turned to Billy. "They might get on you, too, boy."

"What do you mean?" Mom asked.

"Kids will hear their folks talking. Somebody at school will say Billy's old man is a coward. So he'll be supposed to fight."

"If anybody says that," Billy snapped, "I'll knock—"

"You are to do nothing of the kind, boy." He pointed a finger. "Don't let them suck you into it."

"But I won't let 'em talk bad about you, neither!"

Billy looked at his father. Their glances locked. Billy held his breath, and then the question came out. "Paw, *why* won't you sign the oath? You wouldn't have to ride with 'em—all you'd have to do is say they're okay!"

"I saw a mob once, boy. I won't ever support anything like mob action again." Paw's eyes had gone suddenly far away—to that other place and time, and that mob that had somehow changed his life. Billy wondered what it had been, and whether he would ever know. He saw from Mom's expression that she knew. Whatever it had been, clearly it had been very, very bad. "If some people want to think I'm a coward," his father said now, stiffly, "let them."

It was a chilling thought that went deep through Billy: *Was* his father a coward? A possum avoided death by pretending to be dead already; did cowardly men hide their weakness by *talking* about it, as if it were an illusion?

"Just as long," Paw added, "as you don't think bad of me."

"Is that important?" Billy asked, startled.

"Of course. What do you think a man works for? He wants for his woman to look up to him, and his sons to admire and follow after him. You're my firstborn, Billy, our only child so far."

As he spoke, Paw squatted in front of him, making their faces at the same level, and close. He squeezed Billy's arm, and waited.

Billy was supposed to tell him how brave he was, how sure Billy felt about that. He *knew* this was what the silence was for. He felt strangled inside. Because he couldn't do it. He wasn't sure how he felt about Paw right now, and he couldn't lie.

"I better," he said hoarsely, "see about the pets an' stuff."

His father's face reddened, and he stood abruptly. "Yes. Good." He had been hurt. And Billy knew *he* had done the hurting.

Heading for the barn, he struggled to get the heavy weight off his shoulders. Messing with animals had always been his escape. He hoped it worked this time, because he felt so terrible.

Rex, the hound, followed him, as usual wagging all over with friendliness and falling down every ten seconds to scratch fleas. His antics made Billy grin and feel better. Rex meant king, and Billy had always wondered whether Paw had shown a sense of humor or a huge potential for disappointment in naming him. The only kingly thing about Rex was his unmatched capacity for fleas. Paw said if fleas were cows, they would be millionaires.

Crooning nonsense to Rex, Billy walked around the barn to the shaded green enclosure where he kept his pets. Five or six cats snoozing in a sunny patch watched with their usual distant interest as Billy went to his mouse cages, hung on the barn wall. He made sure the mice had fresh water, and checked to see if they still had any of yesterday's cake. They did. Then he went to the rabbits. In his two-tiered row of cages made from crates he had ten rabbits, and by the looks of a couple of them, he was going to have a lot more pretty darned shortly. Pulling off some weed tops that the rabbits liked, he stuck them through the wire openings. "Here you go, Big Boy. How's that for supper? Hello, Queenie. Boy, are you ever fat."

Next he called on Alexander the Great. You couldn't keep a raccoon, everybody had said. A coon would claw out or attack you or go crazy and die. But Alexander the Great had been hurt when Billy found him, and had never been much problem, really. Except like now. His cage looked like a plowed field, and a freshly dug tunnel led under the wire and outside, to freedom.

Billy sighed and refilled his food and water bowls.

"Alexander the Great?" he called softly. In the weeds outside the pen there was a rustling. "All right, you big ole dummy. I'll give you about one minute, boy, and then I'm going to give your supper to Rex." The weed patch rustled more fiercely, there was a flash of gray, then Alexander the Great shoved in through the tunnel under the wire to squeeze up inside the cage. He looked bright-eyed at Billy. He was so fat it was ridiculous. If his belly had been half an inch bigger he would have had to wriggle along like a snake, because his legs wouldn't have been long enough. He was one sorry-looking coon, but friendly. Looking at the ham bone Billy had brought him, he positively grinned.

"Go ahead, fatso," Billy told him.

Alexander the Great started snarfing in the food. Rex, keeping a polite distance, began yelping as he always did when he saw Alexander the Great getting food. "Go on back to the house, Rex."

The dog obeyed, loping off.

Heading for the hawk's nest, Billy saw that clouds were gathering. If the storm approached with the usual way of mountain rains, however, he had time yet to satisfy his curiosity. He hoped the smallest hawk had flown. That would sort of put an end to it—get his mind off this idea of having a hawk of his own. He mustn't cause even the smallest kind of bother. It was hard to believe, but his father might be in real trouble, and it worried him. He had to be available if Paw needed him.

As he climbed higher, he began thinking more about hawks and less about other things. He hoped he could see his hawk's first flight; yet he didn't know if he *really* wanted to, because when the hawk flew, it became its own creature, free. And yet, Billy was telling himself, this had to happen; he was dumb to think of might-have-beens.

Going up through the ravine, he saw no hawks, but he caught a flash of red-tan in the deep brush and recognized a young red fox hurrying off for parts unknown. He shinnied on up the crack in the face of the cliff to his hiding place. Crawling out on the rock shelf, he peered down at the nest. It was empty.

149

He felt his insides lurch. He had missed the first flight, and his loss was now definite and final. He scanned the cloud-gathering sky. There were some birds far away to the north, but they didn't soar like hawks. Nearer he could make out crows.

Below his perch somewhere he heard some scrambling, thrashing sounds and looked down through the branches of the juniper into the shaded gully, which contained a tiny stream and a few deep pools of water. The sounds were not far off, and they puzzled him. Then, at the edge of his vision, he saw a slow movement in the brush. Riveting his attention on it, he saw the fox coming back, moving with infinite care, placing each paw very slowly, stalking something in the brush below the cliff.

Billy scrambled back off his rocky place and down the cliff face, banging up his elbows and knees. As he ran around to a place under the nesting tree, he came in sight of the fox about twenty feet away.

The fox turned and saw him and went stiff. "G'wan!" Billy yelled, and swung his arm. The fox bolted to cover.

Billy moved cautiously toward the gully—the place the fox had been approaching. Some creature was in there, probably hurt. The thought darted across his mind that it *might* be—but he figured that was ridiculous. He paused to get a stout length of old broken limb, just in case. Waist-high brush blocked his view into the gully until he moved around it, stick in hand.

There, on the shale incline halfway between his position and the pebbly stream a dozen yards below, sat his hawk.

Sat was not quite right, though. The hawk was *sprawled,* its back to Billy, one wing canted out at a bad-looking angle. Its feathers and remaining fluff were coated with dust and bits of leaves. It was trembling with fright and excitement. As Billy watched, it made a wild attempt to get airborne, flapping its wings furiously and trying to hop. One of its legs didn't support its weight and it fell on its side, tumbling a few feet down the slope and getting dirtier and more excited.

"Aw!" Billy gasped. He guessed that almost as soon as the hawk got into the air on its practically uncontrolled first flight, it had

150

either run smack-dab into a branch or gone into a spin. Either way, it had come crashing down to the earth and had hurt itself in the fall. It was lost, scared and without defenses, which was why the fox had been after it.

It made, now, another attempt to fly and tumbled farther down the slope, making the scrambling sound that had first caught Billy's attention. One more try and that hawk was going right into the stream.

Billy went down the slope fast on his heels, slid to a halt beside the injured bird and put a firm hand on its back. The hawk turned its head sharply, and its keen, wild eyes studied Billy. It tensed and tried to lunge away, but Billy pressed it down more firmly, feeling the hot body tremble under his hand. "You're gonna be okay, you ole dummy," he crooned. "Just take it easy."

The hawk fought again, writhing and jerking to get free. Billy flung his leg over the bird's back, pinioning it, while he snatched his shirt off over his head and folded it around the hawk like a sack. Sliding one hand under the bundle, he tried to pick it up, but through the shirt he was startled to feel talons grasp his wrist and hang on. A little shaky, Billy raised his arm, bringing the hawk up to the level of his chest. The grip of the talons was tight—the left clinging considerably tighter than the damaged right—but not really painful. The hawk, covered up and confused, was clinging for dear life but not struggling.

Billy sat down in the sun-warmed pebbles and tried to figure out what to do next. He was so excited, he had to urge his brain to think. If he let the hawk go, it would keep on trying to fly until it either hurt itself fatally or got caught by the fox. He peered up at the huge old juniper. To get the bird back in the nest was impossible. Should he climb the cliff, maybe, and put the hawk on a safe-looking shelf? It was hurt. It would starve. Or something would get it there, too.

The only thing to do, Billy thought, was take it home. But he had his orders about that, and Paw had enough troubles.

The hawk stirred on his arm, clasping and unclasping its talons, redistributing its weight. It was a young bird, and so completely

151

helpless. Billy felt such a sudden burst of sheer love for the dumb old thing that he was jolted.

Whatever he did was going to be awfully, awfully wrong. He could try to save the hawk and disobey his father. Or he could leave the hawk and try to pretend it wouldn't die as a result. The more he thought about it, the worse the alternatives looked. He knew he was a silly fool to get involved. But it was *his* hawk, and—

Overhead, a sudden slight commotion caught his attention. Looking up, he saw the adult red-tails swoop back to their nest. The two younger hawks swung through the trees, and followed. The family preened and started to settle down.

His hawk clung to his wrist. Quiet, out of it, and depending totally upon him. Billy got awkwardly to his feet, balancing the hawk under the shirt, and trudged up the gravel slope. He knew he was going to regret this, but he just had to do it.

FOUR

By LATE afternoon, Billy had done everything he could. He knew it was not going to be enough unless he found some kind of help.

"Where are you going?" his father called as Billy started across the yard. His father was working under the wagon, bracing a spring, and Billy could see only his legs sticking out.

"I'm just going up the road awhile," Billy told the legs.

"To the Sled place?"

"Yes, sir."

Pause. Then: "If they ask you about the vigilance committee, remember what I told you. No fighting."

"Yes, sir."

Another pause. Then: "Maybe they won't mention it."

Maybe, Billy told himself, the Sleds wouldn't. They were good folks, and Jeremy was his best friend. He had to count on Jeremy . . . had to take the chance.

The Sled farm was smaller than Billy's, and poorer. The house was a soddy, dug out partially in the side of a hill and then built up with earthen walls. Mr. Sled was building a log house, but work

152

on it had been abandoned until the crops were in. The yard was littered with toys and junk strewn around by the many Sled children, several of whom were playing in the dirt. Billy stopped at the open front door of the soddy. "Jeremy," he called.

His friend appeared at once. He was a year older than Billy, and a foot taller. Until a few months ago he had been the same size. Now he was over six feet, a bony scarecrow, with yellow hair and protruding teeth and bare feet and a lazy, insolent smile. He had always been a kind person, though, both when he was four feet eight and when he had suddenly become six feet one.

"Hullo, Billy," he grunted.

"What would you say we, uh, walk out back?" Billy asked.

"Yuh, okay." They walked around by the barn, from where Billy could see his place and the mountains beyond. Behind the Sled place, the prairie just seemed to extend for a million miles. Jeremy looked at the infinity of grass and kicked at a pebble.

"I have a problem, Jeremy," Billy told him. "I've got a hawk, and I don't know what to do with it."

"You got you a hawk? Aw! You always was lucky, as well as smart with critters."

"I don't know if this is lucky or not. See, my paw said I couldn't keep him at the house. But he's hurt. So I've got him in the woods, in a box, covered up with old rags to keep him quiet. But I can't leave him that way. And if I'm gonna keep him, I got to train him some, and I don't know how."

Jeremy nodded. "You got a problem, sure enough."

"Do you know of any expert hawk person—anybody around here that I could take this ole bird to, so he wouldn't die?"

Jeremy scratched his head. "The only hawk person I ever heard of," he said finally, "is the crazy man."

"The crazy man!" Billy gasped. "You ever *seen* him?"

"Shoot, no! But they say he keeps lots of critters. I heard some-wheres he knows hawks."

"I *can't* ask the crazy man! He'd probably *eat* it!"

Jeremy did not smile. "Dunno."

Billy thought about it some more. He was shaken.

The crazy man lived in the mountains north of Springer. It was said he had a cabin inhabited by dozens of wild animals. He looked fairly wild himself: long hair going to gray, woolly beard, penetrating dark eyes. He stayed to himself, except to go into town about quarterly to get a few basics.

"The crazy man's yur onliest hope," Jeremy pronounced solemnly. "You afraid to go up there?"

"I might be," Billy admitted. "Want to make something of it?"

Jeremy grinned. "I might be afraid, too," he admitted.

"Maybe *you* could just take the hawk—" Billy began.

"Nope, *no* way. My daddy said if I brang in any more critters, I'd haf to eat 'em for supper."

"Well then, I've got to think about what to do."

Thunder rumbled across the big sky. Jeremy held out his hand, catching a raindrop. "Yur ole hawk might git hisself drownded before you've made up yur mind."

THE rain began steadily about six o'clock, and then pelted down in earnest when Billy was up in the sleeping loft. He lay and listened to it pounding on the roof and imagined the hawk in the box he had rigged out in the woods. The box was nailed to a tree, fitted into a crotch so it could not fall. The lid was tight, nailed in. Billy had left airholes, using his shirt as a curtain to keep the light out, and he had put some roofing paper over the box; it would not get too wet inside. But the tree would be swaying in this wind. The poor hawk would be scared, Billy figured.

Later he roused from worried sleep to hear the rain light on the roof. The storm was passing. Knowing that the worst was over for his hawk, he dropped off to deeper rest.

In the morning little rivers ran through the yard in all directions. A limb was off the elm tree, and there were leaves everywhere. The garden looked beaten, plants bent over and dragging in puddles. But they would come back. The rain would work magic in the long run. The earth glistened, the bare mud gleamed. The wet odor was fresh and bracing.

Paw stood at the window. "No farming today, boy. Inside work,

154

and maybe later some relaxation." Paw turned and looked at Billy, and Billy looked away, embarrassed.

Paw was thinking about checkers. They did that, sometimes, on bad days: worked in the house and the barn in the morning, then hunkered over the board near the fire in the afternoon. It was always good, with the smell of Paw's pipe in the room.

It wouldn't work today, though, and in the instant their eyes met and slid off, they both knew it. Their relationship was too strained. It all went to the vigilance committee questions, Billy thought, *and it's all my fault for not having faith!*

"I've got . . . some stuff to do with the pets," Billy lied.

"All right. Do what your mother wants done. Then go."

Before eleven o'clock he was finished and headed out across the icy-wet meadow for the woods, his boots already clogged with mud. So many things could have gone wrong with the hawk that he approached the tree with dread. The box was firmly in its place, the lid seemingly intact. He raised a corner of the shirt curtain, letting in some light. The hawk flustered around inside, making a big racket. Satisfied, Billy quickly restored darkness.

The whole idea of approaching the crazy man was bad enough, but the idea of going by himself was even worse. Well, there wasn't any help for it. Working gently to avoid frightening the bird, Billy got the box loose from its moorings, then secured it against his chest with both arms. It made for awkward walking.

Heading north, Billy took the shortcuts he knew well in the local terrain. After about an hour he was just out of familiar territory. Rain clouds hung against the sides of the mountains like gray-blue blankets, but no rain yet fell.

Billy had only a general idea where the crazy man's place was. He moved up the foothill slopes, through conifer forests, and out the far side onto sloping grassland studded with big boulders. As he trudged upward, holding the hawk box, his breathing began to get harder—the altitude. He was tired, too, but it would be worth it if he could get the hawk cared for. If the crazy man wouldn't help, Billy had no idea what he'd do. He was pretty amazed that he was doing *this*—going to see the crazy man—it

155

showed the things you could do if you had to. His lungs were throbbing with every breath by the time the crazy man's house came into view. No one else had anything this high on the mountain, so Billy knew at once what it was.

It was against a dirt cliff, and appeared to be an old cave dwelling with a new door, axe-hewn logs forming the front wall. Two small log outbuildings and a pen stood nearby, protected by the cliff's overhang. A few buckets and boxes and some rolled wire lay around, but in general it was a remarkably neat camp for a man who was supposed to be crazy.

Billy was glad to be here, but his insides quaked a little, too. He *supposed* the crazy man was friendly, though. A little late to wonder, everything considered.

Billy walked across the clearing, passing the pen between the two sheds. A fawn stood quietly in the pen, one leg splinted and neatly bandaged. What was amazing was that she looked right at Billy and didn't appear nervous at all. On the side of the larger shed there was a shelf, and a big brown owl stared from this perch sleepily. A couple of squirrels sat on the roof, arguing over a nut. But there was no sign of the crazy man.

"Hello?" Billy called, not too loud, so as not to spook any critters. There was no reply. In the distance came some thunder.

Billy put the hawk box down on the steps of the house. It felt mighty good to stretch his arms. "Anybody home?" he called.

Something rustled behind him and a feathery shadow went over his head. Startled, he began to turn. The shadow became a rope that sang over his shoulders and around his waist, pinning his arms to his sides as the noose was jerked closed.

"That's enough!" a male voice boomed behind him. "Don't try to get away, young feller! Just stand still, now, I mean business!"

Tingling with fright, Billy turned toward the voice.

Coming into view from behind the larger shed, the crazy man kept the rope taut in his hands. He looked very upset, his long hair standing out in all directions, his beard bristling.

He was a fairly large man, the crazy man was, with a slight beer belly bulging under his baggy gray flannel shirt. He wore

156

black pants, very old, and clodhopper-type shoes that laced up the side, and a pearl-colored vest with yellow lining. His shaggy hair and beard made his head look even larger than it was. He looked a little like a lion, but a pretty old lion; Billy could tell the crazy man was sixty if he was a day.

"Just don't think you'll get away, young feller," the crazy man said, hopping around Billy. "You'd better just stand still!"

"I am!" Billy protested. "I'm just standin', see?"

."What did you think you'd do, eh? Come up here an' bother the crazy man, eh? Steal his pets? Throw rocks, eh?"

"Did somebody do that stuff?" Billy asked, amazed. He swiftly imagined how some of the older boys might have.

"Yes, indeed! Caught you this time." The crazy man chuckled. "Now what have you got to say for yourself?"

"I didn't come to cause trouble. I came to get some help."

"Help?" The crazy man cocked his head at a wild angle. "What do you mean by help? What kind of prank did you plan, eh?"

Billy was getting over his initial fright and was getting irritated. "See this box? *That's* why I came. It's a young hawk. A red-tail."

"In that box?" The crazy man frowned, his eyes alert.

"It fell," Billy said. "Hurt itself."

"And you come to me? Why?"

"My father says I can't have him. I heard you were good with critters. I didn't want to just let this hawk die. . . ."

"What's your name?" the crazy man asked. Suspiciously, as if he had trusted once too often.

"Baker, sir. Billy Baker."

157

The crazy man, frowning, came to the porch steps and raised a corner of the box lid to peer inside. He looked sharply at Billy, evidently flabbergasted. "You come to *me*."

Billy said nothing.

Quickly, gently, the crazy man pulled the rope from around Billy's arms and lifted it over his head. "I'm sorry. You okay?"

"I'm fine. You scared me for a second."

"Meant to," the crazy man grunted with satisfaction. "Oh, not *you*, of course; the ones that've been comin' up here, messing everything up. Guess they think it's funny." By now his eyes had become pleased and thoughtful. "My name is McGraw, sonny. You can call me Mac or McGraw, but I'll take it very personal if you call me the crazy man, leastwise to my face."

"Pleased to meet you, Mister McGraw. About the hawk, sir—"

"Yes. You say he's hurt? You want to tell me about it?"

"You can help?" Billy asked. "You know stuff about hawks?"

McGraw smiled. "I know *everything* about hawks."

Nor quite willing yet to believe his luck, Billy told McGraw all he knew about his hawk. McGraw watched him keenly through the recitation, paying close attention both to him and his story.

"You've done you a lot of observing, sonny. You must like wild things. Most boys your age figure creatures are just moving targets for their guns."

"I'd never shoot something like a hawk, sir!"

McGraw smiled faintly, then shook his head as if to assure himself of reality. "Tell me this, sonny: What do you want to do? Get this hawk healed up and then let him go?"

"Well," Billy admitted, "I've heard about training hawks to fly free—to come back when you call."

"Falcon can learn that," McGraw said, his eyes alive with speculation. "It's not as easy to train this kind of hawk."

"I'd sure like to try, though," Billy breathed. Then, catching himself: "I mean I can't with *this* hawk. My paw made that clear. But boy, *some*day! . . . I dunno how you do it—do you?"

"I've trained a few hawks in my time, if it comes to that."

"You *have?*" Billy cried. "Then, I mean, *could* you . . ."

"Now, *listen*, boy! We don't even know if your stupid hawk is going to live. I haven't even examined him yet!" McGraw threw up his hands. "Bring the box into the small shed."

The shed had contained birds of some kind before. It was hot and dim and closed off to most outside light, and the odor was of bird dung and feathers. McGraw had Billy place the box in the center of the floor while he picked something up from a far corner. Billy saw it was a T-shaped leather-covered perch, the butt of which fitted neatly into a hole bored in the floor. Some thin leather straps and a leather pouch were attached to the perch.

"All rightee," McGraw said, when he had the perch set up. "I'm taking your little hawk out of the box, now, to get him inspected. Stand back. It can be dangerous. Even," he added quickly, "for a boy as expert as you are."

Billy, pleased by the compliment, backed off against the wall.

McGraw carefully lifted the lid, sliding his hand inside. Dim though the light was, the hawk started to panic. McGraw held the bird down while he reached back with his free hand to get the hood off the perch. "Bird's a little thin," he remarked.

"He was the runt—" Billy began.

"*Shhhh*, now."

McGraw expertly maneuvered the small leather pouch over the hawk's head and somehow, one-handed, he managed to tie the two small strings to keep it in place. The hawk struggled for an instant, then, fully blinded, settled down. McGraw gently picked it up and sat it on the perch. The hawk hung on and stood erect.

With quick movements McGraw examined it. Then he reached for two thin leather loops—called jesses—that were hooked around the perch and got them fastened to the hawk's legs. He stood up stiffly, rubbing his back and looking down at the hawk thoughtfully.

"Wing is hurt. Leg, too. But he holds the perch all right, and he didn't flinch too much when I got the jesses on him. I'd say there's nothing major wrong with that bird."

159

Billy stared at the hawk on its perch, hooded and fastened, just like it had been that way all its life, and he was as amazed as he was thankful. "You just *put* him there—and he stays?"

McGraw chuckled. "He's tired and confused and some hurt right now. He might fight the jesses later. C'mon out. Let's let him rest."

Billy squinted in the sun. "You'll help him get well, then?"

"I'll try. I think this hawk will be okay."

"Then you'll . . . you might let me learn how to train him?"

"Now *that's* a different deal," McGraw said firmly. "Training a bird of prey is dangerous. It takes technique. Some birds won't train. Sometimes you train one perfect and it goes sour overnight, sulks, and takes off for the tall timber. And that's it."

"I would sure work hard," Billy said eagerly. "I've got to work with my paw, and my mom has jobs for me to do, and I've got the pets to feed and water, but I could get up here *pretty* often. I could run most of the way—"

"And what will your parents think, you coming to visit the crazy man?"

"I didn't think I'd tell them," Billy blurted.

McGraw's fine white teeth showed. "Just lie, huh?"

"No, sir! Just—well—just *not tell*."

McGraw shook his head slowly. "Looks to me like a bad deal all around. The bird goes bad, you're disappointed. Your folks find out you're coming up here, you get tanned, and I get burned out or something."

"There won't be any trouble," Billy said. "I *promise*."

McGraw soberly tapped him on the chest with his index finger. "Your parents object, you got to quit coming."

"Yes, sir!"

"The hawk goes bad, we let him go. And no hysterics, see?"

"Yes, sir."

"You do what I tell you, because I know hawks."

"Yes, sir! Right!"

McGraw glowered at him. "You like cookies?"

Startled, Billy didn't understand. "Sir?"

"I said—oh, tarnation—come on in the house!" McGraw turned and strode up the porch of the cave-dugout, jerked the door open and went in. He had to bend slightly to duck the ceiling.

Following him, Billy went into a large, single room with rock walls and floor sloping gently toward darkness at the back.

McGraw's furniture was very simple: a lamp from an old tin can; a stove for cooking, also made from cans; some box tables and box chairs; and a bed rigged from ropes and axe-squared logs. What struck Billy was how neat it was, cleaner than any house he had ever been in, even his own. McGraw gruffly ordered him to sit down. He brought him some cookies on a chipped plate. Billy tasted one to be polite, and it was just about the best cookie he had ever stuck between his teeth. "Hey! These are *great!*"

"Of course," McGraw grunted. "I made 'em, didn't I?"

For a crazy man, Billy thought, he was awfully smart.

FIVE

It was an uneasy feeling, having a secret.

Billy's impulse was to tell his parents about the old man and the hawk, but he kept quiet. He sensed that his father's reaction would be bitter—he'd give Billy a hiding in the shed for disobeying, and then he'd insist that the hawk be turned free. But fear quickly passed into something else, a secret knowledge that, in this one thing, *he might know better than his father*. Billy had never had this feeling before. It was disconcerting.

On Tuesday the family went into town for the week's shopping, always a major event. His father would mingle with other men, talking about crops, prices, the cattle market and other matters. And his mother could be counted upon to make her shopping last much longer than seemed sensible for the few items she bought. Billy usually got stuck with his mother, but sometimes he got to stand outside with his father and listen to the talk.

Springer was a small town in one of the valleys, beside a creek. Main Street—the wide part—was two blocks long, with one street intersecting in the middle, where the fancy church—as Billy's

162

mother called it—put up its steeple against the mountain sky. First there were barns and storage buildings. The street got busier as one approached the church corner. There was Carson's store, flanked by the gunsmith's shop and dress shop on the left and Doc's Confectionery and Springer Feed and Seed on the right. On the far side of the street were the post office, the barber shop, three saloons and Bainbridge's Hauling Company. The commercial buildings sort of petered out near the church, as if out of respect, and the area around it was broad and grassy. On beyond were more one-story buildings, and well up at the end of the block, the jailhouse. Billy had never been to the jailhouse, nor to the fancy church. Their church was more modest, and on the outskirts. The bank was near the fancy church, on the side road that led to the bigger, grander houses belonging to some of the merchants and to the banker.

All of this suggested to Billy, vaguely, that Springer was not the simple community he had once imagined. He knew there were *layers* of people in the town: drunks and drifters and people who got arrested a lot on the bottom; then probably the cowboys and others who didn't stay long but seemed to spend a lot of money; then the sheepmen, and then the start of the *real* people: farmers like his family; merchants like Mister Carson; then folks like the banker; and then the preacher and schoolteacher and people like that, way up on top, practically out of sight. That these layers existed did not bother Billy much; he knew his was the best.

The street was fairly active on this sunny Tuesday. Several horses were tied in front of the saloons. Wagons were scattered along the side of the street. There were some farmers standing in the road talking, women bustling around on the board sidewalk and kids playing in the dirt.

As usual, Billy was riding in the back of the wagon, and he hunkered to the side to greet people, but he didn't see any of the kids his own age he was seeking. His father pulled the wagon up between two others, and the horses settled in, clomping and shifting in their harness. It was then that Billy realized things were not quite normal. People who had been talking when they pulled up stopped and turned to stare at them, then turned away again. When his father swung down off the seat and walked around to help Mom down, nobody said anything. But a number of the private conversations got started again, all at once. Billy looked hard at his father and saw that his face was all squinched up, not quite angry, but sort of on the defensive.

Mom *seemed* not to notice anything. She caught one lady's eye. "Hello there, Mrs. Madison!"

Mrs. Madison hesitated just a moment, then smiled. "Hello, there!"

"Lovely day!" Mom beamed.

"Oh, yes. Lovely."

Billy's father seemed to take the cue. Stepping up onto the sidewalk, he caught the arm of a man. "Morning, Stanley!"

Stanley turned with a show of surprise. "Why, hello, Dan!"

Paw grinned at the other men, his eyes like metal. "Hello, Frank. How are you, Archie?"

Billy noticed that people's smiles seemed strained and that they didn't look his father in the eye. There was another eerie silence, and from outside a saloon across the street came a burst of male laughter that sounded like a thunderclap.

"Come, Billy," Mom said, and swept into Carson's. Paw, who sometimes was not against slipping away for a quick beer, kept close beside her. Billy followed.

The first step into the big store had been frightening when Billy was younger, and it was still dramatic. Most of the lower floor was open up to a loft, and there were barrels and boxes everywhere, with huge bales and rolls of wire and rope hanging overhead. It was dark inside, and the effect was of having walked from the normal world into a cavern peopled by shadowy giants. Billy's senses drank in impressions: the faint odors of hemp, earth, spices and cloth; the feel of the sawdust floor loose and crumbly underfoot; the mutter of voices and chunking of items into sacks. Then his eyes began to adjust and he saw his mother leading the way, under an enormous hanging display of saddles and livery gear, toward the yard-goods section in the far corner. Two house-

164

wives were looking at material, and Mister Carson himself was cutting from a bolt of calico. They all looked up as if greatly surprised.

"Hello!" Billy's father said, as if challenging them.

They chimed in with their hellos. One of the women moved away promptly, and the other worked her way to the far end of the tables as Mom began looking at some cloth. Billy noticed that his father stood closer to Mom than he usually did, his face grim.

Mister Carson came over to them, scissors in hand and tape measure over his shoulder. "Morning, folks. How are you today?"

"Fine," Paw said.

"Word with you, Dan?" Carson said. "In private?"

"No need to exclude the family. What is it?"

Carson seemed to steel himself. "Well, sir, it's about your bill. It's—getting on toward fifty dollars. I'd appreciate it if—"

"Our bill has been higher before," Paw said quietly, his face absolutely flat with what had to be rage. "You know we've always paid as soon as we were able."

"I understand that," Carson said. "Times are hard. But—well, they're hard on businessmen, too." He took a breath, put down the scissors and jammed his hands into his apron pockets. "I'm just having to reduce my credit business, folks."

Mom's hand went up to her throat. "Cash only?"

"That's the size of it."

The color went down out of Dan Baker's face, and it shocked Billy. Out of the deathly gray flesh, his father's eyes looked like fire. "Reducing everybody's credit, Mister Carson?"

Carson's hands bulged in his apron. "Most."

"Especially people who don't sign the pledge?"

"It's my store, Baker. I run it as I see fit."

Billy's father took a step toward Mister Carson. Billy's mother caught his sleeve. "Dan!"

Paw froze, and the look of anguish and anger on his face cut Billy in a way he had never experienced before.

Paw whispered, "You can't wait, can you? Can't see that there's an election coming? You could deal with the problem legally."

165

"Anything we do will be legal. I've told you that."

"*Rope* legal?"

Carson stiffened. "I came over here to tell you, nicely, Baker, that business is bad and I have to reduce credit. The other matter has nothing to do with this."

"Maybe you want to pretend that, but I won't play along."

"Sorry," Carson snapped, and turned to walk away.

Billy's father made a slight, convulsive move. Mom's hand clutched tighter at his arm, holding him back.

"Damn him," Paw whispered. "*Damn* him!"

"*Don't,* Dan," Mom said urgently. "It's all right. Really."

She was about to cry. But she clung to Paw, as if to convince him by her fragile strength that it really *was* all right. Was that what moms did? Say it was all right when it wasn't? *Why?*

BILLY told McGraw about it in the early evening cool of the mountainside as they squatted beside the outdoor perch where the old man had put the hawk.

"Mister Carson sure didn't back off. All we bought was some salt. Paw said we'd just haf to do without some stuff for a while."

"Your paw think about signing the vigilance pledge?"

"Heck no! If they wanted to make it a war on *him*, he told Mister Carson, that was just okay by him."

"Your father isn't likely to win with the power of the town against him. One by one, they'll get the other neutral families to sign up to save their credit." McGraw sighed. "He's a good man, your daddy. You're lucky, you know. I sure hate to see a good man getting things turned around where everything's against him."

"Do you think he should join?" Billy asked.

McGraw grinned. "If I had a lot of answers to life's problems, sonny, maybe I wouldn't live on the side of a hill by myself."

It raised the question Billy had been wondering about, and although it was very early in their relationship to ask, he blurted it out. "How come you live by yourself this way, anyhow?"

Their glances locked for an instant, and Billy had a very strange, frightening feeling that he was looking through McGraw's eyes

166

into an old and private place of pain and regret. *Something* had happened to McGraw once. Like Paw's bad thing with the mob. Billy wanted desperately to know the secret, and simultaneously he knew it was probably better that he didn't.

McGraw answered his question with the quiet irony of a man who knows he is not to be believed. "I like it alone, sonny."

"Aw," Billy growled, embarrassed.

McGraw patted him on the back. "Besides, it keeps me out of trouble. Tell me, don't you figure your hawk looks a little better?"

Billy accepted the change of topic. The hawk *did* look better. Sleeker. It sat its perch strongly, calmly.

"Do we take the hood off now?" Billy asked eagerly.

"We'll take him in where it's real dim and see how he does."

Billy watched McGraw slide his left hand and arm into a stout leather glove and gauntlet, then cautiously move the protected forearm in front of the hooded hawk, nudging its talons and legs. The hawk struggled briefly to keep from being pushed backward off the perch, then saved its balance by stepping onto the glove. McGraw deftly unhooked the jesses from the swivel on the perch, twisted them around his fingers and led the way to the shed.

It took just a minute to install the hawk on its inside perch. The shed was so dark, Billy could scarcely see. McGraw discarded the glove and picked up a long feather, which he used to stroke the hawk's throat and chest. "Gentling him a mite," he explained, his voice crooning for the hawk's benefit.

"Shouldn't you use your fingers?" Billy asked. "Get him used to your touch?"

McGraw chuckled. "You might get a chunk out of your finger. More important, the oil in your hand would mess up the natural waterproofing in his feathers. He'd get soaked in the rain, couldn't fly, would probably die."

Billy pointed to a long, slender stick that McGraw had put beside him. "You use the stick for stroking him, too?"

McGraw made the funny snuffing sound through his nose that Billy had learned was laughter. "Not hardly! See that fruit can there by the door? Bring it over, all right?"

Obeying, Billy saw strips of raw meat lying in the can. The hawk seemed to stir, as if catching the scent.

"Now you just sit back there real easy," McGraw told Billy, "and don't look right at him if he looks at you. Hawks take fright if you stare right at them, sometimes, and no telling how spooky old dimwit here is going to be with the hood off."

Very gently McGraw untied the hood. As he lifted it off, the hawk jerked up and looked around. It had a wild, magnificent tilt to its head, and its body trembled. It did not try to fly. Its head turned from side to side, and those blazing eyes gave Billy a deep thrill.

Now McGraw picked up the thin stick and reached the tip toward the hawk's chest. The hawk looked at it uneasily, then struck down hard with its beak, catching the stick and trying to bite the end off.

With a wink at Billy, McGraw gentled the stick loose from the hawk's grasp. He impaled a tiny strip of meat on it and slowly pushed it forward. The hawk tilted its head nervously, then viciously grabbed the stick. The meat came off in its beak. It chewed and swallowed sharply.

"That's how you teach it to take food from you?" Billy guessed.

"It's a real important step," McGraw told him, baiting the stick again. "You go from stick to string to lure. I'd say this hawk is taking to the first step in good shape."

"I guess we go real slow, huh?" Billy said, as he prepared to head for home.

"The whole training takes just a few weeks," McGraw said. "You know how to carve you a whistle?"

"A whistle?" Billy echoed, puzzled. "What for?"

McGraw's eyes twinkled. "At some point, I reckon, you're going to want to fly this hawk. You'll need your whistle then."

"You mean I blow a whistle and he comes back from *flying?*"

"Boy, if that hawk takes a mind to clear out for the tall timber, ain't nothing you or anybody else can do; whistle or no whistle, he'll *go*. Though a whistle helps sometimes, it's part of the conditioning. But never mind, I'll carve you one." McGraw smiled.

"I'll appreciate it."

"You figure on using this hawk to hunt for you, Billy?"

"No!" Billy gasped. "I just want to have him—train him."

"Your daddy thinks it's nonsense, eh?"

"Well, he would," Billy admitted, "if he . . ." Then he stopped, realizing his mistake. "If he, uh, thought about it, or, uh . . ."

"He doesn't know you brought this hawk up here," McGraw said solemnly. "What do you suppose he'd think if he knew?"

"I don't know, sir," Billy admitted.

"I don't want to get you in any trouble, boy," McGraw said sadly. "And I don't want to get me in any trouble, either."

"I've asked you for help. It's not like *you* asked *me*."

"A lot 'of folks," McGraw explained, "will blame your daddy for not joining the vigilance committee. They'll be mad because he'll be acting *different*—not one of the herd, you see?"

"Some people oughtn't to be in the herd," Billy said.

McGraw smiled sadly. "The herd seldom thinks so. And that's my point. Just as some folks don't like your daddy for not joining them, why, it's natural for your daddy to distrust *me* some, because I'm a loner, right? Folks mistrust folks that are different, especially loners. And you can't blame them, either."

"My paw wouldn't mind about me and you and the hawk."

McGraw inclined his head at an angle that said he was skeptical. "He's got plenty on his mind without hawk or crazy-man trouble. Just you make sure you don't mess up any of us. Right?"

Billy didn't quite understand, but he nodded agreement.

"Might be some bad times ahead, boy. If they do come, you just don't worry about this hawk. Or me. Right?"

"I really don't know what you're talking about now."

"Just promise me," McGraw said sternly.

"I promise," Billy said, confident that he couldn't hurt anything by promising on something he didn't know anything about.

"Better get your rear end home now," McGraw added, swatting him. "Must take you an hour to hoof it back and forth."

It took an hour and twenty minutes, but Billy didn't admit it. He thanked McGraw rather formally, and sped away. He was late.

Night caught him in the foothills. He was still well off from home when he saw the glow of the flames near town, and heard the horsemen coming, and suddenly realized that blind luck had placed him right in the center of something he wanted no part of whatsoever. When the horsemen exploded out of the night on the road behind him, he only had time to dive behind some rocks as if his life depended on it—which, for all he knew, it did.

HE HIT the erosion ditch, rolling between boulders and jagged rocks still hot from the day's sunlight, just as the horses pounded past, astonishingly close. He had the impression there were about two dozen riders, and the clatter of hoofs, groaning of saddle leather and clink of metal were tremendous.

The horsemen were not, however, going by. They were reining up, wheeling, bumping into each other, and yelling instructions as they tried to get some semblance of organization. The dust thickened, choking Billy's throat and nostrils. Most of the riders wore hoods and were heavily armed. In the center of the melee were four riders without hoods: young men, strangers, their clothing in shreds, faces hideous with blood, tied in their saddles and reeling like grotesque rag dolls as their frightened mounts pivoted.

"All right!" a man bellowed, swinging his horse around near the center of the roadway. "Line 'em up there!"

The voice sounded like Mr. Carson's. It was darker, though, with passion, and Billy thought, Maybe I'm wrong. . . .

"Swing 'em around!" the man ordered. "Get them ropes up!"

Through his peekhole in the rocks, Billy watched with horror as arms swung and ropes snaked up and over branches. This high road, this spot of wind-blasted old cottonwoods, could be seen for miles in the daytime. The prisoners, their faces ghastly with fear, were going to be strung up for all to see tomorrow.

"Make a noose," the leader yelled, swinging out of his saddle. "Somebody get some of those torches going. Set a guard back down the road, there! Hurry it up!"

Everything was already a hurry and a confusion. Horses bounced into one another, riders cursed and muttered and maneuvered, fashioning nooses out of the ropes dangling from branches.

"Shove them into line, there, and get the ropes on them!" the leader ordered. The hooded horsemen forced the prisoners' horses together under the trees, pressing them forward so that the nooses hung across the prisoners' faces. One of them brushed against the heavy rope, uttered a strangled cry, and started to fall, un-

conscious, in the saddle. Hands shot out and held him upright.

"All right!" the leader shouted.

The hooded riders stilled. The prisoners stared, haggard with the gaunt pallor of doomed men, as the leader strode across to face them under the nooses. Torches cast yellow shimmers. Smoke curled redly against flames. It was, for an instant, very still, and Billy watched between the boulders, his heart hammering.

"We've burned down your squatter shacks," the leader said. "We are the new law in Springer. No deputies, no hearings, no paroles!" The hooded figure seemed to swell with a deep breath. "You four stole food tonight. Your guilt was judged by the vigilance committee. We set our own penalties; it's our land, our law."

171

He paused, and the sparks and hissing of smoke from torches was the only sound in the vast, nightmare night. "We can hang you now, until you are dead, to show we mean business."

One of the prisoners moaned. Billy, watching, tried to think of a way to escape. He didn't want to see this.

"We can—but we choose not to—*this* time." The voice boomed again. "You're to go. Warn the others. We want no bloodshed, but we're going to protect our own."

Then, before Billy could quite comprehend it, the leader made a slashing motion with his hand. From all sides, knives appeared and sliced through ropes that held the prisoners. One of them keeled over and hit the earth like a sack of feed.

The leader swung into his saddle. His companions followed suit. Dust exploded from the roadway. They were off in a rush.

Grabbing the chance, Billy scrambled along the ditch and started for home. Partway down the hill, in the greeny-wet meadow, he looked back. One of the torches had been dropped on the roadway, and it cast an eerie pinkish light against pluming smoke and the undersides of trees, where the nooses hung. Two of the prisoners sat in their saddles, heads down, stunned. One was out of sight, his horse standing riderless. The fourth man stood beside his horse, arms hanging limp, shocked, unmoving.

Far off toward Springer the glow of the fire, the one that had burned them out, was now a dull coal.

Billy hurried on, and when he saw the lights of the windows of home, he felt a relief so intense it was painful. The war in the valley, he knew now, was on. Tonight his father had been allowed to remain a neutral. Tomorrow—nobody could guess.

SIX

ON THE morning after the first strike by the vigilance committee, Billy's father had visitors again—two men who farmed on the far side of Springer, Judkins and Braithwaite. Billy's father invited them in, but they seemed reluctant to go near the house; they stood uneasily by their wagon.

"You heard about the action last night?" Judkins asked.

Dan Baker looked angry but controlled. "I heard enough."

Judkins spat. "Vigilance committee. Nobody hurt, but those boys ain't around today."

Braithwaite mopped his forehead. "Some of the neighbors, seeing how the committee got something done, joined right up this morning. Sled, down the road there a piece, for example."

"I guess they needed their credit at the store," Dan Baker said sharply. "What do you want with me?"

Judkins raised his eyebrows, as if offended. "Just paying our respects. The committee wants to make sure every citizen understands what's going on. You changed your mind about joining?"

"No."

"Look at this boy." Judkins inclined his head toward Billy, who stood listening. "Haven't you got an obligation to him?"

"Thanks for telling me my obligations as a father," Dan Baker said. "I really appreciate it, gentlemen."

After the two men had been gone a short time, Billy was down by the barn when a visitor of his own appeared. Jeremy Sled squatted against the barn wall and looked down at his splayed bare toes. "Those guys come to yur house, too?"

"Yep."

"Yur daddy join?"

"Nope."

"Mine did. He had to, Billy," Jeremy said quickly.

Billy was stunned at his friend's reaction. "You act *embarrassed!* Like joining was *bad.* I wish *my* paw would join! The vigilantes might do bad stuff—but maybe it has to be done."

"If it was a good bunch of people, would they hold up your credit to make you join? My daddy called it caving in."

"I hadn't thought of it that way exactly," Billy admitted.

Jeremy sighed. "How's your hawk? And the crazy man?"

"He ain't crazy, Jeremy," Billy said, glad to change the subject. "His name is McGraw, and he's real nice."

"How does he look? What's he done to the hawk so far? How long does it take to get there? Could I go with you?"

"I don't see why you couldn't," Billy said, answering the last question first. "And the hawk's fine. We're training him."

"You *will* take me? Boy, howdy! I won't tell my daddy!"

"Why not?" Billy demanded. "You don't have to hide it."

"Well, have you told *yours?*"

"No," Billy admitted. "Because he told me, Paw did, not to mess with any more animals."

"My daddy would be mad about that old man. My daddy says, don't mess with people that are different from you."

"*Why?*"

Jeremy hesitated. "Well—don't take no chances, he says." But when he finally left, Jeremy came right out and admitted he'd like to meet McGraw, Daddy's objections or no. Billy said he would see if McGraw minded.

HIDING his actions from Paw continued to bother Billy. But even with all the trouble building in town, he found he was more and more preoccupied with the project of getting the hawk manned. That, McGraw said, was what you called the first stages of training a hawk. You manned him. It was no mean trick, he said, because that meant building trust and confidence between a person and a wild thing.

"It takes a special kind of man, too, sonny. You see, the hawk has senses we don't even know about. Just look at your hawk, there. He's listening. He's beginning to know you. He's making up his mind. If he can't *feel* you're the right kind of person underneath, then there's no way he'll ever train for you."

"Do you think he knows I saved his life?" Billy asked.

"Ah, he knows, sonny. He *knows*."

It was a mysterious, almost frightening thing, but Billy knew it was true. Hawks were not just another kind of wild creature. They were special, having those keen, keen eyes, and being able to soar; they were very special. How could you ever be sure what a hawk might know? And McGraw said some hawks would simply die rather than accept manning. At first, Billy thought this was dumb, but now he saw it as noble.

"Do you suppose," he asked McGraw, "we could unhood him again?"

McGraw nodded. Gently he untied the leather hood and flipped it back off the hawk's head. The hawk's feathers spread out, magically, as if some new inner fire had suddenly swollen from within. The size of the bird seemed to double, and it trembled on the perch. Its head turned, ever so slightly, toward Billy.

Billy looked away, as McGraw had told him to, his heart thumping. The hawk partially spread its wings, allowing them to unfold and droop downward. It froze in that position. Its eyes focused on Billy, looking not only at him but *into* him, he sensed, filtering out false impressions, picking out those things that were true.

"Am I good enough?" Billy asked McGraw impulsively. "Am I good enough *inside*, I mean?"

"I hope so, sonny," McGraw replied. "We're gonna find out."

That afternoon Billy's mother was at the Sleds', quilting, and Paw was off in the gullies somewhere, looking for a cow. That was when Sheriff Ad Sweeney came, riding up on his swaybacked gelding. Billy had never seen him before, but there was no mistaking him.

"Your daddy here, sonny?" he panted.

"No, sir," Billy told him. "But he ought to be back soon."

"I'm Sheriff Sweeney," he said, swinging out of the saddle. "I don't look much like a lawman, but I am, by grannies."

Billy grinned and stuck out a hand for a shake. This gave him an instant to study Ad Sweeney, who was about five feet eight inches tall, about four feet six inches wide, and as bald as a billiard ball. Sweeney wore pants that looked like circus tents, and he had big silver spurs on his boots, which had to be size fourteen triple wide. He wore a six-gun, all right, and a badge on his suit collar, but he looked like a disaster waiting to happen. No wonder his horse was swaybacked. The miracle was that it was still alive.

"Heard your dad wouldn't join the vigilance bunch," Sweeney said, leaning against the fence, which creaked. He inserted a quarter of a pound of chewing plug into his mouth. "How come?"

175

"He told them he don't like mobs."

"They've cut off his credit. Given him a bad time."

"Yes, sir."

"He hasn't give in."

"Heck, no! Are you kidding?"

Sweeney spat. "How about you telling him I was by, and if he could come to Springer for a talk, I'd be mighty appreciative."

"Are you gonna be around our town for a while?" Billy asked.

"Guess so. People that stand for regular law and order have to get together," Sweeney muttered somberly.

"Because of last night, you mean?"

"Naw," Sweeney said, and heaved up into the saddle. "This afternoon. You don't know about poor old Deputy Plotford, then."

"No, sir. What happened?"

"What happened," Sweeney said, "was six bullets in the back."

"Aw!" Billy stared up, fighting to get it figured out. The vigilantes had struck, and somebody had struck back—at Plotford. And now Sweeney was here, calling on Paw. *Why?* "You looking for help, Sheriff Sweeney?" he asked. "You're not thinking of asking *my paw!*"

"You just tell him I'd sure admire to see him before nightfall."

"I'll tell him, Sheriff."

Sweeney, slumping as if he carried the weight of the world, rode away. Billy turned back to the house and saw that his mother had come home and was signaling to him from the porch. He told her what Sweeney had said. As he got to the part about Deputy Plotford, she stiffened.

"Your paw was right. This is how it goes. The sheriff will hire more men, the vigilantes will strike back, the others will counterattack. . . ." She slipped her arm around his shoulders and squeezed him, hard. "I want you to stay close to home, Billy."

Billy thought about how far he had to trek to get to McGraw and the hawk. Maybe it was silly to be so caught up in this whole hawk business when so much was going wrong. But the hawk *was* important. Maybe this was the last real pet he would *ever* have. And the hawk wouldn't have been *alive* except for him. Now it

176

was up to him and McGraw to make it a trained hunter, sort of a *completed* hawk.

"Do you think the sheriff is gonna ask Paw to be a deputy?" Billy asked.

His mother's face drew together and revealed a dozen fine lines of worry that he had never seen before. "I don't know."

Billy had the feeling of things closing in on them. If Paw became a deputy, he became like Plotford, and Plotford was—

"Get your chores done," his mother said. "He may want to take you to Springer with him."

Billy went out to the pet pens, fed and watered everybody, picked some ticks off Alexander the Great, and had even hoed the corn patch a little, before his father came back with the stray cow. Billy told him about Sheriff Sweeney's visit. Paw looked grim and said he would appreciate company into town. Right, Billy said.

A STRANGER, Billy thought, could have told instantly that something was badly wrong in Springer. Riding in with his father, he knew at once. But how? It wasn't easy to pin down. Horses stood at racks along Main Street, as always, and a couple of wagons were at Carson's for loading. The old-timers sat where they usually did, by the old cannon in the square. Dust skittered along.

Everything normal. But not really.

The only thing Billy could put his finger on was the lack of movement. It was a little like an election day, where everything looked fine on the outside, but anything really going on was going on behind doors someplace. Billy thought of the hooded men of last night. It didn't seem right, them being hidden that way and violent by night, and now just as hidden—but behind a veneer of business respectability—by day.

As his father reined up outside the jail, the door opened and Sheriff Sweeney strode out. "Dan! Thanks for coming. Can we, uh, talk without the boy?"

Dan Baker hesitated.

"I'd just as soon set out here, Paw," Billy said.

Baker nodded and went into the jail with Sweeney.

Settling down against some feed sacks in the wagon, Billy thought about his hawk and then about the town's troubles. From inside a saloon came laughter and the clatter of a piano. It seemed hard to believe, from the peaceful look of things now, that violence walked in the night. He was sitting there, thinking about that, when he heard a faint tinkling sound from the street behind him. He turned.

Coming up the street was a big raggy man carrying a crooked walking stick. He had a floppy black felt hat and floppy brown leather boots, and he was leading a pack mule that was about the sorriest creature Billy had ever seen. The man slumped along steadily, minding his own business.

"Hey, Mister McGraw!" Billy called delightedly.

It took McGraw a second to spot Billy. Then his grin shone. He waved his hand in a slow salute. "Hello, young feller!"

"What're you doing?" Billy asked.

"Well, sir, even the crazy man has to get a few supplies now and then. Might even splurge and get me a touch of red-eye whiskey." McGraw winked. "Just for snakebite, naturally."

"Naturally."

"What brings you to town, anyhow?"

"Aw, my paw's inside, talking to the sheriff. Last night the deputy got killed."

McGraw jerked. "Killed! Poor old Plotford?"

"Yes, sir."

McGraw shook his head sadly. "He was a good man. He didn't try to run me off, like some lawmen would. He liked fishing. Never had much luck, he said." McGraw tipped his hat back and scratched his head. "Guess his luck is *all* run out, now."

"It looks like I won't be up to see you today," Billy said.

"No need to worry. The hawk's coming around real fine."

Billy felt a chill of pleasure. "What do we do next?"

"Well, we keep adding light, getting him used to being carried and handled, and we'll be making his food bigger, you know, so he has to learn to tear it apart with his beak and—"

"What are you doing there, mister?"

178

The voice was so close and so unexpected that McGraw and Billy turned to face it in the same instant.

Standing by the back corner of the jail, his butcher's apron around his ample middle, stood a man Billy knew only as Chafflin. He was heavyset, bald, about fifty. He had small, close-set eyes, and the only time Billy had ever seen him before, those eyes had been jolly. They were anything but jolly now; they looked angry, perhaps scared. Billy saw, with a shock, that Chafflin had a revolver belted around his middle under the bloodstained apron.

"What are you doing to that boy?" Chafflin demanded.

McGraw smiled. "We're passing the time of day, friend."

"What's your business here?"

"I live here." McGraw pointed to the mountains. "Up there."

Chafflin's eyes widened. "You're the crazy man."

"He's not crazy!" Billy protested. "He's my friend and we're talking, and you better butt out, mister!"

"Boy," Chafflin said, moving in, "you need some manners."

"Don't bother him," McGraw said with a sudden sharpness.

Chafflin looked from Billy to McGraw and back, clearly uncertain about how he should proceed. He took a breath and started again. "I'm a member of the vigilance committee," he announced stiffly. "Our pledge is law and order, and people living together so as not to bother each other."

"What law were we breaking?" McGraw asked.

"You've got no business bothering this boy."

"Friend, I'm not bothering this boy."

"You don't belong here. Move along."

"Who decided which people belong here?"

What Chafflin would have responded, Billy would never know; for at that moment there was a sound behind him, on the porch of the jail. Chafflin glanced up and immediately began smoothing his hands on his apron in a nervous way. Billy turned.

Sweeney was on the porch. "Well, now, let's not have any fuss here, shall we?" He was smiling.

Behind Sweeney stood Billy's father. He looked unhappy. He had a deputy's badge pinned on his shirt.

179

"I DIDN'T WANT IT and I'm not qualified," Paw said at supper. "Maybe I don't even have a right to take the risk, with you two to watch after. But Sweeney has to have support."

Seated in front of a plate of food she hadn't touched, Billy's mother had never looked any more solemn or anxious. "I know you had to accept it, dear."

"Sweeney said I won't keep regular duty. All I really have to do is to *be* here—in this part of the

county—and keep him informed. There has to be a— a representative of the real law, you see?" Paw turned to Billy. "I meant to ask you earlier, who was that old man you were with when I came out of the jail?"

"That was Mister McGraw," Billy told him, worried. "We was talking, and old Chafflin came over and butted in."

Dan Baker shook his head. "Some of the roughest element are already gone. But it won't stop now. Chafflin and others like him will try to drive out everyone who isn't exactly what they want. Who is this man McGraw, Billy?"

"He's sort of a friend of mine," Billy hedged.

"A friend? Where does he live?" Paw asked sternly.

"Well," Billy said, giving up, "he lives up in the mountains."

"Is he the *crazy man?*"

"He ain't crazy, Paw!"

"The one people *call* the crazy man? How did you meet him?" Paw demanded.

"Well," Billy said slowly, feeling trapped, "I had this hawk that was hurt. It fell out of its nest and I couldn't just let it die, and you'd said I couldn't bring home any more animals. Jeremy suggested

180

the crazy man. So I took the hawk to him. He's a nice man, Paw! We're training my hawk. It already wears a hood and eats meat you give it on a stick, and—"

"Are you still that much of a baby?" Paw snapped.

"Huh?" Billy said, shocked. "What are you *mad* about?"

Paw threw up his hands. "Will you grow up, boy? The town is torn to pieces, the valley is going up in smoke, a deputy is dead and I'm forced to take his place, the vigilance committee cuts off our credit—and *you're* out playing with a hawk!"

Billy's mother stirred. "Dan," she said in soft reproof.

"No! When is he going to start accepting responsibility?"

The anger in Billy was like a flash of sunlight from a mirror. "When are *you?*" he shot back.

"What?" Paw said, startled.

"When are you going to join the vigilance committee so you can help get something done around here?" Billy demanded. "I know they're rough, but they're getting the job done, right?"

"That's like saying I can butcher a pig by shooting it full of buckshot, since all that matters is getting it dead," Paw told him.

Billy shook his head. "That kind of stuff has nothing to do with what we're talking about. I'm big enough to know that much. You tell me to take responsibility—but you don't."

"I've told you I'm against mob action!"

"Is that it, Paw—or is it just a way to hide?"

"I've heard all I'm going to hear," Paw said hoarsely. He was shaking. "You'll do as I say, young man. Is that clear?"

"Yes, sir," Billy choked, afraid he was going to blubber.

"If you won't grow up on your own accord, I'll make you."

"Now, Dan," Mom said tensely. Her hands were knotted.

"You stay out of it," Paw snapped. "He can't be sneaking off to play with some damned bird when we have all this trouble!" He turned to Billy, his face tight with anger. "You are not to go up there again. Under any circumstances."

"What about *my hawk?*" Billy gasped.

"You're not going to have a hawk. Forget it."

Billy looked at his father, then at his mother, and he was thinking of what he had to say to make them change their minds. One moment he thought he had everything under control, and then, shockingly, he was crying. It was awful—he had thought he would never get caught crying like this again. The tears seemed to spurt from his eyes and splash all down his cheeks and chin. "I'm *not* going to forget it, Paw! I'm not hurting anything. I'm getting all my chores done, and you—you got no right, telling me to stop doing something that isn't even bad."

"We'll see about that!" Paw started to leave his chair.

"Dan!" Ellen Baker's voice was very sharp.

Dan Baker glanced at her and paused.

"Leave the boy alone," she said softly, with great firmness. "Let him work with that hawk, if that's what he wants."

Paw's face was cloudy. "You'd cross me on this?"

Billy had never seen his mother look as hard, or as serene. Her tone was velvet. "I seldom question you, Dan. But when you're wrong, you're wrong—and someone has to make you see it."

"You're challenging my authority over my own son!"

"He's my son, too."

Fascinated, Billy watched his father stare a long time, in silence, at his mother. A lot of things were almost said, but got held back, and the struggle showed in the muscles of Paw's face. He was on his feet, and he towered over Billy's mother. But the way she stood, slender and straight and so *calm,* made it seem as if she were surrounded by an invisible wall of quiet and strength.

"All right!" Dan Baker shouted finally. "All *right!*" He whirled on Billy. "But no shirking of chores, boy!" And he stormed out of the house. The door slammed, shaking the pans on the wall.

Billy's mother began cleaning off the supper table.

"He's really, really mad," Billy breathed. "He—maybe I ought not to go to the mountain, after all."

She turned to look at him with eyes he could not read. "It means a lot to you, doesn't it?"

"Oh, *yes,*" he admitted with a burst of candor that was rare between them. "I've always wanted a hawk. And McGraw's—"

"Then go when you can, son," his mother told him calmly.

"You'll lose your last chances to play—and laugh—soon enough."

"But I hate for Paw to be so mad."

"He is under a terrible strain. But as for being mad at you, or me"—she smiled a secret little smile—"he'll get over that, darling."

Later, in bed in the loft, Billy heard his parents talking softly below, and there was no anger in either voice. He felt better, hearing this. Maybe everything was going to work out.

He imagined his hawk in the sky, flying free, then hurtling back to his signal, and he felt a renewal of spirit. The way he loved the hawk was just unbelievable. You could do anything if you tried hard enough, and he was going to make the hawk perfect.

It was going to be great fun, all of it. Maybe even enough to compensate for the trouble with Paw—and the feeling that came when he thought about it.

SEVEN

DESPITE his chores, Billy managed to get up the mountain every day, and he soon learned that McGraw had plenty of things beside the hawk to keep him busy. He provided all his own food by hunting with simple snares or by fishing, but this was only a small part of his activity. The other animals—the ones he was nursing— were what filled his days.

He had five "patients" in what he called his animal hospital. There were the fawn, recovering from a near-fatal attack by a mountain lion; the owl, which had tangled with something much too mean for it and lost part of a wing; a wolf cub whose paw had been mangled in a metal-jawed trap; a fat old bobcat who was too lazy to hunt for food anymore; and Bodacious, the mule, McGraw's property by right of the fact that the original owner had planned to shoot it and McGraw had intervened. Bodacious knocked down clotheslines and got in the garden quite a lot.

"Get out of there, you old ninny," McGraw bellowed one day when Bodacious was waltzing around through the bush beans.

"Why don't you use bob wire to keep him out?" Billy asked.

"I don't hold to barbed wire," McGraw told him. "Have you ever seen a cow or a deer that caught its leg in barbed wire? Even if it wasn't cruel, I still wouldn't like it. It's cutting this whole country up," McGraw said, his eyes distantly angry.

"The country's gotta be tamed," Billy pointed out.

"Who says so?" McGraw shot back.

"Well, my paw, for one."

"Well, I wouldn't argue with your paw. This used to be a big land, though, you know that? You could go from the Bravo to Canada and never touch wire. But by the time you're grown, you won't be able to walk a hundred yards without a 'pardon me.'"

"It's gonna be all right for me," Billy told the older man, "because I'm gonna live on a mountain. Like you."

The weathered face split in a grin. "Oh, you are, are you?"

"Right. And I'm going to help sick animals, too. There'll always be plenty of animals!"

McGraw squinted at the sky. "Not as much ducks and geese as there used to be. They'll cut down woods, shoot eagles and birds like your hawk, so there won't be any natural habitat, and no parents to continue the strain. They'll finish them off, like the buffalo, and it'll be all over." McGraw's voice took on a bitter ring. "Trappers ought to be happy then. *Nothing* out here, just them and their traps, waiting in case something gets born and needs killing off real fast."

"You don't like folks too much, do you?"

McGraw shrugged. "I don't dislike 'em, boy. Don't talk foolishness. I *know* them, that's all. Do you cuss the wolf because he hunts a rabbit? That's the way nature *is*. Not good, not bad, it just *is*. Man is the worst hunter because he's the smartest and he likes killing more than any other creature—even kills off his own kind." McGraw sighed. "But that's just nature, like I said. Do you want to work some with your hawk?"

Once they started working with the hawk, the cynicism fell away from the old man, and he was like a boy again—chuckling, smiling, gently teasing, exercising infinite patience.

It seemed there was a tremendous amount for both Billy and the hawk to learn. Training a hawk, McGraw told Billy, was not a thing that dragged out. A hawk would either train or he wouldn't. You pushed right along and found out fast. Each day another step was added. McGraw tied food chunks to a string and showed Billy how to tease or jerk it, giving the hawk some added sport in making tiny midair adjustments. Getting it to grab food on a line was important, McGraw pointed out, in terms of steps still to come.

"As I see it," McGraw told Billy thoughtfully one evening, "you're about the stubbornest kid with wild creatures I've ever run into. But sometimes things just don't work out, boy. You ought to *remember* that."

"I will," Billy said, ignoring the thought that McGraw was trying to tell him something he deemed most serious.

While the new feeding process was going on, they also worked on getting the hawk to carry more calmly without the hood. At first, in the dim shed, it flapped its wings wildly and hopped onto McGraw's gloved forearm only long enough to catch balance and hop right back onto the perch. McGraw had Billy work on the technique until one day the hawk stepped up calmly, as if he had been doing it all his life, onto Billy's arm.

"He's doing it!" Billy whispered delightedly. "Look! Hey!"

"Be quiet," McGraw counseled softly. "Let him get used to it slow. Then see if he won't let you carry him around a little—"

But when Billy tried this, the hawk practically went berserk. It flapped its wings frantically and jerked on the ends of its jesses and ended up hanging upside down, virtually pulling Billy's arm off and scaring him half out of his wits before McGraw could grab it and swing it back to its perch.

"I messed it up!" Billy cried disgustedly. "I got scared."

"You did fine, sonny," McGraw murmured. "He might have learned something, falling off." As McGraw spoke, his voice crooned to the hawk, which trembled and spat fire from its wild eyes. "You're going to make mistakes, Billy. Everybody does. Let's not be feeling bad, okay?"

Billy watched the hawk calming down, and began to feel his own insides settle. But he still felt it was all his fault.

"I'd say you ought to be walking this old bird outside in three or four days," McGraw went on. "Might bring that friend of yours up with you. Show him all the hawk's learned."

Billy felt a flush of thankfulness and love that almost bowled him over. It was days ago that he had mentioned the possibility of Jeremy visiting, and McGraw had shown no sign he even heard. Now McGraw was using this moment to cheer him up. It was no small thing, letting another person come here, Billy realized. This was a favor, to let Billy share a moment of triumph. "It's *really* all right?" he asked.

"Dadblame it, boy! If I didn't think it was all right, I wouldn't *say* it was all right!"

McGraw, Billy was learning, could be tough and cranky. The language he used on Bodacious would have made Billy's mother faint. Yet this same big man could turn from a seeming tantrum and be, within seconds, exquisitely gentle, soothing a frightened animal or doing some aspect of training with a care and sensitivity that seemed almost unreal. Billy also knew that McGraw needed him, somehow, liked him, took pride in him. It was good, the way they worked together. "I'll probably bring Jeremy someday real soon," he told McGraw now. But faced with the genuine possibility, he suddenly wasn't sure he wanted to *share*.

"You better be heading out now, young feller," McGraw said as they left the hawk in the shed. "I'd say everybody ought to be home by dark these nights. They're out, the vigilantes."

"Things is quieter in town," Billy said. "A lot of rough guys up and left."

"Don't doubt it," McGraw murmured.

"My paw is right, I guess," Billy said thoughtfully. "But it sure does look like Mister Carson and his vigilance committee has done some good at that."

"Might be," McGraw grunted. "But I side with your daddy."

"He's been real busy, riding around where Sheriff Sweeney tells him, and stuff. But what's gotten done, the vigilance guys have done it. Ole Sheriff Sweeney and my paw haven't."

"No. All *they've* done is try to uphold the law." McGraw's tone was whip sharp.

186

"What're you mad about?" Billy asked. He was upset and hurt.

McGraw tossed an arm over his shoulder, "I suppose I just don't like the idea of them smart alecks taking the law in their own hands and getting kids like you to thinking it's all right. You just don't criticize your daddy, boy. Not even indirectly. Right? Your daddy has needed a lot of courage, going against his neighbors and all. One day you'll understand that."

"Okay." Billy flushed. "I'll keep my big trap shut."

He hurried down the mountainside as fast as he could jog. It was going to be touch and go, whether he made it before dark. He had cut it close several nights, and had gotten good and bawled out for it. He knew his parents' anger was in direct proportion to their worry. Running along a hill saddle, Billy got busy imagining what he would show Jeremy about the hawk, how Jeremy and McGraw would get along. It would be good to have company on these long hikes home, too.

Not that walking alone worried him, because the way things looked, despite McGraw's warnings, the trouble in the valley was definitely easing off. Even his father had evidently begun to worry less. With that relief, and his hawk, and McGraw for a friend, Billy felt it could be the best summer he had ever known. The positive feelings were so strong that he got a second wind, jogging through the meadow toward the creek line and trees, and he ran harder and faster.

He was running just about full out when a rope or branch or something hit him across the chest and knocked him sprawling.

EIGHT

BILLY hit the dirt hard, shocked out of thought. Spitting dirt, he rolled over and saw that a rope had jerked tight across his chest. He pulled at the loop to free himself.

"Just leave it there and don't move."

The voice was close, in the trees, and before he located its source he knew the speaker was Morrie Carson.

Carson it was, all right, coming out of hiding, lariat in hand.

He grinned down at Billy. "You're in an awful hurry, Billy boy."

There were some horses back in the trees, and Billy realized that Morrie was not alone; three other boys were with him, one of them Bobby Robertson. "What do you want?" he demanded. "Git that rope *off* me!"

Robertson stepped forward and nudged him with the toe of his boot. "Where you been and what've you been doing?"

Billy hesitated. All four boys were a good head taller than he, and two or more years older. He decided to play it cautiously. "I've been out looking for berries," he lied.

"*This* time of year? That's pretty stupid," Morrie said.

"A family can use all the food it can get," Billy shot back, "when your paw cuts off credit at the store."

"Don't talk against my father, buddy, unless you want—"

"Take it easy," Robertson cut in nervously. "All we're trying to do is collect information, remember?"

Flushed with anger, Morrie nodded and pulled his rope off over Billy's head. "This is the second time we've seen you come down this way in the past few days. Where have you really been? What's going on with you and the crazy man?"

"What business is it of *yours?*" Billy fired back. "Who do you think you are? What are you doing out here like this, anyway?"

"Everybody does his share," Morrie said grimly. "If a person collects information that leads to an arrest or an action by the vigilance committee, there's a ten-dollar reward."

"What are you going to do?" Billy asked sarcastically. "Collect for saying I like to walk in the woods?"

Morrie balled a fist. "You little punk, I ought to—"

"Morrie, take it easy!" Robertson pleaded.

Morrie walked around Billy, kicking dirt insolently. "You'd better stay away from the crazy man. It's not smart to arouse suspicion right now."

"Thanks for the advice." Billy, a new worry striking him, forced himself to be about a hundred percent more polite than he felt.

"Just remember it," Morrie said.

Billy watched them swing into their saddles and head toward

town before he resumed his jogging. It was so dadblamed stupid, he thought, the four of them almost grown men, riding around, playing vigilante. But Morrie had a genuine cruel streak. They could cause him more trouble than he wanted, if they set their minds to it. He had to start taking them into consideration, especially if he planned to continue visiting McGraw. Rex, hearing or seeing him coming half a mile away, started barking like mad. "Aw, shut up, you big dummy!" Billy yelled. The hound loped out to meet him and raced him to the house. Rex won, naturally, and was sitting on the porch when Billy got there.

His mother was at the fireplace, swinging a kettle of beans and pork off the wood flames. It smelled good, and the mountain evening had turned just cool enough for the fire to feel good, too.

"You're late," she said sternly.

"Yes, ma'am." He knew better than to argue.

"Hurry and wash up," she said.

"Where's Paw?" he asked, pumping up water at the sink.

"He had to go to town. I'm going to go ahead with dinner because I don't know exactly when your father will get back."

"Is there trouble?"

"Not that I know of," she said in a tone that made it clear she was not at all sure. "Sit down. The corn bread's done."

"How come we have all this?" Billy asked, taking his place at the table. "I thought we were out of both beans and cornmeal."

"Well," Mom said, "we have our credit again at the store." She put a plate of steaming food in front of him. "Mister Carson said he knew everyone has to follow his own conscience. Most people around here are really nice, son."

"Oh, yeah," Billy grunted. "As long as you do what they want. Or if they finally decide that what you do doesn't make any difference to them one way or the other."

"I'm not sure I approve of this cynical attitude, young man."

He decided to be smart and say absolutely nothing at all.

The aroma of the corn bread was sweet and overpowering. While she cut slices of it, he gouged big chunks of fresh butter out of the deep dish and piled them on. It seemed strange to be

189

home, having a feast, just a little while after being scared to death by Morrie Carson and his stupid buddies. The corn bread, soaked clear through with butter, was *so* good.

"I suppose you've been off with that strange man," his mother said. "Is the hawk going to live?"

"Oh, sure! It's fine! We're training it now."

"Son—after it's trained"—her expression showed strain—"will you leave it with the cra—with your friend up there?"

"*Mister* McGraw would keep it if I asked him," Billy said with dignity. "*Mister* McGraw is a real nice man: kind,. gentle, smart, and he minds his own business and doesn't spend half his time gouging folks in a store, like *some* folks."

"Billy," she said, coming out with it, "are you *sure* your Mister McGraw is all right? Does he act all right? No one knows where he comes from, or why he insists on living alone. Is there a chance he might have something—criminal—in his past?"

"He lives alone because he likes it," Billy said angrily. "His past is his own dadblamed business. And he always acts fine. Don't *worry*, Mom!"

She sighed. "I do, though. All mothers worry. Now, with the investigation—" She stopped suddenly.

Billy chilled. "The what? Is somebody investigating Mister Mc-Graw? Mom, *tell* me!"

She frowned. "Not just him, dear. Your father said the vigilance committee is investigating a lot of people. They're determined to find any undesirable element—"

"What are they doing? How are they doing it?"

"Writing letters, finding where people came from, talking to—"

"Yeah! Snooping!"

"I want you to be calm about this, Billy. Whatever happens, you just be polite, and tell the truth."

"What do you mean, 'whatever happens'?" He was thoroughly alarmed now. He still didn't know why Paw was in town, or why Mom was making such an issue of Mister McGraw. Remembering Morrie Carson, he had an idea about it which he didn't like. Her expression confirmed his suspicion. "What do they want to do? Ask me questions about him? Ask me to *spy* on him for 'em?"

"Your father won't let them question you. You know that."

He stared at his mother, thunderstruck. Paw could keep them from bothering him, but that didn't mean they would leave Mc-Graw alone. There were grown men in Springer with the instincts of Morrie Carson, merely more developed and honed.

McGraw, Billy saw, was on the brink of serious trouble.

JEREMY's eyes shone with controlled excitement as Billy proudly made the introductions. "How do you do, sir," Jeremy said.

McGraw shook hands. "I'm pleased you could visit. Jeremy, is it? Fine name. Biblical. Billy tells me you like animals."

"Yessir," Jeremy said, "but I don't have a bunch like Billy."

"Tell you what," McGraw said with a smile. "I've got a pretty fawn in that pen over there, and if you move slowly, you'll get a close-up look at the ugliest owl you ever saw. He sits on the side of the chimney and pretends he's invisible. Meanwhile, I'll give your partner, here, a hand in bringing out the hawk."

"Yessir," Jeremy nodded, pleased.

"Come on, falcon master," McGraw said, putting an arm over Billy's shoulder, and they walked to the shed.

Billy opened the door slowly, as he had been taught, to make sure the hawk did not panic at the change in light. It sat calmly on its perch, watching them. "Hello, you ole dummy," he said. He could have sworn the hawk showed recognition.

"I guess the best thing to do," McGraw said softly, "is for you to carry him out and put him on the perch. That way your friend Jeremy can get a good look. Then we can go ahead with some food training." McGraw handed him the glove and armguard. "Let's try it without the hood."

"It's *bright* out there!" Billy protested. He was always tense when he was to handle the hawk, but McGraw, in suggesting that they carry it out of the dim shed into the bright light, and without the calming device of the hood, now was pressing him into a new and scary trial. "This ole hawk might go loony when I carry him out there!"

"Well now," McGraw said softly, "he might at that. But I don't think so—not unless you show how nervous *you* are. This hawk is learning real fast. He knows you. He likes you."

"As big as he's gotten, I don't even know if I can carry him that far! I mean, he's gotten to be a big ole hawk!"

"If you don't want to try it, Billy, then don't." McGraw was watching him closely, compassion and a lively amusement in his crinkled eyes. "A man should never do something he really doesn't want to do."

"I *want* to," Billy breathed. "I'd sure like to have Jeremy see me do it. But I just don't know if the ole hawk—"

"He's ready, Billy. You both are."

Billy struggled with himself. He trusted McGraw. McGraw just wouldn't be wrong about something like this.

"Whatever you think," McGraw told him softly. "If you want to give this hawk another few days, it won't hurt to wait."

McGraw, Billy realized, was giving him an easy out. That somehow helped him decide. "I'll do it." He put the glove and gauntlet on his right arm, then walked very slowly up to the hawk. It watched him, unblinking. Sweat stinging his eyes, he unsnapped the jesses from the perch. This left over a foot of twin leather lines attached to the hawk's legs, and these he twisted around his thumb and pinched inside his palm to make sure that the bird would not get away if it panicked. The hawk stepped onto his gloved arm with perfect ease and calm.

"Did you see that?" Billy said, thrilled.

"Go nice and slow, now," McGraw said, "and don't look right into his eyes, remember. If he starts to flap, stand still and keep your face turned. I'll help you. Don't worry."

Billy moved toward the door.

"Okay," McGraw murmured.

Billy walked on outside, flinching as the sun struck him and the bird on his arm. The hawk did not budge.

Jeremy looked on in awe. "Gosh!" he said huskily.

"Nice and quiet, boy," McGraw told Jeremy. "Just stay put."

Billy, holding his breath, walked across the yard. He was so

192

proud he felt like he was going to just blow up and go all over the sky in pieces. The hawk rode on his arm as if they had been doing it for years. *This* was what having a hawk was all about, he thought with a thrill. In the weight and the slight, living tension of talons on heavy leather glove, there was a communication. They knew each other. They were partners right in this very instant, and they both understood it.

Billy walked to the outside perch, knelt, and carefully moved the hawk toward it. He held his arm still and didn't rush things. The hawk stepped off his arm and onto the perch. Billy untangled the jesses and snapped them onto the new perch swivels.

"Good work, boy!" McGraw said proudly, clapping him on the back as he got shakily to his feet and removed the leather glove.

"Gosh, Billy!" Jeremy gasped. "That's a real beautiful hawk, and you really know how to handle him, don't you!"

Billy's knees, if they had been any more watery, would have pooled out onto the ground.

McGraw shoved his hands into his pockets and stood there lackadaisically, like nothing unusual had taken place. "Good thing the bird's in such a good mood today." His lips quirked in a smile. "He's got a couple new lessons coming this afternoon."

"What're they?" Jeremy looked to Billy for an answer. Billy did his best to freeze his face and hide the fact that he didn't know.

"Billy figures the hawk needs exercise," McGraw said quietly. "And we keep adding new little deals to the feeding. Right, Billy?"

"Uh, right."

The question of exercise began to be clarified before Billy could wonder about it. McGraw squatted in front of the hawk and fitted swivels from a vee tied to the end of a long, coiled line of tough, woven twine to the jess swivels that held the hawk to the ground perch. This gave the hawk as much as fifty yards of potential freedom. McGraw signaled to Billy to put the glove back on and pick the hawk up once more. Billy did so carefully. McGraw carried the coiled twine and led the way to a spot on the sloped clearing about midway between the cliff behind him and the edge of the woods below.

"What we do," McGraw said, "is fly the hawk on the line. He gets exercise, and he gets the idea that he can't just fly off when we let him go. I hold the end of the line, here. Billy flies him. You give him this little warning by lowering the arm—see, like this—and then you toss him."

"I don't know if he's ready," Billy said nervously. "What if he can't fly?"

"If he's not ready, he'd better *get* ready. He can fly. But Jeremy, you might want to stand back there against the shed. The cord won't let this fool bird get quite that far."

"Okay, and I'll stand real still, so's to not spook him any."

"Good," McGraw said. "It's nice to work with people who understand nature and animals."

Jeremy was grinning with obvious flushed pride when McGraw looked back to Billy. "All right, boy. Any time."

Billy looked at the hawk. The hawk seemed to have no idea that he was now attached to a long cord rather than the few inches that usually held him to the perch or the arm. He looked just a little sleepy. Billy mightily hated to toss him. He was afraid it was going to be a real mess.

"You can do it," McGraw said gently.

Billy took a breath and lowered his arm somewhat. The hawk widened his eyes and got slightly unsettled, fluttering one wing. Billy lowered his arm a little more, thinking, If you've got to fly, the higher I throw you the better your chances are. He threw his arm upward so hard that he left the ground with both feet.

The hawk went into the air, straight up, and his big wings unfolded fully for the first time Billy had seen them. They made an incredible commotion, and the hawk began to drop, then caught itself and started out across the clearing, rising as it flew hard and steadily, its wings rhythmic. It was so lovely that it made Billy's throat ache, the way the hawk climbed in this moment's flight, its head forward, leaner and wilder in flight than at rest.

Beside Billy, McGraw raised the end of the line and made a quick pumping action, sending a wave out along the cord. The wave action shortened the line and the hawk felt the tug, then

the wave straightened out so that the hawk had some leeway before actually reaching the end of the cord. The warning broke the hawk's flight and it fluttered to the ground and sat still.

"*Gaw!*" Billy gasped. "Did you see how he *flew?* I mean, he's *strong!* And fast—he was starting to pick up speed and altitude! He'd have just taken off and gone over the mountain!"

McGraw chuckled. "I noticed."

Their eyes met, and Billy burst out, "Aw, he's so *beautiful!*"

"You want to go get him, sonny, so he can fly again, or do you figure on letting him sit out there all night?"

Billy ran down the slope with the exuberance he felt, before he remembered he had to approach the hawk slowly. But if he was worried about the hawk getting too excited, he had again underestimated the bird. It stepped right up onto the glove.

Billy carried him back to the center of the clearing, made sure McGraw was ready, and tossed again. The hawk took off to the right, and again he landed at the end of the line.

On his third flight, the hawk headed for the cliff; on the fourth, for the woods. On the fifth, he merely skimmed the ground and landed before he reached the end of the line.

"What's wrong with him?" Billy asked.

McGraw guffawed. "He's fat and lazy, that's what's wrong!"

Billy decided that getting tired was no big disgrace for a hawk that had really never flown before. He *was* fat. He would get leaned out now, though, because Billy intended to fly him plenty. This was going to be one champion hawk before he got through!

With the flying done for the day, McGraw brought out the hawk's food. There was one more lesson to go. He fastened a piece of meat to an odd-looking chunk of leather, balled together and tied with thongs and covered with feathers taken off small birds. He then attached this contraption to a length of twine and tossed it onto the ground in front of the perch. The hawk came down off the perch for it. McGraw jerked the string, making the bird grab at the gadget repeatedly before letting him catch it.

Watching the hawk tear the meat off the leather object, McGraw explained to Jeremy, for Billy's benefit, "It all goes a step at a

196

time, youngster. We taught it to eat strips, then to jump on chunks and tear them up. Now we're teaching it that its food comes looking like natural prey, and that when we show it this lure—that's what the leather deal is called—then it has to grab it to be rewarded. A little later, see, we'll be swinging the lure and having the hawk catch it in flight. When we get *that* far, we're almost all the way." He rummaged in his pockets and brought out a small wooden object. He handed it to Billy. It was a whistle, delicately carved out of pine. "Try it," he suggested.

Billy blew; a high, piercing note sliced the early evening air. The hawk looked up sharply from its feast.

"You'll call him with the whistle, eventually," McGraw explained. "'Course, that's a ways off yet. But we'll get there."

Jeremy, who had been watching with eyes that grew wider and wider, finally broke through. "Golly, if a hawk can be trained that good, maybe I could—if I located me a nest . . ."

"No reason why not," McGraw said. "But I'll tell you what. I think *this* old bird has had about all the work he wants for one day. I'd like you to help me with one little job, and then we can have us some cookies."

"It sounds good to me," Billy admitted. "What's the job?"

"Need to walk the fawn down the hill a ways," McGraw said, just as if it were nothing, "and turn 'er loose."

"*Loose!* But heck, that little thing's *yours!* I mean, if you hadn't helped it, it'd be dead! Don't you *want* it anymore?"

"I want it," McGraw said gruffly. "I'm a jelly heart inside. But it's time this critter was turned loose."

Billy wanted to ask why. But the expression in McGraw's eyes precluded that. Even Jeremy, new to the entire setting, seemed to recognize that this was no ordinary moment; he watched with big, solemn eyes, his raw-looking hands lax at his sides.

"Not much to the job," McGraw said cheerfully enough, leading them to the pen. "She's mighty tame, and all I want you boys to do is walk along her flanks, just in case she decides to try to run off before she gets her balance."

The chocolate-colored fawn, with no sign of alarm, allowed

197

McGraw to walk up to her in her pen, stroke her, talk gently to her. Then he slid an arm around her neck and led her through the gate and down the slope toward the woods.

"A wild thing has got to be wild, my lady," the gentle voice was saying, and Billy realized that part of this was for him. "You have to be turned back to the wild now, while you can still learn to defend yourself. I'll miss you. Sure I will. But it's best. A deer can't have a working deal with a man, the way a hawk can."

They reached some waist-high brush and ten-foot saplings, and here the ground tumbled downward into genuine woods.

"Step back now, boys," McGraw said softly. Billy and Jeremy obeyed. McGraw hugged the fawn's neck. "Go on now, old girl."

The fawn stood there, quiet, watching him. She looked into the woods, but turned back to McGraw. She did not want to go.

"Go on, old babe," McGraw said.

Still the animal stood quiet, lovely and sleek and brown.

McGraw quickly slapped her flank, hard. She bolted. Two side-stepping leaps, a zigzag motion that was pure grace, and she was into the woods. Gone. Billy felt empty inside, like something had really gone out of him. He stared at the dark woods, knowing the fawn might be standing there nearby, watching, or might be running with silent, gliding freedom a mile away by now. He felt—bereft. He had been thinking, earlier, that he would ask the old man about his past, and warn him that the vigilantes were checking up on him. But he knew now he was not going to broach the subject today. Not after the fawn.

"What do you say we get those cookies, eh, fellers?" McGraw patted his belly. "I can use a snack, can't you?"

There were tears in his eyes behind his smile.

NINE

SHERIFF Ad Sweeney had spent more than a week straight in Springer, but on the day after Billy first flew his hawk, Sweeney was at the house before dawn, saying he had to ride to the county seat. Billy heard him from the loft.

"I hope to be back before nightfall," he told Dan Baker. "I'd appreciate it if you'd go into town and make your presence known. I don't expect a thing. But you being there might reduce the chances. There's still a few rowdies around, and some of our brave citizens are awful excited about running them out."

"I'll go on in, then," Billy's father said. "Have a good ride."

When he came back into the house, Billy slid down the ladder from the loft. "Paw," he said, "can I go to town with you?"

Paw was surprised. "What for, son? I'm not going to be doing a thing but sitting on the porch of the jailhouse, wearing my badge."

"That's okay. I'd just like to—go along." Which was true. He hadn't seen much of his father in the past two weeks. "I won't be any bother, Paw," he said. Possibly, he thought, they could talk about stuff. McGraw, the hawk, Jeremy, even Morrie Carson. Things he needed to talk about.

"Well, all right, if it's all right with your mother."

Mom smiled wanly, betraying worry, but she didn't say no.

DAWN was breaking over the long mountain range to the east when they set out. The air was still and cool. Meadowlarks sang.

"Going to be a pretty one, Billy," Paw said. "Hot, though. We could use some more rain."

"Yes, sir, we sure could."

"Fourth of July celebration next week. Guess you're looking forward to that."

"Well, I know Mom plans to enter her quilt in the contest."

Paw sighed. "Yes. And it's a fine quilt. She should win. But I don't know, there's a chance some judges won't vote for her even if her work is the best."

Billy nodded. "Because you're a deputy now?"

"That, and not joining the committee."

"The vigilantes are just about done, though, ain't they?"

His father grunted. "I'd like to think so."

Ordinarily, Springer was already draped with red, white, and blue bunting this near the Fourth of July. When Billy rode in this

200

morning with his father, however, he saw no signs of preparation, except for one tattered banner across Main Street and two or three fair booths partly constructed in the park. It seemed like the town wasn't getting ready at all.

They went to the jail, which was empty of prisoners at the moment. It smelled musty and sour. Billy got the side window open and propped the door back with a rock. His father, moving with a curious stiffness, as if the badge on his shirt were sticking him, made coffee and then swept the place out. "What do we do now?" Billy asked.

"Nothing. If we're lucky."

The town began to awaken. Several people passed by and gave Billy and his father, sitting on the porch, curt nods. Two men left Carson's store and walked up the street toward the jail. One was Carson himself, the other was Layden, who operated a small fix-it shop on the side street. "Morning," Carson said gruffly to Paw.

"Morning, sir," Paw said, with extra politeness. "Morning, Mister Layden."

Layden took his hands out of his pockets. They were shaking. "Somebody broke into my shop last night. Busted the back door in. Took a clock and most of my tools and eleven dollars. And what are you gonna *do* about it?"

"I'll go right down there and have a look-see," Paw said.

"It was done hours ago! What good is you *looking* gonna do?"

Paw's eyes got flinty. "What do you suggest?"

Carson said, "We know who broke into Joe's place. We want to know if you're going to get them, or if we have to. Someone saw them leave the boardinghouse empty-handed and go back later with a sack. They're in the boardinghouse now. We've got the front and back covered, and a man on the roof next door."

"When you say 'we,' you mean your people."

"I mean the vigilance committee, good citizens willing to do their part for law and order. I told the boys since this is right in Springer, we ought to give you a chance to go in and get them before we do. I consider this a real move toward reconciliation. But we're moving. I'm warning you."

"That sounds like an ultimatum to me."

"Call it anything you like. If you don't want the chance—"

"The fact that two men carried a sack into their room," Paw cut in, "doesn't prove they stole anything."

"What do you think it was? Their family silver? They're drifters." Carson looked toward the boardinghouse with disgust. "Strangers. All they've done in town is idle around."

"Have they caused any trouble?"

"Do you call breaking into this man's shop trouble?"

Paw looked like he sometimes did at the end of a long day in the fields. "I'll go talk to them."

"That's not enough. We want them arrested, charged—"

"I'll *talk* to them."

Carson's face reddened. "We go with you, or we go alone!"

Billy expected Paw to argue. For some reason, he didn't. "I'm the constituted law. I talk to them. All you do is observe." He walked into the jail and came back with a double-barreled shotgun, broken open. He punched a fat shell into each chamber.

"That's more like it," Carson said, eyeing the gun.

"I'll *question* them," Paw snapped, and the shotgun clamped shut with a bright metallic ring for emphasis.

His stomach in his mouth, Billy trailed along. Paw noticed him when they were almost to the church. "Billy, you go back."

"Paw!"

"All right. But when we get to the boardinghouse, you stand where I tell you. You savvy that?"

Billy nodded. There was no arguing with that tone.

He did not really know what he *hoped* might happen. A part of his mind saw Paw going in, arresting the men and being a hero. Another part saw him proving the two were innocent. But over both of these fantasies was this growing, smothering *fear*.

His father, he saw, was all alone. Carson was not really on his side. The men in the boardinghouse might do anything. And Paw was no lawman. It showed in the way he walked, his shoulders uneven from the work behind the plow. Paw was not ready for this in any way. But he was going. Billy's mind reeled.

It was not the best boardinghouse. It had once been a barn, and it still looked like one, with a few windows cut in it and a rickety outside staircase to the second floor. Across the street from its silent front entrance, Carson stopped. Four men with rifles leaned against the wall of a shed. Another man was sitting in a wagon, the barrel of his gun bright in the sun. And then Billy looked up and saw the man on the roof of the store to his right.

Chills raised goose-pimples on his arms and back.

Carson pointed. "Their room is up there, Baker. The first one off the side stairs."

"I'll go up," Paw said.

"We go with you," Carson said.

"*I'll* go up," Paw snapped.

"You're a real fool. **You really** want to go alone?"

Paw's face surprisingly split in a slight grin. "I do."

Carson stepped back. "Okay, then."

Billy watched his father walk across the street, test the first step of the old stairs, then go up slowly. It was very quiet. He could hear the stairs creaking. Oh Paw, he thought, why don't you let them do it? Why are you so dadgummed stubborn?

He saw his father reach the little landing, pause, then open the door and go inside. The door closed behind him.

Carson called out softly, "Everybody ready!"

The men at their stations hefted their guns. Carson pulled Billy back against the shed. "Now you stay put."

From deep inside the boardinghouse came a muffled shout. Then—no one would have heard it unless it were this quiet—something hit a wall, or a floor. Carson, his hands shaking, shaded his eyes as if to see better, although there was nothing to see.

Agonizing moments fled by. Then the door on the little landing flew open. A tall, red-haired man dressed only in baggy long underwear ran out onto the platform, making the whole staircase shudder. He looked confused, sleepy. He had no gun, nothing. He started down the stairs, three at a time. Above him, a second man appeared on the landing. He was buck naked. He had what looked like a bridle in his hand.

203

"That's them!" Carson yelled. "That's them, men!"

The man on the stairs froze, halfway down. He looked around, trying to locate the voice. On the roof opposite him, the man with a rifle stood. A puff of smoke issued from his weapon, and there was a sharp, clapping sound. The man in the underwear was slammed into the wall.

On all sides the other guns opened up. Billy saw it all at once— saw the slugs ripping into the man as he fell, saw the other man, the naked one, freeze in terror and hold his arms up in surrender, saw the first blast of fire take him full in the face.

Men were running forward, pausing to fire, yelling. A pall of smoke blued the sunlight as the first man tumbled down the stairs, crashed to the earth, and rolled completely over as more bullets hammered into him.

Then, by a miracle, it was still. Somebody coughed. A man worked his carbine lever, and a spent shell glittered as it ejected. Now the naked man, too, tumbled down the steps, then lay still.

Billy turned to stare at Paul Carson.

Carson held his gun just as he had held it earlier. He had not fired a shot. His face was the color of raw dough.

A man nearby laughed. "Looks like we need an undertaker."

"Much lead as they got in 'em," another called, "we might need a winch to pick 'em up."

There was an outburst of laughter that sounded obscene. Paul Carson stood there, vacant-eyed. His mouth worked, but no words came out. He looked like a man who had received a mortal blow.

Above, on the landing, the door opened again. Billy's father, his face bloody, staggered out. Carson made a sound like something dying and rushed forward to help him.

In the doctor's office it was quiet. The doctor expertly taped the bandage on Paw's head. Billy and Paul Carson stood watching. The only sound was the soft tick of an old clock in the corner. Outside, faintly, came the sound of excited voices.

"Listen to them," Carson rasped. *"Celebrating."*

"It was my fault," Paw said. "I got too close when I went into the room. They panicked and one of them hit me with the lamp."

Carson's eyes were far away. "Celebrating!" he repeated, as if he could not comprehend it.

Paw looked sharply at him. "Well, as it turns out, they were the thieves, you know. If you wanted to set an example—"

"Don't," Carson said softly. "Just—don't. All right?"

The two men exchanged looks.

Carson said huskily, "I thought it was the right thing to do. Crime just keeps getting worse. You see stores being broken into, even your own son running crazy, refusing to obey . . ."

"Everybody makes mistakes, Mister Carson."

"But when I saw what our people did out there . . . and then *joked* about it!"

Billy saw his father watching Carson with compassion in his eyes. "Maybe you can shut down the committee. People will listen to you."

Carson shuddered. "I'm not in charge. I don't know who is. Chafflin could be. I don't know. Maybe nobody is in charge."

The doctor finished bandaging. "Ought to heal fine, Baker."

Paw nodded. He was pale. "I'll pay you just as soon as I can."

Carson said, "*I'll pay*. Let me do that much, anyway!"

Billy saw his father consider it soberly. "Mister Carson," he said finally, "I'm very much obliged."

Carson's face was haunted. "I don't know what else I can do."

"Maybe this will be the end of it," Paw said.

But even Billy knew his father had spoken to try to make Carson feel better. The end was nowhere in sight.

STUBBORNLY, Billy's father went back to the jail and sat on the porch, his badge catching the sun now and then. As the afternoon moved along, Springer seemed to return to near normal.

Later, the Sled family wagon came in. John Sled walked up to the jail. He looked at his feet as if hesitant, but then raised his head almost defiantly. "We need to talk," he announced.

"Sit down," Billy's father said politely.

"I found out that my boy went up on the mountain yesterday

with your boy, and messed around with that crazy man up there."

"He's not crazy," Billy said, "and we didn't mess around."

"Billy," his father said quietly, "shut up."

"'S aw right," Sled said. "I admire the boy for speakin' up. But I wanted you to know—jus' to be sure your boy, here, gets the message—that he ain't to invite Jeremy no more."

"The boys are training a hawk," Dan Baker said. "I don't think you have to worry about Jeremy getting into trouble."

"Maybe so. But Jeremy's not to go up there, an' that's final!"

Dan Baker drew a slow breath. "You heard, Billy. If Jeremy wants to go, you understand you're to tell him he shouldn't."

"Yes, sir."

Sled said, "If my boy tries to go anyhow, I want you to tell your daddy, boy, so he can tell me."

"Well now, just a minute," Dan Baker said. "I'll not ask Billy to report on Jeremy to anybody. They're *friends,* John!"

"Aw right," Sled said grudgingly. "But I mean it about Jeremy not going up there. I feel strong about it."

"I understand that, John."

Billy stood with his father and watched as the tall, slope-shouldered man shambled down the street. Dan Baker sighed and touched the bandages on his face.

"Why, Paw?" Billy asked.

"I guess he wants to—protect Jeremy. See, every man wants his son to believe what he does, do what he does, but go farther with it, be able to give *his* children more. Jeremy's dad figures his son might end up a tramp, a crazy man on a mountain himself."

"That's funny! I mean it ain't very likely!"

Paw smiled. "Fathers worry about a lot of things, son."

A new thought crossed Billy's mind. "Paw, do you worry about *me* like that? I mean—afraid I might be a crazy man someday?"

Paw frowned. "I might."

"Then you don't know me at all!"

Paw looked at him thoughtfully. "We've drifted apart lately. Once I thought I knew you well. Now—I'm not sure."

It was true, Billy thought with a pang. He didn't feel he knew his father, either. Desperate for conversation to gloss over this feeling, he said, "I just hope Jeremy ain't too disappointed."

"You'd better just hope he obeys his dad. If Jeremy keeps going up there, then Jeremy might not be the only one to suffer."

"Mister Sled wouldn't do anything to McGraw!"

"In the mood this valley is in right now? Wouldn't he?"

TEN

SPRINGER'S Fourth of July was the quietest on record. People stood around on Main Street under the tattered banner and told each other that it was nice, having such a quiet celebration.

There were all the usual elements—the quilting bee, baking contest, pie-eating competition, sack races, speeches, prayers, horseshoe pitching, band concert, picnic and square dance. Billy's mother did not win the quilting bee, as his father had predicted.

To Billy, it just seemed a little forced this year. He knew his parents were forcing their gaiety somewhat, and Jeremy was, too. Jeremy was depressed. "Did you tell Mister McGraw I'm sorry?" he asked for the tenth time.

"I told him," Billy assured him, "and he said you're sure welcome to visit later, if things straighten out."

"I don't know if they ever will," Jeremy said despairingly.

"They will, Jeremy."

Each day, Jeremy stopped by for a report on the hawk. Billy told him carefully each time, in detail, torn between his own enthusiasm and the fear of seeming to boast. The hawk was learning fast. They were trying now to get him to respond to Billy's whistle, even when the lure was not in evidence.

This was proving difficult.

"He'll get it, he'll get it," McGraw had said patiently.

"But you can't be *sure*. You said that sometimes a hawk will go just so far, and then just stop learning, right?"

"Not this hawk. Look at him setting there, watching for you. He's practically grinning. I've never seen a hawk like a person the way this hawk likes you. He'll keep learning for you."

207

"I wish you'd tell *him* that!" But McGraw just chuckled.

McGraw had not been surprised to hear that Jeremy couldn't come back. And Billy's report on the vigilance committee's checking into people's backgrounds didn't dismay him. He had merely shrugged. "You know," Billy had told him finally, driven to candor, "those folks could get after *you*. If you got anything in your past, that is, that they might not like," he added, fishing.

"I'll tell you something about dealing with people, sonny," McGraw said after a long silence. "You've got to act like they're going to be rational."

"What do you do when you count on 'em to be, and they're not?"

"You adjust, sonny. You adjust."

It was just one of three or four times Billy made a strenuous attempt to get McGraw excited about his own potential danger, or to find out about McGraw's background. The man refused to get excited about anything. And he might as well have had no past.

However subtly Billy probed, there was simply no way McGraw could be tricked into revealing anything. Worried as he was about the vigilance committee, Billy consistently imagined the worst: McGraw was wanted for a crime somewhere, or actually did have crazy moments and had to be put away periodically, or had run off from a wife and six children. Theories such as these were hard to square with experience, however. McGraw had to be the kindest, gentlest man in the world.

"I think this ole hawk likes me," Billy said once. "That might mean I'm a good person, if he likes me."

"Billy, you're a good person whether a hawk sees it or not. I want you to remember that."

Billy thought about it, and the thoughts felt good.

"Mister McGraw, don't you ever get lonesome up here?"

"I used to," McGraw said with a smile, "before you came."

"Why do you like to live alone the way you do?"

"Sonny, some men are like some animals; they have to live in a pack. Others are like other creatures; they have to stay alone. If we're ever going to be happy, we have to learn to be true to our own nature and not fight the way we are."

208

"People get worried about hermits," Billy pointed out.

"Animals that run in packs get nervous about ones that don't—unless the one alone is a doe or something helpless."

"I guess if you're going to stay out of the pack, you'd better be as strong as you can. And not be afraid."

"Or *control* the fear. The man who said he wasn't ever afraid is the biggest liar the Lord ever created."

"What are you afraid of?"

McGraw's face lined with serious thought. "Of getting hurt. Of being chased. Of everything staying the same. Of everything changing too fast. Of living too long or not long enough. Of being misunderstood. Of being loved or of being hated."

"I don't think people in town hate you, but I think they're afraid of you, some."

"You may be right. I made some bread. Come and try it."

During the week or so after July 4, Billy made it to McGraw's every afternoon, and the training of the hawk progressed swiftly. In town, things were quiet. There had been two nights when distant fires stained the horizon, and Billy's father rode out, to return hours later, gaunt and bitter-eyed. The vigilantes had located just about all of those they didn't approve, Paw said. He did not elaborate. Billy didn't really want to know.

One afternoon Billy got home to find Jeremy waiting for him in an unusual state of excitement. "I've got me a hawk of my own," he burst out. "It flew in our barn. It's hurt, can't fly. I've got it hid out in the crick bottom, in a crate."

"Is it gonna live? Are you gonna be able to feed it?"

Jeremy's long face got longer. "I don't know. I'll do what I can, but . . . could you come down and have a look at it?"

"I will, after supper," Billy decided, checking the low sun. "I don't suppose your daddy would let you take it home."

"He'd kill it," Jeremy said somberly.

Jeremy's hawk was a kind Billy had never seen before. It had a yellow bill and eyes, yellow feathers in its wings and a pure white body. It was about fourteen inches long, almost a third smaller than Billy's red-tail. It was one extremely scared hawk, and its wing seemed to be badly beaten up. It wouldn't eat. Jeremy was excited and proud, but worried sick. Billy told him everything probably would be fine, but he was not sure of that at all. The hawk was going to die fast if it refused to eat.

The next afternoon, McGraw wasn't very encouraging. He agreed with Billy's diagnosis, judging by his description, and he was worried not only about the hawk, but about how Jeremy would take it if he lost the thing. There was also something else on McGraw's mind, and for once Billy managed to pry it out of him. Some pranksters had been around in the night, shooting into the clearing and throwing empty cans off the cliff. Billy wanted to tell his father, but McGraw said if things ran true to form, the pranksters wouldn't be back again for three or four months, and let sleeping dogs lie.

Getting home by a new, circuitous route to avoid any possible meeting with Morrie Carson or his friends, Billy found Jeremy waiting for him again. "He's worse," Jeremy said. "*Real* worse, Billy. You've got to help me. You've got to."

"Help you do what?" Billy thought he already knew.

"Help me get my hawk up to the old man," Jeremy said.

"Your paw will take your hide off," Billy pointed out. But finally he said yes. He knew he was taking a chance. He just didn't know how much a chance it was.

In the morning the leaden sky dripped a steady, bleak mist. It made work on the farm impossible. Finishing his inside chores as quickly as he dared without raising questions about his unusual efficiency, Billy hightailed it to Jeremy's house. The rain had already made the road a red slime, and by the time Billy had gotten to the neighboring farm he was beginning to wonder if there was really much chance of climbing to McGraw's place before the weather broke. One look at Jeremy's face settled that.

"He didn't eat anything, Billy. He's just layin' there, hardly moving. He just sorta rolls his eyes. He's dyin', Billy."

"Well, he ain't going to die," Billy said, as if he believed it.

Jeremy cast a worried glance toward the embankment that hid

210

his hawk. Then he looked back at the house. "My daddy's inside."

"Well, look, Jeremy. If you're too worried to go, that's all right. I think I can get your hawk up there okay."

Jeremy's jaw set. "No, sir. It's my hawk. I'll go with you."

So they slipped down to the gully and collected the box, which Jeremy had wrapped as best he could in some old canvas. They headed out northwest, staying to the creek bottom, moving as fast as they could without jostling the hawk to death. Mud stuck heavily to their boots. The going was hard, and Jeremy kept glancing back, as if expecting to see his father coming after him. Billy felt sorry for him. As they worked their way up, the rain thinned. Deep gray haze masked everything and isolated them on the side of the old mountain, as if they and their sick hawk were the only creatures remaining in the world.

Taking his turn with the box, Billy noticed an ominous thing: even when he happened to tip the box a little, there was no movement within—no sign that the hawk was alarmed by the jostling, or was moving around to try to stay upright. But Billy was not about to mention this to Jeremy.

They had just reached the band of evergreen forest that led to McGraw's when a brisk, cool wind developed, making Billy shiver as his clothes dried. The sun broke through. It was going to be a clear, cool mountain day.

Billy and Jeremy got out of the woods and looked up the last slope to the cliff house. A wisp of woodsmoke issued from it.

"Mister McGraw!" Billy called, hurrying up the slope.

A voice *behind* him, in the woods, called quietly, "No need to yell, boy." And there was McGraw, coming out of deep brush. He walked bent over, like a man carrying a tent, which he virtually was. He had a heavy canvas draped over him, its edges dragging the ground; but despite the tarp, his clothes were soaked through. Billy was shocked to see how tired he looked, with a bluish tinge to his lips.

"They've been back?" Billy guessed.

"Afraid so." McGraw glanced at Jeremy. "Glad to see you again, youngster. Your daddy had a change of heart?"

211

"Not exactly." Jeremy flushed. "But I've got something—a hawk." He took the box from Billy and put it down in front of McGraw. "It's *real* sick, Mister McGraw. The only thing I could think to do was bring it up here to you."

"Well, now," McGraw said softly, squatting to remove the canvas from the box on the wet earth. "I guess we'd better see." He removed the canvas and cautiously lifted the lid.

Jeremy saw it first. "*Aw*," he said huskily. He turned to Billy, his eyes mirrorlike with surprise and pain. His lips turned down at the corners, and then his eyes changed again, filled.

"I'm afraid we started a little late, youngster," McGraw said regretfully, examining the small body with tender hands. "He'd had a bad accident, Jeremy. He was too badly hurt to save."

"He was just a little guy." Jeremy choked.

McGraw's forehead wrinkled massively. He licked his lips and seemed to make at least two false starts at saying something. "I had a pet kitten," he murmured. "I called her Sheba. She got sick. I did everything I could, but sometimes there just isn't enough you *can* do. I buried little old Sheba back there by the cottonwood. You get shade and you can hear the creek real nice."

Jeremy said nothing, just kept crying silently.

"Would you like to bury your hawk back there?" McGraw asked.

"Yes, sir, I guess I would." And then there was a silence.

It might not have been so bad for Jeremy, Billy thought, if he had ever had many pets before, or if his father hadn't told him not to come back up the mountain. Jeremy had risked just about everything, and now he had nothing to show for it.

With the silence dragging out, McGraw asked softly, "Would you like some help burying him, Jeremy?"

Jeremy squared his shoulders. "No. I'll do it just fine."

"The spade is beside the bigger shed."

For an instant Billy felt a rush of wild rage; he wanted to strike at McGraw for his uncharacteristic callousness. What was the hellfire rush about getting the dead hawk into the ground? Why didn't McGraw stop pushing Jeremy?

Woodenly, Jeremy picked up the crate containing his dead

hawk. His feet dragged at first, but as he walked, he seemed to move with more determination. Which was when Billy got it: You had to go ahead and *do* something when it hurt like this, and McGraw knew that. What seemed callousness was kindness.

"Billy," McGraw spoke soberly. "I think we ought to give your friend something to think about. Let's fly your hawk and give Jeremy a job to do to help us with it."

"Do you think that's what we really ought to do?" Billy asked.

"Yes, sir," McGraw said with great dignity. "I do."

By the time Jeremy had come back from his job with the shovel, Billy and McGraw had the red-tail out and waiting for its morning's work. He sat his perch handsomely, the slight, high breeze riffling his feathers, his head fiercely erect and alert. Jeremy got an oddly stricken expression as he saw Billy and McGraw playing out exercise cords and readying the lure. McGraw turned to him with a matter-of-fact expression.

"Will you help us do some work with this hawk?"

Jeremy looked at Billy and the hawk. "Sure," he said firmly.

The way McGraw set it up, he was to toss the hawk, Billy was to lure and whistle it, and Jeremy was to bring it back when it flew to the end of its cord and landed. The large bird moved restlessly on its perch. Jeremy, with a carrying glove McGraw gave him, hurried to the edge of the rocks; his eyes had come partly alive again. "Everybody ready?" McGraw asked.

"Ready!" Billy said, swinging the lure.

McGraw tossed the hawk. It flapped its wings eagerly and ignored the lure and Billy's piping whistle. It caught on the end of the line and fluttered to the ground.

"Dummy!" Billy yelled, letting the lure swing to the earth.

Jeremy was already hurrying over to the hawk. As he held his arm down in front of it, it hopped obediently up.

"Good boy!" McGraw said easily, as Jeremy returned the hawk to him. "I think he'll play the game right this time. You ready, Billy?"

Billy began swinging the lure in a wide arc, lengthening the cord as centrifugal force took the lure farther and higher, out twenty feet or more from his body. "Yes!" he called. "Ready!"

McGraw tossed again. The hawk started for the trees once more. Furious, Billy blew hard on the whistle. The hawk veered slightly in his flight, banked upward, then swung around and down again, diving for the lure. Both lines—the hawk's and the lure's—went slack and became crazy coils in the air. The hawk bore the lure instantly to the ground practically at Billy's feet.

"That's the boy!" Billy yelped. "That's more like it!"

"He's learning." McGraw chuckled.

"If the lure had been a real bird," Jeremy enthused, "it wouldn't have had a chance!"

But the next toss was a failure. The hawk again ignored both lure and whistle and fluttered to earth only a few paces from the edge of the woods.

"Well." McGraw frowned. "He's acting strange today."

Jeremy hustled over to retrieve the bird.

The brush near the hawk became the scene of a commotion, and then it parted and two figures stepped into the clearing so casually that Billy for a moment could not quite understand what was going on. He saw it all at once: Jeremy stop in midstride and stare; the young men stand there, legs spread, grins cocky over the surprise they had provided; the hawk ruffle its feathers nervously not far from where they had emerged; and McGraw stiffen, his face a thunderhead.

The intruder was Morrie Carson; his companion, Robertson.

SEVERAL things clicked into focus for Billy. He knew from McGraw's expression that it was these two who had harassed him in the night. Morrie looked very pleased with himself because he felt so much in command of the present situation.

The two young men appeared to have been out much of the night; they looked tired, worn from a hunt, but strangely alive with new excitement. Robertson now led the horses into view from the woods. Both he and his companion carried rifles.

"What'd you do, old man?" Morrie called. "Send for help?"

"You two better just get out of here," McGraw said. "These boys and I are minding our own business."

"What're you going to do? Have Billy tell his old man? Some deputy!" Robertson giggled and reeled slightly. He was a little drunk, and Billy, as he saw this, realized that Morrie was in the same shape. It struck a chill into him. A sober Morrie was bad enough. Drunk, either of them might do anything.

"Yeah." Morrie grinned. "Your daddy won't save you, Billy."

Jeremy sang out, "You guys leave him alone."

Morrie turned to Jeremy. "Listen, Sled, I happen to know *your* daddy told you not to be up in these parts. You're in plenty of trouble already, without shooting off your face."

"That's my business," Jeremy said stoutly.

At this moment Billy's hawk evidenced its nervousness by unfolding its great wings and moving a few inches on the ground.

"You *playing* with this ugly thing?" Morrie asked.

"Training him," Billy shot back.

Morrie looked at Robertson. "Want to have some more fun?"

McGraw took a step forward and pointed a stubby finger. "This is your last warning, boys. You two had better get out of here."

It was so obviously an empty threat that Billy's insides sank. Morrie grinned. His rifle was aimed in McGraw's direction with a frightening casualness. "You talk real big."

Jeremy started toward the hawk—which was also toward Morrie and Robertson.

"What're you doing?" Robertson snapped nervously.

"I'm getting the hawk."

"No, you're not," Morrie said. "You just stay right there."

"I'll get it," McGraw muttered, and took a step.

"*Hold it,*" Morrie said.

The rifle now pointed at McGraw's chest, and whatever light lived in Morrie's eyes was a dancing flame. McGraw froze. "I don't like you, Billy boy," Morrie said quietly. "And I don't like this freaky clodhopper"—nodding toward Jeremy—"and I don't like *him,*" his eyes on McGraw. "Living by hisself, like he's too good for ordinary folks, with his stupid pets."

The hawk, increasingly restive, opened its wings again and moved around in a circle, dragging its swivels and line. Morrie watched it an instant, then brightened. "Although I guess we can't complain, huh, Bobby? We sure wouldn't have had such a good dinner if that meat hadn't been so tame."

"What are you talking about?" McGraw asked.

"Our supper last night," Morrie said, the light brighter and wilder. "This little ole fawn come right up to us, like she expected a handout or something. Funniest thing I ever did see."

Billy, suddenly sick at his stomach, looked at McGraw. The man's face seemed to go to pieces. "You didn't shoot her!"

Morrie's face showed the pleasure he was deriving from the obvious pain in the man's expression. "Sure was tasty meat."

"You bastards!" Billy screamed. "You rotten *bastards!* You git out an' stay out, or my paw *will* throw you in jail!"

Morrie grinned. "Right, Billy boy. We'll leave." Putting the rifle in his left hand, he stepped toward the hawk. "We'll just have some fun with your bird, here, first—"

"*Stop it!*"

Morrie grabbed the hawk by the legs and swung it up as one might swing a chicken about to be tossed onto a chopping block. The hawk screamed and its wings exploded in terror and fury. Morrie yelled angrily and dropped the rifle to grab the hawk with both hands. Billy, thinking the hawk was being torn apart, ran forward.

At that moment, Morrie lost his grip. The hawk got its wings straightened out as if for flight and shot upward a dozen feet. Morrie staggered backward a step. Robertson's face was agape. The hawk swung in the air and turned—*not* toward the woods, or toward seeming freedom . . .

It dived on Morrie. At the last second of the brief dive, it rotated its wings and body so that its talons lashed down into his face.

The talons dug, the wings beat a mad rhythm; Morrie flailed his arms and screamed. The hawk described a blindingly swift arc low to the ground and landed at Billy's feet.

Morrie screamed again with the pain and fell.

216

With Morrie Carson thrashing on the ground, bubbling sounds coming from his throat, McGraw rushed to him. "Here, let me—"

"No closer, old man!" Robertson, in panic, raised his rifle.

"I want to try to help him! Let me look—"

But Morrie shoved McGraw's hands away furiously and struggled to his feet. He whipped out a bandanna and pressed it against the bloody wounds on his jaw and throat, crying frantically to Robertson, "Let's get to town—to the doc!"

"I'll help you here first," McGraw argued. "Let me at least make sure there aren't any veins punctured."

Morrie swung into the saddle, and his horse staggered in a half circle. Dazed, bleeding around his hands and the bandanna, the youth shouted, "I'll get you for this, old man! And you wait, Billy!" Further words were cut off as Morrie touched his spurs and his horse charged into the brush. Robertson, pale with panic, jumped into his saddle and hurried after him, leaving Morrie's rifle on the ground in his haste.

Billy felt rooted to the spot as he and his companions listened to the thrashing of the horses fade down the mountain.

Jeremy recovered first. He hurried across the clearing and picked up the rifle. "They forgot this. It's yours now."

"*Put it down!*" McGraw's words were so sharp that Jeremy, stricken, dropped the gun.

McGraw pressed fingertips to his temples. "I don't know how badly hurt that lad may be. Your hawk struck back, Billy!"

"I can't say I'm exactly sorry."

"I know," McGraw replied sadly, looking down at the hawk, now as calm as if nothing had happened.

Billy bent to pick up his hawk, which hopped up the moment he offered his arm. McGraw looked carefully at its wings and body to see if there was any injury. He couldn't see any. They put the hawk on its perch in the shed and went back outside. Only then, standing there in the vast, morning silence, did Billy begin to realize what had happened. "They'll get to town inside an hour,"

217

he said. "They'll raise the biggest commotion anybody ever saw."

Jeremy's eyes widened. "And they'll make it sound like—"

"—like my hawk attacked him for no reason," Billy supplied bitterly. "They'll make it sound bad—for you, too, Mister McGraw."

"Then you need to get down to your folks," McGraw replied. "You need to let people know what really happened."

"What if they don't believe us?" Jeremy asked.

"They will. They'll see that you two boys aren't liars."

It was just almost unbelievable that McGraw should have this faith in people. And yet Billy saw that his suggestion made sense. Paw had to be told. Sheriff Sweeney, too. Because now they—the law—had to prevent Morrie and friends from coming back for revenge.

"We'll tell them," Billy decided. "If there's any kind of bad reaction, one of us will git back up here and let you know."

McGraw took a deep breath. "You sure you'll tell, Jeremy?"

Jeremy's Adam's apple went up and down. "I'll git a lickin', no question about that. But I'd rather tell Daddy than have him hear it from somebody else first."

"Jeremy," Billy said, "we better git moving."

When Billy reached his house, the first thing he saw was Sheriff Sweeney's swaybacked gelding. He hurried inside. One look at Sweeney's face, and his father's, told him the trouble had already reached town, and Sweeney was here because of it.

"Billy," his father said, "tell us exactly what happened."

The two men sat at the table over their coffee cups, glancing at each other now and then with expressions that grew grimmer as Billy's story unwound.

"Well, the punk asked for it, sounds like," Sweeney grunted when Billy concluded. "But tell that to those people in town."

"We could do just that," Billy's father snapped. "Take Billy and Jeremy to Springer, have them tell their story."

Sweeney tipped his head back and drained his mug of coffee. "Dan, I know this isn't the first time Morrie and his buddies have been out harassing folks. But do you figure anybody else is going to believe it? They'll say it's just an attempt to discredit Paul Carson."

"That doesn't even make sense!" Dan Baker said disgustedly.

"It don't have to make sense," Sweeney said. "Morrie and his buddies have been going around having the time of their lives, raising hell, and everybody has been blaming somebody else."

Billy saw his father's face go slack with a startling new thought. "Why, those boys might even have pulled some of the rough stuff in town that got the vigilante business stirred up in the first place. How is Carson acting now, about Morrie getting clawed?"

"Quiet. He told me he don't believe Morrie's story. He's scared, though, what some of the others might do."

Billy blurted, "They wouldn't go after Mister McGraw! Not if Mister Carson doesn't tell them to!"

"Mister Carson isn't in charge anymore, Billy. A boy comes in, clawed by a hawk. The hawk is being kept by a crazy man, so-called. The town has a group that's already running off everyone who even looks a little different."

Sweeney said, "It can't hurt to take Billy and the Sled boy into town. Get them to tell their version."

"Are you willing, boy?" Paw asked.

Billy thought about it. He was scared. "Yes, sir," he said.

Paw nodded. "We'll go collect Jeremy, then."

Billy's mother was hoeing around the corn in the garden. Paw leaned over the rickety fence to talk earnestly to her for a minute. Then he hurried into the barn to saddle the gray gelding that had been his to use since the deputizing. In a minute or two he swung onto the horse and held down a hand. Billy sprang up and got on the horse's hindquarters. The sheriff led the way and they cantered up the road, which the sun was fast drying after the morning rains. Off in the mountains, Billy noticed, were new clouds. By nightfall it was going to get bad again. He thought of McGraw up there alone and felt a stronger pang of worry.

The whole Sled family was outside their house, waiting. John Sled, his face set grimly, looked up at the sheriff. "Git down if you like," he said.

Sweeney did not move. "We need Jeremy's help, John. The boys need to tell their story in town—"

"The boy disobeyed me. He's staying right here."

"Unless these two boys tell their side, and convince folks, some of those hotheads might try to take it out on old McGraw."

Sled did not blink. "No concern of mine."

"We're asking your help, John. It's serious. We'll have him back in an hour or two."

"Mister McGraw might git hurt—" Jeremy began to plead.

"Shut your mouth, boy," Sled said.

Billy's father said, "I know how you feel, John. But if it might head off some violence—"

"He stays here," Sled said.

Sweeney's heavy hands rested on the horn of his saddle like chunks of meat, and his eyes were just as dead. "You won't help?"

"Nyawp."

Sweeney sat still a minute, then touched his hat. "Mrs. Sled." He turned his horse. "You go on home, Dan," he said bitterly.

"What will *you* do?" Paw asked.

"Go back to town. See if I can find out what they mean to do." Sweeney spat soundlessly. "Most of the people in the vigilance group are good people pushed too far. Some ain't. Some have mumbled against that old man on the mountain for a long time. And now the ball's been opened on killin' or anything else, ain't it?"

"If some of them try to do anything to that man—"

"I'll stop 'em," Sweeney cut in, as if saying he would churn some butter, or chop some wood.

Billy's father sat straighter. "I'll help you, if I can."

Sweeney looked at him. "Mob action is like a sickness. If they get going, they don't stop easy. It's not really your fight."

Billy saw his father's rueful smile. "I've been dealt in."

Sweeney thought about it, then nodded. "I'll let you know."

By HIS father's solemnity, Billy knew the situation was potentially far worse than anything in his experience had led him to expect. There was a conference between his parents—words that

220

the turning of backs and lowering of voices declared private. Then Billy's mother returned to cleaning vegetables. His father took a deep breath, seemed to shake himself, and walked down to the garden. He began hoeing, but not as if his heart was in it.

Billy joined him, and for a long time they worked in silence. The sun had begun to peep through the swollen clouds, making it humid and hot. Billy saw his father mop a shirt sleeve across his forehead, feel the bandage there, and frown.

"You all right, Paw?" he asked anxiously. "You look kind of peaked."

"You do, too, as a matter of fact. Why don't you go in?"

"Well, I guess I'll just stay here with you."

His father smiled. "You're a good boy, you know that?"

It unaccountably embarrassed Billy. "I shouldn't of done all that with the hawk."

"What's done is done. We've got more important things to worry about right now."

"They wouldn't really bother Mister McGraw, would they? He hasn't done anything!"

"You don't have to do much for some people to fear you, son."

"I thought they had killed you in town, Paw!"

His father grinned. "It takes a lot to kill an old cuss like me."

It struck Billy forcibly: the way his father stood there, grinning, bandaged, leaning on the hoe—some new glimpse into *what his father was*. It had to do with coming here to claim new land, and fighting it for survival. It had to do with a lot more. All of it went to a sudden knowledge of the kind of man this father of his might really be. Billy sucked in a sharp breath because the vision was not clear, and he was not sure of it. Could he *ask . . . ?*

But his father turned then toward the road. A man was coming on horseback. There was no mistaking the thick silhouette.

SWEENEY stood with one foot hiked up on the edge of the stoop. "Carson tried to calm folks down, but nobody would listen. Not the hotheads, anyway. Mister Chafflin got going. About old men corrupting little boys. Then something else came up. The town clerk had written to Washington, and a letter came back just today. It's not good—McGraw's war record. He was a deserter."

"No!" Billy shouted the denial.

"It's true. The letter covers it," Sweeney said, looking as if the taste of every word was foul in his mouth. "He was with our side— the Union—at Vicksburg. He was listed as a deserter, and later they tried him. I've just been up there to see him."

Paw said, "He admitted it?"

"He wouldn't talk about it—said there was some truth in it, it was his business. He's a tough man, in his own way."

Paw took a deep breath and glanced worriedly at Mom. "Even if it's true, that's no excuse for anybody in town to do anything."

"Ordinarily," Sweeney said, "right. But now, *anything* is an excuse. Some of them have the bloodlust. Some go along because they're scared of reprisals. They're going to run him off."

"We can't let them," Paw said. "I know how they'd do it. With guns, or torches. He could be killed."

"He could."

"What do you plan to do about it?"

Sweeney's face twisted in anger. "Back them off, if I can."

"I'll help you," Billy's father said after a slight pause.

"You've done enough, Dan."

"I said I'd help. Don't give me a good chance to back out. I don't have a very long gut, and I may take you up on it."

Sweeney's eyes flashed approval. "The west slope. Near the road. They'll do it at night, the way they always do. And probably tonight. I could give you a flare—you could watch—"

"I'll be there tonight."

"I'm going to ask Carson if he wants to help me keep watch in town. If we see any sign of the vigilantes moving, we'll either head them off or be on the mountain before them. I know I'm asking a lot of him. But I think Carson really has turned around on all of this. And a man needs a chance to redeem himself. As for you, Dan, I'm still not sure I know why you're giving us so much help."

"I'm crazy," Paw said, "that's why." And he smiled.

TWELVE

With the approach of nightfall a cold drizzle began. In the house, Billy watched his father solemnly put on the old slicker and check his rifle. He wore his oldest clothes, all gray and thick, for warmth, and his sturdiest work boots.

Billy's mother, standing by the fireplace, betrayed her worry in the ashen color of her face. "How long will you be out there?"

"Until daylight, unless something happens. So hope, will you?"

She nodded. "I'll hope." Her smile was a failure.

"Paw?" Billy said. "*Please,* can't I go? I could help."

"I know you could. But you stay here." His father picked up the brick-red cylinder off the table and started rolling it in waxed paper. "I hope this flare stays dry and works if I need it."

"You got matches?" Billy asked.

His father patted a pants pocket. "Plenty."

Billy stood with his mother as his father put the wrapped flare and the rifle under his slicker and pulled his hat down low over his face. He turned to them. "Don't worry." Dan Baker's grim smile flashed and he opened the door, letting in a flurry of icy rain. The door closed and he was gone.

Billy's mother stirred the fire with the poker for a few minutes, although the fire didn't need stirring. Then she sat down in the rocker with her sewing and looked at Billy. "He'll be all right," she said.

Billy, his tension almost more than he could handle, went to the loft ladder. "I'll see him down the road from my window."

She nodded silent assent.

Climbing into the loft, he crawled over his sleeping pallet to get to the small window in the peak of the roof. Through the drizzle-streaked glass, he couldn't see a thing but blackness. Disappointed, he rolled over onto his pallet and lay looking up at the rafters, close enough that he could reach out and feel their rough texture. Lying still, he could hear the hiss and sputter of the fire below, the draw of it through the chimney that went up through the loft, and the creak of his mother's rocker.

He was so worried that he felt sick at his stomach. It was so dumb of his paw not to let him help. There were various approaches up the mountain, and he knew them better than practically anyone else, but they weren't giving him a chance. He decided he would go anyway. The problem was with his mother, and getting out of the house undetected. Of course, you *could* slide this window open enough to squeeze out, and you *could* get down the side of the house. The question was whether you could do it quietly enough. He lay there listening. His mother, judging by the sounds, rocked for a while, then moved about the lower room nervously, with no pattern to her actions.

"Billy?" she called just then. "Are you going to go to sleep?"

"Yes, ma'am, I guess so. Soon."

"Billy . . . good night . . . don't worry, son."

"Yes, ma'am. 'Night." And he heard the big bed creak lightly as she got into it.

Billy had not undressed. If he *were* going, he would have to put on his heavier boots. So just for practice he put them on and laced them up. And he would need his sweater, for sure, and an extra pair of pants over the others. He just managed to squirm into them in such close quarters and put on his jacket and hat.

He sat on his pallet, overclothed, feeling like a mummy, and wrestled with himself about going. He ought to obey Paw. He ought to be where he could help. Should. Shouldn't. Yes. No. Until he thought his brain was going to burst. In an instant—knowing he had just been postponing it—he slid the window open cautiously. The air and drizzle that swept in were cold. But not half so cold as the rain and wind that began pelting gently, insistently, against him as he climbed down the side of the house with fingers already starting to go numb.

He knew where his father would be on the ridgeline that guarded the approach to the mountain. There were only three or four spots where boulders were piled high enough to provide both cover from the weather and good observation of the road. So finding Paw, to help him, wasn't likely to be hard. He was already soaked and shivering, slogging through the wet blackness,

224

before the *real* problem occurred to him: how to get Paw to accept his help and not send him packing down the mountain again. Billy had been so anxious to have a part in whatever might go on that he hadn't considered how unlikely it was that Paw would change his mind.

The rain pelted down, stinging coldly through his jacket. The wind picked up. A vein of lightning splintered across the sky, then everything was black again as the thunder clapped sharply. He lost track of time. His teeth chattered and he was shaking all over. He knew where his place was, however, he kept telling himself. It was with Paw, where he could help McGraw—

"Billy!"

The voice was right next to his ear, shouting over the wind and startling him badly. Strong hands grabbed his shoulders, turning him, and he stared up into his father's gaunt face.

"What are you doing out here?" Paw yelled. "You crazy kid!" He hauled Billy across the muddy road to a place between huge rocks where the wind whipped the edge of a canvas. His father shoved him into a rocky grotto, where they were protected by boulders from the wind on two sides. At the back and front and over the top his father had lashed canvases, making a tentlike roof. The canvas to the front was gaped about a foot, allowing a view outside, down the slope. The protected area was about six feet square, and although the ground was muddy from leaks, and the wind whistled right through once or twice, it was like a fortress compared with what Billy had come through.

His father turned Billy to face him. He looked grimly angry. "You should have stayed home, boy."

"I wanted to help, Paw!"

Dan Baker seemed to be thinking hard about what to do, possibly weighing the danger of sending Billy back to the house in the storm. He opened his coat and spread his arms. "Get inside here and try to get warm."

"I'll get you all wet."

"Will you do what you're told? Once?"

Billy obeyed. His father's body felt big and hard, and he was,

225

Billy saw, soaked through, too. But there was warmth inside the coat, heavy though it was with rain. Warmth—and security. His father closed the coat around both of them, squatting behind the front gap in the makeshift tent. His father said nothing and he said nothing, but he kept peering into the night, trying to penetrate the darkness. He wanted to help.

His father, he thought, was the brave man he had always—until

this had begun—assumed. There could be no doubt of it now, and he was proud. But their relationship had been damaged. He felt a great sadness. Could something as fragile as this ever be repaired? Was love like a fine piece of glass, which, once broken, could not be made as it was again no matter how great the effort?

It was a terrible thought. He would try, he told himself, he would go on trying as long as he lived. And right now, the way to try was to watch the night with this man, stay close to him. He huddled closer.

Time passed. The rain thrummed on the canvas. Billy's eyes grew sticky and his eyelids became heavy. It wouldn't hurt, he thought, to rest his eyes just a minute. He drifted.

He slept—a moment, an hour—then awoke with a start.

They were coming.

The sky had a pearly sheen in the east. From wispy, fast-moving clouds, only a light drizzle fell. He had been awakened, he imagined, by the stiffening of his father's body in alarm. Now his father was reaching for the wax-papered package that contained the flare. Billy saw all this in a second, however, because his attention was seized by movement and illumination about three hundred yards down the hill. There were horsemen there. He couldn't tell how many, but one held a smoking torch, shielded somehow from the rain. It gave little light, but whatever it provided was probably necessary; the wet brush and rocks were treacherous and the horses were laboring.

Hurrying, Billy's father unwrapped the flare, which would act like a rocket once the wick had been lighted. Pressing the fuse out straight, Paw stuck the end of the firework into the soggy ground just outside the tent. He found his matches, gave Billy a warning look, and cracked the match head on the rock.

The match didn't light.

Frowning, Paw whipped the match over the rock again. It left a long streak on the boulder, but didn't even spark. Despite the chill predawn wind, sweat stood out on his face. He rummaged through his pockets and tried different matches. Not one would begin to light. Paw had forgotten to take care of the matches. They had soaked all night in his wet pockets.

"It's not going to work," Paw muttered, hurling a match away.

Meanwhile, the riders were moving higher. They would pass near this spot, and their path could lead to only one place: McGraw's. "I don't see any sign of Sweeney," Billy's father said. "These must have gotten away without him seeing them. If I could make the damned flare work!"

"I could run for town," Billy suggested.

"By the time you could get there, it would be all over."

The simple statement shocked Billy. *McGraw didn't have that much time left.*

Below them, the horsemen were now about two hundred yards distant. Billy watched his father's face harden in desperation. "What are you going to do, Paw?" he asked.

"When they get up on the road here, I'll identify myself and order them to turn back. It looks like five or six of them. They won't be able to see how many of us there are."

It sounded like a desperate gamble, but Billy accepted it immediately. "If you've got an extra gun, Paw, I—"

"No. You've got to get up there. Fast. Let McGraw know."

"And leave *you?* No, sir! I—"

His father grabbed his arm so roughly that he almost yelled. "Boy, don't argue! Our job is to save that man's hide. *Your* part is to warn him. I'll probably bluff them right out of here."

"Then why should I have to go warn—"

"Billy, damn it, *will you do what you're told?*"

Billy stared into his father's eyes. He understood that he *had* to obey. "Yes, sir," he said.

His father glanced out the front canvas. The riders were moving very slowly on the difficult, wet terrain. "Boy, if all's quiet, you wait up there for me. If you hear shooting, that means I haven't bluffed them into turning back. In that case get McGraw clear of his place until we can get things straightened out."

"If I hear shooting! That'd mean they was fighting you!"

"Not necessarily," his father said, with that soft, ironic smile. "They start giving me a bad time, I'll shoot a couple rounds into the sky, hoping the noise will carry down to town." He saw that Billy wasn't buying it. "They might shoot at *me*, too, of course, to try to scare me off. But they wouldn't want to hurt me, son. You *know* that. I'm the real law around here."

Billy's teeth chattered. "Are you sure *they* know that?"

Paw grinned. "You'd better git. Good luck, boy."

Hearing the distant sound of the horsemen, the jingle of spurs and clopping of hoofs, Billy felt a stab of fear for his father and the need to say something—he didn't quite know what it was. "Paw," he said thickly, "I—"

"I know, boy. Now will you *git?*" He reached out and caught Billy startlingly close in an instant's bear hug. When he pushed his son back, his eyes looked bright. "Go," he said.

Billy crawled out the back of the tent on his belly, looked around to make sure he had his bearings, then moved up through the rocks. By the time he had gone a hundred feet, he glanced back and could no longer pick out which set of boulders sheltered his father. The horsemen's torch shone below in darkness. The sky to the east was touched now by the faintest bands of pink.

Turning, Billy scrambled up through more rocks.

"Mister McGraw! Mister McGraw!"

First dawn light etched the face of the cliff. As Billy reeled into the clearing, the door of the cabin burst open. McGraw came to meet him. "What's happening, sonny? You're out of breath!"

Billy gasped for air. "They're coming after you! My paw is trying to hold them off, but you got to git out of here. . . ."

McGraw's arms engulfed him in odors of tobacco and wood-smoke and sweat. "Easy, son. Take it one step at a time."

Billy struggled to tell it clearly. McGraw, his face growing harder as he listened, started to turn away. "I'd better be getting down there to see if your daddy's all right."

"No! Paw wanted you *warned.* That's why he took the chance. If you go down now, you're just messing things up worse!"

McGraw looked somber. "What is it I should do, then?"

"Run."

"That don't set right, youngster."

"They'll burn your place. They might—hurt you."

The older man heaved a sigh and looked off into a distance of time as well as space. "A man gets tired of moving on." McGraw returned his gaze to Billy and smiled briefly. He reached out and tousled the rain-soaked hair. "I guess you and your daddy have gone to a right lot of trouble to try to save me, haven't you?"

"You'd better *run.* I can help you git ready," Billy told him. "Maybe you'll just have to hide a few days, and then—"

"No," McGraw said firmly. "You can't leave a place and be gone, and then go back. When a man moves—he has to move."

Billy stared at him, not fully comprehending, but seeing that this meant he would never see McGraw again.

McGraw said, "You'll have to take care of your own hawk."

"I can't," Billy said, surprising himself with how certain this knowledge had been within him all this time.

"Of course you can. You've finished the training. He's ready to fly free. You can keep him at your house."

"No. Somebody would just shoot that ole hawk down in the valley. They'd shoot him because he hurt Morrie, or just because he's big and fine and strong and flies around, free. Somebody would have to *git* him, down there." Tears blurred Billy's vision. "You'd better hurry, Mister McGraw."

McGraw went quickly into his house in the cliff.

Billy took the glove off the nail outside the hawk shed and put it on. The hawk stirred on its perch when he went in. Billy knelt beside it. "Okay, you ole dummy," he murmured. "This is a big day for you. Come on, now." He held out his arm and the hawk stepped onto the glove. Outside, the hawk turned its head sharply, pivoting about to see this cooler, wetter world. Its talons gripped Billy's arm through the glove with familiar tension.

McGraw appeared in the doorway of his house with a burlap sack over his shoulder. He saw Billy and the hawk, and walked over to them. He stroked the hawk's breast with the back of his index finger. "S'posed to use the feather, of course, but I s'pose it don't hurt once in a while."

"Is that stuff all you're taking?" Billy asked.

"That's all."

"Will you hide, or are you really going for good?"

"For good, Billy."

"I want to—thank you for all the help. . . ." Billy took a breath. "Only—now I'm turning this hawk loose."

"You don't have to do that, youngster!"

"No, like I said, they'd shoot him. And right now my daddy— see, I don't know where Paw *is*, or if he's even alive, and he didn't want me to have no hawk—" Billy broke down and sobbed.

McGraw put a heavy arm around him. "Aw, sonny—"

"I'm okay," Billy insisted, shrugging him off. "You better git going. I've got to let this ole hawk loose before somebody gets here."

Solemnly McGraw backed away and watched. Billy unwound the swivel line from his hand and gently slipped the jesses low on the hawk's feet so they would drop free when the bird took flight. Without thinking, Billy reached into his pocket to check for the whistle. But then he realized that he didn't need it anymore.

"You have a nice life, you ole dummy, you hear?" Billy lowered his arm. The hawk stirred. Billy tossed. Its wings working strenuously, the large bird remained low to the ground for about twenty feet, heading for the brush as it often did on the tether line. But as if remembering the lure, it swung upward, turning, almost going upside down as it swooped back toward Billy. It came low past him in a rush, looking for the lure, rose in a beautiful turn, and came back a second time. Its eyes, as it shot by, watched Billy with a bright intensity.

"Go on, go on!" Billy yelled. "You ain't tied, you dummy!"

The hawk pivoted overhead and landed midway between Billy and McGraw. "Go *on*, hawk!" Billy yelled.

"I dunno about the hawk," McGraw said, "but I'm on *my* way." He turned and vanished into the brush, then reappeared, working his way up the cliff. In a few minutes he would be gone.

The hawk fluttered its wings nervously and walked around. "You *fly!*" Billy told it, being as tough as he could.

The hawk looked at him. There was so much intelligence in those eyes, it was heartbreaking. The hawk *knew*, Billy thought. It knew something unusual was taking place and was looking to him for a signal of what to do. It hurt to see it *depending* on him that way. The hawk was so beautiful, it had flown so perfectly.

Billy scooped up a small rock and hurled it. "Go on! Go *away!*"

The hawk took to the air in alarm. It rose higher this time—higher than it had ever flown, rising almost vertically. Then it turned and swooped, looking down at Billy again.

Out of the woods below him, Billy saw another movement, which drew his attention from the hawk. It was his father, hatless, his clothing soaked from tearing through wet brush.

"I turned them back," he said with tired satisfaction. "But I'm afraid they'll return after a while."

"It's all right, Paw. Mister McGraw is gone. For good." Billy pointed to the top of the cliff, where the landline moved across toward the edge of the mountain saddle. "There."

His father shaded his eyes to look. McGraw moved into view, against the sky, striding fast along the saddle line. And the hawk wheeled through the sky above him, balanced on the strength of its broad wings.

"That's not your hawk, is it?" Paw asked, surprised.

"No, sir," Billy choked. "Not now, it isn't."

Paw's face showed he understood. "I'm sorry, boy."

"I am, too, Paw." Then he added in a burst, "I *doubted* you."

"We all have doubts. They're part of living—of growing up."

"I'll never doubt you *again!*" And with these words the tears came, and he fiercely hugged his father's waist. "I love you, Paw! I'm sorry! I'm *sorry!*"

His father's big arms closed tightly around him. "It's okay, Billy. It's okay, son."

Billy sobbed with hurt and regret and relief. McGraw vanished over the ridge. The hawk swung once through a broad orbit of the sky, circling, uncertain, lost. Then it, too, went out of sight beyond the line of rocks. Billy clung to his father. It was over.

THIRTEEN

WILLIAM R. Baker, attorney-at-law, had gone to sleep very late, kept awake by the flood of old memories, and he awoke early, the memories still strong in his mind.

Dressing, he packed his suitcase carefully, because he would be concluding the land talks today and heading back toward Colorado. It struck him that it seemed like much more than a dozen years since that morning on the mountain overlooking the little town of Springer.

He had never seen McGraw again. The vigilantes had done their job, burning his sheds and house the same afternoon. But in the process one of the vigilantes was accidentally burned, badly, on the face. After that, there was an inevitable reaction to the outburst of violence. The reaction got a mighty boost when Robertson, Morrie Carson's companion, had too much to drink and told the truth about the hawk's attack—telling all of it in a crowded saloon that became deathly still as he babbled the tale. Following this, Sweeney's reelection had been easy; a new, regular deputy had been named; things had begun to settle down.

But the loss of both McGraw and the hawk haunted the grown-up Billy still, though he knew it should be long behind him. He was thinking about it when he met Chumley, the land group's representative, in the hotel lobby to go to breakfast.

"Say." Chumley grinned at him. "You must be more worried about *some* part of this deal than you let on. You look like you didn't get too much sleep last night."

Baker smiled, and over their coffee he told the rancher part of the old story. "I've been in a hundred towns west of Denver since I began law practice," Baker admitted. "And it keeps crossing my mind that in one of them I might run into McGraw again. But I suppose he's dead, like the hawk."

Chumley nodded solemnly. "That's true. Though I started to say—but no . . ."

"Started to say what?" Baker asked.

"Well, believe it or not, we've got *us* a crazy man of the mountain here. Hard to say how old he is. He's got a gray beard. He lives up on that slope. See through the window where I'm pointing? It's a couple of hours' ride. Nobody bothers him, he don't bother nobody. But—" Chumley looked startled. "It would be too much to ask that he'd be *your* mountain man—right?"

IT *would* be too much to ask. But within thirty minutes Baker had rented a horse and was on his way. He felt strung tight and eager as he rode, although he knew the odds were a thousand to one against him. He had made other rides to see mountain men. He had had his share of disappointments, looking for McGraw. Still, it felt good to be alone in the woods on horseback.

Ahead, through high virgin timber, Baker spied a wisp of woodsmoke. He rode for it, letting the horse pick its pace across beds of pine needles toward a snowy peak thousands of feet above. Then he came out onto a shelf and saw, just ahead, a log cabin with two outbuildings. It was a poor place, but kept up so neatly that it looked like more than it was.

Baker dismounted. "Hello!" he called. "Anyone home?"

For a moment there was nothing. Then the door of the cabin swung open. The man who stood there had a gray beard and long, straight gray hair. His shoulders slumped a bit, and there was a potbelly. He wore heavy gray pants and a red flannel shirt, and there was absolutely no question about it.

"McGraw!" Baker burst out incredulously.

The old man squinted at him. "What? Who are you?"

"I'm—Billy," Baker said, struggling for the best way to make himself remembered. "Billy Baker. I knew you in Springer, Colorado. You lived on the mountain, and I brought you a hawk—"

"*Billy?*" McGraw gasped. And then he straightened up and strode with the stride of a young man across the front yard of the cabin. He grabbed Baker in his arms and they embraced.

After the first burst of questions, McGraw invited him into the cabin for coffee. It was an immaculate little place, and the coffee was as good as the cocoa and cookies used to be.

"I can't get over it," Baker told the old man with a grin. "I had really given up ever finding you!"

"What brings you here?" McGraw asked. Baker told him about his law degree and the land deal pending here in Oregon. Then impulsively he told McGraw how the vigilantes had burned the cliff house, and about the good that had come of it all finally.

McGraw's face was a thousand happy wrinkles. "Your daddy?"

"He died four years ago. Mother and my ten-year-old sister live in Denver now."

McGraw narrowed his eyes, remembering. "There was another lad who brought a hawk once, but it was sick—"

"Jeremy. Jeremy Sled. He still lives near Springer. He has his own farm now. He's married, with four children. But what about you, sir? What happened to you when you left Springer?"

"I came here and had this very place built within a few months." McGraw smiled. "Times are changing, a little. People don't think an old man is crazy just because he wants to live alone on a mountain. And now and again some boy comes around, asking me to help mend a rabbit's broken leg or a bird's wing."

"You still work with wild creatures, then?" Baker smiled.

"I always did, you know. That was why I was a scout back in the war—maybe why that thing happened that let some people think I was a deserter. You heard those stories," McGraw said.

"Right at the end—someone said something."

McGraw nodded sadly. "Of course. To justify getting rid of me."

Baker drained his coffee cup. He wanted to ask more about it, but couldn't. The old sense of loyalty was back full strength.

Suddenly McGraw's eyes danced. "Remember that hawk of yours?"

"Every day," Baker admitted. "If there's anything I'll ever regret, I guess it's that—somehow—I didn't keep that bird, or at least get to see him work."

"It took courage to release him. You did it to save his life."

"I don't know if it worked, though. I never saw him again."

"The hawk followed me all that day," McGraw said. "Kept landing near me, begging. I finally took the poor, dumb thing in."

Baker was delighted. "You mean you took the hawk along? I'm glad it didn't die in the wild. What did happen to it?"

"Well, hawks live a long time, you know. Fifteen or twenty years." McGraw paused and watched Baker with lively eyes.

Baker was puzzled. "I don't get what you're driving at."

McGraw heaved himself out of the chair. "Come with me."

Following the old man outside and around the cabin, Baker

had a fleeting suspicion that the hawk might somehow—but that *was* impossible. Was he going to see a grave? McGraw was a sentimental old fool, just as he was a sentimental young one.

They reached the back of the cabin. There was a small cleared area. There was a perch on the ground. On the perch was a hawk. It was heavier, but it *did* look the same. Baker's mind reeled. Unable to believe the pleasure detonating through him he stood rooted, staring. The hawk was regal, ignoring him.

"Would you like to fly him?" McGraw reached for a glove.

"I don't know—if I could," Baker admitted huskily. "I haven't worked another hawk, I—"

"I think he'll work for you," McGraw said with a smile. "I'll toss and you can call. I'll just find you a whistle."

"You don't have to do that." Baker fished in his coat pocket and took out the whistle he had carried ever since that morning.

"So you saved that, did you!" The old man chuckled. He walked to the perch and, bending low, let the hawk step up onto his gloved arm. The hawk was watching Baker now, but showed no alarm. Baker pulled his glove on, a tumultuous gladness within him. It was his hawk. They knew each other still. No one would have believed that, he thought. But he knew it.

McGraw, beaming, walked out to the center of the clearing, the hawk riding easily on his arm. Baker moved across the clearing, the whistle ready to call, his own glove in place for the hawk to come to him and land. The sunlight poured down on him, and he was sweating with joy and a feeling that a dozen years had never been, and he was a boy again, but this time *completed*.

McGraw poised with the fine, strong, beautiful hawk.

"Are you ready, then?"

"Yes!"

236

Jack Bickham

Jack Bickham pursues a dual career. An associate professor of journalism at the University of Oklahoma, he is also a widely published author with fifty novels to his credit, ranging from standard Westerns (which he writes under pseudonyms) to mysteries, comedies and serious contemporary works.

Like the fictional young hero of *Baker's Hawk*, Bickham has an impressive assortment of pets: two dogs, two cats, and scores of tropical fish, among which is a prized collection of Japanese ornamental carp. When he learned that a local boy was training a hawk he arranged to meet the youth, and under the lad's direction, flew the bird on a tether. As he thrilled to the partnership between hawk and flier, the central theme of *Baker's Hawk* was born.

To Bickham the dilemma of Billy Baker's father represents the struggle of a growing number of Americans to maintain a perspective of justice in the face of rising crime. And like Billy, Bickham says, "We all have to come to the fact that our parents are human, that they deserve a better kind of love than mere blind love."

Married and the father of three sons and a daughter, he now lives in Norman, near the University of Oklahoma.

BRING ON THE EMPTY HORSES

A veteran actor recalls,
with wit, charm, and candour,
the glitter and the heartbreak
of Hollywood's golden days

A condensation of the book by

DAVID NIVEN

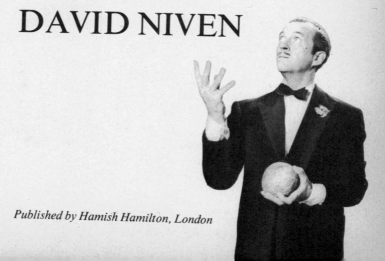

Published by Hamish Hamilton, London

"This is a book about Hollywood. It is *not* a book about me . . . at least, it is not *meant* to be. Unfortunately, the actor's urge to take centre stage is strong, so if I have on occasion, despite valiant efforts to remain in the wings, eased myself forward, then I apologize.

"The years covered in this book—1935 to 1960—are often hailed as 'The Great Days of Hollywood'; perhaps they were, perhaps not. Certainly Hollywood was Lotus Land, and though two hundred million people paid each week to see its products it bore little relationship to the rest of the world.

"I was there from 'extra' on up, and I have described people and events just as I saw them, making little effort to keep things in chronological order. For me it was an exciting, fascinating canvas, there will never be another like it, and I hope, by trying to add a little first-hand light and shadow, that I have not spoiled it."—DAVID NIVEN

The author with his Oscar for best actor for his performance in Separate Tables *(1958)*

1. The Playpen

To try to describe Hollywood, the self-styled glamour capital of the world, it seems best to do so as it appeared when I arrived there in 1934 before the outbreak of World War II, when there were still plenty of room and fresh air for everyone, very little industry, and clear blue skies without a hint of smog.

Greater Los Angeles was not a city remarkable for its beauty, and it was necessary to disregard the temporary appearance of the buildings and the unsightly forests of overhead wiring and concentrate on its truly remarkable setting in the horseshoe of the San Gabriel mountains, and the sunsets.

Everything in Southern California seemed to me to be outsize—the bronzed and sun-bleached girls and boys on the beaches were representatives of a master race bred in freedom, sunshine, and clean air; the robins were the size of pigeons and the butterflies had the proportions of bombers. And in the scrub-covered hills above the suburb of Hollywood was a forty-foot-high wooden sign: HOLLYWOODLAND.

The film folk, I discovered, unwound at their favourite playgrounds: the beaches, the mountains at Lake Arrowhead and Big Bear Lake, and a tiny colony in the desert at Palm Springs. Santa Anita Race Track was also very popular, and there were various country clubs. Not one had a black member, and several refused to admit Jews, prompting the Jewish community to start its own country club and to exclude Gentiles.

A home in Beverly Hills was the status symbol in the pre-war motion-picture industry, and the area boasted more private swimming pools and detectives to the square mile than anywhere else in the world. Beverly Hills had gone against the haphazard planning of Greater Los Angeles, and in developing its gently sloping acreage it had the good taste to send for an expert from Kew Gardens, who planted a different species of tree on every street: maples, magnolias, palms, corals, pines, sycamores, flowering eucalyptuses, elms, olives, jacarandas, and oaks.

The relaxed villagelike atmosphere of Beverly Hills was very contagious. In the Brown Derby restaurant the men wore loafers, open-neck shirts, and sports jackets, while the girls, lately liberated by Marlene Dietrich's earthshaking appearance in a man's suit, appeared enthusiastically in slacks. The waitresses were pretty would-be actresses in varying stages of disenchantment.

The home of the phoney phone call was the over-chlorinated pool of the Beverly Hills Hotel, around which little-known agents reclined, red-eyed and sweaty, waiting for the loudspeaker to relay messages which they themselves had carefully arranged to have broadcast: "Mr. Bleepburger, please be good enough to call Mr. Darryl Zanuck when you have a moment—urgent." All the time the long-legged high-bosomed girls in swimsuits and high heels ebbed and flowed hopefully around the water hole.

In the late 1930s the twice-weekly programme presented by most American movie theatres consisted of a newsreel, a cartoon, a short, the second feature, and the first feature. The whole show lasted for a bum-numbing four hours, and as a result, Hollywood was booming; Metro-Goldwyn-Mayer, one of the seven major studios, boasted that it alone turned out one feature film each week.

Edmund Lowe was famous in films then, and he and his secretary befriended me soon after my arrival, because she decided that I looked like her employer. She had noticed this resemblance when she saw me standing outside the main gate of Paramount Studios, watching for the stars in their fancy automobiles. The likeness made me stand out, apparently, from the throng of sight-

242

seers and out-of-work extras, and so intrigued the lady that she
brought me before her master.

Eddie Lowe was a friendly, smiling man and in the next few
weeks he taught me much about Hollywood, tried valiantly but
unsuccessfully to arouse the interest of his producer friends in my
career, and personally gave me a conducted tour of one "dream
factory" in which he worked. He drove me around the cozily
named "back lot"—a two-hundred-acre spread upon which stood
the permanent sets, including the streets of New York, the villages
of New England, France, and Spain, mediaeval castles, a railroad
station complete with rolling-stock, lakes with wave-making
machines and rustic bridges, a university campus, an airliner, a
section of jungle and another of pine forest, a Mississippi steam-
boat, a three-masted schooner, native canoes, a submarine, and a
stretch of desert with a ruined fort. In addition—carefully
dismantled, docketed, and stored—were acres of mud huts, dance
halls, Southern plantations, and Oriental palaces.

Lowe also took me to the studio's Western ranch: several
hundred acres of rolling hills in the San Fernando Valley upon
which stood the permanent sets—townships and Indian habitations.
Huge tracts of make-believe were necessary to film production then,
because air travel was in its infancy and distant locations had to
be conjured up locally. Small wonder that *Gone with the Wind*
was filmed in Culver City, *Mutiny on the Bounty* just off Santa
Catalina, and *The Adventures of Marco Polo* a hundred yards from
the city gasometer, while *The Charge of the Light Brigade* was
photographed in the San Fernando Valley, *The Hunchback of
Notre Dame* adjacent to Vine Street, and Scrooge's frozen breath in
A Christmas Carol captured in a vast refrigerator near the Ambassador Hotel.

The main studio resembled a mixture of the business district of
a thriving small town and the maintenance area of a busy airport.
Twenty or thirty towering, hangarlike sound stages dominated
the centre, surrounded by the fire department, the power plant,
camera and electrical stores, wardrobe departments, legal departments, furniture repositories, tailoring and dressmaking shops,
and ever-widening circles of photographic studios, cutting rooms,

243

makeup departments, projection rooms, rehearsal halls, accommodations for set designers, the story department, accounting offices, publicity offices, casting offices, greenhouses, restaurants, a hospital, a gymnasium, and a shoeshine parlour.

In the outer circle, rather stately by comparison, green lawns softened the barnlike dressing rooms allotted to the swarming extras and the double-deck rabbit warrens which housed the small-part actors. The bungalow dressing rooms of the stars, shaded by trees, gave an outward impression of peace and tranquillity, but inside, as I was to learn, their walls bore the scars of countless exhibitions of temperament, noisy moments of triumph, and far too many lonely heartbreaks.

I was also to learn that writers got drunk, actors became paranoid, actresses pregnant, and directors uncontrollable. Crises were a way of life in the dream factories, but by some extraordinary mixture of efficiency, compromise, exuberance, gambling, shrewdness, experience, strong-arm tactics, psychology, blackmail, kindness, integrity, luck, and a firm belief that "the show must go on", the pictures came rolling off the production lines.

The first question asked by investors when it was hinted that they might put money into a film—or by moviegoers when it was suggested that they should buy tickets—was "Who's in it?" The star system was the logical answer. The studios expended immense sums in signing established stars to long-term contracts and in discovering young unknowns to take their places when they faded. Once a studio was convinced that a performer had caught on with the public, great care was taken to maintain his popularity by presenting him only in roles in which his special talents would be displayed to the maximum advantage.

On the other hand, when a studio felt that a star's popularity was waning, a wide variety of manoeuvres was employed to bring their mutual contract to a speedy conclusion. The easiest way, of course, was to give the actor an inferior part to play. He would fluff up his feathers of hurt pride and "refuse to be seen in such a lousy role". The studio would then suspend the actor's contract for the duration of the picture (probably at least four months) and instruct its publicity department to leak the news to the

244

public that their hero refused to honour his obligations. He would also be suspended for an additional fifty per cent of that time as a punishment. . . .

There were, of course, iniquities on both sides—many stars behaved abominably to those who had discovered them. But the classic use of a contract as a one-sided weapon has to be this. An actor made a great hit in a play at the Shubert Theatre in New York and celebrated the fact by entering into a not-too-well-camouflaged affair with the wife of a Hollywood producer. One day a representative of the producer appeared at the theatre and offered him a very lucrative seven-year Hollywood contract. The actor, overjoyed, kissed New York audiences goodbye and prepared to become the darling of the world.

On arrival in Hollywood he was accorded the "A" treatment: press interviews, publicity layouts, and so forth. Then the boom dropped. One day he was called to the makeup department at six thirty a.m. to be prepared for photographic tests at eight. In a high state of excitement he arose at five and drove to the studio. For seven years thereafter he was called to the studio six days a week. For this he was paid handsomely, but he never appeared in front of a camera. When last heard of he was a moderately successful and devoutly alcoholic real estate salesman in Canoga Park. His actor's heart had been broken.

WHEN A film was completed, the next trick was to sell it to the public, and to this end studios allocated millions of dollars to their publicity departments.

In the earliest days circus-type ballyhoo had been employed. In fact, Harry Reichenbach was lured away from Barnum and Bailey's Circus to publicize a Tarzan picture, and his method was effective. He checked into a smart New York hotel just across from the theatre where the picture was opening, and a large wooden crate was delivered to his room. At lunchtime he called room service and ordered fifteen pounds of raw meat. The waiter who brought it let out a piercing yell and dropped the meat—a large lion was sitting at the table. The waiter sued Reichenbach, and the headlines blossomed.

Publicity departments went through their most difficult period when the studio heads decided that their stars must be presented to the public as the all-American boy or the girl next door, and should represent the sum total of all the virtues; they should not drink, swear, or, above all, copulate. Self-inflicted dents in the façades of these paragons had, therefore, to be papered over without delay, so close contacts were forged with the police departments of Los Angeles, Beverly Hills, and the San Fernando Valley. Over the years only a thin trickle of the actual number of brawls, attempted suicides and scandals was reported.

A quite extraordinary rapport existed between many stars and the publicity chiefs of their studios—the sort of understanding that soldiers develop for one another. Many stars found themselves disproportionately dependent on the counsels of the men who had nursed them through marriages, divorces, disasters, scandals, tremendous triumphs, and dreadful deflations. It was a risky arrangement, when one considered the number of closets that were clanking with skeletons. With puritanism rampant across the country, how fatal to careers it could have been if the keys had been misused. But there was a flamboyant honour among the publicity men, and I never heard of one of them breaking his vow of silence.

Occasionally publicity plans misfired. Mae West, at the height of her popularity, started a picture at Paramount titled *It Ain't No Sin*. One hundred and fifty parrots were placed in intensive training to learn to imitate her sexy drawl and to repeat endlessly, "It ain't no sin". The birds would be placed in theatre lobbies and public places to coincide with the openings of the picture.

All went well, and at last the proud trainers reported their troops were ready for action. But on the same day the Motion Picture Production Code Administration (charged with keeping Hollywood's public image clean) announced that the title of the picture must be changed because *It Ain't No Sin* was too suggestive. The new title was *I'm No Angel*, and the parrots were given a crash course in that phrase. But the theatre lobbies and public places reverberated only with frustrated whistles and rude noises, and the dejected birds were sent home in disgrace.

Walt Disney's publicity department had its problems, too. For the New York opening of *Pinocchio* it was decided to hire eleven midgets, dress them in Pinocchio costumes, and have them gambol about on top of the theatre marquee on opening day. Food and light refreshments, including a couple of quarts of liquor, were passed up to the marquee top at lunchtime. By three o'clock in the afternoon a happy crowd in Times Square was treated to the spectacle of eleven stark-naked midgets belching loudly and enjoying a crap game on the marquee. Police with ladders removed them in pillowcases.

Starting with Clara Bow as the It Girl, individual girls were built up with catchy titles. Jean Harlow became the Platinum Blonde and Betty Grable the Pin-up Girl. Finally, lovely red-headed Ann Sheridan (at a highly publicized dinner party paid for by the Warner Brothers publicity department) was voted by the ten most eligible bachelors in Hollywood as the Oomph Girl. The eligible bachelors, it is worth noting, were purely a Warner Brothers selection and included Edmund Goulding, Errol Flynn, myself, and seven others who just happened to be making pictures at Warner Brothers—a good "double play".

As press and public grew more cynical the publicity gimmicks gave way to publicity junkets. Warners splurged on a five-day junket to publicize *The Santa Fe Trail*, and reporters eagerly accepted invitations to congregate in Santa Fe, New Mexico. The studio, wary of Errol Flynn's capacity as a roisterer, assigned three men to work in shifts around the clock to keep him sober and in his own bed, but Errol outdrank and outmanoeuvred the three men, and the junket lasted twice as long as planned.

Errol was a friend of mine; for a time a very close friend. We started together in Hollywood at exactly the same time, and after his first superproduction, *Captain Blood*, I joined him in his second, *The Charge of the Light Brigade*. Mike Curtiz was the director, and his Hungarian-oriented English was a source of joy to us all. One day he decided the moment had come to order the arrival on the scene of a hundred riderless chargers. "O.K.," he yelled into a megaphone. "Bring on the empty horses!"

Flynn and I doubled up with laughter.

247

Towards the end of the picture Errol and I were placed in a large basket atop an elephant. For some obscure reason Warner Brothers had decided to twist history and let the Light Brigade charge across India instead of the Crimea. The elephant, driven mad by the arc lamps and by Curtiz's megaphone, went berserk and dashed all over the back lot trying to scrape off the basket—with us inside it—against trees and archways. Only the astute closing of the gates by the studio police stopped us from trampling our way out into the traffic of Pico Boulevard.

And then there were the parties. Christmas parties, birthday parties, parties to celebrate the end of a picture, the signing of a contract, the birth of a baby! There was always an excuse for a party in Hollywood, and at the end of the strenuous six-day week Saturday night was dedicated to letting off steam. Income tax was low, salaries were high, and if a few of those entertained could be deemed "helpful to the career", the cost of the binge could be deducted from tax. An essential was to invite a few Press photographers so that the presence of the "useful" guests could be proved.

Parties, of course, varied enormously in size, from a super bash for two thousand in costume at Marion Davies's beach house (built for her by her boy-friend, William Randolph Hearst), to half a dozen eating Mexican food prepared by Aldous Huxley in his tiny stucco pad on the wrong side of the Beverly Hills tracks.

Basil Rathbone and his Russian wife Ouida were inveterate middle-sized party givers, and several times a year this kindly man, the highest paid freelance actor in the world, who specialized in playing mean, hiss-provoking villains, provided extravaganzas into which went a great deal of inventive thought.

He badly misjudged the climate one Christmas, however, when he covered his lawn and driveway with three hundred tons of snow trucked down at high speed and great expense from Big Bear mountain. Torrential warm Southern Californian rain took over the arrangements, we splashed and skidded through thick brown slush, and the city of Beverly Hills sent Basil a ferocious bill for clearing up the mess.

Many parties were given with full Press coverage to publicize

Niven and co-star Errol Flynn go over the script of The Charge of the Light Brigade *(1936) with director Michael Curtiz, whose call for riderless chargers gave both stars a laugh—and Mr. Niven the title for his book.*

the emergence of a finished film, the theme of the production being worked into the decor.

The first night Deborah Kerr spent in Hollywood, I took her to one such affair being given by the producer, Nunally Johnston. We arrived early and found half a dozen sour-faced, topless blondes lying outside his door with everything below their hip bones squeezed into shiny green fish tails.

"We're waiting to be carried in and propped up at the bar," they told us. Nunally was launching his picture *Mr. Peabody and the Mermaid.*

When Jimmy Stewart was getting married, about twenty of us gave him a bachelor party. It followed predictable Hollywood lines with the usual jokes, speeches and gags, including a huge covered dish which was put before the bridegroom-to-be: inside was a midget dressed as a baby.

I sat next to Spencer Tracy that night and he gave me a jarring insight into his great personal problem.

"What's this?" he asked me, pointing to the dessert.

"It looks like a trifle," I answered.

He sniffed at a spoonful like a bird dog.

"There's something in it," he said. "What is it?"

I too sniffed.

"A touch of rum—I think," I said.

Spence pushed his plate away.

"Jesus!" he said, "that's all I need . . . one mouthful of that and I'd be gone for a week."

When I looked disbelieving he elaborated: "I'm not kidding. I have to fight it all the time. I'm a real alcoholic and just that little bit would start me off."

Years later Mike Todd, always flamboyant, had steaks flown out from Kansas City on his private plane for a party of six, and proudly displayed them to us. He was going to cook them in a new way, he announced, and at his barbecue pit on the hillside he left them surrounded by sauces, oil and brushes, while he took us into the house to wait until his charcoal fire was perfect. A fox ate the steaks and Todd sent out for Chinese food.

The big "black tie" parties for two or three hundred usually followed the same pattern . . . men in white coats parked the cars, the food and drink was catered by Romanoff's, the swimming pools were boarded over to make dance floors, and marquees were erected in the gardens. In the early mornings fights and scandals were frequent.

HOLLYWOOD was a village, and the studios were the families. We were all in the same boat, involved in the early years of a terribly exciting experiment; it was an international community, and there was a maximum of camaraderie and a minimum of bitchiness. Employees from the most glamorous stars to the lowliest riveters on the heavy construction gangs felt they were members of a team; they gloried in the success of their hit pictures.

250

Hollywood was also a hotbed of false values, it harboured an unattractive percentage of small-time crooks and con artists, and the chances of being successful there were minimal, but it was fascinating, and if you were lucky it was fun, and anyway it was better than working.

2. *Clark*

Chet Liebert was a loathsome human being, gross, pig-eyed, and rude, but he had one great asset—a forty-five-foot fishing boat named *König*. He also had an undeniable talent, and by the other charter boat skippers working out of nearby Balboa, he was grudgingly acknowledged to be the most successful. Every year his clients caught more broadbills and marlins than theirs did. He paid deckhands generously, and this attracted me like a moth to a flame. In 1934, as a $2.50-a-day Hollywood extra who worked only spasmodically, I was in no position to be choosy, so I eagerly grabbed the six dollars a day he gave me for ten hours of dangerous, dirty, backbreaking work.

"O.K., so you're late," Liebert said when I showed up for work at five o'clock one morning. "Get her cleaned up, gut a dozen flying fish, and check two sets of gear. Make sure the head is spotless, too, dammit, because we've got a charter today and the guy is bringing a broad with him. They'll be here at six thirty, so see that the coffee's ready, and stand by with ham and eggs. They're picture people," he added, "so keep your trap shut about being a lousy phoney actor, and get on with the job."

By six o'clock on that still and cloudless morning *König* was

251

swabbed down, and by the time a large open Packard turned onto the dock, the aroma of good coffee was rising from the galley.

"O.K., fetch their gear," Liebert ordered.

When I approached the Packard I saw what he meant—the girl was blonde and willowy, with a fresh, fun-loving face. She wore a blue reefer, red slacks, and a yachting cap. A large, muscular man was opening the boot of the car, and when he turned around, smiled, and said, "Hi, it looks like a good day," I nearly fell into the harbour. The man was Clark Gable.

I relieved him of rods, various professional-looking tackle boxes, a large ice bucket, and a bottle of Scotch, and watched him stride purposefully towards *König*; the blonde held on to his arm.

"O.K., Chet, bait 'em up and let's go," he yelled happily as he leaped aboard.

We had a lucky day. Gable landed two big blue marlins and a gigantic mako shark. Even the blonde, amid shrieks of excitement, landed a couple of twenty-pound yellowtail tuna. The deckhand was working at full throttle—looking out for fins or telltale swirls, baiting hooks, gutting and cleaning the catch, making sandwiches, mixing drinks.

When Gable heard my voice he immediately pinpointed my accent and expressed mild curiosity as to why I was there. Liebert gave me a long, hard look as I prepared to answer, but suddenly the first marlin hit, and Gable's curiosity vanished.

Six months later, in the spring of 1935, I landed something myself: a small contract with Samuel Goldwyn. The doors of Hollywood began to open, and I met Gable again.

It was the Academy Awards dinner, and the iron man from Ohio was looking rather trapped in white tie and tails, but the occasion demanded such discomfort. Hollywood was honouring its own with its strange tribal rites, and excitement ran high among the two hundred tribesmen and women who filled the private banquet room downstairs at the Ambassador Hotel.

Gable was seated with a party from his studio. I was remembering with pleasure his unaffected friendliness aboard *König* when suddenly he glanced directly at me. For a moment he looked puzzled; then my face must have clicked into place, because he waved, smiled, and mimed the hooking of a big fish. I nodded and waved back. After the presentations were over, he came over to the table where I sat with Goldwyn and others from my studio and shook my hand.

"Good to see you again," he said. "What are you doing here, trying to get Sam to go tuna fishing?"

I explained that I had changed my job and had lately landed a contract with Goldwyn.

"Well, that's just *great*," he exploded. "Lots of luck, kid, and don't forget—the first thirty years are the hardest." Then he added quite seriously, "I'm moving over to the Goldwyn lot for the next one, so I'll hope to see you around. We can forget about making pictures for a while and yak about fishing—is that a deal?"

The author's friendship with Clark Gable began aboard a charter fishing boat where Niven (above) was a deckhand.

"Fine," I said, delighted at the prospect of seeing "the King" again and not unaware of the soaring of my personal stock among my high-powered dinner companions. Several weeks later Goldwyn gave me my first speaking part in *Barbary Coast*.

I had only one line. I was to be a sailor who was thrown out of the window of a waterfront brothel in San Francisco; as I sailed past the madam I was called upon to say, "Orl right—I'm goin'!" Then, as I lay face down in several inches of mud, the two stars of the picture, Miriam Hopkins and Joel McCrea, accompanied by several donkeys and a posse of vigilantes, walked over me.

Gable was by now making *The Call of the Wild* at the Goldwyn studio. On the morning of my big moment he, the greatest star in the Hollywood firmament, took the trouble to come over to the back lot to wish good luck to a beginner. He insisted on stills being taken of the two of us, and the Goldwyn publicity department gleefully grabbed the opportunity to rub off a little of the King's glamour onto their nameless charge.

ONE JANUARY day Gable's excited voice came over the telephone.

"Hey! Let's go! I've just been talking to some pals who have a trout fishing camp on the Rogue River in Oregon—the steelheads are running! I'll pick you up at noon, we'll spend the night in Frisco and be at Grants Pass by tomorrow afternoon."

He was a fast and dedicated driver, and he made it clear that he could do without small talk because it ruined his concentration. This was perfectly all right with me, and I sat back and revelled in the glories of California.

At Grants Pass we were joined next morning by a squat, unsmiling, flaccid-faced Indian who smelled heavily of spirits. He was, according to Clark, the best guide on the river. He was also the worst driver in the neighbourhood and in the semi-gloom of that freezing winter dawn his dilapidated Chevy, unbalanced by the heavy fishing skiff trailing behind it, swung terrifyingly around icy mountain bends.

As the sky began to lighten we came to rest on a sandy beach between towering grey cliffs and manhandled the skiff into the water. Gable was wearing a heavy checked Mackinaw and his "lucky" long peaked cap. He had not bothered to shave.

"What are you giving us for breakfast, Chuck?" he asked.

"Small trout fried in butter," said the unsmiling one, "but you've got to catch 'em before I can cook 'em, don't you?"

"Sure thing," Gable grinned. "Let's get going."

The Indian knew the likely pools and, using wet flies, we soon had half a dozen beautiful brook trout about eight inches long. We pulled over to a sandbank, and while Gable and I collected dry driftwood, the guide cleaned our catch.

On the east ridge high above us the sun was backlighting the snow-covered firs. We huddled gratefully around the fire, sniffing the coffee. A family of seven deer came down to drink, a pastoral scene that was rudely shattered when an eagle picked up a large rattlesnake from the rocks beside them and spiralled upward. When the sun caught them, we could see the silver underbelly of the reptile writhing in the great bird's talons.

You learn a lot about a man in four days of strenuous fishing and four nights of medium to heavy drinking. There was not a phoney bone in Gable's body. Around the log fire, or drifting down calm broad reaches between the tumbling rapids of the aptly named Rogue, he would talk frankly and unemotionally about Hollywood and the people who controlled it.

Clark had a moderate opinion of studio heads. "They're bastards," he said flatly. "They encourage people to be larger than life, but the moment you slip—oh, brother! Look at the kids working now—Judy Garland, Robert Taylor, Mickey Rooney. Great kids, but they'll probably ruin 'em all."

I asked him how it felt to be in the number one spot in the whole industry.

He laughed. "Well, as sure as hell there's only one place I can go from where they've got me now! So I just go along with Spencer Tracy's formula and hope for the best."

"Tracy's formula?"

"Sure. Get there on time, know the jokes, say them the best way you can, take the money, and go home at six o'clock."

Gable remained completely unimpressed by his success. "Look," he said, "so they call me the damn king at the moment, but there are dozens of people warming up in the wings, and anyway I'm just out in front of a team, that's all. Metro has half a dozen people whose only job is to find the best possible properties for me.

"Don't ever let your studio kick you around," he warned. "They squeeze people dry and then drop them. Be tough with them if you get up there, because it's the only language they understand. Remember you're dealing with people who believe that a two-thousand-dollar-a-week writer is guaranteed to turn out better stuff than a guy who is only asking seven fifty. Most executives at the big studios have no guts. They're so busy holding on to their jobs they never stick their necks out."

Acting did not come naturally to him, he admitted. "I worked hard to learn a few tricks, and I fight like a steer to avoid getting stuck with parts I can't play."

He never agreed that his breakthrough into the Hollywood big time was the glamorous rocket-propelled affair claimed by the MGM publicity department and always gave credit for it to two people: Lionel Barrymore and Joan Crawford. Barrymore got him a test for the native boy in *Bird of Paradise* and directed it himself. According to Gable, "They curled my hair; then they stripped me and gave me a G-string; a propman stuck a knife in my G-string, which scared hell out of me in case his hand slipped; then he stuck a goddamn hibiscus behind my ear and told me to creep through the bushes."

Irving Thalberg, the boy-wonder producer and vice-president of MGM, saw the result and told Barrymore, "You can't put this man in a picture. Look at his ears . . . like a bat!"

Nevertheless, a short time later, MGM hired him to play a laundryman in a Constance Bennett picture and a small contract followed. This brought in its wake the all-important contribution by Joan Crawford. She bullied the studio till Gable was given a major part in *Dance, Fools, Dance* as a tough, hard-boiled character. His success was instantaneous.

When *Gone with the Wind* was about to be published in 1936, producer David Selznick snapped up the film rights. So great was the impact of the novel on the American public that the casting of the roles of Rhett Butler and Scarlett O'Hara took on the proportions of a national pastime.

There was never any doubt that Clark Gable was the perfect Rhett, but the identity of the actress who would play Scarlett remained an international question mark, and Selznick greatly enjoyed the publicity. He made scores of tests for the role of Scarlett. There was hardly an actress who did not covet it. I was making *The Prisoner of Zenda* for Selznick at the time, and whenever I had a day off he would stuff me into a Confederate uniform to play Ashley Wilkes with my back to the camera, while the female elite of Hollywood hacked their way through dozens of versions of Scarlett O'Hara. After *The Prisoner of Zenda* I moved back to

256

the Samuel Goldwyn lot to make *Wuthering Heights* with Laurence Olivier, and it was there that Scarlett was finally found. The delicious and kittenlike Vivien Leigh had come out to Hollywood to be with Olivier during the shooting of *Wuthering Heights*—they were deeply and touchingly in love.

Myron Selznick, the top Hollywood agent and David's brother, happened to visit the set one day, and within minutes of meeting Vivien he put her firmly into a black limousine, whisked her across town, and paraded her before his brother. By evening, much to the fury of countless local ladies, it was officially announced that the search for Scarlett O'Hara was over.

Next to fishing and hunting, Clark loved to play golf, and we played a great deal together. He was a splendid sight at Pebble Beach, his favourite course. He didn't walk between shots—he strode. He had a fearsome slice, which he never completely corrected, and we bent the rules slightly so he could continue to play his ball when it drifted out-of-bounds onto the beach. There he hacked happily away among the small tidal pools.

He was a doughty opponent, but at golf he lacked concentration. Some years later, in an important foursome match, I gleefully saw him falter. My partner was Group Captain Douglas Bader, the legless RAF fighter pilot who, fitted with artificial legs, had come out to tour the hospitals after World War II and encourage other double amputees.

Bader pulled his first ploy on the second tee. Just as Clark was about to drive, Bader, with a noise like a machine gun, tapped the ashes out of his pipe against his artificial thigh. On the fifth green he winked at me and tightened a little wheel in his knee; then, by moving very slightly just as Clark pulled back the head of his putter, he produced a high, penetrating mouse squeak. Bader and I coasted to an easy victory!

Clark never went out of his way to make friends. He reckoned that he was what he was, and people could take him or leave him; if they preferred to leave him, that was perfectly O.K. with him. Above all, unlike so many big stars, he felt no need to bolster his ego by surrounding himself with sycophants, so his circle of friends was small and independent.

257

It was difficult to paint a fascinating picture of a man whom nobody seemed to dislike. As producer David O. Selznick was to remark during the filming of *Gone with the Wind,* "Oh, Gable has enemies all right—but they all like him!" However, wherever there is competition there is jealousy, and where there is jealousy the knockers will knock. So in Hollywood people occasionally nudged each other and said, "Gable only likes older women."

It was the understatement of the century—Gable loved *all* women: older, younger, blondes, brunettes, redheads . . . the lot. He was strangely fatalistic when his marriages broke up, which they did with great regularity.

True, his first two wives, Josephine Dillon and Ria Langham, were older. The knockers said that Josephine, a well-educated drama teacher, had "invented" Gable, and that Ria had paid to have his teeth capped. Clark just laughed. "My mom and dad invented me," he said, "and L.B. Mayer paid for my teeth."

Both times, after obtaining his freedom from Josephine and then Ria, he issued the same hopeful statement: "I don't intend to marry again—ever," but each time he soon forgot what he'd said. One of the ladies to whom he was attached for a while observed rather sourly, "Of course, Clark never really *married* anyone. A number of women married *him* . . . he just went along with the gag."

THEN CAROLE LOMBARD entered his life. For a time, apart from a few games of golf, I saw little of Clark. He and Carole were completely happy in each other's company and needed no stimulation from outsiders. Carole had everything Clark wanted in a woman: supreme blonde good looks, a sense of humour, lovely wild bursts of laughter, his own brand of down-to-earthness, and, most important, his love of wild country, hunting, fishing, and the same determination to separate her public life from her private one.

In September 1939 they invited me for a farewell dinner. I was off to the war, but we talked of other things. They were so happy that I wondered aloud if there could be anything they wanted.

"I'll tell you what Pappy wants," Carole said quietly, "and I just hope I can give it to him. . . . He wants a kid."

"Yeah, that's right," said Clark, stroking her hair. "I'd give my right arm for a son."

There was a semi-embarrassed silence till Carole let out one of her famous yelps of laughter. "And he's sure working on it!"

Shooting had just finished on *Gone with the Wind,* and Clark had nothing but praise for Vivien, insisting that his only contribution to the success of the picture had been arson. Before shooting could start, it had been necessary to pull down a big cluster of old sets at the Selznick studios in order to make room for the building of Tara and parts of Atlanta. "Why not put a match to the whole damn lot of 'em one night and photograph it?" Clark suggested to Selznick. "It'll look like Atlanta going up in smoke."

Selznick was delighted with the idea, and with some fire-proofed stunt men doubling for Rhett and Scarlett making their horse-drawn getaway from the burning town, that's exactly how flaming Atlanta came to the screen.

During our last evening together Carole had talked a little about Hitler. She hated everything he stood for. On the day after Pearl Harbor she wired President Roosevelt offering both her own and Gable's services in any way they could be useful, and they were invited to go on a bond-selling tour. Clark was finishing a picture, so Carole went alone.

The final stop was Indianapolis, Indiana. Carole booked sleeper accommodations for Los Angeles, but at the last second, anxious to get home, she changed her mind and caught a milk-run plane instead. Gable was delighted when she phoned him before takeoff. He began sprucing up to meet her at the airport.

He was just getting into his car when a call came from the studio. Something had gone wrong with Carole's flight. There were no other details, but Edgar J. Mannix, an MGM vice-president and a close friend of Clark's, was on his way out to the house. A terrible chill settled on Clark.

Mannix arrived and told him the latest news. Someone had seen an explosion in the sky thirty miles from Las Vegas, the last airport Carole's plane had left from, and another pilot had reported a fire burning fiercely on Table Rock Mountain.

Gable and Mannix reached Las Vegas in a chartered plane to

find a search party with packhorses preparing to make the ascent to the summit. Mannix joined them after talking Gable out of going. After hours of toiling through deep snow the searchers found the smoking debris scattered over a large area; Mannix was able to identify Carole chiefly by a pair of earrings he had helped Clark choose for her.

Ice-cold and monosyllabic, Clark supervised everything, from ordering a hot meal for the exhausted search party on that dreadful night to choosing hymns for Carole's funeral three days later. Then he went to the Rogue River, holed up at his favourite fishing camp, and for three weeks drank himself into a stupor.

MGM, with the soaring costs of an unfinished picture very much on their minds, dispatched emissaries to inquire as tactfully as possible when their star might be expected to return to work. Clark never saw them, he just roared through the locked door of his cabin, "I'll be back when I'm good and ready—now beat it." Finally he showed up unexpectedly, outwardly unchanged and kidding with old friends. He was always on time, always knew his lines, and as always he was the complete professional. Grief, like everything else, was very private to Clark.

The day his picture was finished he enlisted in the air force, asking to be trained as an aerial gunner and posted overseas.

BY THE summer of 1943 I had offset the misery of military life by the happiest of all acquisitions: a beautiful wife, Primula, and a baby son, David, Jr. They lived in a thatched cottage two miles from Windsor Castle, and whenever I got leave I rushed to join them. One summer evening I came home to find a large American air force officer sitting under *my* beech tree; on his knee was *my* little boy. It was a great reunion. Clark was stationed in the Midlands, and from then on our cottage became his refuge.

In his own deep misery he found it possible to rejoice over the great happiness that had come my way, and he became devoted to my little family, always showing up with goodies from the bountiful American PX. But sometimes the very happiness of our little group would overwhelm him. One evening Primmie found him on an upturned wheelbarrow in the garden, his head in his hands, weeping uncontrollably. She held the huge bear of a man in her arms and comforted him.

He had had a difficult time, he told me; becoming an officer. Passing the written exam had been hell, but he had managed it by memorizing textbooks like scripts. He found it rough being Clark Gable in the service. He was caught between those who fawned on him and those who thought he ought to be chopped down. It was impossible for him to be what he longed to be—just an ordinary guy.

Clark did several bombing missions over Germany, and one flak-shredded plane he was in nearly disintegrated over the Ruhr. He was no false hero; he admitted he was scared stiff the whole time. But what really put the fear of God into him was the thought of having to bail out. "That son of a bitch Hitler'll put me in a cage and charge ten marks a look all over Germany."

With the end of the war in sight, Clark was released from the service. He lived on his ranch at Encino in the San Fernando Valley, where before the war he had spent his happiest days. Carole's room was a shrine, and her clothes, photographs, and perfume bottles all remained exactly as she had left them. But the sprawling white house did not become a mini-monastery. Far from it—its steps were polished by the expectant arrival and disappointed departure of a steady stream of carbon copies of Carole Lombard. They laughed with him, drank with him, even donned blue jeans and safari jackets and

Gable and his wife, Carole Lombard. Her death in an air crash devastated Clark.

261

went duck hunting with him, but each in turn failed to measure up.

When I returned to Hollywood after the war, Clark seemed to be withdrawing more and more into his shell. I think the arrival of Primmie and me, by now with a second little boy six months old, provided him with a tiny port in his personal storm. At any rate, hardly a day went by when he did not drop in at the house we had rented in Beverly Hills; always he arrived loaded with goodies for the children and played with them for hours.

One weekend we all drove north through Big Sur along the high, winding, scenic route to Monterey, with the Pacific crashing against the rocks far below. We caught very few fish and laughed all the time. Clark was at his best, revelling in showing Primmie such a spectacular section of his beloved California. During the weekend she wrote to her father in England saying she had never been so happy in her life. Two days after we returned to Beverly Hills, as the result of an accident, she died.

During my long period of utter despair Clark was endlessly thoughtful and helpful, and he checked up constantly to see if I was all right. Without my realizing it, he was drawing on his own awful experience to steer me through mine, and for the next eighteen months I saw a great deal of him. But he seemed to have lost interest in making pictures. He drank more than before and gained weight, which worried him.

I went to Europe for six months to make a film, and when I returned, Clark seemed to have perked up. He was even getting away from the ranch occasionally and being seen in public with Anita Colby, a beautiful New York cover girl. He also seemed to take heart from the fact that—after two years—I had remarried while in Europe. He approved mightily of Hjördis, and he was our first guest at the house we bought in Pacific Palisades.

Clark made no bones about it—he was longing to be married again. But when a man nearing fifty is looking around desperately hoping to fill a void, he is usually not seeing too clearly.

Sylvia Fairbanks, the widow of the inimitable Douglas, fascinated Clark from the moment he met her, and because of her ravishing blonde beauty, and her outspokenness, she seemed to have come from the same mould as Carole. A few weeks after they

262

met they called us. "Guess what?" yelled Clark. "We're married!"

I had known both of them for many years, and I marked them down as a high-risk combination. Clark lived for the open air, blood sports, the big country, and large dogs. Sylvia was devoted to the great indoors, to her milky white skin and flawless complexion; she was happiest amid the chattering chic of café society and owned a Chihuahua the size of a mouse and named, of course, Minnie.

Three weeks after they were married Clark was looking grim. Sylvia had blithely revamped Carole's room at the ranch and invited some smart friends from the East to come out and stay in it. The King, with the expression of a man wearing a dead fish for a tiepin, was occasionally seen carrying Minnie. After seventeen months Sylvia, claiming she had been locked out of the ranch, instituted divorce proceedings.

Once a settlement had been arrived at, he issued his customary statement—"I don't intend to marry again *ever*"—and took off for Africa to make *Mogambo* with Ava Gardner and Grace Kelly. It was a big hit, and MGM wanted him to sign a new long-term contract. But Gable was sick of the studio and its petty politics. So after fifty-four movies and twenty-three years he left MGM.

His choice of pictures thereafter was not inspired; in his mid-fifties even the King was finding it difficult to land good roles. A long love affair with Scotch was beginning to show, too; he was becoming heavy and bloated. But above all, he was lonely, and his dream of a happy marriage and a son was fading rapidly.

Then, when he was fifty-five, the sun came out for Clark. One day he ran across Kay Williams. Kay was his type in looks—blonde and beautiful, with periwinkle-blue eyes. But she also possessed qualities which Carole had had in abundance; she didn't kowtow to anyone, and she was prepared to give as good as she got. She had a couple of other assets, too, that Clark liked—a little boy of four and a girl of three. Kay was now in her mid-thirties, and had decided that her acting career would never amount to much, so she was ready to settle down. A year later they married.

Kay was perfect for Clark, and she set out intelligently to make him happy and content. Instead of sweeping the memories of

Carole under the rug, she encouraged them. She played golf with him and became a good shot and an excellent fisherwoman.

Engrossed as he was in his marriage, he did film jobs as they came along, and his popularity remained enormous. He was approaching sixty now, but in spite of the rather mediocre material he selected, he seemed indestructible.

One day a script arrived on his desk that really fascinated him. The screenplay of *The Misfits* had been written by America's number one playwright—Arthur Miller. John Huston was to direct, and for co-stars Clark would have Marilyn Monroe and Montgomery Clift. The role was perfect for Gable, the best he had been offered in years, and in a high state of excitement he got into top shape before shooting started. He played golf every day, watched his diet, and cut down on the booze; the professional was getting down to his fighting weight for a special job.

In July 1960, when he reported to the location near Reno, Nevada, he was the picture of health and vitality and was looking forward eagerly to the start of the film. That same day a radiant Kay arrived with the best possible news; she was pregnant. That was a lovely day for Clark. He felt sure that his longing for a son of his own would at last be fulfilled.

John Huston was not happy with Arthur Miller's script, but the annoyances of rewrites paled into insignificance with the arrival of Marilyn Monroe and Montgomery Clift. Marilyn had become a mass of terrors and indecisions, and the poor doomed girl was headed for a breakdown. Montgomery Clift had been in a car wreck some years earlier, and his face was badly disfigured. Plastic surgery had done miracles, but the shock and the painkilling drugs had changed him terribly. Now he was subject to the blackest depressions, and he frequently found it unbearable to show up on the set.

On the Reno location Miller kept rewriting the script and Huston kept rewriting the rewrites; then either Monroe or Clift would be hours late—sometimes they wouldn't turn up at all— but every day Clark was there on time, ready to start work. Never once did he say a word against the others, though. He understood their problems.

264

At long last the picture was finished. Clark saw a rough cut, and although he usually didn't discuss his work, he told one and all that this was the best thing he had done since *Gone with the Wind*. Then he sat back and waited contentedly but impatiently for the birth of his child.

One morning Kay woke to find him standing by the bed half dressed, his face chalky white. "I've got a terrible pain," he said.

It was a massive heart attack. Kay moved into the hospital with him, and he improved steadily over the next nine days. On the tenth day he asked Kay to stand sideways against the light so he could see her silhouette. Laughing happily, he used the doctor's stethoscope to listen to the heartbeat of the little boy he longed for so much but would never see. During the night he was struck down a second time.

In Clark's copy of *The Misfits*, Arthur Miller had written: "To the man who did not know how to hate."

3. *Garbo*

In our itchy fustian trousers and jackets, we extras working on a "period" potboiler were making the most of our short lunch break on the MGM back lot, stretched out on the grass and eating dispiritedly out of the small cardboard boxes provided for our refreshment. A dusty road separated the well-tended lawns on which we sprawled from the fronts (no backs) of a row of prim New England houses.

"Here she comes!" somebody suddenly announced, and the message spread among us half-hundred depressed citizens with the rapidity of a forest fire.

"Who?" I asked my neighbour, a large Mexican lady.

265

"Garbo!" she replied, rising to her feet. "Every day at lunchtime she takes her exercises."

The extras stood respectfully and watched in fascinated silence as a slim figure wearing dark glasses, a baggy sort of track suit, and a large floppy hat strode purposefully past along the dusty road. Upon the hardened, cynical faces of those extras, long exposed to every great star in the business, were looks of wonderment and awe. Suddenly the spell was broken. A young boy broke from the ranks and, brandishing a pencil and a grubby piece of paper, ran across the grass towards the road. "Miss Garbo!" he called.

The trim figure lengthened her stride. Leaving the youth pounding along in her wake, she disappeared at a graceful gallop towards her dressing room. She had never looked around, but when it came to avoiding contact with a stranger, she had the radar system of a bat.

When the panting and crestfallen boy returned, the Mexican lady cuffed him hard and shook him.

"Why you not leave her alone?" she demanded loudly. "She likes be *private!*"

She did indeed. She also liked to work always with the same crew and demanded that the redoubtable Bill Daniels photograph all her pictures. A great professional, she seemed perfectly at ease among others working on the same film, but as Bill said, "She could sniff an outsider a mile away, and if anyone, no matter who, came on the set to get a peek at her, she'd sense it even with a couple of hundred extras around and she'd just go and sit in her dressing room till they'd been put out."

Stories of her elusiveness were legion. She probably never uttered the great Garbo quote, "I want to be alone," but there was no question that she was a loner—painfully shy with those she did not know and preferring her own company to that of most people. "Making a film with Garbo," said Robert Montgomery, "does not constitute an introduction."

Garbo had an icy look in her eyes when anyone sought to impose upon her, as Groucho Marx discovered one day. He saw the well-known figure approaching in slacks and floppy hat, waylaid her, bent down in his famous crouch, and peeked up under the brim. Two prisms of pure Baltic blue stared down at him, and Groucho backed away, muttering, "Pardon me, ma'am. I thought you were a guy I knew in Pittsburgh."

When the talkies came in, there were many casualties among the great silent stars, but none suffered a more dramatic and humiliating decline than John Gilbert. Somehow his light, pleasant voice did not suit the dark flashing eyes of the great screen lover, and the established number-one male box-office attraction of the MGM Studios was wrecked upon the rocks of his first talking film. Gilbert's first squeaky declarations of passionate love brought down the house.

Some years before, he and Garbo had embarked on a highly publicized love affair. Too highly publicized, perhaps, for Garbo's taste, because at the very moment when Gilbert thought that all was set for a wedding and a honeymoon in the South Pacific, Garbo took to her heels. Now with his career in tatters, Gilbert was badly in need of a friend.

At the height of her popularity, Garbo was preparing to make *Queen Christina*, and with great fanfare Laurence Olivier was brought over from England to play opposite her, but for some reason the studio decided at the last minute that he was wrong for the part and sent him home again. Meanwhile Garbo informed the bosses that she would make *Queen Christina* only with John Gilbert.

The picture was a triumph for Garbo, but although Gilbert, now in his mid-thirties, was still a man of sparkling good looks, his performance failed to rekindle the flame with his fans, and he sank back once more into despondency.

Around this time Ronald Colman, who had befriended me, took me frequently to Gilbert's house to play tennis. It was a sombre place, a rambling Spanish-style structure at the end of a long, winding, highly dangerous mountain road. When Gilbert showed up to play, the tennis was desultory. Often he did not appear at all, and Colman and I would take a swim in his sad, leaf-filled pool.

Once or twice I caught a glimpse of Garbo's beautiful face

267

watching us from a window, and on one occasion, as we were climbing into Colman's car, a figure in a man's shirt, slacks, and a big floppy hat approached from the scrub-covered hills and, with head down, hurried past us into the house.

"When Jack's drinking, she goes walking," said Colman. John Gilbert made only one more film before his heart gave out.

MY NEXT mini-glimpse of the famous recluse came when Edmund Goulding, the director, invited me for a weekend at his desert retreat above Palm Springs. I arrived hot and dusty after a long drive and went to cool off in his swimming pool in the palm trees below. As I neared the pool I saw standing in the shallow end a naked female figure. As this incident took place in the mid-1930s, the reader will understand that I retreated to the house and asked my host for a clarification of the situation.

"Oh," he said, "it's only Garbo. She's staying somewhere down there and uses the pool when she feels like it."

I hastened once more down the garden path, but I was too late. All that remained was the disturbed surface of the water.

Garbo was finally dethroned as an actress. Her dethronement was sudden and remarkable, because she apparently went down without a struggle. It could have happened to anyone—and frequently did. She chose the wrong film. Nothing in show business is more horrendous than a farce when it is not funny, and *Two-Faced Woman* was a four-star, fur-lined, oceangoing disaster. Garbo, instead of drawing comfort from her record of success and resolving to be more selective in future, just stopped making films.

Certainly she was as sensitive as a seismograph, but her extraordinary abdication rocked Hollywood to its foundations. Possibly she reasoned that she had always longed for privacy and could afford it now; this may have seemed to her the ideal time to go.

She did not go far—just to New York—and she came back occasionally to haunt Hollywood like a lovely ghost, nonchalantly pushing aside a hundred offers to return to the screen. Hollywood could not believe she would not make a well-timed comeback—not to do so was contrary to all Hollywood thinking. So the longer she stayed away, the stronger grew the Garbo myth.

The newspapers printed reports of her walking the New York streets aimlessly and alone, or haggling over the price of carrots. Her apartment there was reputed to contain a priceless collection of Impressionist paintings stacked on the floor, facing the wall.

Our house in Pacific Palisades had been built by Vicki Baum, the author of *Grand Hotel*, which had been made into a hit film starring Garbo. A neighbour of ours was that rarity—a Hollywood hermit. Richard Haydn was a much sought-after director and character actor, but his joy in life was to be alone tending the most beautiful collection of flowers in California, and I suspected that he went near the studios only in order to earn money to buy seeds and fertilizer.

One evening some years after Garbo's retirement Hjördis and I were sitting on our terrace when Richard materialized suddenly. "I've brought someone who says she spent some of her happiest days in this house," he announced. "She would like to see it again if it's not inconvenient." Behind him stood Garbo.

My wife, being Swedish, took over the tour of the house, and by the time they came back the two of them were jabbering away like two Scandinavian conspirators. Garbo told us about our house during the Vicki Baum days—it must have been a fascinating place, a rendezvous for Leopold Stokowski and a host of European writers and artists.

During subsequent years, Garbo often came to see us. Always the same, of undiluted beauty but with something held back in reserve.

People who have climbed a cliff have been known to glance casually down into the void below and for the first time realize to their horror that they suffer from vertigo. With knees of jelly, pounding hearts, and spinning heads, they then inch their way down—and never climb again. I often wondered if something of the sort had overtaken Garbo at the peak of her career. Just once I dared try to find out. "Why *did* you give up the movies?" I asked her.

She considered her answer so carefully that I wondered if she had decided to ignore my question. At last, almost to herself, she said, "I had made enough faces."

4. The Prince

IN the hot summer of 1947 I was settling myself luxuriously into a booth in the bar of Romanoff's Restaurant in Beverly Hills. It was lunchtime, and the best-known faces in Movie Town were making their "entrances" in droves into the main dining room. It was nice to be in the dark, air-conditioned cool of the bar, nice to be out of the glare of the midday sun; above all, it was nice to be in the company of the diminutive proprietor of the joint—His Imperial Highness, Prince Michael Alexandrovich Dmitri Obolensky Romanoff.

"Old boy," my host intoned in his deep, slightly "off" Oxford voice, "your emperor has ordered an ice-cold bottle of Dom Pérignon and some grouse which were flown in specially this morning from your native Scotland."

The headwaiter approached with a deferential inclination of the head. "We must find room for this party, Mr. Romanoff. They're very important . . . eight of them."

"Who are they?" demanded Mike.

"Oilmen from Texas and society people from Pasadena."

"Peasants," said His Imperial Highness. "To hell with 'em."

Ten minutes later the scene was repeated. "There's a general waiting in line, too, Mr. Romanoff . . . from St. Louis. . . ."

"Cannon fodder," commented the prince. "From the interior, too," he added with disgust.

Harry F. Gerguson of Chicago, as Mike was known to the New York City police, had been described officially by Scotland Yard as "a rogue of uncertain nationality". He had been jailed countless times in the United States and in France and had received two suspended sentences in England. He had been deported regularly from all three countries and had been caught twice on transatlantic liners, a stowaway using empty cabins. All his crimes had been what he termed "moves of self-preservation" —selling *objets d'art* which did not belong to him or passing rubber cheques. All these misdemeanours had been perpetrated to help Harry F. Gerguson live in the style to which Prince Michael Alexandrovich Dmitri Obolensky Romanoff would have been accustomed.

I first met Mike in New York at the tail end of Prohibition; we frequented the same speakeasy, Jack and Charlie's, at 21 West 52nd Street, where I had just been taken on as their first salesman of legitimate booze. I was not selling very much, and after an initial effort Mike realized that putting the bite on me for ten bucks was living in Mother Hubbard land; thereafter we became good friends in need.

Depending on whom he was talking to and his estimate of their gullibility, he operated a sliding scale of claims of kinship to the murdered Czar Nicholas II. Sometimes he was the czar's nephew; often he was the son of Prince Yusupov, who had pumped booze and bullets into the czarina's adviser, the mad monk Rasputin; on particularly low-risk occasions, Mike became Yusupov himself. When he operated in the "interior", he occasionally took on a British aura, wearing a monocle and calling himself Sir Arthur Wellesley.

With New York harbouring countless Russians of authentic noble birth, Mike was again and again denounced as an impostor. But on these occasions he conducted himself with such immense dignity that he added to his growing coterie of admirers.

One day somebody invited the Grand Duke Dmitri of Russia to meet his kinsman. The grand duke peered suspiciously at the top of Mike's hairbrush crew cut and spoke to him rapidly in Russian. Mike made for the door, raising a languid hand to silence the duke. "I don't think," he said, "that we should insult our hosts by talking in any language but theirs." Later he confided that he had never much cared for that branch of the family.

It was inevitable that sooner or later anyone with Mike's flair would feel the call of the Hollywood wild. In 1927 His Imperial Highness arrived aboard the Santa Fe *Chief*, took a large suite in the Ambassador Hotel, and started dispensing princely amounts of champagne and caviar to all and sundry. Vowing haughtily that the Romanoffs never dirtied their fingers with common currency, he tipped the headwaiters and bellhops with great abandon—by cheque.

The prince was lavishly entertained by Hollywood hostesses, and after Mike had admitted modestly that he had served with the British Army in the Great War and knew the Sudan like the back of his hand Warner Brothers begged him to be their technical adviser on *The Desired Woman*, a picture with a Sudanese background and a British Army foreground. He pulled down a royal salary for many weeks and became much sought after by the studios as technical adviser on pictures with Russian overtones. One of them proved his undoing. An old friend of the late czar—an ex-general named Theodor Lodijensky—was working as an extra on the film, and he alerted the Los Angeles *Examiner*. The next day a front-page story exposed Mike as an impostor.

Finding Southern California suddenly uncomfortably warm, Mike decided to disappear, and soon he was papering the interior with his phoney cheques. He kept on the move, however, and usually stayed ahead of the sheriff. But well into his forties by now, Mike was longing to settle in one place, and soon he was back in Los Angeles, broke but with a new light in his eye—he had determined to go straight. Instead of borrowing money, he now preferred winning it at backgammon or at chess—he was a chess expert, playing several games at once all over the country by telegram. Throughout his metamorphosis he clung tenaciously to his Romanoff fantasy, but he now traded on it openly and became more widely admired and entertained as a famous impostor than he ever had been when he was accepted as the real thing.

FOR A time I was living in a house on the beach at Santa Monica. Mike was a frequent and welcome visitor; occasionally he requested the loan of a bed "on which to lay the imperial head"

He made the trips to Santa Monica by bumming lifts.

One day, however, he drove up to the door in an immense Dusenberg.

"Greetings, old boy," he said smugly.

"Whom did you borrow it from?" I asked.

"It's mine," said the prince. "I bought it last week. Allow me to show you the pink slip," he said, and displayed the document proving that he had indeed made the purchase.

I goggled. "Where are you sleeping?" I asked.

"In the Dusenberg, of course," said the imperial motorist.

EVEN THOUGH by now he was playing his impostor role for a different effect, he still used the trappings of his calling, wearing an Old Etonian tie one day and a Brigade of Guards scarf the next. His conversations still pulsated with "when I was up at Oxford", "during my time at Sandhurst", or "he was a classmate of mine at Harvard".

It was no easy job to catch him out; many tried and failed. There were dozens of witnesses to prove that in 1923, for a few months at least, he had indeed studied at the Graduate School of Arts and Sciences at Harvard. As a Sandhurst man myself I found his knowledge of the procedures at the Royal Military College, and of the habits and hideaways of its cadets, to be just as extensive as my own.

"How many schools and colleges *have* you attended?" I asked him once.

"Let me see," said Mike. "St. Paul's, Andover, Choate, and Harvard in the United States. Eton, Harrow, Winchester, Oxford, Cambridge, and Sandhurst in England and, of course, the Sorbonne and Heidelberg. Believe me, old boy"—he chortled—"this business of being an impostor is a full-time job!"

In 1937 Mike struck gold. He obtained an option on the lease of a defunct restaurant on Hollywood's Sunset Strip. His friends became stockholders in the shoestring enterprise, and the place reopened in a blaze of black ties, mink, well-known faces, and publicity.

The invitation was a classic:

I AM COMMANDED BY HIS IMPERIAL HIGHNESS PRINCE MICHAEL
ALEXANDROVICH DMITRI OBOLENSKY ROMANOFF TO REQUEST YOUR
PRESENCE AT A SOIREE HE IS GIVING IN HIS OWN HONOUR . . .
COUVERT FIFTY DOLLARS
BRING YOUR OWN WINE AND KINDLY FEE THE WAITERS

HARRY GERGUSON
COMPTROLLER TO THE IMPERIAL HOUSEHOLD

All Hollywood turned out, and so many people brought wine
that few realized the place had no arrangements whatever for
cooking. A sparse menu was serviced by a nearby hash joint on a
strictly cash basis. (The money collected for the first two *couverts*
started the ball rolling.) But a riotous evening was had by all, and
enough money was raised to install a kitchen and launch Mike on
a successful career as a restaurateur.

In 1939, when I was headed for Europe and the British Army,
Mike came to say goodbye.

He also gave me a hand-knitted Balaclava helmet ("saved me
near St. Petersburg, old boy"), and a large blue and white spotted
scarf with a burn in the centre ("mustard gas . . . Cambrai . . .
silk is the only thing against it"). I lost the hand-knitted Balaclava
helmet but I still have the blue and white spotted scarf: a laundress
told me that careless ironing was responsible for the burn.

Restaurateur Mike prospered during the Second World War and
by 1945 he was firmly established as the owner-manager of the
highly lucrative Romanoff's in Beverly Hills, the imperial *R*
emblazoned on the front door. When he branched out into an
even larger and more elaborate establishment, his loyal staff and
clients and the imperial *R* made the move with him. Around that
time he also started a subsidiary on an escarpment near Palm
Springs called Romanoff on the Rocks and accumulated a bulldog
named Confucius and an extremely attractive young wife, Gloria.
His Imperial Highness had made the big switch from con man to
capitalist and, in a strange reversal of form, had not lost a friend
in the process.

One of my reasons for visiting him in his establishment on that
hot summer's day had been to ask his help for a project of my own.

In 1937 Mike Romanoff, tired of impersonating Russian nobility, "went straight"—in the restaurant business. Niven and his date, Jacqueline Dyer, helped launch the operation by bringing their own wine.

Robert Laycock, my good friend and Primmie's uncle, was coming to visit me, and I wanted Romanoff's to cater a party for him.

"Ah, and how is young Bob?" asked Mike the minute he heard the name. "I haven't seen him since he was at Eton."

"Now, Mike," I said patiently, "Bob Laycock is twenty years younger than you. You were never at Eton with him—or with anybody else for that matter."

Mike looked pained. "I did not suggest that young Bob was a schoolmate of mine—I merely mentioned the fact that I had not seen him since he was at Eton."

It was always fun to play along with Mike, so I tossed him a cue. "And where did you meet him while he was a schoolboy?"

"At Wiseton, of course. He was home after the summer half and Sir Joseph had invited me for the weekend for a spot of country-house cricket."

275

Wiseton was indeed the Laycock home in Lincolnshire, and Sir Joseph was certainly Bob's father, but the mental picture of Mike in blazer and white flannels, sitting in a deck chair awaiting his turn to bat, was too much even for me.

"Mike, please," I said, "please don't get into a thing with Bob Laycock, because he's a very rough character indeed—he was the chief of all the commandos, you know."

"And the youngest general in the British Army," said Mike, unmoved. "I'm very proud of him."

I shook my head. "Mike, please, on this one occasion, *please* don't press your luck."

"After luncheon," said my host, "we will go to my house—I have something to show you which may put your mind at rest."

At his white stucco residence on Chevy Chase Drive, Mike took me up to his bedroom; there he nonchalantly displayed a pair of ivory-backed hairbrushes. The ivory was a little yellow with age, but what brought me up short was the insignia in worked silver. It was something I knew very well—the Laycock crest.

"A present from old Joe," said Mike smugly.

Bob Laycock arrived, and the party was a great success. For a large part of the evening Mike cornered Bob, who seemed to be thoroughly enjoying the company of the mini-monarch. Judging by Mike's expressive gestures, both cricket and hairbrushes were being discussed at length.

Nothing awful happened, however, and after the happy guests had gone, Bob and I had a nightcap. "What did you think of Mike?" I asked.

"Fascinating," said Bob. "There is no question but that he has been to Wiseton and no question at all that he has played cricket there. There is also no question that long ago a team of Durham miners came over to play. I well remember it because Father was so furious. When they left, it was discovered that someone had swiped his favourite hairbrushes."

Prince Michael Alexandrovich Dmitri Obolensky Romanoff remained enigmatic when I tried to pump him. "Golden days, old boy," he would say dreamily. "Golden days."

And that was *all* he would say.

5. Bogie

Humphrey Bogart was born in December 1899, which up to a point was perfectly all right with him. The thing he deeply resented about it was that it happened on Christmas Day. "Got gypped out of a proper birthday, dammit."

His famous lisp was caused by a badly performed operation on his lower lip, in which a splinter of wood had become embedded. I asked him how the piece of wood had got into his lip in the first place. He shrugged. "Accident as a kid." The Warner Brothers publicity department improved upon this and announced that it was a "shrapnel wound suffered in combat during World War I".

Bogie endured a well-to-do upbringing on the eastern seaboard, attended Andover, and headed for Yale. He didn't make it there, much to his mother's annoyance. She told him he was a failure and ordered him to go get himself a job. He complied, enlisted in the U.S. Navy the next day, and in the closing months of World War I, did indeed see service—aboard the troop carrier *Leviathan*.

After the war he was employed as a runner for a Wall Street brokerage house. He didn't run fast enough, apparently, and he openly resented the financial establishment, so to the accompaniment of catcalls from his mother, he drifted into the theatre. By the age of twenty-six Bogie was regularly employed as a sleek juvenile lead, complete with white tie, tails, and occasionally a tennis racket. These being the Roaring Twenties, he also set about making a name for himself in the speakeasies of Prohibition. Bogie maintained from then on an awe-inspiring level of Scotch consumption, but he never allowed it to interfere with his work.

277

Bogie married a successful young actress named Helen Menken. The marriage fell apart after eighteen months, with Bogie blaming himself for putting his career first. It was the depths of the Depression, and work for actors was scarce. One year later he married another successful young actress, Mary Phillips, and they moved into crumbling lodgings on the East Side and for a while were supported solely by Bogie's prowess at chess, which he played for fifty cents a game in Sixth Avenue dives.

To be over thirty years old, an unemployed married actor, small in stature, short on presence, with a pronounced lisp and limited professional experience, must have been daunting even for Bogie, but he gamely plodded off on his rounds of agencies and producers' offices, and in 1934 he struck theatrical oil. Arthur Hopkins was casting *The Petrified Forest* by Robert Sherwood, and Bogie was given a chance to read the part of the sentimental killer, Duke Mantee. He delivered his lines with a snarl made even more menacing by his lisp.

Neither Hopkins nor Sherwood was impressed. But Leslie Howard, the star of the play, had been sitting quietly in the back row. Now he urgently begged the others to reconsider. He was convinced that Bogie was ideal for the part.

The play was a huge success, and at the end of the Broadway run Bogie was signed with Howard to make the picture for Warner Brothers. But when he and Mary arrived in Hollywood, all set to knock the film world for a loop, he learned to his stunned dismay that the studio had decided to put one of its biggest contract stars into the role—Edward G. Robinson.

Bogie fired off an SOS to Leslie Howard, who unleashed a return salvo at Warner Brothers: "It's either with Bogart or without me." Bogart it was, and film history continued smoothly on its way. He never forgot the helping hand, and as a gesture of his gratitude, he named his second child Leslie.

The brothers Warner, never renowned for the delicacy and foresight with which they handled their contract players, decided that they had hatched a golden egg, so in the next four years Bogie pumped out more than twenty gangster films in which he played a carbon copy of Duke Mantee. This nearly finished his

278

career, and it completely ruined his marriage. Seeing nothing of her husband except glimpses of a zombie who worked punishing hours, Mary took off for New York to do a play—and to divorce Bogie. He consoled himself with a blonde of conspicuous cleavage named Mayo Methot.

Mayo was a hard case, a drinker who went refill by refill with Bogie, but unlike him she was unable to handle it. In 1938 Mayo and Bogie married, and the partnership soon developed into the toughest situation Bogie had ever had to handle.

I had met him two years before, when he had been lent by Warner Brothers to Goldwyn to make *Dead End*. We did not like each other very much. I found his tough manner and his habit of needling people rather tiresome, and he marked me down as a prissy Englishman. We parted with expressions of mutual respect and a determination to avoid each other like the plague.

Humphrey and "Betty" Bogart with Stephen and Leslie. They named their daughter in honour of Leslie Howard, who had helped Bogie get his first big part—in The Petrified Forest.

One time I ran across Bogie and Mayo in a restaurant on the Sunset Strip. It was a favourite hangout of the younger Hollywood group because it boasted the best music in town, but the place also catered to the gangster element of Los Angeles.

Bogie, like all movie mobsters, was plagued by drunks who would lurch up to him in public and try to pick a fight in order to impress others, but he was adept at avoiding physical combat. It was not that he was cowardly; it was just that he was a bantamweight who had not the faintest intention of being knocked around by people twice his size. His fondness for needling, however, sometimes led him into dangerous brinkmanship.

That night at the restaurant Bogie was confronted by a large man with a flushed face wearing an open-neck shirt. I was sitting a few tables away with the Oomph Girl, Ann Sheridan. Suddenly all hell broke loose. Bogie threw a full glass of Scotch into his aggressor's eyes, and at the same moment Mayo hit the man on the head with a shoe. I caught a glimpse of flinty-eyed characters rising purposefully from the table whence the large man had come, and of a solid phalanx of waiters converging on the battle area. Soon the air was thick with flying bottles, yells, plates, left hooks, and food.

"Quick!" screamed the Oomph Girl. "Under the table!"

We had not been installed there for more than a few seconds before Bogie came crawling over to join us, laughing like hell. "Everything's O.K.," he chortled. "Mayo's handling it."

Mayo was indeed. The attacker and his party were ousted.

AFTER THAT night Bogie nicknamed Mayo "Sluggy", and she lived up to it. The skirmishes between the Battling Bogarts, as the Hollywood press corps christened them, were noisy, and complaining neighbours insisted that they were nonstop. Jealousy on the part of Mayo seemed to be the spark that ignited the flames. Bogie and Mayo would drink; then her jealousy, generally of his current leading lady, would come to the boil, and the bottles started whizzing past his head. On one occasion Mayo slashed her wrists, on another she set fire to their house, and on a third she stabbed him in the back with a carving knife. "Only went in a little way," he said as he was being stitched up.

The Battling Bogarts were still at it hammer and tongs in September 1939, when, in a moment of military lunacy, I departed for Europe. I did not see Bogie again till I returned in 1946, but a friend had kept me up-to-date.

Bogie, he told me, had widened the area of conflict and had decided to take on the studio at the same time as he was conducting his running battles with Mayo. He had realized that he must get away from his gangster image because, with the wartime carnage being fully reported, the "mob" had become tame stuff indeed. So he refused to work at all and was suspended. After much resistance from Warner Brothers, John Huston was allowed to put Bogie into *The Maltese Falcon*, and its success opened up a new career for Bogie; within a few months he played a romantic soldier of fortune in *Casablanca* opposite Ingrid Bergman. He became the pet of the Warner Brothers lot.

As Bogie's film popularity soared, his homelife deteriorated. Mayo became an alcoholic; her looks and figure collapsed, and she made an increasing number of hideous scenes in public. It couldn't last at that pace, of course, and when in 1944 Bogie made *To Have and Have Not*, he fell head over heels in love with his nineteen-year-old leading lady, a former theatre usherette and cover girl named Lauren Bacall. "Betty" Bacall was equally in love with Bogie.

Divorce became inevitable, and Mayo, a classic Hollywood casualty, departed for her Oregon birthplace. There, six years later, she died—all alone in a motel.

When Betty and Bogie married, there was exactly twenty-five years' difference in their ages, and the Hollywood smart money went on an early breakup. But they underestimated Betty. In spite of her youth she had a mountain of common sense and the guts to put it to work. She never kowtowed to Bogie, she never nagged him, and above all, she truly admired him as a man and as an actor. For his part he adored her and was proud of her looks, her talent, and her spirit. He never looked at another woman. He cut back conspicuously on his whisky consumption too because "Betty doesn't go for it too much, and it's no fun drinking alone." Her explanation was probably nearer the mark:

"Bogie drank a lot because he was unhappy. Now he's happy."

Betty was the perfect mate for Bogie, although as they were both completely honest with each other and utterly straightforward in their approach to life, there would occasionally be an almighty explosion. But it never lasted long.

This then was the couple that I visited when I returned to Hollywood in 1946. Betty had arranged a surprise party for Bogie on his forty-seventh birthday—a potentially dangerous tactic. When Bogie walked in and discovered thirty people hiding in closets or under beds he became loudly abusive, and no amount of singing "Happy Birthday" could soften his attitude.

Betty finally won the day by playing it his way. "All right then, you SOB," she yelled. "You stay here alone, and we'll all go out for dinner."

He bared his teeth in the famous wolf grin and snarled, "O.K., you bastards—you're welcome." The party went on till dawn.

BOGIE bought a sixty-five-foot ketch, *Santana*, and next to Betty she became the most important thing in his life. He was a first-class sailor, and his love of the sea was deep, almost mystical. Betty was smart enough not to be jealous of this other love and realized that he derived much peace and strength from his weekend voyages.

During that surprise forty-seventh birthday party, Bogie had learned that I, too, had sailed all my life, and his face softened. "There's hope for you yet," he growled. "Come to the island next weekend."

I enjoyed the trip immensely, but I subsequently discovered that while I had been told to take the helm or put up a spinnaker, I had in fact been under Bogie's microscope. His theory was simple —if a man could handle a boat in rough weather, he should be awarded one star, like a reliable restaurant in the *Guide Michelin*. If in addition he proved to have interests, experience, and curiosity outside the small world of film making and enjoyed a game of chess, he might receive a higher rating. I never learned my own classification, but imperceptibly, almost, our understanding prospered from then on, and one day I looked up to find Bogie

282

and Betty among my closest friends. This was flattering, because Bogie did not really like actors as a breed; apart from Tracy, Sinatra, and Peter Lorre, he usually kept his distance.

On my many trips aboard *Santana* I grew to realize what a very special man Betty had married. To Bogie things were either black or white; he had little patience with the greys. To sort people out quickly, he used the shock technique. Early on in the acquaintance he would say or do something completely outrageous and the reaction of the other told Bogie most of what he wanted to know about them.

He loathed the phonies and the pretentious. People in movie theatres saw him as the personification of the tough and the sardonic, and up to a point they were not far wrong. He gamely presented the same façade in real life, but he had a difficult time covering up the fact that he was really kind, generous, intelligent, and deeply sentimental.

Bogie set himself up as a nonconformist, and this was no act. He really intended to do his own thing and despised those who pandered to the Hollywood code of good behaviour. "I'm not one of the boys next door," he would say. "I leave that to all those good-looking bastards with their button-down shirts." And he would go on his merry way, arriving at nightclubs with giant panda dolls, arguing with all and sundry, championing left-wing causes, and making heavily quoted statements about the unreliability of people who never drank.

Although right at the top of his profession, Bogie also possessed the actor's Achilles' heel—he was jealous and showed it. The actor he admired most was Spencer Tracy. Both were highly professional performers, and both despised the stars who were not. Bogie wanted to make *The Desperate Hours*, and the "dream casting" was to have Spencer and Bogie in roles that seemed tailor-made for them. Each wanted badly to play with the other. Again and again they got all steamed up about the prospect, but each time it mysteriously collapsed, the reason being that the moment they parted they quickly contacted their respective managers—neither of them would take second billing. They never did work together.

BOGIE became increasingly exercised over the fact that a successful actor's life is a series of short bursts of high taxation, with no chance to spread the earnings over the lean years. "I've got to get some decent dough put away for Betty and the family." He worked continuously towards that end, making pictures through his own company and finally selling the company with the rights to all his pictures for a very large sum.

Betty, meantime, was champing at the bit to break out of his small gloomy canyon house with its disturbing memories of Mayo, but for a long time her pleas for more elbow room fell on deaf ears. "You were raised in one room in the Bronx," he would insist, "and there's nothing wrong with *you*."

Finally, with the help of his business manager, Morgan Maree, who touched a nerve by persuading him that it would be an excellent investment—"something to leave to Betty and the offspring"—he forked out a down payment on a beautiful house with tennis court and pool in the high-tax area of Holmby Hills. Bogie felt he was being conned into joining the Establishment, but Betty smiled like a big cat and soothed him down—this was when she was pregnant with their second child. Bogie grew to be obsessively proud of his new acquisition. He never dressed the part of a Holmby Hills squire, however, and slopped about the place attired in a grisly selection of antiquated moccasins, sweaters, windbreakers, and dungarees—usually with a battered yachting cap on his head. Dogs and cats were everywhere. He was a good father, though his idea of entertaining his children on a free day was odd—he would take them to lunch at Romanoff's.

I DON'T remember when I first noticed Bogie's cough; probably it was while we were sharing sleeping quarters aboard *Santana*. I thought it was just a smoker's cough, for he used up a great number of "coffin nails" as he called them. But the cough got worse, and Betty prevailed on him to see a doctor. The news was as bad as a man could hear.

There followed an eight-hour operation, and the slow slide began. "I've got it licked if I can put on some weight," he said, but as the weeks went by he lost weight steadily. His eyes became enormous in his pitifully gaunt face, but his courage shone out of them.

At the funeral service on January 17, 1957, his friends were determined that his departure should be dignified and purged of all Hollywood bad taste, and when several newsmen attempted to enter the church with concealed cameras we unceremoniously bundled them outside.

John Huston had always been a joy to Bogart, probably his favourite companion and certainly his favourite director. Huston got the most out of Bogie as an actor, and together they turned out classics like *The Maltese Falcon, The Treasure of the Sierra Madre, The African Queen,* and *Beat the Devil.* So it was right and fitting that Huston should speak a few words of farewell at the service. He said, in part:

"Bogie's hospitality went far beyond food and drink. He fed a guest's spirit as well as his body. . . . This tradition of wonderful hospitality continued on to the last hour he was able to sit upright. He would lie on his couch upstairs until five o'clock, when he would be shaved and groomed in grey flannels and scarlet smoking jacket. Then, as he was no longer able to walk, his emaciated body would be lifted into a wheelchair and pushed to a dumbwaiter on the second-floor landing. The top of the dumbwaiter had been removed to give him headroom. Sitting on a little stool, he would be lowered down to the kitchen, and again by wheelchair he'd be transported to the library and his chair. And there he would be, sherry glass in one hand and cigarette in the other, at five thirty, when the guests would start to arrive. They were limited now to those who had known him best and longest; and they stayed, two and three at a time, for a half hour or so until about eight o'clock which was the time for him to go back upstairs by the same route he had descended.

"No one who sat in his presence during the final weeks would ever forget. It was a unique display of sheer animal courage. After the first visit—it took that to get over the initial shock of his appearance—one quickened to the grandeur of it, expanded, and felt strangely elated, proud to be there, proud to be his friend, the friend of such a brave man."

6. Mr. Goldwyn

When a history of Hollywood is written, the name of Samuel Goldwyn is bound to get top billing.

For half a century he towered like a colossus above his contemporaries, and the results of his taste and his single-minded determination to settle for nothing short of his own ideas of perfection are preserved on film for all to see.

It was long a habit among the jealous in the Hollywood jungle to ridicule Goldwyn and try, by the all-too-easy manufacture of Goldwynisms, to diminish his stature. "Include me out," "I'll tell you in two words—impossible," "A verbal contract is not worth the paper it's written on," "We can always get more Indians off the reservoir"—all these have become part of the Goldwyn legend. But who can claim to have been present when these pearls of wisdom were dropped? Another alleged Goldwynism—"Elevate those guns a little lower"—was actually an Andrew Jacksonism which erupted from the lips of the future seventh president at the Battle of New Orleans in 1815.

Goldwyn did have a problem remembering names. He invariably referred to Joel McCrea, who was under contract to him at the same time I was, as Joe McCreal, and Goldwyn's European public relations chief, an impeccable and immaculate Welshman named Euan Lloyd, became resigned to being addressed as Urine.

When I was leaving Hollywood to go off to war in 1939, I went to Sam's office to say goodbye. He was very put out that I was leaving voluntarily and not waiting until I was called up, so he put me on suspension till the end of the war or my life, whichever came sooner. "I'll cable Hitler," he said, "and ask him to shoot around you."

Six and a half years later, when I returned to the Goldwyn fold, a broke and forgotten commodity, Goldwyn sombrely pointed out that during my absence there had been a change in the law, as a result of which my suspended contract had lapsed. Then, unpredictable as always, he laughed at my stricken face, gave me a new five-year contract at a greatly increased salary, and lent me enough money to make the down payment on a house.

A SPECIAL determination of his was to be a great gentleman, and in his own home he was. Even if, an hour before, he had been banging his office desk and hurling imprecations at you, once you arrived at his house on Laurel Way he would meet you, smiling, at the door, look after your every need during the evening, and personally escort you to your car when it was time to depart. People found this Jekyll-and-Hyde quality disconcerting, because the reverse could happen; lulled into false security during a cozy dinner, they could find themselves facing accusations and abuse from the boss at the studio the following morning.

Goldwyn had immense presence and a great dignity. His head was almost completely bald from an early age, and his eyes were dark, small, and deep-set. His jaw was pronounced and very determined indeed. Above average in height, deep of chest, and high of voice, he was always dressed in suits, shirts, and shoes of perfect fit, clothes being one of his few personal extravagances. He also took great trouble to remain trim. His light, almost Spartan luncheons at the studio were served in his private dining room, and every evening on his way home he ordered his car to stop as soon as he reached the city limits of Beverly Hills so that he might walk briskly the remaining mile and a half to his house.

In everything, competition was his lifeblood. Playing croquet with Sam could be a real hazard. He had a beautifully manicured lawn, and the best players in Hollywood gathered there on Sundays, but it was necessary to have an extra man stashed away in the trees, because after a disagreement Sam frequently stalked into the house and locked the front door. Nobody would have accused him of actually cheating at games—he just had to come out on top.

Fred Astaire and I witnessed another bit of Goldwyn gamesmanship—on a golf course. Sam sliced his ball into some trees, and it ended up in an unplayable position. Fred grabbed my arm, shaking with laughter. "Look at him," he said. Very methodically, Goldwyn was moving stones and fallen branches so that he had an unobstructed view of the green. Then he produced a wooden tee from his pocket and put the ball upon it.

"Sam!" I yelled. "You can't *do* that!"

"I know," he shouted back. "My caddie *told* me I shouldn't."

If he was competitive at games, he displayed the toughness of steel in business, and the fields were littered with the vanquished. Ronald Colman, after years under contract to him, refused ever to speak to him again, and Eddie Cantor swore that working for Goldwyn put him in a hospital. Sam's rows with his top director, William Wyler, were so noisy that Merritt Hulbert, the head of Goldwyn's story department, asked to have his office moved to another floor. "Quiet conferences make quiet pictures," retorted Goldwyn firmly, but eventually he and Wyler arranged a truce.

"Look, Willie," he said, "from now on we each put 'a hundred-dollar bill on my desk, and the first one to shout loses his money."

As a result Hulbert stayed in his office, while next door appalling insults were traded in whispers.

I don't believe Sam was rude on purpose. I think his thoughts flashed through his head with lightning speed, and sometimes he just didn't give his tongue enough time to check its possible effect on people.

Goldwyn's employees from top to bottom were in awe of him, and for a very good reason—there was not a technical job on the lot that he could not fill perfectly himself. He was well aware of his awesome presence and seldom visited the sound stages, because he knew that his appearance there sowed instant alarm in the breasts of one and all. Directors, actors, cameramen, and sound technicians who had not reached the high standards he demanded of them were "sent for"; invariably they returned looking as though they had witnessed a terrible accident.

He never asked the banks to put up the money for his productions; however expensive, the sole financier of a Samuel Goldwyn film was Samuel Goldwyn himself. "The banks can't afford me," he said.

LITTLE Samuel was born in 1882 in the Warsaw ghetto. At the age of eleven he ran away from home to relatives in Manchester, who quickly "placed him" as a blacksmith's assistant. He saved enough for a steerage passage to New York, where an Irish immigration official, unable to cope with his unpronounceable Polish name, told him that he would be known as Samuel Goldfish.

Young Sam became a glove salesman; he sold enough gloves to be able at twenty-eight to marry Blanche Lasky, whose brother Jesse was a vaudeville producer. In 1912 Samuel Goldfish decided that he could not look another glove in the face and that his future lay with the infant motion-picture business. His brother-in-law was doing quite well, and he was not overly tempted when Sam proposed that they join forces. Lasky, however, conjured up a possible partner for Sam in the shape of a Canadian actor and writer of vaudeville acts—one Cecil B. DeMille.

DeMille fell for Sam's idea, and a year later the two of them prevailed on Lasky to put up $25,000. DeMille was dispatched to California, whence he wired his partner that he had "rented a barn for seventy-five dollars a month in the middle of an orange grove in a place called Hollywood." Hollywood was born.

With Sam Goldfish handling distribution and exploitation, the company made twenty-one films that first year. Samuel Goldfish became allied with a theatrical producer from New York, the quiet, self-effacing Edgar Selwyn. Using half of each of their names, they registered their combine as the Goldwyn Company. Its name became a household word, whereupon Samuel Goldfish, with what quiet Edgar Selwyn described as a piece of monumental treachery, legally took the name of Goldwyn for himself.

The Goldwyn Company boomed, and more changes followed. Goldwyn discarded his wounded partner, Selwyn, but was himself bought out by new associates who merged the Goldwyn Company with Metro and L. B. Mayer. Goldwyn agreed to this

289

merger but cagily insisted that his name should remain in eye-catching sloping letters between the stereotyped ones of Metro and Mayer. Then he left Metro-*Goldwyn*-Mayer with its snarling-lion trademark and became in 1924 what he was to remain until his retirement in 1965: the greatest independent producer the world has ever seen. With other independents—Douglas Fairbanks, Charlie Chaplin, and Mary Pickford—he formed the United Artists Company, and they bought studios on Santa Monica Boulevard. Before long Goldwyn realized that he was the major contributor to the company's output and in a final major convulsion he unloaded his partners and wound up owning the studios.

IN 1925, several years after he had been divorced from his first wife, Blanche, Sam married a calm and beautiful young actress, Frances Howard, who presented him with an enchanting male heir, Samuel, Jr., and provided him with an enduring Hollywood marvel, a happy married life.

The house they built together on Laurel Way was charmingly unpretentious, surrounded by an attractive garden, a pool, and a tennis court—the croquet lawn came later. Decorated by Frances with a light and happy touch, it had none of the traditional trappings of the typical movie mogul, though there were a few good Impressionist paintings and a comfortable projection room.

Goldwyn loved this sanctuary and guarded it jealously against all intrusion. One evening, sitting on the veranda with him, I pointed out the splendid spectacle of a family of quail parading across his lawn. Father was in front, proudly bearing his antennae head-dress; mother walked fussily at the back, and in between were eight scuttling little babies.

"They don't belong here," said Goldwyn coldly.

The Goldwyns entertained quietly—no big ostentatious parties, no striped tents covering a boarded-over swimming pool—just a few friends on a Saturday evening invited to enjoy dinner and afterwards a movie or cards.

All the top producers and stars had projection rooms either inside their houses or as outcrops of their playrooms or pool houses; collectively they were known as the Bel Air Circuit, and the competition to display the latest film to weekend guests was intense. Often a movie was heckled, mocked, and torn to shreds by loud-mouthed and over-lubricated know-it-alls talking back to the screen. The reputation of a picture was frequently blackened before the paying customers had a chance to judge for themselves, and it was not uncommon for a studio head, hearing of such a hostile reception, to turn chicken-hearted and downgrade the film's advertising budget.

This never happened in Goldwyn's house. Once the guests were comfortably seated, Sam manned the sound controls himself, and the film, good or bad, was unfolded with dignity. Afterwards Goldwyn might invite discussion of its merits or demerits, but always his was the most constructive of criticism. Secure in his own integrity as a film maker, he felt no need to chop down the opposition.

"The play's the thing," Shakespeare said, and Goldwyn early believed him. Although he entered into long contracts with big established stars such as Ronald Colman and Gary Cooper, his major outlay was always for authors. Frequently he would have several screenplays prepared by different writers from the same material; then he would choose the best. Employed by Goldwyn, but never incarcerated in the chicken-coop writers' buildings, were, among others, F. Scott Fitzgerald, Robert Sherwood, John Huston, Maurice Maeterlinck, Lillian Hellman, Ben Hecht, and Thornton Wilder.

Goldwyn's formula for making a successful movie was simple:

1. Forget what other people are making.
2. Never worry about trends.
3. Buy a property that *you* think will make a good picture.
4. Hire the best writer or writers to give you a screenplay.
5. Employ the best director to translate that screenplay onto celluloid.
6. Give him the cast he wants and the cameraman he believes in.
7. Control the whole thing yourself, and *above all, take the blame if it goes wrong.*

291

But even Goldwyn was fallible, and inevitably he suffered a few disappointments. In 1934 he signed the Russian actress Anna Sten, who had appeared in a silent version of *The Brothers Karamazov*. She duly arrived in America long on avoirdupois and short on English. She remained incomprehensible for several films. The whole operation cost Goldwyn a small fortune. Gable he once turned down because "his ears are too big", and after buying *The Wonderful Wizard of Oz*, he decided that it would never make a picture and sold it, at a bargain price, to MGM.

One setback particularly irked him. He was trying to coax the elusive Garbo into working for him and managed to lure her up to his house for dinner—a carefully prepared meal catering to her Nordic taste—intending once she had thus been softened up to persuade her to sign a contract. After dinner, however, Garbo spent two hours talking to his Swedish cook, then slipped out through the kitchen door and went home.

"THE GOLDWYN TOUCH" became legendary, and Sam spared no expense to perpetuate it. We were rehearsing that subtle fantasy *The Bishop's Wife*, in which I was playing the bishop, Loretta Young the wife, and Cary Grant the angel. Bill Seiter, normally a director of broad comedy, was at the helm.

The day before shooting was to start, Goldwyn decided that the interiors of the bishop's house were not ecclesiastical enough and ordered several sets to be torn down and rebuilt. Then, two days after the cameras had finally begun to turn, Goldwyn decided that Seiter's hand was a little too heavy on the tiller; he was removed, paid his full salary, and Goldwyn hired Henry Koster to start again from scratch—with another two weeks of rehearsal. All this must have cost Goldwyn several hundred thousand dollars, but in the end he got what he wanted.

Goldwyn was always a perfectionist. When we were preparing a picture in which I had to age from twenty-five to seventy, he talked me into having my hair bleached white for the last scene instead of wearing a wig. He examined the result, ignored the fact that my own dog had attacked me on sight the night before, and said, "It looks good."

When the picture was finished, I said, "I'm glad you're happy. Now what are you going to do about my hair?"

"What's the matter with it?" asked Goldwyn.

"I want it put back the way it was," I said.

A makeup man was instructed to dye me back to normal, but my hair came out jet black and shiny, like that of a Japanese general. A two-week holiday in the sun and salt water of Bermuda turned it into a metallic magenta. I was stuck with it for a year.

The review I liked least appeared in the Los Angeles *Examiner:* "A pity Goldwyn allowed Niven to ruin his performance by wearing an appalling wig."

This, of course, is not intended to be a portrait of Samuel Goldwyn. At most, it is a few hesitant lines of a preliminary drawing, because in spite of many years of close association with him, I was never able to see him clearly.

To me Samuel Goldwyn was like *crème brûlée*—rock hard on the outside and surprisingly soft underneath. When he first pulled me out of the extra ranks and offered me a contract for seven years starting at a hundred dollars a week, I was so excited that I failed to notice I would have to face twelve weeks of layoff without pay each year. I just signed the contract with a heart pumping at the unbelievable good fortune that had befallen me. Then I did something I had always wanted to do: I went to a Ford dealer and, flashing my golden credit card—my contract with the great Samuel Goldwyn—pointed to a two-seater convertible and said, "I'll take *that* one."

I drove slowly back to the studio to display my shiny beauty before the admiring employees in the casting office. Bob McIntyre, the kindly head of that department, looked embarrassed. "Take it back again, son," he advised. "Mr. Goldwyn has just called down. You're on layoff for six weeks."

So much for the hard outside. The soft inside was often revealed by massive and unpublicized donations to charities and by unexpected generosity to the people who worked for him. To them Sam Goldwyn was a father figure who demanded, and got, an awesome standard of professionalism. They gave him their best, and he looked after them. For a beginner it was incredible luck to be picked off the floor by Goldwyn. From 1935 to 1950 I had happy times with him and sad times, some dizzy heights and some heartbreaking lows.

The key to understanding Goldwyn was to know that his total obsession was making pictures of which he could be proud, and apart from his private moments with his family and friends, every waking minute of his day was dedicated to that end alone.

In the end I repaid the man to whom I owed so much by getting too big for my boots and was, with great justification, fired. Only then did I really find a friend.

7. Bobbie

It will never be known if Utrillo or Van Gogh would have painted better pictures if they had drunk less, nor if Picasso would have excelled even himself if he had drunk more. Many modern musicians are convinced that they play finer music when high, but when Artur Rubinstein or Yehudi Menuhin perform they are stone cold sober. Certainly surgeons, airline pilots and racing drivers avoid the stuff, but for writers and actors it presents a rather special problem.

How much of Scott Fitzgerald's brilliance was aided by the bottle? How much of John Barrymore's or Spencer Tracy's was dimmed? Certainly, if the actor is not at ease the audience is restless, so the temptation to relax oneself artificially is considerable. On average, I suppose, actors expose themselves to the hazards of drink more than most.

Bobbie Newton was a brilliant actor, but in his case the bottle little by little took charge. With just the right amount on board he could be fascinating, for he was a highly intelligent, kindly and knowledgeable man, but once he had taken the extra one and his Plimsoll line had disappeared below the surface he became anything from unpredictable to a downright menace.

When the Germans launched World War II upon a trembling and ill-prepared world, Bobbie was near the peak of his career as a London stage actor and was already receiving the most flattering offers from Hollywood. He promptly joined the Royal Navy as a stoker in a minesweeper.

For four long years he ate, slept, and presumably stoked encased in a hideously bulky and uncomfortable life-jacket, the official theory being that there was always the possibility that the ship might hit a mine instead of sweeping it. It was only later, fortunately for him, that he heard the story of one Herbert Mundin, another great entertainer of legendary conviviality, who had volunteered for the Royal Navy in World War I and had served on minesweepers in a similar capacity. He too had been obliged by regulations to wear a life-jacket in which he ate, slept, and presumably stoked. He too grew to loathe that life-jacket with passion but, this hatred notwithstanding, for four long years, day and night, he was trapped inside it.

On November 11, 1918, in the middle of the North Sea, he was called on deck with the rest of the crew and after triple rum rations had been issued the captain announced that the war was over. In the midst of the general excitement, the cheering and the back-slapping, Herbert Mundin quietly looked down at his detested life-jacket, his prison for four long years. He undid its canvas straps one by one, slid the loathsome garment over his head and approached the rail, smiling secretly to himself. Then, holding it in both hands and looking it right in the eye, he flung it far out into the cold, grey northern waters.

The life-jacket sank like a rock.

When Bobbie Newton was demobilized from the Navy in 1945, and before he took off for a sparkling career as a character actor in Hollywood, he made a film of Noel Coward's *This Happy Breed* and at the same time performed each evening in a play in London's West End.

It could have been brought on by overwork or a longing for the play to close so that he could leave for California, but one Saturday night at the St. James's Theatre the curtain did not rise. The audience became restless, then impatient, and finally slow hand-clapping started in the gallery and spread to the dress circle and the stalls.

At last the middle of the curtain wobbled uncertainly and a pair of shoes appeared beneath it. Sensing an announcement, the audience hushed itself into silence. Unsteady hands pulled the curtain apart just enough to frame the purple countenance of the star.

"Ladies and gentlemen," roared Bobbie Newton, rolling his eyes at every corner of the house, "the reason this curtain has so far not risen is because the stage manager . . . has had the damned impertinence to suggest that I am *pissed*."

Very shortly after this episode, Bobbie was on his way to Hollywood.

He did well there and his work was greatly admired, but as word of his bar hopping and extravagant behaviour got around, the bush telegraph between studios signalled a preliminary warning and producers began to ask embarrassing questions about his reliability. With millions of dollars being spent on production the last thing anyone wanted was to have precious shooting-time wasted because of an actor's self-indulgence.

It was dreadfully sad to see such a glowing talent being destroyed, and Bobbie's friends tried hard to stop the rot. He would listen to us with great solemnity and agree with everything we said, and for weeks on end he would keep his promises. But sooner or later some little bell inside would summon him to the bar and off he'd go again.

The astonishing thing was that though drunk he could still give great performances, so long as his memory remained unimpaired, but gradually that vital part of an actor's equipment showed signs of stress and the bush telegraph beat out another set of warnings.

As he became more and more eccentric assistant directors watched the clock apprehensively every morning. During the filming of the Kipling story, *Soldiers Three*, at MGM, he arrived

296

on several occasions just in time for the first shot but still in pyjamas.

Throughout the long weeks of shooting on that picture I dreaded the magic hour of six o'clock because at the close of work Bobbie had accumulated a giant-sized thirst but he hated to drink alone.

"Dear fellow," he would wheedle, "a little light refreshment this evening? A tiny tipple on your way home to the old ball and chain?"

I made up a variety of excuses; they were coldly received.

"Getting a little settled in our ways, are we? A little sedentary perhaps? No sense of adventure any more?"

On the last day of shooting Bobbie made it crystal clear that he had no intention of letting me slip away without a "farewell posset".

"I know a little bistro, dear fellow, it's just around the corner— come, let us away."

He shovelled me, protesting, into his car, both of us still wearing the khaki uniforms, pith helmets and drooping moustaches of Queen Victoria's army in India.

The car was a 1921 Rolls which he had found in a junkyard and had renovated at huge expense. The chauffeur in full regalia was an ex-stunt man whom Bobbie had befriended when he found him working as a bouncer in a gambling hall. The "bistro" turned out to be thirty-three miles away, in Long Beach. The Rolls had a top speed of about twenty-five miles per hour, and the honest citizens of Southern California blinked in amazement as we rolled sedately through their communities perched up like two visiting generals with the chauffeur pinching a big black rubber bulb at the end of a long brass horn and coaxing therefrom a mournful upper-class braying.

On arrival at Long Beach I warned Bobbie for the umpteenth time that I had no money on me.

"My treat, old cock, and I'm loaded with the good stuff. We'll only stay a few minutes."

We entered Bobbie's little bistro and I shuddered. It was a long, dimly lit, evil-smelling bar. There were many customers, some on stools, others playing cards at tables. All were fishermen from the big tuna boats: Russians, Yugoslavs and Japanese. They looked a little perplexed at the entrance of two soldiers of the Queen but soon returned to their drinking and playing.

"I knew you'd love it, dear fellow," said my host. "Full of colour, don't you think?"

We gave our order to the barman who prepared it in sulky silence. He was blue-black and would have made Sonny Liston look like a choirboy. The chauffeur remained with the car. "Can't have people removing souvenirs from Old Mary, can we?" said Bobbie.

He called for constant refills and for the first half hour the time passed pleasantly enough, but quite suddenly he interrupted himself to roar at some Yugoslavs the opening lines of a lengthy poem by Thomas Lodge:

"Love, in my bosom, like a bee,
Doth suck his sweet.
Now with his wings he plays with me,
Now with his feet. . . ."

The Yugoslavs backed away in some alarm and the barman muttered, "Hey, you—cut that out, willya!"

Bobbie fixed him with a stony eye. "If you don't like Lodge, dear fellow, then I shall give you a taste of Andrew Marvell," and off he launched into the interminable *Nymph Complaining of the Death of her Faun*.

"The wanton troopers riding by
Have shot my fawn and it will die."

By the time he had finished there was no doubt that Bobbie had lost his audience. I had a nasty feeling that things were getting out of hand and said so to Bobbie.

"Let's pay and get the hell out of here."

"On the contrary," said Bobbie firmly, "the greatest joy an actor can have is to tame a hostile audience. . . . I now propose to deliver to this scum the Gettysburg Address."

"Let's deliver everyone a drink first," I pleaded.

"Good thinking," said Bobbie with enthusiasm and ordered drinks all round. Then, an incongruous figure in his creased drill

298

uniform, he began pacing up and down the bar roaring and declaiming.

He did not finish to a standing ovation it's true, but at least he came to the end in a respectful, perhaps a slightly embarrassed hush because the Russians, the Japanese and the Yugoslavs, whether they understood what he was saying or not, had caught on to the fact that tears were streaming down his face.

"Let's go, Bobbie," I begged.

"Of course, dear boy. . . . Do you have any money, dear fellow?"

"No," I hissed. "I told you forty times that I haven't."

"Ah!" he said, pressing a forefinger against the side of his nose and rolling his eyes, "we have a tricky situation here. . . . Nip outside, dear boy, and prepare the getaway car, then call me from the door."

I wandered away looking vaguely at my watch and caught a last glimpse of the huge barman, arms akimbo, staring straight into Bobbie's face from across the bar. Bobbie was smiling back uneasily. Outside, the ex-stuntman caught the urgency of the situation and cranked the starting handle. The Rolls stood throbbing as I hurried back to the entrance, leaving both car doors on the kerbside open.

"Bobbie!" I yelled, making ready to flee.

Newton started towards me and I heard him get off his exit line.

"Barman dear—just put it all on my mother's charge account at Harrods."

The barman's roars, like those of a wounded stag, we heard for quite a while as we motored peacefully away.

In 1956 Mike Todd, New York's super showman, was bringing to the screen Jules Verne's classic, *Around the World in 80 Days*. A key role was that of Mr. Fix the detective, and Todd wanted to cast Bobbie Newton in the part. The red flag warning of Newton's unreliability had been waved, however, and Todd could ill afford delays in his shooting schedule. He called Newton in and said, "I hear you're a lush."

"An understatement, dear fellow," said Bobbie blithely, and was hired on the spot.

Todd extracted a promise from Newton that he would go on the wagon for the entire four months of his engagement, and Bobbie stuck manfully to his word. He completed his role in the picture and left the company looking fitter than I had seen him for a long time.

Two weeks later he was called unexpectedly for an added scene. At seven thirty in the morning I was sitting in the makeup room when the passage outside was shaken by a roaring delivery from *Henry V*:

> "We few, we happy few, we band of brothers;
> For he today, that sheds his blood with me
> Shall be my brother. . . ."

I was horrified at Bobbie's blotched and puffy face when he lurched into the room.

"Don't chide me, dear fellow," he said. "Please don't chide me."

Tears coursed down his cheeks.

Not long before he had told me that his doctor said if he really got at the drink again he would "very likely leave the building for good". Within a very short time, alas, the doctor's diagnosis was proved tragically correct.

8. *The Agent*

Many people were fond of Samuel Goldwyn, and everyone loved Clark Gable, but hardly any were devoted to their agents. All actors, writers, and directors had contracts with agents, and all, with varying degrees of resentment, paid them ten per cent of everything they earned.

At the beginning of a career it was virtually impossible to get started without an agent, because he knew about the pictures that were being planned and had contacts among those doing the planning. The giant step was, of course, the first good job, but if that job led to a coveted seven-year contract, the agent who had found it became a financial albatross around one's neck, and was entitled to his ten per cent for the next seven years without any further obligation to the client—not even to send him a Christmas card.

The spectrum of agents went from the cheap little flesh peddler to the big wheel who could walk unannounced into the sanctums of the moguls and play power politics for the services of his high-priced stable of stars. In between these two extremes were agents who worked hard to find and develop talent, but who became resigned to seeing ambitious clients drifting away from them to join the stables of the big wheels.

A particularly unattractive example of this was the behaviour of an actor I knew very well. This man was under contract to an excellent, hardworking, clear-thinking, honest, middle-of-the-spectrum agent named Phil Gersh, under whose guiding hand the client's career had prospered exceedingly. They had been together for some years, and although their contract had only a few more weeks to run, both knew it would be renewed, for neither had any intention of dissolving the association; also, the men had become good friends. The actor, however, like most in his profession, was made uneasy by suggestions that his progress up the ladder could be accelerated by a new approach.

One night, in a house on Mulholland Drive, with the lights of Los Angeles twinkling like a million stars on one side and those of the San Fernando Valley glowing like the Milky Way on the other, the actor was listening with rapt attention to the siren words of one of the big wheels—Bert Allenberg. Tall, good-looking, charming Bert Allenberg personally guided the fortunes of half a dozen of the biggest stars in Hollywood, and to be one of his hand-picked clients was the dream of every actor.

"I'd like to handle you," Allenberg was saying. "I have a whole lot of ideas for you. . . . What d'you say?" The actor had visions of being catapulted into the very forefront of the Hollywood galaxy. He thought about the offer all evening, carefully weighing his ambition and greed against his integrity.

Finally, as he was saying good night, he told Allenberg, "I'll talk to Phil Gersh tomorrow and tell him I'm leaving him."

The confrontation between the actor and Phil Gersh was unpleasant for both. The agent listened in amazement as the actor explained that he would not be renewing his contract. "But why?" asked Gersh.

"Of course, it's nothing personal," said the actor. "It's just that . . . I feel like, er, changing my butcher," he finished lamely.

The agent rose to leave. "You were the first actor I ever *really* liked . . . ever *really* trusted," he said quietly. "Now I know you're just the same as all the rest. . . . I'll stick with writers and directors from here on in. . . . I'll never handle another actor."

In his comfortable leather-bound office, Bert Allenberg lolled back in an armchair and listened as the actor recounted the scene. "Gersh'll get over it," he said flatly. Then he broke out the champagne and outlined his plans for the future. "I'm meeting with Darryl and L.B. tomorrow," he said. "I'll have big news for you by Wednesday. Call me first thing in the morning."

The actor slept little on Tuesday, and on Wednesday morning, in a high state of expectancy, he called his new agent's office.

The secretary's voice was muffled. "Mr. Allenberg died last night," she said, sobbing.

The actor can be found in the photograph on the facing page.

David Niven

In 1915, when David Niven was only five, his father was killed in the war. The loss didn't mean very much to him—he hadn't seen his father much, except when brought down to be shown off to dinner-party guests who smelled, he remembers, strongly of soap. In due course a stepfather appeared, a frosty Conservative politician who quickly packed young David off to an unspeakable boarding school in Worthing. (He still has one ear he claims sticks out almost at right angles on account of the pulling it received there.) With such a start it is hardly surprising that the lad's subsequent school career was stormy, to say the least.

His subsequent army career in the Guards was hardly better. Still, it took a man with an unusual turn of mind to end it with a telegram to his Commanding Officer: DEAR COLONEL, REQUEST PERMISSION RESIGN COMMISSION. LOVE. NIVEN. Wisely he was on a boat to Canada next morning.

Once there he found that, in spite of introductions to all the very best people, he was still in need of a job. He drifted to New York, but in the Depression New York was short on jobs—especially for unqualified English ex-Guardsmen. He tried unsuccessfully to sell liquor to men who'd much rather buy from the established gangsters. Then he ran a kind of indoor rodeo. It folded.

It was a surprise legacy that suddenly rescued him, paid his debts, and set him on the road to a place called Hollywood where he had a vague sort of idea that he might become a movie actor. . . .

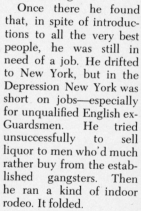

Robert Newton *Treasure Island* photograph
on page 238 © 1950 Walt Disney Productions

Lord of the Far Island

A CONDENSATION OF THE BOOK BY

Victoria Holt

ILLUSTRATED BY
Ron Lessor

Published by Collins, London

Ellen Kellaway's life as a Poor Relation seemed about to take a dramatic turn for the better when handsome Philip Carrington singled her out and proposed marriage. But fate was to intervene—twice—first tragically, then with an intriguing invitation that drew Ellen to a remote island off the coast of Cornwall and into the orbit of her newfound cousin, Jago.

A recurrent nightmare of Ellen's since childhood is finally put to rest as the discovery of past secrets and the dawn of love come together in Victoria Holt's new romantic mystery.

PART ONE: THE POOR RELATION

*A Proposal of
Marriage*

THE dream disturbed my sleep on the eve of Esmeralda's coming-out ball. It was not the first time I had had that same dream. It had come to me periodically over my nineteen years. There is something vaguely alarming about these recurring dreams because it seems certain that they have a significance which one must discover.

When I awoke from it I would be trembling with terror and I could never be entirely sure why. It was not exactly the dream itself, but the impression it brought of impending doom.

I would be in a room. I knew that room very well by now, for it was always the same each time I dreamed. There was a brick fireplace with chimney seats, a red carpet, and heavy red curtains tied back with thick cords. Over the fireplace was a picture of a storm at sea. There were a few chairs and a gate-leg table, and in one corner was a rocking-chair. Voices came and went in the dream. I would have a feeling that something was being hidden from me; and suddenly there would come this overpowering sense of doom from which I would awake in horror.

Afterwards, lying in my bed, I would ask myself why my imagination had conjured up that room and why I should have dreamed of the same room over the years. I had talked to no one of this, though, for the whole matter seemed so foolish in the daytime. Yet somewhere deep in my thoughts was the conviction that a strange and as yet incomprehensible force was warning me of impending danger, and that perhaps someday I should discover what.

I was not given to wild fancies. Life had been too grim and earnest for that. Ever since I had been cast on the mercy of Cousin Agatha I had been encouraged to remember I was that most despised of creatures: a Poor Relation. Even the claim that I was a member of the family was frail, for Cousin Agatha was in fact merely my mother's second cousin, a very slender bond indeed.

Everything about Cousin Agatha was outsize—her body, her voice, her personality. She dominated the household, which consisted of her small husband—perhaps he only seemed small compared with his wife—and her daughter, Esmeralda.

Cousin William Loring was a wealthy man, a power outside his home, though inside it he was completely subservient to his forceful wife. He was quiet, and always gave me a weak smile when he saw me; I think he would have been a kind man if he had had the strength of will to oppose Cousin Agatha.

Poor Esmeralda, with the splendid name which didn't fit her one little bit! She had pale blue eyes which watered frequently, as she was often on the verge of tears, and wispy hair. I did her sums for her and helped her with her essays. She was quite fond of me.

Cousin Agatha would be very annoyed when people mistook Esmeralda for the Poor Relation and me for the daughter of the house. Actually, Esmeralda's lot wasn't much better than mine. It would be: "Don't slouch so, Esmeralda." Or "Don't mumble."

It was one of Cousin Agatha's regrets that she had only one daughter. She had wanted many offspring whom she could have moved about like pieces on a chessboard. That she had only one rather fragile daughter she blamed entirely on her husband. The rule of the household was that good flowed from Cousin Agatha's actions and anything that was not desirable from other people's.

Cousin Agatha was noted for her good works. She surrounded herself with a perpetual haze of virtue. Small wonder that both her husband and daughter felt at a disadvantage. Oddly enough, I did not. I had long made up my mind that her good works were done for the satisfaction they brought to herself as much as to anyone else. She often must have noticed the smile which I could not keep from my lips when she was talking of her newest schemes for someone's good. She deplored this lack of appreciation in me. No doubt she sensed in me a reluctance to conform. She would convince herself, of course, that it was due to the bad blood I had inherited from my father's side, though she protested she knew nothing else of that family connection.

Her attitude was apparent when she first sent for me.

There I was, a sturdy ten-year-old with a mass of almost black hair, dark blue eyes, a short nose and a rather long stubborn chin. I was made to stand before her on the great Persian rug in the room she called her study, where her social secretary wrote her letters and did most of the committee work for which she took the credit.

"Now, Ellen," she said to me, "we want to make clear your position in the household. I am sure you are grateful to me and to Cousin William Loring for taking you in. We could, of course, on the death of your mother have put you into an orphanage, but because you are of the family—though scarcely a close relation—we have decided that you must be given our protection. Your mother, as you know, married a Charles Kellaway. You are a result of this marriage." Her large nose twitched a little, which showed the contempt in which she held both my parents and their offspring. "A rather unfortunate marriage."

"It must have been a love match," I said, for I had heard about it from Nanny Grange, whose aunt had been Cousin Agatha's nanny and was therefore knowledgeable about family affairs.

"Pray," went on Cousin Agatha, "do not interrupt me. Your mother, against her family's wishes, went off and married this man from some outlandish place. In something less than a year you were born. When you were three years old your mother left her new home irresponsibly and came back to her family, bringing you.

She had simply nothing. You and she became a burden to your grandmother. Your mother died two years later."

I had been five years old at the time. All I remembered about my mother were the embraces which I loved and the feeling of security which I did not recognize until she was gone. There was also a vague memory of sitting on cool grass, with her beside me, a sketchbook in her hand. I often wondered about my father, but he was never mentioned and I could discover nothing about him. As for my grandmother, she was a formidable old lady. Fortunately I was resilient and had managed a stoical indifference to all her reproaches and appeals to God as to what would become of me.

"Just before your grandmother died," added Cousin Agatha, "she asked me to care for you, so I took you into my house as a member of my family. I do not ask for gratitude, but I expect it. Do not think that you will have the same advantages as my own daughter. That would not be good for your character. When you are of age it well may be that you will have to earn a living, either as a maid in some household or perhaps, if you show an aptitude for learning, as a governess. You will share Esmeralda's nanny and her governess, so that by the time you reach your eighteenth birthday you will be an educated young woman. Learn all you can and always remember that these opportunities are due to my bounty."

I was meant to go away and marvel at my good fortune and to cultivate humility, in which, alas, I seemed sadly lacking.

At first the threat of the orphanage hung over me, but I quickly learned that Cousin Agatha could never allow her friends to know that she had disposed of me in such a way. I came to understand that the more of a burden I was, the greater her virtue in keeping me. And I did grow shrewd and naughty, "artful as a wagonload of monkeys," as Nanny Grange put it. If there was mischief about, I'd lead Cousin Esmeralda to it.

In the winter we lived in London in a tall house opposite Hyde Park. Esmeralda and I used to sit at one of the topmost windows and watch the hansom cabs clopping by. We both shed tears when we saw a man running behind a cab on its way to Paddington

310

Station, where he hoped to earn a few pence by carrying the luggage. I made up a story of heartrending squalor which had Esmeralda weeping bitterly. She was so kindhearted and so easily swayed. It was a pity that she was so ineffectual; it gave me an exaggerated idea of my own cleverness.

In the summer we went to Cousin William Loring's country estate in Sussex. There Esmeralda and I learned to ride, visit the poor, help at the church fête and indulge in the usual activities of the gentry. And it was there that I became aware of the great importance of the Carringtons. They owned most of the Sussex hamlet and the surrounding farms, and they lived in Trentham Towers, a very grand mansion on a hill. Like Cousin William, Mr. Josiah Carrington had big interests in the City and an elegant London residence in Park Lane.

Mr. Carrington's wife, Lady Emily, was the daughter of an earl. One of Cousin Agatha's great ambitions was to live on terms of familiarity with the Carringtons, and she would be most disconsolate if they were not present at her dinner parties and balls.

Philip Carrington was about a year older than I and some two years older than Esmeralda; Cousin Agatha was very anxious that he and Esmeralda be good friends. I remember meeting Philip for the first time. It was early summer and Esmeralda had been formally introduced to him in the drawing room; I had been excluded. Then Cousin Agatha had instructed Esmeralda to take Philip to the stables and show him her pony. I waylaid them and joined them.

Philip was fair, with freckles across his nose, and light blue eyes.

"I suppose you ride ponies," he said rather scornfully.

"Well, what do you ride?" I asked.

"A horse, of course."

"We shall have horses later on," said Esmeralda.

He ignored her. Obviously he had already decided to despise her, this puny girl he'd been sent off with.

I said, "We could ride horses just as well as ponies."

He looked interested in me. But we bickered all the way to the stables. He sneered at our ponies, and I was angry, because I loved my Brownie passionately. Then he showed us his horse.

311

"A very small one," I pointed out.

"I bet you couldn't ride it."

That was a challenge. Esmeralda trembled with fear and kept murmuring, "No, Ellen, don't," as I mounted his horse bareback and rode it recklessly around the paddock. I must admit I was a bit scared, but I wasn't going to let him score over me.

Then Philip mounted and did some tricks, showing off blatantly.

Despite our not getting along in the beginning, we saw a great deal of Philip that summer. And this was when I first heard of Rollo, his elder brother. Philip was about twelve then and Rollo was twenty-two. He was a student at Oxford and according to Philip could do everything.

"What a silly name," I said just to plague Philip.

"It's a great name, you silly thing. It's a Viking name."

"They were pirates," I said disdainfully.

"They ruled the seas. Everywhere they went they conquered."

And that was how it was, Philip and I sparring all the time. It used to upset Esmeralda because she thought we hated each other.

Once she said to me, "Mama would be cross if she knew you quarrelled with Philip. You ought to remember he's a Carrington."

I first saw Rollo as he was riding in the lanes with Philip. His horse was white, and if he had had one of those helmets with wings at the side, he would have looked just like a Viking. Philip called a greeting as he passed; Rollo scarcely looked at us.

When we returned to London that year I saw more of Rollo. Once, while he was on vacation from Oxford, he even called on us with his parents. Cousin Agatha fawned on him, and Nanny Grange said that Madam had her claws out to pick him up for Miss Esmeralda. The idea made me want to laugh and I debated whether to tell Esmeralda. But there was no point in scaring her completely out of her wits.

Those were enjoyable days. Life was full of interest, especially that part I spent belowstairs in the servants' quarters. If Esmeralda were with me, the servants would be self-conscious; but they talked quite freely in front of me, perhaps because my fate would one day be not dissimilar to theirs.

312

I was particularly enthralled when the servants talked about the market. Once I prevailed on Rose, one of the parlourmaids, to take me there. She was a flighty girl who had at last found a lover who wanted to marry her. He was Harry, the Carringtons' coachman, and she was going to live in a mews cottage with him.

I shall never forget that expedition to the market with Rose. It was November, and already holly and mistletoe were being displayed among the goods. The naphtha flares were like erupting volcanoes, and people bargained at the stalls where raucous cockney voices called their goods. I admired the crockery, the ironmongery, the secondhand clothes, the mounds of polished fruit, the stewed and jellied eels to be eaten on the spot or taken home; and I sniffed ecstatically at the cloud of appetizing steam which came from the fish-and-chips shop. Most of all I liked the people, who bargained and jostled and laughed their way through the market. I thought it was one of the most exciting places I had visited.

I returned starry-eyed, and my outrageous stories about the market had Esmeralda breathless with excitement. I promised that I would take her there, and soon the perfect opportunity came along. It was about a week before Christmas—a dark misty day—and there was to be a dinner party that night. The household could think of nothing else. Nanny Grange and our governess had been pressed into service to help. It was the very day when we could get away and be back before they noticed.

I told Nanny Grange that Esmeralda and I would look out for ourselves, and soon after tea, taken at half past three that afternoon to get it over quickly, we set off. I had carefully noted the number of the omnibus and the stop where Rose and I had got off, and we reached the market at about five.

I dragged Esmeralda through stalls piled with fruit and nuts; then we watched the organ-grinder with his little monkey, into whose cap people dropped money. Esmeralda loved it. As we stood there listening, a cart brimming with rattling ironmongery came pushing its way through the crowds.

"Make way for Rag and Bone 'Arry," cried a cheerful voice. "Stand aside, please."

I leaped out of the way and was caught up in the press of people. Suddenly I realized that Esmeralda was not beside me. I looked around; I fought my way through the crowd; I called her name, but there was no sign of her.

I didn't panic immediately. I had told her to keep close to me and she was not adventurous. But after half an hour of frantic searching I began to be very frightened.

Esmeralda was clearly lost. I must go back to the house and confess what I had done, so that search parties could be sent out. And I knew it might even result in my being sent to an orphanage.

I finally left the market and braved the journey back, to discover that the striped awning—for important receptions only—was up and the red carpet down and that guests had begun to arrive. I ran around to the servants' entrance and made my way up the stairs to the hall, and then I heard voices.

A policeman stood there, and beside him, looking very small, was a pale-faced Esmeralda, who immediately began to cry.

"Lost," the policeman was saying. "We brought her home as soon as she told us where, ma'am."

It was a tableau I believed I should never forget. Cousin Agatha, very stately in a low-cut gown twinkling with emeralds and diamonds, and Cousin William Loring, immaculate in his evening clothes, had been summoned to the hall from the top of the staircase, where they had been receiving their guests, to receive instead their truant daughter, brought home by a policeman. Several guests stood on the stairs, including the Carringtons.

Cousin Agatha's emerald earrings quivered with passionate indignation. When Esmeralda saw me through her tears and called my name, Cousin Agatha turned and directed her basilisk gaze straight at me. "Ellen!" she said in a voice full of evil omen.

"We only went to the market—" I began.

"Wilton!" There he was, in all his butlerian dignity.

"Yes, madam," he said. "I will have the young ladies taken to the nursery."

Then Nanny Grange appeared. "This could very well cost me my job," she muttered venomously as she hustled us up the stairs.

315

We were packed off to bed without supper, and I lay there wondering what life was like in orphanages.

Cousin Agatha sent for me the first thing next morning. She looked as though she had had a sleepless night.

"Such conduct, such deceit," she began. "Do you know I despair of you. I know that these inclinations come to you. It's in the blood. Most people would send a wicked child like you away. After all, we have our own daughter to consider. But blood is thicker than water and you are of the family. Nevertheless, I must warn you, Ellen, that you will have to mend your ways if you wish to stay under our roof. What the Carringtons thought of you I can't imagine. I shan't be surprised if you are not allowed to be with Philip again."

However, by Christmas the affair of the market began to be forgotten. Philip appeared during school holidays and was allowed to play with us in the park. I told him how Esmeralda had got lost in the market and in an excess of contempt he pushed her into the Serpentine. He laughed as I waded in and dragged her out. Then Nanny Grange came along and rushed us back to the house to get our wet things off before we caught our deaths.

Poor Esmeralda! I'm afraid we were very careless with her. It was not exactly that Philip and I banded together against her, but simply that she lacked our adventurous spirit.

THE years sped away. My eighteenth birthday came and went. The time when I must earn my own living was coming nearer and nearer. Esmeralda used to comfort me. "When I'm married, Ellen," she would say, "you'll always have a home with me."

I didn't envy Esmeralda; she was so mild. It was true she had grown a little pretty, but I couldn't help noticing that when we were out together it was at me that people glanced. But at least *her* future was secure. Soon she would be coming out into society and we were beginning to be segregated. Esmeralda was taken visiting and to the theatre with her parents, and I was left behind. Tilly Parsons, the dressmaker, settled in for a spell and worked on lovely clothes for Esmeralda. There was nothing special for me.

316

I could feel that vague doom. It was as in the dream.

The Carringtons were now Cousin Agatha's closest friends. Lady Emily's name was mentioned twenty times a day. Philip was often a member of a family party and he, with Esmeralda, visited the theatre with Cousin Agatha and Cousin William. I longed to go to see a witty comedy and laugh with Philip.

The day after they had attended an unusually sparkling comedy, Esmeralda and I walked in the park with Nanny Grange, who was still with us. However, now that we were older she walked a few paces behind us like a watchdog. We met Philip and he said accusingly to me, "Why didn't you come to the play?"

"Nobody asked me," I replied. "Didn't you know I was the Poor Relation?"

"Oh, Ellen," wailed Esmeralda. "I can't bear you to talk like that."

"Whether you can bear it or not," I said, "it's true."

"When my parents return the visit to the theatre I shall insist that you are included," Philip assured me.

"That's nice of you, Philip," I said. I felt very pleased because at least he didn't see me as the Poor Relation. Before we parted he gave me a playful push, just as he had when we were children.

THERE was going to be a grand dance, Esmeralda's coming-out ball, and I was to be allowed to go. For this I was to have a new gown. I dreamed of deep blue chiffon which would heighten the colour of my eyes.

Cousin Agatha sent for me. "Ah, Ellen. You may sit down."

I sat nervously.

"You realize, of course, that you are now of an age to go out into the world. My efforts to place you have been rewarded."

My heart started beating fast with apprehension.

"Mrs. Oman Lemming—the *Honourable* Mrs. Oman Lemming— is losing her governess in six months' time. She is willing to see you with the possibility of giving you the post. I have known her well all my life. I had thought it would not be good for you to be in a house which we might visit, but these are special circumstances.

317

You will have to be discreet and keep out of the way if we should be there. Mrs. Oman Lemming will understand the delicacy of the situation. She is taking tea with me next week. While she is here she will look you over, and I trust you will be mindful of your duty to please her. Such posts do not grow on trees."

I was dumbfounded. My absurd optimism had let me believe it would never come to this. But now my approaching doom was but six months away.

Cousin Agatha, who had clearly expected me to express my gratitude, sighed and lifted her shoulders. "I should not wish you to go ill equipped to your post, and that brings me to the matter of your ball dress. I have chosen the material for you and I am asking Tilly Parsons to make it in a style which will not date."

The dress would be expected to last a long time. My heart sank.

Then, to make matters worse, when I met the Honourable Mrs. Oman Lemming I could see a kindred spirit to Cousin Agatha. She was a large woman with sweeping feathers in her hat; a heavy gold chain descended the mountain of her bosom; a large brooch sparkled on her blouse. Her eyes were too closely set together, and her mouth when she studied me was thin and cold.

"This is Ellen Kellaway," said Cousin Agatha.

Mrs. Oman Lemming raised her lorgnette and studied me. "She is very young," she commented.

"It is so much easier to mould the young to our ways, Letty," said Cousin Agatha, and I thought how incongruous the name sounded for such a militant-looking female.

And so it was arranged that in five months' time I should enter the Oman Lemming household and be instructed by the departing governess as to my duties.

When Esmeralda and I walked in the park the next morning Philip joined us.

"You look like thunder today," he said to me.

"It's this wretched governessing," put in Esmeralda. "Mama found a place for Ellen with Mrs. Oman Lemming."

"You . . . a governess!" Philip burst out laughing at the idea.

"If you find it amusing, I don't," I snapped. "Cousin Agatha says it's time I earned a living, that I've lived on charity too long."

"Never mind," said Philip, slipping his arm through mine, "I'll come and see you at the Honourable Lemmings'."

"You'll forget all about me," I said angrily.

He didn't answer, but he continued to hold my arm.

IT WAS through my parlourmaid friend Rose that I heard the gossip. She got it from the Carringtons' coachman.

"Oh, there's been some conferences going on, at Park Lane as well as here. My word, they're planning an early wedding! Young people are impatient, they say. 'Impatient!' I said. 'Why, Miss Esmeralda don't know what she's got to be impatient about!' "

"You mean they're planning Esmeralda's wedding?"

"To Philip," whispered Rose. "Of course your Cousin Agatha would have liked the elder brother, Rollo, for a son-in-law."

"Why don't they try for him?"

Rose pressed her lips together to indicate that she was about to divulge a secret. "Well, about a year ago Mr. Rollo got married . . . runaway match. Eloped and all that. Such a to-do in the family. Outside it was very secret. Oh, very. Then Mr. Rollo persuaded them that it was all right and they all got reconciled. But no one ever saw *her* at the house. That was what was so odd. It was just said that Mr. Rollo was abroad with his wife. . . . Then we found out why. It seems there was something wrong with the marriage. She's somewhere, but she don't come to the house."

"Then he's still married to her?"

"Of course he's still married to her and that's why your family has got to have Mr. Philip for Miss Esmeralda."

I had always thought there was something so unusual about Rollo that nothing ordinary could happen to him. I had been right.

A week or so passed. There was a visit to the theatre with the Carringtons and to my delight I was a member of the party. Cousin Agatha was most put out. "I cannot think why Lady Emily should have included Ellen," I heard her comment. "It's really quite unsuitable, considering that she will soon be working more or less in our own circle." My effort to thrust aside the unpleasant was not

319

quite so successful as usual. But my spirits rose that night of the performance at the Haymarket Theatre. I was greatly excited by the play and between the acts I discussed it animatedly with Philip and Mr. Carrington.

The next day Cousin Agatha took me to task. "You talk far too much, Ellen. I think Mr. Carrington was a little put out."

"He didn't seem to be," I couldn't help retorting.

"My dear Ellen," said Cousin Agatha in a tone implying that I was anything but dear, "he is a gentleman, and therefore would not dream of expressing his disapproval. I really must ask you to assume a more modest role in future."

The night of the dance was fast approaching. The folding doors of the three large drawing rooms had been thrown open to make a magnificent ballroom. There were balconies in all three rooms, and these gave a view of Hyde Park and of gardens and some rather fine buildings. Evergreen plants ornamented the balconies, and the rooms were decorated with flowers.

There was to be a buffet supper in the dining room, and musicians for the dancing. No expense was to be spared; Cousin Agatha wanted all to know, particularly the Carringtons, that from Esmeralda's parents a very good dowry could be expected.

I was caught up in the excitement although I was not at all pleased with my dress. It was black, heavy velvet, and only just managed to creep into the ball-gown category. When I saw Esmeralda's beautiful concoction of sea-blue silk and lace I knew it was just the dress I should have loved. But it wasn't serviceable, whereas mine would stand up to the years.

The night before the ball I had dreamed once more of the room with the red carpet. I was standing near the fireplace and I heard the whispering voices. Then suddenly that feeling of doom overtook me. I was staring at the door and—this was new—it started to open. A terrible fear possessed me then, for I knew that whatever it was I dreaded was behind that door.

I woke up trembling. It had been a very vivid dream, as always, but on this occasion the doom had come a little nearer.

I tried, but without success, to shake off the feeling of approach-

320

ing disaster. And I kept reminding myself that this coming night would be that of the dance.

The next morning Rose brought up a little box. "My word, Miss Ellen," she said. "It's for you. Admirers, is it!"

And there, nestling in the box, was a delicate pinkish-mauve orchid—just the decoration I needed to liven up my dress.

I thought, It's from Esmeralda, and hurried to thank her. But she looked blank. "I wish I'd sent it, Ellen. I assumed there'd be flowers provided for anyone who wanted them."

I enjoyed trying to think who had sent it to me. I decided it must be Cousin William, because I fancied he was a little disturbed at my going to work for Mrs. Oman Lemming.

The orchid transformed my dress and, piling hair high on my head, I actually thought I looked quite elegant.

Esmeralda looked pretty in her magnificent gown, but she was very conscious that she was the reason for the ball and she was apprehensive at the notion of receiving a proposal. The prospect of a grand marriage appalled her. "They all think I'm going to marry Philip, but I know he doesn't like me very much."

I tried to comfort her. There was no reason, I told her, why she should marry anyone she didn't want to marry.

Cousin Agatha had given me my instructions. "Make yourself useful, Ellen. At supper, be sure that people are well served, especially Lady Emily. I shall introduce you to one or two gentlemen, and perhaps they may even ask you to dance." I could visualize it all: Ellen in sombre black to distinguish her from the real guests; "Ellen, do tell Wilton we need more salmon," "Ellen, old Mr. Something is alone. I'll introduce you." And there would be Ellen stumbling around with old Mr. Something, longing to be gliding over the floor with a kindred spirit.

How different it was. Right from the first, Philip was beside me.

"So you received my orchid," he said.

"Yours!"

"No one else would send you flowers, I hope."

We danced the first waltz and our steps fitted perfectly. After all, we had gone to dancing classes together.

"Do you know I am here with the duties of the Poor Relation?" I asked. "I have to keep my eyes open for neglected guests."

"That's all right. You keep your eyes on me, for if you don't I shall feel neglected. Now listen," he went on, "I must talk to you. It's deadly serious. Where can we get away to be quiet?"

"There are one or two smaller rooms on this floor."

"Let's go then."

We sat on a settee in a room filled with potted plants.

"Ellen," he said, "we've got to put a stop to this governessing thing. We're not having you sent away to that poisonous woman and her dreadful brood."

I turned to him and my fear of the future suddenly enveloped me in earnest. "What authority have you to stop them?" I asked.

He took me by the shoulders and held me against him. "The best of all authority. You and I are going to get married. I always meant we should."

"But . . . but you're going to marry Esmeralda. That's what this dance is for."

"What nonsense!"

"That's where you're wrong. During this dance or after it, they are hoping to announce your engagement to Esmeralda."

"But 'they,' by whom I presume you mean the Lorings, are going to find they have made a mistake. Engagement yes, but to Ellen, not Esmeralda."

"You mean you'd announce your engagement to *me* tonight? At *her* coming-out ball?"

"Of course. I have a sense of the dramatic. You know that."

"What will your parents say?"

"They'll be delighted."

"To accept *me!* You're joking."

"I am *not*." He looked very serious. "My father likes you. And my mother will too. She wants me to be happy above all else."

"Perhaps, but they can't possibly want me as your wife."

"I've already hinted to them and they're full of approval. They've been at me to marry soon."

Cousin Agatha had so impressed on me my inferior status and

the glory of the Carringtons that I could never imagine myself marrying into that family. Now the prospect excited me, not, alas, so much because of Philip—whom I liked very much, of course—but because marrying him would mean that I did not have to take up the post of governess with Mrs. Oman Lemming. Chiefly, perhaps, I was savouring the triumph of being the chosen one. The sight of Cousin Agatha's face if our engagement were announced would compensate me for all the years of humiliation.

"You seem at a loss for words. I've never known you to be so."

"It's the first time I have ever had a proposal of marriage. And I hadn't thought of you as a husband," I said.

"Why ever not? I thought it was obvious." He took my hands in his and kissed me. "Well?" he said.

"What about Cousin Agatha? She has set her heart on a Carrington son-in-law. And what she wants she usually gets."

"Well, who cares about her anyway?"

"I'm liking you more every minute."

He put his arm about me. "We'll have fun together, Ellen."

He went on to talk of what our life would be like. We would travel a great deal—to places like India and Hong Kong. It would be necessary, for he was learning all about his father's business. We would have an establishment of our own in London where we would entertain frequently. And Philip would see that I was introduced to the most exclusive dressmakers. "You'll be stunning in the right clothes, Ellen," he said. "You're a beauty, only it's never shown to advantage."

"You know I have no dowry. Esmeralda has a good one."

"I'm not tempted. It has to be Ellen or no one."

I put my arms about his neck and kissed him heartily; at just that moment Cousin Agatha appeared.

"Ellen!" Her voice was shrill with disbelief and anger.

I broke away from Philip and stood up uneasily.

"This is disgraceful. I shall talk to you later. In the meantime, guests are being neglected."

"Not all of them," said Philip cheekily. He had always liked to disconcert Cousin Agatha.

323

I said, "I'll go and see what I can do."

I wanted to get away because I still could not entirely believe that Philip was serious. But I was in a whirl. I caught a glimpse of myself in one of the mirrors. My cheeks were flushed, my eyes brilliant. The black gown was not so unbecoming after all.

Then Mr. Carrington asked me to dance with him. He was courteous and charming, and I sat out with him afterwards. Soon Philip joined us. "She's said yes, Father."

Mr. Carrington nodded, smiling. "I am very happy. Ellen is a remarkable young woman."

"Your Cousin Agatha is glaring like a gorgon," Philip informed me as we started to dance.

"Let her," I answered. "I think I know just how Cinderella felt when she went to the ball."

"I must make a delightful Prince Charming," Philip said.

When the waltz was over he escorted me in to supper. Mr. Carrington made the announcement. He said that this was a very special occasion for his family because his son Philip had confided to him that he had asked for the hand of a young lady who had promised to be his wife. He wanted everyone to drink to the health and future happiness of Miss Ellen Kellaway and his son Philip.

What a hush there was in the dining room, where the great table, so expertly dressed, was laden with cold salmon, meats of all descriptions, salads and desserts; and where the black-gowned, white-capped staff stood like sentries waiting to serve.

All eyes were on me. Philip gripped my hand firmly and I sensed that he was proud of me. Yes, I was happy as I had rarely been. For there was Philip beside me, and in my mind he *was* Prince Charming, fitting the glass slipper on my foot.

Lady Emily wafted up and kissed me. Then Esmeralda threw her arms about me. Dear Esmeralda! Even though she had not wanted to marry Philip, she might have felt a little piqued. Not she! She could see that I was happy, and she was contented too. Cousin Agatha tried bravely to hide the fury in her heart, but when I met her gaze it was quite venomous.

Mr. Carrington said he thought there should be no unnecessary

324

delay in the marriage. Once two people had made up their minds, why should they hesitate?

Philip said good night and told me he would call the next day. We had so many plans to make, and he agreed with his father that there should be no delay.

I went to my room. I took off my serviceable ball gown and was in my petticoats when Cousin Agatha burst in. She was breathing deeply. "Well, you have made fine fools of us all."

"I?" I cried. I could not resist adding, "Why, I thought you would be pleased. It gets me off your hands!"

"My, but you have suddenly grown innocent. You must have known all this time, and poor Esmeralda has been thinking it would be her wedding that would be announced. You are wicked and I'm sorry for the Carringtons."

"You have always led me to believe that the Carringtons are one of the most important families," I said. "I scarcely think they will want your pity." I was thoroughly intoxicated with my success. "I know such a marriage was not what you intended for me," I went on. "To be governess for the Oman Lemming children was not what I wanted for myself. But fate has raised me from the status of Poor Relation, which I can assure you, Cousin Agatha, has sometimes been hard to bear."

"When I think of all I did for you . . . I took you into my home, because you were of the family. . . ."

"Though the connection was not strong," I added.

She knew she was beaten. She turned and went out.

How life had changed for me! Josiah Carrington was not only a financier of great standing in the City, he was also an adviser to the government and a power in diplomatic circles. Cousin William, although comfortably off, was small fry in comparison.

Philip said we would set about choosing a house right away. I had to keep assuring myself I hadn't imagined the whole thing. There I would be, the Poor Relation who had never been sure of her room, with a house all my own!

I had taken on new status. Esmeralda was delighted. She said how happy she was for me. "You two always went so well together. It's right, Ellen. You'll be ever so content."

I kissed her. "You are a dear, Esmeralda. Are you sure you really don't love Philip?"

"*Quite* sure," she answered emphatically.

Cousin Agatha had soon got over the first shock and was now swallowing her disappointment. I wondered whether she was consoling herself that even a Poor Relation's link was better than none. "Of course," she said, "you will have to have some clothes. We can't have people saying that we kept you short. After all, it will reflect on us, and we have Esmeralda's future to think of."

I'm gloriously happy, I thought. I suppose this is being in love.

Philip was always calling at the house, and because he was a Carrington we were constantly being talked about. We rode together in the Row in Hyde Park. I had a new riding habit—a present from Cousin William, prodded no doubt by Cousin Agatha, for riding in the Row made one suitably prominent.

Philip was very happy and it was wonderful to know that he was so much in love with me. I was nineteen; he was nearly twenty-one, and there was not a cloud in my sky during those first weeks of our engagement. I believed it would go on like that for ever.

We went down to Sussex for a week as the Carringtons wanted to celebrate our engagement among their friends in the country. I had always been attracted by the house, but now that it would occasionally be my home too, I was more than ever excited by it.

Trentham Towers was an old Tudor mansion. It was built on a hill and looked imperiously down on the countryside in what I had thought of as a true Carrington manner. But it was Cousin Agatha who had given me my opinion of them. No family could have welcomed me more warmly, which was really very remarkable considering the circles in which they moved.

Philip was delighted to show me the house. We explored the great hall and the chapel and the dining room, where the portraits of his mother's family were displayed. Then he led me down a stone staircase and, throwing open an oak door, said, "This is the old armoury. It's now our gun room."

"What a lot of weapons!" I cried. "Just ornaments, I hope?"
He laughed. "They're used during the season."

"I hate shooting things," I said vehemently.

"I don't suppose you mind partaking of a succulent pheasant now and then," he said. He had opened a case lined with red satin, in which was a silver-grey pistol and a place for another. "Isn't that a beauty?" he demanded.

"I'd scarcely call it that. And where's the other one?"

"It's in a safe place. What if I'm alone in a wing of the house? In comes a man in a mask. He's going to steal the family treasure. I feel under my pillow and draw out my pistol. 'Hands up,' I cry. And the family treasure is saved." He touched the pistol lovingly before he closed the case.

"You don't really keep a pistol under your pillow, do you?"

"Yes. But after we are married I'll have you to protect me."

"You are an idiot," I said. "Let's continue exploring."

I was enchanted by the old butteries and storing houses, but most delightful was the room in which Queen Elizabeth was reputed to have slept; it was here that I turned to Philip and said, "When shall I meet Rollo's wife?"

Philip looked uneasy. "We don't see her. We don't even talk about her. It's a most unfortunate affair and so unlike Rollo. One couldn't imagine him involved in anything like that. He's always been so wrapped up in business . . . every bit as much as Father . . . dashing about the world. . . . To marry like that, so hastily. . . . And then, after the honeymoon he found out."

"Found out what?"

"She's . . . unbalanced."

"Mad, you mean?"

"She has to be under restraint. There's someone who looks after her. They were here at one time, but it was difficult when the family came. So now Rollo has moved them somewhere else."

"Where?"

"I don't know. We don't discuss it. It's Rollo's affair. He wants it that way."

"He must be very unhappy."

"You never know with Rollo. He never did show his feelings."

"I wonder how *she* feels?"

"Perhaps she doesn't know. People like that don't sometimes."

"I'd like to see the rooms she occupied when she was here."

"Whatever for? They're right at the top."

"I've just a feeling I'd like to. Come on."

We mounted the oak staircase almost to the top of the house. From there a spiral staircase took us right to her rooms. There were four of them together—a sort of small apartment. Two were bedrooms. One for Rollo's wife, I thought. One for her keeper.

I am sensitive about dwellings and I fancied I could detect suffering here. I shivered, and Philip said, "Let's go down. I can't tell you anything more about her."

We don't even talk about her, Philip had said. That was the Carrington way of life. When something was unpleasant you pretended it didn't exist. I could never be like that and I couldn't stop thinking about Rollo's wife. I wanted to know about her. Perhaps I could talk to her, help her in some way.

BACK in London, Philip and I liked to walk in the park and talk about our plans. It was during one of our strolls that I became aware of a man watching us. There was nothing remarkable about him except his unusually bushy eyebrows. He was seated not far from us. He gave me an uneasy feeling.

"Philip," I said, "do you see that man on the bench over there? He seems to be watching us."

"Yes, he must be thinking how pretty you look." Philip squeezed my arm. Soon the man got up and left, and we forgot about him.

The House in Finlay Square

WE WENT to see a house in a Knightsbridge square. I was so excited when Philip produced the key and we went in. It was a tall white Queen Anne house with a small garden in front.

There is something about empty houses; they can be welcoming or forbidding. I don't think I have any special perception, perhaps merely an overcharged imagination, but this house affected me as the top rooms of Trentham Towers had done, and for the second time in my newfound happiness a coldness touched me.

Philip was saying eagerly, "Do you like it?"

"I haven't seen it yet. You can't judge a house by the hall."

We went through the lower rooms; they were far too intimate—their walls closing in around me. No, I thought. No!

We rushed up the stairs—there were four storeys—and the rooms on the first floor were light and airy. I liked them better.

"We'll give our parties here," he said. "Elegant, isn't it?"

We climbed higher. There were more big rooms and on the top floor more, and above that attics.

"It's too big," I said, finding an excuse.

He looked startled. By Carrington standards it was quite small. "We shall need these rooms. There are the servants to be accommodated, and guests. . . . And you want a nursery, don't you?"

"Yes, very much. But I feel there is something . . . not quite right about this house. It looks so"—I floundered—"empty!"

He laughed. "What do you expect it to be, you goose? Besides, the sooner we get a place, the sooner we can get married."

He took my hands and kissed me. Then we raced downstairs.

I couldn't shake off my uneasiness about the house in Finlay Square. It was to be Mr. Carrington's wedding present. Philip was eager to acquire it and I hated to curb his enthusiasm. I couldn't find anything specific to dislike about the place; yet when I imagined myself alone there I had the same feeling as in the dream.

It was very disturbing. Even though I knew this could never be the house for me, I became so obsessed by it that one day I went to the agent and asked if I could look it over alone. So I got a key.

It was afternoon, about three o'clock, when I arrived at Finlay Square, determined not to give way to my odd misgivings.

I let myself in and stood in the hall. Then I mounted the stairs slowly, and on the first floor I studied the elegant drawing room. I furnished it in my mind and imagined myself as the hostess—a graceful Carrington hostess, I thought with a curl of the lips.

Then I felt my heart leap in terror, for I had the uncanny feeling that there was someone else in the house. I stood very still in the centre of the room; I heard a sound. Someone *was* in the house.

My heart began to hammer painfully. Who? It couldn't be Philip. He was at his father's London office.

I listened. There it was again. A muffled sound, then the creak of an opening door, and footsteps on the stairs.

I found it difficult to move. I was petrified. The footsteps were coming nearer. Someone was immediately outside the room.

The door slowly opened. I gasped. Rollo Carrington stood there.

"I'm afraid I startled you," he said. "I thought no one was here."

Although I had glimpsed him before, I felt I was seeing him for the first time. He looked so tall, and he exuded a sort of magnetism. I said, "You are Mr. Carrington, Philip's brother. I am Ellen Kellaway, his fiancée."

"Yes, I know. Congratulations."

"Thank you. I didn't know you were in London."

"I arrived from Rome last night. Philip told me about the house and I said I'd look it over, so he gave me the key."

"I wanted to see it on my own," I explained. "Shall you advise your father to buy it?"

"It's very likely a sound proposition."

He kept his eyes on me and I felt uncomfortable because he seemed to be assessing me, and I was not at all sure what he was thinking. He appeared so cool, so much in command of himself, that it was impossible to imagine him caught up in a love affair passionate enough to make him marry so hastily. I thought I detected a certain bitterness about his mouth. He was no doubt reviling fate for making his beautiful wife unbalanced and allowing him to discover this only after he had married her.

"Shall we look around together?" he asked.

"Yes, of course."

"Come then, we'll start from the top."

He talked about the snares to watch for. He'd had some experience in buying property, he said. But I was hardly paying attention. I just wanted to hear his voice, which was deep and authoritative; he was so mature compared with Philip and me.

We went through all the rooms, then out into the garden. I looked back at the house. It seemed more menacing than ever, even though Rollo was there to protect me.

He stared at me intently. "I'll call a cab and take you home."

A great relief swept over me.

THERE was something enigmatic—completely baffling—about Rollo, and I could not get him out of my mind. He certainly was a man who could conceal his true feelings.

When I saw Philip that evening I told him about my meeting with Rollo. He was amused.

"He came home only last night," he said. "Quite unexpectedly. Mother had written to him about our engagement. He thinks the house is quite a good bargain. He suggests we make an offer for it."

"He doesn't object to our marriage?"

"Object! Why on earth should he?"

"Well, you're so rich and I have no money at all."

Philip burst out laughing. "What notions you get! As if they would care about that. Mother was poor when she married my father and he was already a rich man then."

"She had a title."

"Well, you're beautiful and kind, and kind hearts are more than coronets. You should know that."

Philip was so jaunty, so sure that life was going to be good. How different he was from his brother.

I said, "It's marvellous the way your family has accepted me. Cousin Agatha is truly amazed at it."

"Why, they're delighted. They think it will be good for me. And they'd like some little Carringtons. As for Rollo, he's as pleased as he could be."

And so we talked. He was kind. He was affectionate. I was fond of him. But I was suddenly afraid of the future, for I wasn't quite in love with him.

I wanted to hear more about Rollo. Rose was a good informant by way of Harry, her coachman. "What about the Carrington son?" I asked her.

"Why, miss, you know more about Mr. Philip than anyone."

"I mean Mr. Rollo."

"Oh, him. He's another like his father. All business. Very cool and aloof, and since that mysterious marriage, very touchy."

"Rose, did you ever see *her?*"

"Harry did. He drove them once or twice. But he never heard her speak—never heard him, either. She was just in the carriage with him. Like two deaf-mutes they were. Then she went away."

"What did she look like?"

"I've asked Harry that, Miss Ellen, but men never seem to notice. Just that there was something sad about her. That she was like a grey ghost. She was always dressed in grey."

"A sad grey ghost," I echoed. Then I excused myself. I knew I shouldn't be gossiping with one of the servants in my old manner. I must mend my ways, now that I was to be a Carrington.

STRANGELY enough Lady Emily liked me, which was very comforting since she could hardly have been delighted by my poverty. She encouraged me to visit her frequently. She liked to talk a great deal in a rambling fashion, and from her conversation I learned more about the Carringtons. She confided in me once that it was a Carrington tradition to have boys, and in view of Rollo's misfortune in marriage, Philip and I were to produce the male heirs.

"I do hope I shall have these babies," I said.

"You will, because you're in love. Tell me, have the two of you decided on a date yet?"

"Philip thinks the end of June."

"That's a lovely month for a wedding."

One day Philip took me down to the mews to show me a new horse he had acquired. I immediately noticed one of the grooms because I had seen him somewhere before. Philip introduced me.

"This is Hawley," he said. "He hasn't been with us very long."

Hawley said, "Good afternoon, Miss Kellaway," and I continued to be puzzled.

When we left the mews Philip said, "I think we'll have the house in Finlay Square."

"I'd like to look at it again, Philip."

"Oh, come, Ellen, where are we going to live when we're married if we haven't a house? We'll have to be in my father's house for a while as it is—I doubt everything will be ready by June."

I felt a shiver of apprehension then. June. It was so near and I was very uneasy.

When I went to bed that night I remembered where I had seen the new groom before: he was the man I had thought was watching us in the park.

THERE was to be a musical evening at the Carringtons'. Lady Emily had engaged a famous Italian pianist. Cousin Agatha was delighted to be going. "Half London will be there," she said. "At least anybody who *is* anybody will be."

"I suppose," I retorted, "everybody is somebody, and I doubt whether even Lady Emily's drawing room would accommodate more than seventy people in comfort."

I could never resist the temptation to be what in the old days she would have called pert. I shouldn't have been human if I had been able to resist exploiting my situation a little.

It was amusing how my stature grew daily. Tilly was sewing for me all day and into the night, and I was making frequent informal visits to the house in Park Lane. However, deep down I knew that I was trying to reassure myself. This sudden turnabout provided by the Carringtons was too good to be true.

A few days later, as I stood with Philip at the Carringtons' musical soirée, people came up to congratulate us.

"We'll go on the Continent," Philip was saying. "Venice. Rome perhaps." He turned to me. "Will you like that, Ellen?"

I said it would be lovely.

"Perhaps the house will be ready by the time we come back. Rollo's taking over arrangements for it now that he's in London for a spell. He likes doing that sort of thing and my father hasn't the time. Rollo's most anxious to conclude it all as soon as possible."

I nodded. "It's good of Rollo."

The recital was over and there was a buffet supper to follow.

Everyone was discussing the romantic Chopin preludes, and Philip, having caught sight of an old friend, went over to have a word with him, leaving me temporarily alone.

A voice behind me said, "I've wanted to meet you all evening."

I turned sharply and looked up at one of the tallest men I have ever seen. I knew at once that I had not met him before, because if I had, I could not have forgotten him. There was something unusual about him—an aura of power. His eyes were dark, deep-set, heavy-lidded, but very bright and expressive. His nose was high-bridged and arrogant-looking; his mouth could be either cruel or gentle. I guessed his age to be about thirty. "I have seen pictures of you in the papers," he went on. "May I say that none of them does you justice."

"That's kind of you," I replied. "Are you a friend of the family?"

"A connection."

"I hope you enjoyed the recital."

"Very much, thank you. Have you set a date for the wedding?"

"It's to be in June, but the actual day is not decided."

"I shall be there. I'm determined to be at your wedding."

"Lady Emily is giving my cousin her guest list." Then our conversation ended rather abruptly, for Philip was looking across the room at me.

My companion bowed and turned away, and I went over to Philip. "Who was the tall fellow you were talking to?" he asked.

"I don't know. He said he was a connection of yours."

Philip shrugged his shoulders. "He's probably one of my father's or Rollo's business friends."

"Do you think so? I thought he looked the outdoor type."

We went over to greet old Sir Bevis, one of the most peevish of the family's friends. He congratulated Philip, but I could see that I was the one he was really congratulating. Like many people, he could not understand why the Carringtons were accepting a girl without money. And yet a logical explanation was that they were so rich that another fortune wouldn't make much difference.

When we had left Sir Bevis I noticed the new groom we'd seen in the Carrington stables. I told Philip I thought he was the man we'd seen in the park, but Philip laughed at my being concerned.

"Oh, Hawley. He has many talents. He's butler for us now."

During the rest of the evening I looked for the tall stranger who had spoken to me at the buffet supper. But it was in vain. I wished I had had the presence of mind to ask his name when he'd simply said he was "a connection."

"IT SEEMS," said Esmeralda a few days later, "that one of the Carrington servants is courting our maid Bessie. So there's Rose and her coachman and now Bessie and Hawley."

"Did you say Hawley?"

"Yes, I'm sure that was the name. There seem to be several bonds between us and the Carringtons."

"Isn't that what your mother always wanted?" I asked, and I was thinking: Hawley! The man in the park. Philip might laugh at my concern, but ever since I had first noticed him watching us, I'd been in some uneasy way aware of him.

The time was passing and we were halfway through May. The horse chestnuts were ready to bloom and I should have been joyous, but I would often wake with a vague sense of disquiet.

The contracts for the house in Finlay Square were being drawn up. Philip and I still had a key apiece, and I didn't want to return mine. I visited the house again, trying to get used to the place, trying to reconcile myself to it. Was it really misgivings about the place, or was it apprehension for the future and the life Philip and I would lead there?

Did I want to marry Philip? Certainly, when I thought of the alternative. The past few weeks had made me forget how humiliating my position had been before Philip proposed. And the reason I had forgotten my gratitude to him was that I had seen his brother and realized suddenly that one does not necessarily want an old playmate—whatever affection one has for him—for a husband.

I was marrying Philip to escape. I knew that was not really a good reason for marriage, but how could I possibly back out now? Then it came to me, almost as though the house was telling me: It's not too late. You could escape the marriage.

Escape? Where to? To Mrs. Oman Lemming and the dreary life which I knew I was going to hate? Maybe. But to escape from her is no reason for marriage.

Then, I reproached myself, why was it only at this, the eleventh hour, that I realized I was plunging into marriage without enough experience of life?

And the uneasiness crept over me again. The house was rejecting me. These rooms are not for you, it seemed to be saying.

I clenched my fists. If I want to live here, I will. It's my life. How could I possibly be a governess to that old tyrant's offspring now?

Suddenly I sensed that I was not alone in the house. Then sounds were distinct. The creak of feet on wood. Footsteps coming up the stairs. It's Rollo again, I reassured myself, thinking of the other time he had startled me in the house.

The door opened slowly. I almost cried out, "Rollo!" Then my flesh started to creep, for it was not Rollo. It was the tall dark man who had spoken to me at the Chopin recital.

I stammered, "How . . . how did you get in?"

He held up a door key.

"Where did you get it?" I demanded.

He laughed and answered, "The house is for sale, the agent led me to believe."

"No, it's sold . . . or all but sold."

"That's a pity because *I* quite like it. But you never know. . . . The sale could fall through and then I could jump into the breach. So while I'm here I shall look it over."

As he spoke his hooded eyes regarded me intently. I was sure there was something more in this than he would have me believe.

He advanced. The fact that I was alone in the house with this man struck me forcibly. I desperately wanted to get out.

"I'll leave you to look around," I said hurriedly.

"Couldn't we do so together? I'd welcome your comments."

I thought cunningly that I would pretend to go around with him and when we reached the ground floor I would walk out the front door before he had time to stop me. "I must remind you that this house is definitely not for sale. All the same, if you want to look around, do. Let's start at the bottom."

"You are kind." He stood aside for me to pass, and as I started to walk downstairs I was aware of his being very close behind me. He seemed so powerful that he made me feel helpless. Moreover, somehow I didn't quite believe he had come to see the house, or that the agent had given him the key when the Carringtons had all but bought the place. I had rarely been so frightened in my life. Is he mad? I asked myself. He had a motive for coming, and it was not to see the house. But I could not think what it might be.

I prayed, O God, let me get away. I'll never want to come to this house again. Please let me get away from this man.

He sensed my fear, I was sure. It amused him. Out of the corner of my eye I could see the curl of his lips, the glint in his eyes.

And then my prayer was answered. We were on the stairs, looking down into the hall, when I saw a shadow behind the glass panel of the door. He saw it too. I heard his quick intake of breath as the door opened and Rollo entered.

He seemed as surprised to see us as we were to see him.

As I stood rooted to the stair, I heard myself explaining, "There's been a misunderstanding. This gentleman didn't know the house was sold. He came to look it over."

Rollo frowned. "Didn't the agent explain? He had no right to give you a false impression."

The dark man smiled. "I shall have a word with him. I didn't realize negotiations had gone so far." He bowed to me and went to the door. Then, just before the door shut, he turned and looked straight at me.

"How extraordinary!" cried Rollo. "I can't understand the agent's giving him a key with the deal so near completion."

"Who is he?" I asked. "He was at the recital. He said he was a connection of yours."

"A connection? I've no notion who he is. What's his name?"

"I don't know. We weren't introduced. He addressed a few words to me. The next time I saw him was here."

"How very strange, and you seem so upset. We'll certainly have to find out who he is. Well, I've come to look at the dining-room ceiling. There's a certain amount of damp there. The surveyor pointed it out."

I was still feeling dazed as I followed Rollo through the house. "It's good of you to take so much trouble," I told him.

"For my own brother and his future wife!" He looked at me, his eyes appraising but warm. "I want you to know, Ellen, how very much we welcome you into the family."

Despite his words, I still felt deeply troubled. Nothing could induce me to come to this house again.

We went out and Rollo called a cab. He sat beside me looking satisfied, as though something he had undertaken had succeeded very well. As we turned into the square my heart gave a leap of terror, for standing on the pavement looking into the cab was the dark man. He lifted his hat and bowed to me. I glanced at Rollo, but he had not noticed.

THE wedding was three weeks away. My dress was being made by Lady Emily's own dressmaker. It was going to be one of *the* weddings of the year and even Cousin Agatha was excited, bustling about as if she had arranged it all. Her great sorrow was that all this fuss was for me, but when she convinced herself that it was a rehearsal for Esmeralda's wedding she was somewhat reconciled.

I should have been congratulating myself on my good fortune and at times I did, but into my thoughts would creep an insidious notion that I was making a mistake, a mistake fraught with danger. It's marriage, I thought. I'm not ready for it. What I wanted more than anything was time. I would lie awake at night and my problem would niggle away at me. And adding to my disturbance was that I fancied Rollo had been avoiding me.

It was the Sunday before the wedding. There were six more days to go. We were to be married in London at St. George's, Hanover Square and then go back to the Lorings' house for the reception. In the late afternoon we should leave for Venice.

Philip and I walked through the park to Kensington Gardens. We skirted the palace and then we walked back across the grass and sat by the Serpentine. He took my hand and held it firmly. "Six whole days," he was saying. "It seems a lifetime. I'll be glad when all the fuss is over."

Philip was exuberant. At least *he* had no doubts, capable as he was of complete enthusiasm for whatever obsessed him at the moment. I have never known anyone who had such a capacity for living in each moment and enjoying it. What a wonderful gift! Darling Philip. I was to be grateful later that he had possessed it.

That evening I sat by my window, looking out on the gardens. This time next week Philip and I would be on our way to Italy.

The next morning Rose, her face chalky, came into my bedroom, where I was sorting my clothes. "What's wrong?" I asked.

"There's been an accident. Mr. Rollo's here, asking to see you."

I went down to the drawing room. Rollo was standing by the fireplace, his face drawn and anxious. "Something terrible has happened," he began. "You must try to be calm. It's Philip. . . . He was found dead in his room this morning."

"Philip . . . *dead!* No. How could that be? He wasn't ill."

"He was found shot."

"Shot! But who . . . ?"

Rollo shook his head. "It seems the wound was self-inflicted."

I felt myself growing dizzy. "There's a mistake," I said shrilly. "I don't believe it."

"Alas. There is no mistake."

Everything was collapsing about me. The world had become a strange place full of distorted nightmares. And the greatest of these was Rollo, standing before me, saying in a low tragic voice, "Philip is dead. He took his own life."

I couldn't believe it. Philip dead! Only the day before he had talked exuberantly of our future. What could have happened so suddenly to make him take his own life?

THAT VERY day a newspaper ran the story with the headline SUICIDE OF BRIDEGROOM-TO-BE. "Six days before he was to have married Miss Ellen Kellaway, Philip, son of Josiah Carrington, took his own life. What is the story behind the tragedy?"

339

Everyone believed that there was a story and that I was the one who held the vital clue. Why should a young man who had every blessing shoot himself a few days before his wedding? That he would rather die than marry me was the implication.

Esmeralda told me what had happened. "He was shot with one of the guns from Trentham Towers. He must have brought it with him from the country."

"It's not possible. That would mean that he had planned it."

My mind raced back to that day when we had been in the gun room at Trentham Towers. I remembered the silver-grey pistol he had touched so lovingly. There had been an empty compartment in the case, and he had talked, jokingly I had thought, about keeping a pistol under his pillow. Even if he had been serious, what could have possessed him to turn the pistol on himself?

"Imagine, Esmeralda, the despair a man must be in to take his own life!" I cried out. "Can you imagine Philip in despair? *I* never saw him so. Nobody knew Philip better than I, and I say it's *impossible*. I shall never believe it."

Esmeralda said, "There'll be an inquest. You'll have to go."

"I want to go," I said. "I want to discover the reason for this."

The inquest was like a dream. . . . Mr. Josiah Carrington, his face distorted with grief; Lady Emily more bewildered than ever, with a tragic look in her eyes. And Rollo grown stern, his eyes like ice. They all looked searchingly at me, making me shiver.

There could be only one conclusion. Suicide. I wanted to cry out my protest. But that was the court's verdict.

I begged not to go to the funeral. I just lay on my bed in shocked stillness, weak from despair and lack of sleep.

"The press keep calling," Esmeralda said. "Mother thinks you should go to the country for a while. I'm to go with you."

So we went, and what a comfort Esmeralda was! I felt a little better there, but I could not sleep well. I had nightmares of Philip, the pistol in his hand and the blood on his bed.

I had been in the country for about two weeks when Rollo came to see me. He insisted that we be alone. And as he stood before me in the small sitting room and bowed stiffly, I thought how he had changed. He was not the godlike creature I had seen when we were young.

He came straight to the point. "I want you to tell me why Philip killed himself," he said harshly.

"If only I knew. If I had known what he was going to do, I would have found some way of stopping him."

Rollo kept his eyes on me. "Are you absolutely sure that there were no differences between you? Perhaps you had deceived him."

I cried out, "You can't believe such nonsense!"

"Who was the man with you in the house in Finlay Square?"

"I told you. I don't know who he is. He was at the recital at your home . . . and then he came to the house. That's all I know."

Rollo looked sceptical. "How did he get in?"

"He told you. He got the key from the agent."

"No, Ellen. He met you by appointment and I surprised you."

"That's monstrous."

"I can only draw the obvious conclusions. You had one key, Philip had the other, which I used. There was no third key. I have spoken to the agent and he swears he gave no one else a key. So there was only one way that man could have entered the house. You let him in. Don't lie to me any more."

"This is absurd. How dare you! I was as surprised to see that man as you were. He did have a key and the agent is lying."

"I would have respected you more had you confessed the truth. I wish to God Philip had never seen you."

I was desolate. I had lost Philip and with him everything. And now Rollo despised me and suspected me so cruelly and unfairly.

I went for long walks, but there was hardly any spot in the neighbourhood where I had not been with Philip. In the village where they had known us as children, people looked at me covertly and I knew the thought that was in all their minds: Philip's death had something to do with me.

WE COULD not stay in the country for ever, and after three weeks Cousin Agatha recalled us to London.

I felt a quiver of alarm when I entered the house and was

confronted by her. Her expression was one of exasperation and veiled triumph: exasperation because I had managed to get myself "talked about," as she put it; veiled triumph because I had had to come back to be victimized at her will. My brief glory was over.

It was not long before I was summoned to Cousin Agatha's sitting room. "I suppose," she said with distaste, "it will take us a long time to live down this very unfortunate affair. Of course I never really believed that marriage would take place." She sighed.

I no longer felt the irresistible desire to defy her. In fact, I had lost my spirit and made no comment.

"However, every cloud has a silver lining, they say, and it seems that in your case this may be so. Mrs. Oman Lemming has not yet completed her search for the right governess. She has decided in her kindness to ignore convention and give you another chance."

I looked at Cousin Agatha in astonishment and she gave me a wintry smile. I might have known her pleasure would be my pain. "Oh no," I protested.

"Yes. I know it is unbelievably generous of her. She is of the opinion that in due course this scandal will be forgotten and that it may have a salutary effect upon you. I had to be honest and inform her that you could at times be pert. After all, one in your present position should be especially contrite."

"Why? What have I done?"

"My dear Ellen," she said in a voice that showed I continued to be far from dear to her, "when a man commits suicide rather than marry, people will always look askance at the woman who was to have been his wife."

"Philip wanted our marriage more than anything. And he did not kill himself. I am sure of it."

"No hysterics, please. Remember your place. You are distraught, and the best thing for you is to begin your new life as quickly as possible. Work will help you over an unfortunate spell. I have told Mrs. Oman Lemming to expect you the end of the month."

I felt as though I were drowning in my misery. With Philip's death I had lost my champion. But what saddened me most was that I had not appreciated him when he lived.

I set about preparing my trunk. According to Cousin Agatha, I would need good serviceable clothes. What I did have was a wardrobe of beautiful garments which were to have been my trousseau. Ironically, now that I was about to leave London society, I was better equipped for it than ever before. But what comfort were clothes when one was lost in a cruel world!

I awoke the next day to find a letter waiting. I did not know the bold writing on the envelope.

The letter was headed the Far Island, Polcrag, Cornwall, and ran:

Dear Miss Kellaway,

When you read this letter you will be wondering why I have not written before. The truth is that I only recently discovered your whereabouts. I live in this remote spot which was your father's home. When he died, about a year ago, he appointed me your guardian until your next birthday, when you reach the age of twenty-one. I believe you have been kept in ignorance of your father's family and I am sure would like to know more. It would give me great pleasure if you would come and visit us here.

Jago Kellaway

The Far Island. My father's home! I knew nothing of all this and my first impulse was to ask Cousin Agatha. But I hesitated. She was so set on my becoming governess in the Oman Lemming household that she might do anything to prevent my escaping it.

There was something fateful—and exciting—about receiving a letter so fortuitously. The Far Island sounded romantic.

I said nothing about the letter, not even to Esmeralda, until by good luck I found an opportunity to show it to Cousin William.

"Why, yes," he said, "your mother did marry and go off to that island. Something went wrong and she left, taking you with her."

"Who is this Jago Kellaway?"

"He must be some sort of relation." He looked at me quizzically and I saw the compassion in his eyes. "Unfortunately I can tell you no more, but if your father is now dead and these people are asking you to visit them, perhaps they will make amends for his not bothering with you all these years." He laid a hand on my arm. "It

343

is not my wish that you should take this post as a governess, Ellen."

"Thank you, Cousin William. And you think that I ought to go and see my father's family?"

He nodded and I could see that he thought it might be a fortunate way out of my present difficulties.

That afternoon from my window I saw Mrs. Oman Lemming arrive. Soon I should be sent for, to stand before them, eyes downcast, the Poor Relation to whom they were being so generous.

And so without further delay I wrote to Jago Kellaway, telling him that I should be delighted to come to the Far Island. I had just completed the letter when Bessie came to summon me.

Defiantly I went downstairs, my old spirit briefly reviving. I was not going to Mrs. Oman Lemming's to be bullied and treated with disdain. I was going to join members of my family at the Far Island off the coast of Cornwall.

PART TWO: THE ISLAND

Hydrock Manor and the Castle

IT WAS late afternoon when I arrived at Polcrag with three moderate-sized bags and a purse of sovereigns slipped to me by Cousin William. There was a carriage waiting at the railway station, and I asked the driver to take me to the Polcrag Inn. Jago Kellaway had suggested this procedure when he had written to say he was delighted that I was accepting his invitation.

As we clopped along I took stock of the little town which nestled below the surrounding cliffs. The houses were of grey Cornish stone and many had glassed-in porches, undoubtedly for the dual purpose of catching the sun and keeping out the strong sea winds. The Polcrag Inn, a building of three storeys with an archway at the side, stood in the main street, and we drove under this arch to the

stables. Just as I was about to alight, a man whom I guessed rightly
to be the host came into the yard.

"You'm Miss Kellaway if I be not mistook," he said.

I said that I was indeed Miss Kellaway.

"I've been warned of your coming. Orders is you'm to be well
looked after till the boat do come for 'ee."

"I thought I should cross to the island today," I said.

"Lord love you, no, miss. The sea be proper treacherous. Did
you notice the white horses out there on the water? When you see
them you know 'tis no time to take the boat for the island."

I followed him across the courtyard, through a door and into a
hall, where I was greeted by his wife.

"This be Miss Kellaway," said the innkeeper.

The woman's eyes opened wide as she looked at me wonder-
ingly. "Be it so then?" she said, and dropped a curtsey. "I'd best be
taking her to her room."

As we ascended the stairs she said, " 'Tis a fine room I have for
'ee, Miss Kellaway. 'Twouldn't do to give you aught but the best."

We reached the landing and she opened the door. All this time
she had scarcely taken her eyes off me, and after a second's hesitation she burst out, "I knew your mother. You'm like her. I were
maid to her . . . until she left."

"I'm so glad to meet someone who knew her," I said. "I was five
when she died and one doesn't remember much at that age."

"Time passes," she mused. "It seems only yesterday, though
much have happened since, I reckon. Tom Pengelly and I were
married soon after your mother went off, and I had Augustus.
There be nothing wrong with the lad. 'Twere just that he were
born two months too soon. When he were little he showed himself
not quite like other children, and I used to say 'twere because he
came before he was quite done. I said he was slack-baked and then
people started to call him Slack. He'm a good boy at heart. He's
over there." She nodded towards the window. "He works for Mr.
Jago. I'd take it kindly if you'd look out for him over there."

"I will," I promised.

There was a knock on the door and a maid appeared with hot

water. She was followed by a boy with my bags. Mrs. Pengelly went out and I crossed to the window. I strained my eyes for a glimpse of the island, but all I could see were ominous dark clouds.

As I washed and changed I became more and more excited, for now I should learn something about my parents. All I knew was that they had been unhappy together, and because my mother had left my father, I was sure he had been an ogre. I also wondered about Jago Kellaway. His letter of welcome had been so warm.

As I descended the stairs the savoury smell of roast pork made me feel hungry for the first time since Philip's death. It was early yet and there were no other guests in the dining room. I was glad because it gave me an opportunity to talk with Mrs. Pengelly.

"You must have known my mother very well," I began.

"Oh yes, Miss Kellaway. You too, when you was a little un."

"Why did my mother leave the island?"

Mrs. Pengelly looked taken aback. "Well, my dear, that were for reasons best known to herself."

The innkeeper came into the room to ask how I was enjoying the meal, and when I told him it was excellent, he looked pleased; but before he left I intercepted a look he gave his wife and I wondered whether he had come in to warn her against talking too much.

I finished my coffee and went up to bed. I fancied the sea was calmer and the wind less persistent. It was inevitable that I should have the dream.

When I awoke, my feelings were not so much of apprehension but of excitement, as though I were at last on the verge of learning the meaning behind the mists of my dream. However, I was dismayed to discover that the wind had risen again and the waves were pounding on the shore. Yesterday's white horses had not returned to the stable; in fact, more had come out to join them.

I knew there would be no boat that morning, so after breakfast I decided to stroll out to look at the town.

There was not a great deal to Polcrag when one left the main street, just a few shops and houses. The post office was the general store, and I decided to buy some stamps, for I had promised to let Esmeralda know how I had fared on my journey.

The postmistress looked up when I walked in and, recognizing me as a stranger, asked if I was visiting.

"Yes," I replied. "I'm waiting for the sea to grow calm so I can cross to the island. My family have asked me to stay with them."

"And have you never been there before?"

"Actually I was born on the island but I haven't been back since I was three."

"You can't be . . ."

"I'm Ellen Kellaway."

She stared at me in astonishment. "Well now," she said at length, "that be something!"

"You know my family?"

"Everyone do know the Kellaways. There's been Kellaways on the Far Island for hundreds of years, 'tis said."

"Mr. Jago Kellaway has invited me to stay."

"Well, he be the lord of the island, as they do say."

I was aware that everyone in the shop was interested in me, so I hastily bought the stamps and returned to the inn, where I ate a cold luncheon of ham, cheese and fruit.

The long afternoon stretched before me. The clouds were as lowering as they had been the day before, and the waves, edged with white froth, were thundering on the sands.

I decided to walk again, and took a winding path through some woods, thinking of all I was trying to forget. I saw Philip's face creased in laughter, gently mocking, but he was always ready to protect me; and as frequently I felt Rollo's accusing eyes on me.

I must not get lost, I thought, so I turned and, I assumed, went back the way I had come. But after I had walked for half an hour I was still deep in the woods, and I very soon realized with dismay that I *was* lost. I continued walking, trying to retrace my steps, and eventually I came to a gate. I opened it, passed through and all at once I found myself in a clearing. Suddenly a man on a grey horse rode into sight and pulled up beside me.

"Can you help me?" I asked. "I'm lost. I was trying to find my way back to the Polcrag Inn."

"You are a long way off course," he said. "The easiest way now is past the house. Actually these woods are private because of the pheasants, but it's a shortcut."

"Oh dear, do you think the owner would mind?"

"I'm sure he wouldn't," he said with a smile. "As a matter of fact, it's my house and these are my woods. I'm Michael Hydrock."

"I *am* sorry. I must apologize."

"Oh, strangers often stray in. We should post more notices."

Just then I took a step forward and, as I did so, tripped over an old beech trunk and fell sprawling onto the grass.

The man sprang from his horse and helped me up. I noticed what a pleasant face he had. "Are you hurt?" he asked.

"I don't think so." I stood up, then touched my ankle.

"You certainly can't walk all the way back. I tell you what we'll do. I'll help you onto my horse and I'll lead it back to the house. We'll go in and see how badly hurt you are. Then I could take you to the inn in a carriage."

"This is too kind."

"Not at all," he said as he helped me onto the saddle.

I shall never forget my first glimpse of Hydrock Manor. We had come out of the woods and there it stood—a grey stone dwelling with a gatehouse and a Gothic arch at the entrance.

The place affected me with a profound sense of peace. We followed a gravel path across a brilliant green lawn, then went through the archway into a cobbled courtyard. Michael Hydrock helped me dismount as a groom came hurrying to take the horse.

"Come this way," said my host, and he led me through a doorway and into a hall—not large but beautifully proportioned, with a hammer-beam roof. "I think," he said, "that I'd better call my housekeeper. She would know whether the ankle is badly hurt or not. But first, do sit down."

He pulled a bell rope and a manservant quickly appeared. "Tell Mrs. Hocking to come here, please," Michael Hydrock said.

Within minutes Mrs. Hocking had joined us. She was in her late sixties, I imagined, and there was about her the air of the servant who has been with the family for so many years that she regards herself as privileged.

348

Michael Hydrock explained what had happened, and she knelt and gently prodded my ankle. "Does that hurt?" she asked.

"A little."

"Now stand up and step on it," she commanded. I did that. "All right?" she asked, and I said I thought it was.

"'Tis only a slight sprain," she announced. "Like as not it will be fine by tomorrow. But you oughtn't do any walking today."

"I don't know how to thank you both," I said.

"We're only too pleased to help, Miss . . . er . . ."

"Kellaway," I said. "I'm Ellen Kellaway."

The silence was immediate. Then Michael Hydrock said, "You must be related to the Kellaways of the island."

"Yes. I'm on my way to them. I'm only staying at the Polcrag Inn until the weather permits me to cross."

Mrs. Hocking seemed to be directing a look of cold disapproval at me, and I fancied that the fact that I was Ellen Kellaway had not exactly endeared me to her. I wondered why.

Michael Hydrock said, "I daresay you would like some tea. Mrs. Hocking, would you have it sent to the winter parlour, please."

The winter parlour was an intimate room nearby with an oval table in the centre. We sat down on tapestry-covered chairs and I said I thought the house was delightful, which pleased him. He said, "It has been my family's home for about four hundred years."

Tea was brought by a young girl, and the tray, with its Georgian silver teapot and kettle on a spirit lamp, was set on the table.

I offered to pour, and as I did so, felt completely at ease. I was liking my rescuer more every moment. Suddenly I was talking of my life in London, and before I realized it I was explaining that I had been on the point of marriage when my fiancé died in a tragic accident. I wondered whether he had heard the story. Heaven knew it had been publicized enough. But I realized that Michael Hydrock was the sort of man whose good manners would not allow him to mention that he knew it already.

"As a matter of fact," I went on, "I didn't know I had this family until a few weeks ago, and I'm longing to meet them. What sort of a man is Jago Kellaway?"

Michael Hydrock smiled. "It's hard to describe him. There can't be another person in the world like him."

"Do you often go to the island and do they come here?"

"I do know some members of the household," he said gravely, but there was a hint in his manner which meant that he hoped I would not carry that inquiry further.

He told me about the countryside then, of the places to visit, the customs of the people and how the old superstitions about witchcraft still prevailed here. His company was delightful, but I was staying too long. So I thanked him for his hospitality and said I must be on my way.

A groom helped me into the pony trap. Michael Hydrock sat beside me and took the reins. I studied his clean-cut profile and thought what a kindly face his was. Here was a man who, I felt, could be relied on to act in a predictable manner.

He said, "I fancy the wind is softening a little. The sea may well be calm enough for you to go out to the island tomorrow."

"I had no idea that I should be delayed so long."

"It's the geographical location of the island, actually. You see, this coast is extremely treacherous. There's a mass of rock which has to be carefully skirted, and there are quicksands about a mile or so east of Polcrag beach. It has been said that was why it was called the Far Island, not that it is so very far from the mainland—only three miles—just that conditions so often put it out of reach."

We were entering the inn yard and I was sorry, for I wanted to go on riding with Michael Hydrock.

Mrs. Pengelly looked at us in blank amazement.

Michael Hydrock said, "Miss Kellaway hurt her ankle and I've brought her back." Michael had leaped down and was helping me out. He then took my hand and smiled at me gently. "Be careful of the ankle. And when you come to the mainland . . . or if you feel at any time you need . . . do call. I should be delighted."

"You have been most good to me," I said earnestly.

"It was nothing and has been my pleasure." Then he was back in the trap and turning the horse out of the courtyard.

Mrs. Pengelly and I stood together watching him.

Then I went into the inn and up to my room. I had not been there five minutes when there was a tap on the door and Mrs. Pengelly came in, her eyes alight with curiosity. "I wondered if there was anything I could get you, Miss Kellaway?"

I assured her there was not, but I could see she wanted to talk.

"It was strange that you should meet Sir Michael," she began.

"I had no idea that he was *Sir* Michael."

"Oh yes, one of the Hydrocks was knighted years ago. The Hydrocks have been the squires of these lands ever since—and that's going back a few years—just as the Kellaways have owned the Far Island for about as many years."

"They own the island?"

"Why yes, 'tis often known as Kellaway's Isle."

"There are surely not just Kellaways there."

"Bless you, no. It's a thriving community."

"Mrs. Pengelly, what do you know about my parents?"

She gazed down at her hands as though looking for inspiration. "Your mother just couldn't abide the place. She came from London. She hated the sound of the waves pounding on the shores. She said the cries of the gulls were like voices jeering at her because she was a prisoner."

"A prisoner!"

"That was how she felt. She was always saying she would leave. There were quarrels. Your father was not easy to live with. Then she went away and took you with her."

"She must have been very unhappy."

Mrs. Pengelly raised her eyes and looked at me. "She was so bright and lively when she came here; then she changed. Kellaway's Isle wouldn't suit some people and she was one of them."

"Didn't my father try to bring her back?"

"No, he just let her go."

"So he didn't care very much about either of us."

"He wasn't the sort of man to be very interested in children. And then of course . . ."

She trailed off and I said eagerly, "Yes, what?"

"Nothing. I left and came back here. My father had this inn. I

351

married Pengelly and when my father died the inn passed to us."

"Who is Jago Kellaway . . . what relation to me?"

"Now that's something he'll tell you. He wouldn't want me to be talking too much."

"You seem afraid of him."

"He's not the type a body would want to offend."

"There seems to be a sort of mystery about the island or the Kellaways. I notice a change in people when they learn who I am."

"They'd be surprised, I reckon. Hereabouts people know something about others' business. They're just interested to see what you've grown up like. Oh my dear life, I be forgetting I have work to do. I'd best be off."

The evening passed quickly. I admitted to myself that I should not be completely sorry if the sea prevented my crossing to the island for another day, for I might see Michael Hydrock again.

Next morning I awoke to a calm sea, glittering in the sunshine, and at ten o'clock the boat arrived.

FROM my window I saw a man alight. Two oarsmen remained in the boat. I went downstairs. Then one of the stable hands took my bags, and by that time the man had come into the inn.

Mrs. Pengelly bustled around, very eager to please. "Oh, Mr. Tregardier, Miss Kellaway will be glad to see 'ee."

The man held out his hand and shook mine. "I am so pleased to meet you at last," he said. "I'm William Tregardier, Mr. Kellaway's estate manager. He wants me to tell you how eagerly he is awaiting your arrival. Alas, we have been at the mercy of the sea. But you can be sure we crossed as soon as was possible."

Mrs. Pengelly brought us some of her special bees' wine and saffron cakes, and half an hour later we set out.

There was a light breeze blowing—just enough to ruffle the water—and I felt my excitement rising. It was not long before the island came into sight.

"There it is!" said William Tregardier.

A sudden pride took possession of me. It was thrilling to have my name associated with such a splendid place.

352

"It's beautiful," I cried. "And there's another island!"

"That's the nearest. It's not cultivated like the main island. It's more rocky, and there's some sort of deposit on the rocks which in some lights gives them a bluish tinge. That's why it's known as Blue Rock Island. And now you can see yet another, Sanctuary Island. It's a refuge for birds. It's uninhabited but for the choughs and sea gulls that congregate there."

I turned my gaze back to the main island. The rock on one side rose in a stark cliff face beneath which was a sandy cove where several boats were moored.

"Are we going in there?" I asked.

"No," answered William Tregardier. "We land on the other side. There are dangerous rocks and currents here."

The island was now showing a different aspect. I could see picturesque little houses with whitewashed walls and orange roofs. There was a ridge of low hills running down to the sea—all green and beautiful, brightened by purple heather and yellow gorse.

We ran onto a beach where two men were waiting with horses.

"I trust you ride," said my companion. "Jago was sure you did."

"I wonder how he knew. Yes, I've always been keen on riding."

"That's excellent. It's the best way of getting around the island. We have a docile little mare for you now, Miss Kellaway. Later you can select your own horse. Jago keeps a very good stable."

As we rode up from the beach he said, "The castle is close by."

"The castle?" I asked.

"We always call it that. Kellaway Castle. It's very ancient."

The castle—and it was indeed a castle—was a massive quadrangular edifice with thick stone walls flanked by four circular towers rising above the crenellated parapets of the roof. We passed through a stone gatehouse topped by yet another tower and were in a cobbled courtyard; from there we went under a Norman arch into another courtyard, where a groom was waiting for us.

"Take our horses, Albert. This is Miss Kellaway, who has come to stay with us."

Albert touched his forelock to me. He took the horses and William Tregardier led the way towards a heavy iron-studded door. "I daresay you will wish to change before meeting Jago. I'll get one of the maids to show you to your room."

I was bemused. I had certainly been unprepared for such a castle. It was grander in its way than Hydrock Manor and clearly of an earlier period. We had entered a reception room; there was a suit of armour in one corner and shields and weapons on the walls, and I imagined it had once been a guardroom.

It seemed as though everyone in the house was awaiting my arrival, for no sooner had we stepped into this room than a maid came in from another door.

"Ah, Janet," said William Tregardier, "here is Miss Kellaway. Take her to her room and see that she has everything she needs."

I followed Janet, marvelling. We went through several stone-floored passages and mounted a stone staircase. Then we came to a gallery and were clearly in the residential part of the castle, for the medieval aspect gave way to a more modern air of comfort.

Janet threw open a door and we entered a luxurious room hung with ancient tapestries in shades of red and grey. There was a red carpet on the floor and the curtains were of red velvet trimmed with gold fringe. The four-poster had red velvet curtains about it. I looked round the room at the dressing table and mirror, the big cupboard, the fireplace, and a mantel on which stood large candle-sticks. The ceiling was lofty and ornately carved.

The window—semicircular and cut out of an amazingly thick wall—had a stone window seat reached by three steps. I climbed them and looked out. Although the castle was a little isolated, standing on its incline, I could see that the island was well popu-lated. I made out what must have been a main street with shops. It was like a miniature town. I could see farmhouses surrounded by fields, and there were orchards and even a small forest. I even caught a glimpse of Blue Rock—just a small channel of sea separated us. Then I gazed at the mainland and wondered what Michael Hydrock was doing.

"It's magnificent," I said, turning to survey the room.

" 'Tis one of the best rooms in the castle," said Janet. Then she gave a little giggle. "We've all been warned, miss. We got to take

354

very special care of 'ee. If there's anything you do want"—she walked to the bell rope—"you just pull this and I'll be with 'ee."

At that moment a boy arrived with my baggage.

"I'll bring 'ee hot water, miss," said Janet.

"Thank you," I said.

When she had left, I opened one of my bags and took out a dress which had been made for my honeymoon. Suddenly I felt quite wretched, and I could not stop thinking of our honeymoon plans. "Venice," Philip had said. "Gondoliers. Serenades on the Grand Canal. Very romantic."

While I was standing there, lost in my painful reverie, Janet came back with the hot water. "Mr. Jago has just come in, miss," she said. "He says I'm to take you to him in his parlour. I reckon you'll want to hurry, miss. Mr. Jago isn't one to be kept waiting."

I washed while Janet hung up my dresses. I realized that my hands were trembling, for I was about to see this man of whom I had begun to build a formidable picture in my mind.

And so I went down to my first meeting with Jago Kellaway. That parlour was a gracious, dignified room, with a deep bow window overlooking the sea. There was a big open fireplace with andirons, and a long stool in front. Tapestries covered the walls, and the ceiling was decorated in a pattern that incorporated the arms of the family. But all this I noticed much later.

Janet had knocked at the door and when it opened, as if by magic, I advanced into the room. At first I thought there was no one there and then I heard a laugh behind me. The door was shut and he was leaning against it, studying me with amusement.

"You!" I cried. "You . . . Jago Kellaway!"

For the man who faced me was the mysterious dark stranger who had been at the recital and later in the house in Finlay Square.

My spine tingled in horror and amazement. "But I don't understand," I stammered.

"I thought you'd be surprised." There was laughter in his voice as he took my arm and led me to the window. There he put his hands on my shoulders and looked into my face. "Ellen. At last!"

355

"I should like to know what you were doing at the recital and at the house in Finlay Square? Why didn't you tell me who you were? And who *are* you anyway?"

"You ask too many questions to answer all at once. First, I want to tell you how very happy I am to welcome you to Kellaway's Isle. You are indeed a Kellaway. You take after your father. He was a very impatient man. But come sit down, my dear, and I will answer every question."

He led me to a chair with carved arms and a petit point seat, and almost pushed me into it. Then very deliberately, as though he enjoyed my impatience, he drew up a chair for himself. It was like a throne, that chair—large, ornately carved, and inlaid with lapis.

Jago was even more impressive than he had been in London. His hair was thick and dark. I noticed again those heavy-lidded eyes which could hide so much; they were surveying me with obvious pleasure. He wore a midnight-blue velvet smoking jacket and a white cravat. His hands were well shaped and slightly bronzed, and he wore a signet ring on the little finger of his right hand.

"Now," he said, "you ask who I am and you wonder just what my connection with you is. Well, dear Ellen, it is a complicated but rather common story. Perhaps it is a little indelicate for your ears. But no. You come from the sophisticated London world and will know that matters of this nature arise now and then even in the most sedate families. Am I right?"

"I can't say until I hear it," I replied sharply. Something about him irritated me and made me want to do battle with him. I was eager to understand the mystery which surrounded him, and yet he deliberately took his time explaining it. He had already acted in a strange manner, and it was clear he thought it all a great joke.

"The Bar Sinister comes into this," he said. "One of our ancestors—your great-grandfather—had a much younger sister named Gwennol. Gwennol was beautiful and wild. There is a picture of her in the gallery. The Kellaways were a great family. They owned the islands and they lived here in some state. A grand marriage would have been arranged for Gwennol, but one day she proudly announced that she was going to have a child. She would not name the father nor had she any intention of marrying. Her own father, furious with her, threatened to turn her out of the castle unless she told him who her lover was. She refused and left the castle, taking several of the servants with her; whether they went through love or fear I don't know, for by some she was reputed to be a witch, and it was even said that the devil was the father of her child." Again Jago Kellaway's eyes showed that flicker of amusement. "Well, Gwennol went to Blue Rock Island, which is only a short distance from here. You have seen it perhaps?"

"I have. Mr. Tregardier pointed it out, and I can see it from my window."

"The house Gwennol had built for herself still stands there. In it her son was born. He was my father."

Jago paused. "So, Ellen, you and I are cousins. Several times removed, but we are both Kellaways. My father died when I was quite young and I came to live at the castle and later I shared the management of the island estate for some years with your father. When he became too ill to do much I took over completely. Then last year he died."

"And my father never wanted to know where I was?"

Jago looked at me steadily and shook his head. "But before he died he asked me to find you and to be your guardian until you reached the age of twenty-one. It was not easy to find you. Your mother had determined to lose herself when she left the island. But when I saw the papers and learned that you were about to be married, I came to London."

"Why didn't you tell me then who you were?"

"Ah, a quirk in my nature—to surprise, to be dramatic. I wanted to know you before you knew me. So I came to the recital."

"How? The Carringtons didn't know you."

"Shall we say I was an uninvited guest?"

"What . . . impudence! And the house in Finlay Square. The agent denied having given you a key."

"Well, you know how these agents are. They want to make sure of a sale and apparently there was some hesitation about this one, so the agent gave me a key. Then I waited until I saw you enter

357

the house. Let me tell you this: I had a duty. I wanted to make sure about the family you were marrying into."

"You quickly found out who the Carringtons were, I'm sure."

"Yes, I discovered a good deal about them. Then the tragedy happened and I asked you to come here. Is it clear now?"

"Yes," I answered.

"I hope, Ellen," he said earnestly, "that you will stay with us for a very long time."

"You are kind," I replied with a touch of asperity, for I didn't believe he was telling me the whole truth.

"I want you to like this place," he went on. "You have had a bitter experience, and I hope we'll help you grow away from it."

He looked sincere now. His eyes seemed serene and friendly. His was the most expressive face I had ever seen. A few moments before, he had looked mischievous, almost satanic; now he had become the kindly, protective guardian.

"What shall I call you?" I asked.

"Jago, of course. That is my name. Don't let the fact that I'm your guardian overawe you."

"Indeed I shall not. I have stood on my own feet most of my life. I certainly don't need a guardian at this stage."

"But you have one, Ellen; and as he is a man blessed—or cursed—with a very strong sense of duty, he will feel obliged to honour his promises, however much you object to his guardianship. Now, let me tell you something of the family. There's Jenifry, my older sister. She's a widow who lost her husband some years ago during a typhoid epidemic. You might say that she is the chatelaine of the castle. Her daughter, Gwennol, will be company for you. She's about your age.

"You must," he went on, "discover something of your Kellaway heritage while you're here, Ellen. As to the island, which has been in our possession for centuries, it is wonderfully fertile, for the climate is conducive to growing things. The rock formations on the east protect us from the colder winds, and those on the west from the southwest gales, while the Gulf Stream keeps us warm—I even have palms in my sheltered gardens. We have our township, our church, our cemetery, our inn. We are independent—almost—of the mainland."

As he was speaking his manner changed again. Now he was glowing with pride of possession, and I warmed to his fierce enthusiasm. I waited to hear more. My interest clearly pleased him.

"I shall enjoy showing you everything, Ellen," he continued. "But for now, let us talk about your life in your cousin's house. It wasn't very comfortable, was it? She had a daughter who wasn't half as attractive as you. I saw that much. And she made you feel as if you were living on her bounty."

I was surprised that he had been so perceptive.

"And then," he went on, "this rich young man came forward. They wanted him for their daughter and he chose you, the wise fellow. But then he killed himself."

"He didn't. If you had known him, you would realize he would never do anything like that."

"It's all over." Jago's voice had become soft and soothing. "We will not speak of it again. But tell me, what were your plans before you received my letter?"

"I was going to be a governess."

"You . . . a governess! My dear Ellen, you're too proud for such a menial position. You should be engaging governesses for your own children. An attractive girl such as you are will not remain single long, and as your guardian I should like to see you happily married. Well now, I daresay you would like to go to your room and rest awhile before dinner. If there is anything you need, just ring."

I rose and he did the same. Then he laid his hand on my shoulder, and as we walked to the door I could feel the strength of his fingers.

I went to my room in a strange mood. My guardian-cousin, Jago, was the most unusual man I had ever met. His moods and personality seemed to change so quickly.

I was much too excited to rest. Everything was so different from what I had imagined. A grand castle and a guardian who was not middle-aged, but a gentleman of about thirty who behaved in an unconventional way—a man who liked dramatic happenings. The prospect of living here dominated by such a man stimulated me; I felt more alive than I had since Philip's death. I was also determined to find out why my mother had left so mysteriously.

I had been told that I was to make myself at home. Well, I would begin by taking stock of my surroundings. So I descended the staircase and came to the guardroom. As I stood there the room seemed to take on a menacing aspect. Perhaps I was just feeling uneasy because of the shock of finding that Jago Kellaway was the man who had frightened me in the house in Finlay Square. But then, hadn't I always been susceptible to atmosphere in unfamiliar houses? I shuddered now to recall the repulsion I had felt when I had first entered that house in London.

This room, medieval in aspect, with the weapons on its walls—two crossed swords, an axe, a halberd—reminded me of the gun room at Trentham Towers. This shadowy memory was conjuring up hidden dangers, and I fancied that just as I had sensed a warning in the house in Finlay Square, so I did now in Kellaway Castle. Stupid imaginings, but I was in an uncertain state.

I moved towards the door, and my footsteps ringing on the marble paving stones filled the guardroom with an eerie sound. Then I stepped out into a courtyard and saw an archway which appeared to be cut into the wall. It led to several other courtyards and then to a winding pathway with stone walls on either side.

Suddenly I heard the flutter of wings and the cooing of birds. I had come into another courtyard. Little dovecotes were attached to the walls, and several pigeons were pecking at maize that had been scattered over the cobblestones. Most of the pigeons were bluish grey, but some were brown. I had never seen pigeons that colour before. As I stood there looking at the birds I was aware of a shadow at a lower window. Someone was watching me.

I called, "Are these your birds?"

There was no answer. I went closer to the window, but the shadow had disappeared. There was a little door in the wall and I tapped on it. I realized that it had been slightly ajar, and as I stood there it was quietly shut. Someone on the other side of the door was clearly determined to keep me out.

How unfriendly! I shrugged, left the birds' courtyard and found my way back to my room in time to dress for dinner.

I put on my sapphire-blue silk, and just as I had finished dressing a servant came to conduct me down to an anteroom where the family was waiting for me. Jago was standing in front of the fireplace, his hands clasped behind his back, dominating the room. On either side of him was a woman—the older one about forty years of age, whom I guessed to be his sister, Jenifry, the younger his niece, Gwennol, who he had said was about my age.

"Ellen," said Jago. "This is Jenifry, my sister."

My heart sank a little as she stepped forward to take my hand. She was almost as dark as Jago and had the same high-bridged nose, which gave her the arrogant look I had noticed in him. But her voice was soft and warm. "We are delighted to have you at last, Ellen," she said. However, there was something coolly appraising about her eyes which was in contrast to her words. I felt the same uncertainty about her as I did about her brother.

Gwennol was dark too. Her hair was almost black, her eyes dark brown, her nose a trifle retroussé, her mouth wide. Her face was made striking by her soulful dreamy eyes and the alertness her nose and mouth seemed to betray. "Hello, Ellen," she said. "Welcome to Kellaway Island."

Almost immediately a servant announced dinner, and Jago put his arm through mine and led the way. "We are dining in the hall," he said. "It is a custom reserved for feast days and special occasions, and what occasion could be more special than this?"

There was something royal about the vast hall with its lofty roof, and its thick stone walls partially covered with fine tapestries. At one end was a door leading to the kitchens, through which servants hurried back and forth; above the door was the minstrels' gallery, its balustrade decorated with antlers. Places had been laid at the long oak table and on the dais and already the benches on either side of the table were occupied. These people, Jago told me later, were employed on the estate—those who farmed the land, managers of the various concerns, his clerks, and—I could scarcely believe this—there below the salt, those who worked in a more menial capacity. This was the manner in which kings had feasted in medieval times.

When the minstrels began to play softly I was touched by Jago's determination to create an atmosphere of bygone days, because I knew it had been done to honour me.

All those at the long table rose as we entered. Jago led the way to the dais, his arm still through mine, and he stood at the table with me beside him. "I have great pleasure," he announced, "in introducing you all to Miss Ellen Kellaway, my ward and cousin, who has come to stay with us, I hope, for a very long time. I know that you are as delighted to see her here as I am."

There was a murmur of assent. I smiled and, as Jago held my chair out for me, I sat down. There was a shuffling of chairs and benches, and everyone did the same.

"What do you think of it?" Jago whispered to me.

"It's incredible. I have never had such a welcome in my life."

"Then our purpose is served," he said, patting my hand.

We had excellent soup, followed by venison. Jenifry sat on Jago's left and Gwennol was beside me.

"Christmas is the time when we really go back to the old ways," explained Jago. "Then the hall is decorated with holly and ivy, and the carol singers and mummers perform here. It's been a custom of the family for centuries."

"We are trying to discover the exact age of the castle," put in Jenifry. "It was originally merely a fortress to protect the island."

"I want to show you around myself," Jago said to me. "We'll begin tomorrow. You ride, I know."

"Oh yes. We used to ride in London. And in the country I rode a good deal. But tell me more about the island," I said.

"There are times," interjected Gwennol, "when it's impossible to get to the mainland. And that can last for days."

Jago cut her short. "Ellen knows that. But people here don't feel they're missing anything by not being able to reach the mainland. People come and stay at our local inn to get away from the mainland. It has only four bedrooms, however, for we don't want the island spoiled with too many visitors."

I was learning how obsessed he was with the island. It was his and he was proud of it. To him it was perfect.

"Do you ever have any criminals here?" I asked.

"Hardly ever," he assured me. "I know how to keep the people lawful, but there are dungeons in the castle which serve on the rare occasions they are necessary."

"And the law allows this?"

"I'm a justice of the peace. Of course, in the case of a major crime—murder for instance—the criminal would be taken to the mainland. But we deal with petty matters here."

"Is there anyone in the dungeons now?"

Jago laughed. "No, Ellen, there very rarely is."

Gwennol said, "They're horrible. Dank, dark, and said to be haunted by the ghosts of those who didn't obey Kellaway law. In the past, Kellaways put their enemies there and left them to die."

"I'd like to see the dungeons," I said.

"So you shall," Jago promised me. "The whole place is yours to explore."

"As a matter of fact I did explore a little before dinner, and was surprised to see some brown pigeons. I'd never seen pigeons that colour before."

"We've always kept a few brown pigeons at Kellaway," said Jago. "You tell her the story, Jenifry."

"It's simply that one of our ancestors was saved by a brown pigeon," his sister said. "I think they originated in Italy. He was imprisoned there after being captured in some battle, and a little brown pigeon and his mate perched on his windowsill. He tamed them and used to attach messages to their legs, hoping that some of his friends would see them. When, after a long long time, the message actually did reach his friends, it was regarded as a miracle. He was rescued and he brought the two brown pigeons back to the island with him. And then it was said that as long as there are brown pigeons at the castle there will be Kellaways on the island."

"What a charming story," I commented.

When the meal was over, Jago, Jenifry, Gwennol and I went to his parlour, where coffee was served. The atmosphere there was decidedly more intimate. We talked more about the island, then about my life in London, which now seemed remote.

It was half past ten when Jago remarked that I must be tired.

"Jenifry will take you to your room," he said.

She took a candle from a table. We left them and made our way back through the hall, then up the stone staircase into the long gallery, which, with candles burning in wall sconces, looked more medieval than ever.

I opened the door to my room, but it appeared different and alien now. There were too many dark shadows. The curtains had been drawn, and the four-poster, from which the curtains had been looped back, seemed to dominate the room.

Jenifry lit the candles from the one she carried. There were two on the dressing table and the ones on the mantel. She was smiling at me, her expression benign. "I'll say good night," she said. "If you need anything, ring."

I glanced in the mirror and caught a glimpse of Jenifry's face. Her expression had changed; her eyes had narrowed; her mouth had hardened; it was as though a mask had slipped to reveal a different woman. I turned sharply and looked at her. But again her face had changed and she was smiling once more.

"Good night," I said, "and thank you for everything."

"Sleep well," she said, closing the door behind her. I stared at it blankly for a moment. My heart was beating unnaturally fast. Then I looked back at the mirror and saw that it was a very old one—a little mottled perhaps—and it had probably hung there for two hundred years. It would distort, but had she really looked at me like that? Speculatively, as though she hated me?

I sat down and took the pins out of my hair. It fell to my waist.

The trouble is, I told myself, I'm so used to being unwanted that I can't really believe in all this friendship. That was why I imagined she looked at me as she did.

The flickering candlelight threw long, eerie shadows about the room. I looked in the mirror again, and as I did so I seemed to see Jenifry's face suddenly distorted into an evil smile. It was all fancy, of course. I was overwrought. But as I looked in the mirror I heard

364

a sudden sound behind me. Startled, I grabbed a candle and swung around. No one was there.

I went to the door and turned the key, locking myself in. Then I heard the sound again. I looked around the room and laughed aloud when I realized that the sound had come from the cupboard door, which was not securely fastened.

I opened it. My clothes were hanging neatly, and as I stood there a dress slid slowly from its hanger and fell in a heap on the floor. I picked it up and, in doing so, saw some writing that had been scratched on the cupboard wall.

I pushed aside the clothes and held the candle closer. I read, "I am a prisoner here. S.K."

I wondered what S.K. meant. I guessed that this had been written by a child, because the lettering was childish.

Although the incident had made me feel not at all sleepy, I blew out the candles and got into the bed, which seemed very large. I lay there for some time while scenes from the day's events kept flashing in and out of my mind. I thought of all the people who had slept in this bed over the past hundred years. S.K. had probably been one of them. Finally I was so tired, I suppose, that I slept.

It was inevitable that the dream should come.

The room was as vivid as ever. The wind was blowing the red curtains and the door was moving. Slowly it opened. Now . . . that awful fear, the certainty that I was in great danger.

I was awake. My heart was racing and I was trembling.

It's only the dream, I soothed myself, but the doom seemed to have come nearer.

Discovery in a Sketchbook

SUNSHINE filled my room and the terrors of the night had completely disappeared with the coming of daylight.

When I went down to breakfast I found Gwennol, Jenifry and Jago at the table. "Help yourself from the sideboard," said Jenifry. "There's ham, eggs and devilled kidneys."

I took some and sat down. Jago inquired solicitously if I had

slept well, and said that in an hour or so he would be ready to show me the island.

"Which mount will you give her?" asked Gwennol.

"I was thinking of Daveth for a start."

"Isn't she a bit spirited?"

"Perhaps they'll be well matched." Jago was eyeing me with an expression I couldn't quite understand, but it made me determined to ride the spirited Daveth.

After breakfast I changed into my pale grey riding habit—part of my trousseau. I also had a grey riding hat—tall-crowned like a man's top hat—which suited me well.

Jago looked at me with approval when I met him in the stable yard. "You are so elegant," he said. "The people of the island will be enchanted with you."

He was riding a white horse with a black mane, and I had to admit that horse and rider looked magnificent; they suited each other. I did find Daveth somewhat sprightly, but I was able to manage her. Jago glanced sideways at me, and I was delighted because I believed I had his approval.

We rode first to the highest peak on the island. What a sight lay before us! There was the castle with its grey stone walls and battlemented towers. It seemed impregnable, and in the past it would have been a perfect fortification against marauders. I could also see Blue Rock Island.

Jago followed my gaze. "Blue Rock," he said. "It's a pity we allowed it to pass out of our hands. It belonged to the Kellaways at one time, but your grandfather sold it. He was in financial difficulties; he was a bit of a gambler. And that's Blue Rock House. The one built by the Gwennol I told you about. An artist lives there now. He inherited it from the man your grandfather sold it to. I think he's that man's great-nephew."

"Does he live there alone?"

"Quite alone. But he travels around a bit, I believe. His name is James Manton. Have you ever heard of him?"

"I can't say I have, although I don't know very much about painters. Perhaps I shall meet him one day."

"He doesn't visit the island. He and your father didn't like each other. We're polite when we meet, but we don't visit. Look! You can see the mainland."

"It's a comforting sight," I commented.

"Comforting?" A faint frown appeared between his eyes.

"One doesn't feel so cut off from the world," I explained.

He nodded, and we cantered off across a green stretch and came to the shore.

"I will show you our community," he said. "It is complete in itself. We are a little kingdom, you might say. There is much of long-ago times left on the island and I intend to keep it that way."

We had come to a group of houses surrounded by fields. In the centre was a shop which seemed to be that of a linen draper, hosier, tallow chandler, ironmonger, grocer and baker all combined. I decided to visit that shop as soon as possible.

From one house came the cheerful sound of merrymaking.

"It must be a christening party," said Jago. "There's a new baby in the house. We'll join them for a moment. They wouldn't like it if I passed by and didn't well-wish the baby." He shouted, "Boy!" And as if by magic a boy appeared.

"Take my horse and the lady's," said Jago. We dismounted and entered a small cottage, where several people were gathered.

"Why, 'tis the master," said a woman, dropping a curtsey.

"'Tis honoured we be," said her husband.

"Where's the baby?" asked Jago.

"She be in her cradle, Mr. Jago. 'Twould be an honour if you'd bless the child and take a piece of the cheeld's fuggan."

He would, he said, and I should too.

The cake was cut, and both Jago and I had a piece and also a glass of sloe gin, which burned my throat a little.

"Good luck to the child," said Jago.

"May she grow up to be a good servant to her master," said the baby's mother.

"Aye," said Jago, "so be it."

We came out into the street, where the boy was patiently waiting with our horses. We mounted and continued our ride.

368

"All these people are our tenants," Jago told me. "And every bit of the land is Kellaway land, owned by the family for six hundred years. You'd find most of the houses similar. They're what are known as Lives Cottages. A man who builds one has to start construction after dark and be finished before the next dawn. He thereby has a right to occupy it for his own lifetime, as will his son and his grandson."

"Can people really build a cottage in one night?"

"If they have their materials ready, they can have the four walls standing and the roof on. That is all that's necessary. How did you like the 'cheeld's fuggan'?"

"A little too yellow."

"Oh, that's the saffron—a great delicacy here."

I had learned much about the island that morning. It was a community of about one hundred people, fishermen mainly, although there was some agriculture. There were many little coves where boats were moored, and we passed fishermen mending their nets as they sat among the lobster pots. They all greeted Jago, and I felt a certain pleasure in their respect for him.

He told me of their customs and superstitions. "Fishermen don't like to land with their catch before daybreak. They think the little people might carry them off if they did. And when they are at sea it's unlucky to mention rabbits or any wild animals. Once a superstition is born it seems to live for ever.

"In the old days," he continued, "these islands were a sanctuary for people who wanted to evade the law. Many outlaws found asylum here and became subjects of the ruling Kellaway."

"And the Kellaway line is unbroken through the ages?" I asked.

"Yes. If a female inherited, she was duty-bound to marry and her husband would then take the name of Kellaway."

"It's been a wonderful morning," I said, "edifying too."

He turned to me and laid his hand on my arm. "I can't tell you how much I want you to stay here, Ellen," he said. "When I saw you in London it was the devil's own job to restrain myself from snatching you up and insisting that you come down and get to know your family before you rushed into marriage."

369

"I still can't understand why you didn't tell me who you were."

"It was the whim of a moment. You were so immersed in the prospect of marriage . . . and then, when it fell through, I felt my chance had come. I wanted you to come here freely. . . ."

I was touched by the tenderness in his voice. I was finding his company stimulating. He had intrigued me at the recital; he had frightened me in the house in Finlay Square. But now I decided he was the most fascinating man I had ever met.

He seemed to make a great effort to curb his emotions. "Alas," he said, "we must return to the castle. There is so much more I want to show you, but another day."

"I look forward to that. You must be rather proud when the people show you such obvious respect, as they did this morning."

"They daren't do aught else." He laughed. "I will say, though, that since I've been in control we've prospered. Crops have been good; I've introduced modern farming and marketing methods. Your father and I didn't always see eye to eye, Ellen."

"Oh?" I said, wanting him to go on about my father.

"He was ill for a long time. That left the reins in my hands."

"And it was then that things began to improve?"

"People on the island will tell you so. But let's not talk about the past, Ellen. You're here. Let's go on from there."

He smiled at me, and I fancied I saw in his eyes that which faintly alarmed me. But it had been such a good morning that I was in a happy mood as we rode into the stables.

THAT afternoon Gwennol went to the mainland. "She often gets one of the men to row her over on calm days like this," Jenifry explained. Jago was off on some estate business and Jenifry wanted to rest. So I decided to stroll around the castle by myself.

It was about half past two when I set out—a beautiful September day with the sun picking out pearly tints in the water. Soon I found myself in a familiar-looking courtyard. I heard the cooing of the pigeons and recognized this as the spot I had visited on the previous evening.

Then I saw him. He was very small, with a thatch of almost

370

white hair; his eyes were pale and his fair eyebrows and lashes gave him a look of surprise. I judged him to be about fourteen.

He carried a bowl of maize, and a look of fear came over his face when he saw me. He started to walk towards the outbuilding.

"Don't go, please. The pigeons must be fed," I reminded him. "Do let me watch; I love the way they flutter around you."

While he considered his next move, I had an inspiration. "I think you must be Slack," I said. "I met your mother at the inn."

He paused. Then a smile appeared on his face and he nodded.

"I'm Ellen Kellaway. I'm staying here for a while. I heard the wonderful story of the brown pigeons taking the messages."

"These take messages," he said proudly. "I train them." He then took a handful of maize from the bowl and threw it onto the cobbles. Several of the birds flew down and pecked at it.

"I saw you in there last night," I said, pointing to the outbuilding. "I called you, but you didn't hear."

"I saw you," he replied with a sly smile.

"May I look in your pigeon house now? I am very interested."

He opened the door and we stepped into a small room where sacks of maize and drinking troughs were stored.

"I've been looking after the pigeons ever since I came here," he said. "Now I've got to finish feeding them."

We went back into the courtyard. He held out his arm and two birds immediately alighted on it. "There, my pretties," he murmured. "Be 'ee come to see Slacky, then? You like pigeons, miss. Her liked 'em too. Her'd help me feed 'em. Then her went away."

"Her? Who was that, Slack?" I asked.

"Her," he said, looking bewildered. "Her just went away."

He was so disturbed by the memory that he had almost forgotten my existence, and because I could see that to question him further would only make him less inclined to talk, I strolled off.

THE next day Gwennol gave me a tour of the castle.

"Let's begin with the dungeons," she said.

Clinging to a rope banister, we descended a treacherous spiral staircase. At the bottom was an enclosure with a cobbled floor. It was surrounded by doors, about eighteen in all. I pushed one open and saw a cavelike cell in which it would have been difficult for a man of normal height to stand upright. Fixed to the wall on a chain was a heavy iron ring. I shuddered, realizing that this had been used to prevent the cell's inmate from escaping. The walls were seeping with moisture and there was a damp, noisome odour about the place. I explored other cells, some lofty but all equally dark and dismal. On one wall the sketch of a gallows was cut into the stone; on another an evil grinning face had been drawn.

"It's gruesome," I said. "Imagine yourself a prisoner. You'd call and no one would hear, or even care."

Gwennol nodded. "Ugh! Morbid," she commented. "I can see you've had enough of the dungeons, but you had to have a look at them, of course. They're an important part of the castle."

We climbed the stairs to the upper regions and she took me through so many rooms, towers and galleries that I lost count. She showed me the kitchens, the bakery, the buttery, the winery and the slaughterhouse; she introduced me to the servants, who watched me guardedly and with obvious curiosity.

One room which led off the hall interested me particularly because as we entered, Gwennol said, "I heard this was your mother's favourite room. I don't think anyone has used it since she went."

There was a step leading down to the room, which was furnished as a sitting room with a table and a few chairs. There was also a wooden settle that fitted into an alcove.

I looked around eagerly, trying to picture my mother there. It was certainly not a bright room. The window was small and its panes leaded. I said, "I wonder if any of her things are still here."

"Why don't you look in the cupboard?" suggested Gwennol.

I opened the door and immediately spotted an easel and some rolls of paper. "These must have been hers," I cried in triumph. Then I saw a sketchbook lying on the floor. Written across it was her name: Frances Kellaway. I was so excited by this discovery that my hand shook as I turned the pages. There were paintings and sketches; some were of the castle from various angles. She had been quite an artist.

"I want to take this to study at my leisure. You're probably amused by my excitement, but I knew so little of my mother, and my father I can't remember at all. You must have known him."

"Nobody knew him well. But I don't think he liked young people. He was ill for a long time and mostly kept to his own rooms. I'd see him now and then in a wheelchair. Fenwick, his secretary-valet, looked after him, and he could tell you more about him than anyone else, I daresay. But he left when your father died."

"Do you know where he went?"

"I think he lives on the mainland, but I'm not sure where."

Then, seeming to find the conversation about my father boring, she changed the subject. "Let's go and see Slack," she said. "I want him to row me over to the mainland tomorrow. Would you care to come? I always like to take advantage of calm seas. I shall be visiting friends, so perhaps you'd enjoy exploring a bit. We could go to the inn and get horses there. It's what I often do."

I said I would go along.

"Good. Slack always loves to take me. It gives him an opportunity to see his mother."

"He's a strange boy. I discovered him feeding the pigeons."

"Oh, so you've already met him. They say he's 'lacking', but in some things he's quite bright. It's just that he's different. I think people underestimate him. He came to us when he was about eleven. He had found a baby robin and was looking after it. Jago noticed him and thought he'd be useful to look after the pigeons, which at that time were being attacked by some disease—and you remember the legend about when the pigeons go, the Kellaways will lose the island. Not that Jago would believe it, but he says he respects superstitions because other people believe in them. Well, the pigeons thrived immediately under Slack's care. There's no doubt he's got a way with birds. Come. Let's find him now."

Slack was nursing a pigeon. "She have hurt her leg," he murmured. "But I can heal it. You see, there be this power in me."

Gwennol smiled. "I want you to row Miss Ellen and me over to the mainland tomorrow, Slack. That's if the sea's like it is today."

"I'll have the boat for 'ee, Miss Gwennol."

Gwennol and I went back through the courtyards.

When I retired that night I felt drowsy. But as I was about to get ready for bed, I noticed my mother's sketchbook. So I set the candle down on a little table that stood beside the bed and started to look through it.

She had had considerable talent. One could feel the antiquity of those grey stone castle walls which she had painted so realistically. There was a lovely picture of Blue Rock Island, and there were some portraits too. One depicted a plump child with large inquiring eyes. The caption read: "E. Aged Two." Why yes, I recognized myself. I turned the pages. There was Jago—two portraits of him, facing each other. How she had caught the resemblance! They were like two different people. Strangely enough, he was smiling in both of them, but in one the smile was benign and in the other the eyes had a veiled, almost sinister look; and there was a certain twist about the mouth, as though he were plotting something evil.

Could my mother have been saying, "Beware, there are two Jagos"? I felt uneasy, because I was beginning to enjoy his company more than I cared to admit to myself.

I turned the pages and came to another double portrait. In one of these I saw a rather demure girl, her hair in braids. She was looking up as though in prayer and she held a Bible in her hands. In the picture on the opposite page, her face peeped out from a curtain of unbound hair; the eyes were wild, yet pleading, and the expression was tortured; she looked as though she were trying to tell some secret and did not know how. It was a horrible picture.

Under it was the initial S.

I was quite shaken. I knew this was the S.K. who had written her message on the cupboard wall. Who, I asked myself, was she?

Sleep had completely deserted me. I turned over the pages and studied the peaceful landscapes, hoping they would soothe me. But instead an even greater shock came from that sketchbook.

I gasped in amazement when I first saw it, for there on a page was the room of my dream! The fireplace, the chimney seats, the rocking chair, the painting of the storm at sea . . . everything!

One thought kept hammering on my brain: The phantom room

really existed; my mother had seen it. What did this mean? What *could* it mean? I felt that my mother's spirit was trying to get in touch with me through her sketchbook.

She had seen Jago as two different people; the sinister portrait had taken me right back to those awful moments in the house in Finlay Square. What did she know of Jago? And who was S., who could look so demure and so wild?

But it was the picture of the room which haunted me. One thing I could now be sure of: The dream room existed. But where?

I SLEPT fitfully that night and oddly enough I did not have the dream. The first thing I did the next morning was to pick up the sketchbook. Yes. It was really there—the room I knew so well.

After breakfast Gwennol came to my room to see if I was ready.

"I've been looking through my mother's sketchbook," I said. "Look at this picture. Do you know the room?"

She was puzzled. "Should I? It's just an ordinary room."

An ordinary room! How odd to hear the room that has been haunting me so described! I wanted to say: That room haunts me. If I could only find it, I might understand why I dream about it and always feel such an overwhelming dread. But I found it difficult to talk about, so I merely said, "I wondered if it might be in the castle."

She shook her head as though vaguely surprised that I should make so much of such an insignificant matter.

At that moment there was a knock on the door. I called, "Come in," and Slack entered.

"What's wrong?" asked Gwennol, surprised to see him upstairs.

" 'Tis just I thought we'd best get an early start because of the tide," he said.

"You're right. We're almost ready," Gwennol replied.

On impulse I showed the sketch to Slack and asked, "Have you ever seen that room?"

He stared tensely at the page and did not look at me. It seemed as though a shutter had dropped over his eyes. "I can't tell 'ee about a picture room, miss," he said slowly.

"My dear Ellen." Gwennol laughed. "You're becoming obsessed. Your mother sketched a cozy room and that's all there is to it."

Slack nodded. I thought, He is stupid after all.

"Let's be going," said Gwennol. "Is everything ready, Slack?" They exchanged a glance that seemed to have a meaning from which I was excluded.

"Everything be done and we'm ready to go," said Slack.

We left the castle and went to the shore where the boats were moored. The sea was calm and the boat skimmed lightly over the water. There was a seraphic smile on Slack's face, for he clearly loved the task. He looked different from the way he had when I asked him about the room. I watched him—slack-baked—not finished off, his mother had said. It was an apt description of him in a way. His hands were strong, yet like a child's; his eyes were child-like too, except when the shutter came down.

In due course we ran ashore on a beach, and then made our way to the inn. Mrs. Pengelly came out, beaming with delight. "Welcome to 'ee, Miss Gwennol, Miss Ellen. You'll be wanting horses?"

"I shall," said Gwennol. "And you, Ellen?"

I said I would, for I thought it would be pleasant to call at Hydrock Manor.

"Well, you go to the stables then, Augustus, and tell your father the ladies be here and what they do want. Then come to the kitchen, where I'll have a tidbit for 'ee. And what refreshment would the ladies be looking for? A glass of wine while you'm waiting?"

Gwennol asked, "Has anyone arrived at the inn yet?"

"No, Miss Gwennol. No one be here yet."

"We'll drink a glass of wine then, please," she said.

We went inside to the parlour, and Mrs. Pengelly brought out her blackberry wine and some saffron cakes. We had not been there long when we heard the sound of a horse's hoofs.

Gwennol sat very still in her seat and a smile touched her face, making it not only striking but beautiful.

"In the parlour?" asked a voice which I recognized with pleasure as that of Sir Michael Hydrock.

As he entered, Gwennol rose and went to him, holding out both her hands, which he took and covered with both of his. Then he saw me and a smile of delighted recognition lit up his face.

"Miss Kellaway," he cried.

Gwennol looked astonished. "You . . . you know each other?"

"Yes," said Michael, advancing towards me. "How are you enjoying the island?" he asked.

"I'm finding it enormously interesting," I told him.

"I don't understand," said Gwennol rather impatiently.

"It's easily explained," Michael told her.

And I added, "When I was waiting to come to the island I got lost in Hydrock Manor's woods. Sir Michael rescued me."

"I see," said Gwennol coolly.

"You must come to the manor with us," said Michael warmly.

"Thank you. I should love that."

"Are the Pengellys' horses ready for you?" he asked.

"I've already ordered them," said Gwennol, "but Ellen may have other plans."

"As a matter of fact," I answered, "it had occurred to me that I might call at the manor."

"And I," he said, "should have been very hurt if you hadn't. But now you've lived in the castle. We're not as grand as that."

"The manor is enchanting," I said.

"It's the most beautiful house I've ever seen," added Gwennol fervently.

We went into the yard, where the horses were ready for us. Off we rode, and in a short time we were at the manor.

"By the way, Miss Kellaway," asked Michael, "how's the ankle?"

"Fine, thank you. By the next morning I wouldn't have known anything had happened to it."

"You hurt your ankle, then?" asked Gwennol.

I told her about it; she listened intently, but her expression was less pleasant.

We went into the hall, and I felt the same peace I had experienced when I was there last. "There's something so friendly about this house," I commented.

"We all feel it," said Gwennol shortly.

"Yes," added Michael. "There's a saying in the family that Hydrock Manor will either welcome or reject you. It certainly seems to welcome you, Miss Kellaway. I should like to show it to you. You don't mind, Gwennol? Gwennol is a very old friend," he told me. "She knows the manor as well as I do."

"I'd love to see it," I assured him.

And Gwennol put in, "I can't see enough of the place."

"Look at that armour on the walls," he said. "Those breastplates were worn by ancestors of mine during Cromwell's time. These pewter vessels have been used by the family for hundreds of years. I like to keep everything as it was as far as possible."

"Jago is like that too, isn't he, Gwennol?" I said, for I was anxious that she should join the conversation. I realized by this time that her feelings towards Michael were warmer than those of friendship. The softness of her eyes and mouth was rare with her.

"Jago would like to go back to feudal days," she said sharply. "He'd like to be not only the lord of the manor but of us all."

"He's proud of the island," I said. "He's done so much for the people."

"My dear, they're afraid to say a word against him. He could turn them out of their homes tomorrow if they offended him."

In his easy manner Michael diverted the subject from Jago by saying, "Come and look at the chapel."

We crossed the hall and ascended a spiral staircase.

"There are lots of documents in the vaults under the chapel," said Michael. "Someday I intend to compile a history of the family. And Gwennol has promised to help me."

"There's nothing I should like more," she said, becoming animated. She almost looked as though she would like to get down to the task immediately.

There were about twelve pews in the chapel, and on the altar was a very fine cloth, worked, he told me, by his mother. He spoke then of his mother's illness and her untimely death when he was just ten years old.

I was deeply moved by the story, as was Gwennol. Her eyes

378

never left Michael as he talked. I thought, Yes, she is in love with him. I'm in the way. I ought to have gone off on my own exploring the countryside. Just because he's too polite to show he doesn't really want me, I had imagined he was eager for me to come.

"Now," he said, "we'll go to luncheon."

"How kind of you," I said. "Gwennol was expected, but I . . ."

"We're delighted to have you," said Michael warmly. "Yes, Gwennol was expected. I had the message," he told her. Then turning back to me, he explained, "We've an excellent method of communication. Slack sends messages over by carrier pigeon. We have trained pigeons here too."

I enjoyed the view from the dining room, with its window looking out over smooth lawns. It seemed to me that Michael Hydrock was completely contented. I could not help comparing him with Jago—that restless spirit—whose changing moods and unpredictability were half attractive, half repelling, but always intriguing.

After luncheon Michael accompanied us to the inn, where Slack was waiting. "Come again soon," said Michael, and there was no doubt that I was included in that invitation.

Gwennol was silent as we were rowed back, and I sensed that she was suspicious of me.

When we reached the island we left Slack to tie up the boat and made our way to the castle. Gwennol said, "How strange that you should have met Michael and not mentioned it." Then she gave a little laugh. "You apparently didn't hurt your ankle badly. It must have been one of those convenient little twists." And before I could express my indignation she had turned and run into the castle.

Jago looked at me reproachfully. We were at dinner that night and he had asked how I had been spending the day.

"What, Ellen, deserting us for the mainland already? And where did you go?"

"To Hydrock Manor. I'd met Sir Michael before."

Jago put down his knife and fork and gazed at me. I was aware of Jenifry's eyes on me too.

I explained how I had hurt my ankle.

"It was one of those temporary twists," said Gwennol.

I detected a note of sarcasm in her voice. And I realized that this information had disturbed both Jago and Jenifry.

Jago said, "Tomorrow I will show you more of the island. I've been thinking, by the way, that you should practise rowing. You have done it before?"

"Yes, but not at sea; on a river, which I suppose was different."

"It's the same really," said Gwennol, "only you have to be more careful at sea—mostly because of the weather."

"I'll take you out tomorrow," said Jago. "Until you've practised enough, always have someone with you. Slack will take you where you want to go. But just don't go alone at first."

I was exhausted when I went to my room that night. I had enjoyed visiting Hydrock Manor even though the day had been spoiled by Gwennol's jealousy. I should have to stay away from the manor from now on, which was a pity because it had been rather comforting to have such a pleasant friend on the mainland.

I was sitting at my dressing table plaiting my hair by candlelight when there was a knock on the door. I started up in dismay. I wasn't sure why, but always when the candles were lighted in this room I felt uneasy. There was a further knock and the door was quietly opened. Jenifry stood there holding a candle.

"I want to have a word with you," she said. She set down the candle and drew up a chair, so that we were both sitting at the dressing table. "It's about Gwennol and Michael Hydrock. He's one of the most eligible bachelors in the neighbourhood. He and Gwennol have always been good friends. In fact, general opinion has been that they will make a match of it. But then Gwennol came back today more than a little upset.

"His is a great family," she went on. "There are some who wouldn't think Gwennol quite suitable. The Hydrocks are so proud of their ancestry." Her lips curled in contempt. "That woman Mrs. Hocking, for one. She was his nurse, and still clucks over him, pampers him. Nobody but the daughter of a duke or an earl is good enough for her dear Michael."

"I would think the Kellaways are good enough for anybody."

"Yes, but there's the story of our illegitimate branch, of our having something of the devil in us, and although Michael Hydrock might not believe it, he'd be aware of what people were thinking."

She moved closer to me, but I could not look at her face. If I did, I knew I should see the evil expression which I had caught in the mirror on my first night.

"He was very taken with you, wasn't he?" she said. "I daresay he found you more sophisticated than most of the country girls he meets. And although you're a Kellaway too, yours is the pure strain, isn't it?"

I felt exasperated. "Listen," I said almost fiercely. "I was lost in his woods and he took me back to the inn. I met him again with Gwennol and lunched at his house. I like him. I like his house. There's nothing more in it than that. I am not trying to snatch him from under the nose of an ambitious mother with a marriageable daughter. And I can assure you I am not desperate for a husband."

She rose, and as she stood there I shivered. She was holding the candle in front of her, and it had the effect of lighting up her face while the rest of her was shadowy; the image in the mirror was like a disembodied face. She looked malevolent.

"From what I know of Michael Hydrock," I told Jenifry, "he is a man who will make his own choice."

At that she said good night, and when the door had shut on her, I was certain that there was something more than her fear for her daughter's happiness that had filled me with apprehension. It was as though she were warning me.

That was the night I found the first of the notebooks.

I was so disturbed by Jenifry's visit that I knew it would be foolish to try to sleep, so I decided I would write a letter to Esmeralda. There was a charming desk in my room, with a sloping top covered with leather and inlaid with ivory. I had already put my writing materials inside it. Now I tried to open it but it had jammed, and so I forced it open. As I did so a flap, which I had not noticed in the top compartment, opened and a notebook fell out.

I picked it up and saw that inside was written in a childish hand, "S.K. Her Book." This, I assumed, was the same S.K. who had scratched words in the cupboard and whose picture my mother had painted.

I flicked through the book, and some paragraphs caught my eye.

"I hate it here. I wish I could escape. I am supposed to be writing an essay called 'Life on an Island.' Miss Homer said I shall stay in my room until it is done, but I'm writing this instead. It is a secret and I shall not show her. She wants me to write about crabs and jellyfish and tides and scenery, but I don't care about those things. I'm going to write about Them and Myself. My father hates me. My stepmother doesn't like me very much either. Nobody likes me except Baby and she's too young and silly to know. My step-mother said to me, 'Look at your little sister. Isn't she a love?' I said, 'She's only a half sister. That's not a real one.' Everyone comes and looks at Baby and says how lovely and good she is, even if she has been screaming just minutes before. I bet when I was a baby they didn't say I was wonderful.

"I wish I could *see* my father. He doesn't want to see me, but he sees Baby now and then. The reason he doesn't like me has some-thing to do with my mother. He didn't like her. I heard one of the servants say that. She died when I was seven. Then I became very naughty, like the time I threw Miss Homer's hair dye over the floor and she didn't want anyone to know she used it.

"When my stepmother came it was better for a while. But I knew my father only spoke to me because Stepmother asked him to. Baby came then and everybody made a fuss of her and nobody cared about me. My stepmother only cared about Baby and gave up trying to make my father like me."

I wanted to know more, but the remaining pages were blank. So I put the notebook back into its place and closed the desk. I was in no mood for writing to Esmeralda now.

I took the oars and Jago sat opposite me. We were going to row to the bird sanctuary. It was a beautiful day with a still sea.

"It's the best time of the year," said Jago, "before the October gales set in. They can be very wild. On the other hand, they might not come at all. There's only one thing that's certain about our weather and that's its unpredictability. You row very well, Ellen. You're going to be quite a champion."

"If I'm going to stay here for a while that will be necessary."

"*If* you're going to stay. My dear Ellen, I hope you are going to stay here a very long time." I looked up and was disturbed by his intense gaze. "You're beginning to love the island, confess it."

"I'm finding it very interesting, yes."

Sanctuary Island lay before us, a green hump in the ocean. "Run her onto the beach here," he said.

I was proud that I was able to do so with competence, because I had an absurd desire to shine in his eyes.

Jago secured the boat and we started to walk up a slope to a sort of plateau. "Look at those choughs over there," he said. "There are hundreds of them. We get the occasional storm petrel. She just lands to lay her eggs and then departs."

"I'm surprised you find time to be interested in these birds."

"I find time for anything I want to do."

He put his arm through mine, ostensibly to help me up the slope, but I felt he was conveying the fact that he was going to find a great deal of time to spend in my company.

"Let's sit here," he said. He had brought a travelling rug, and now he spread it on the grass. We looked over the sea to Blue Rock Island, and I thought I could make out the artist's house. It was sheltered by tall trees and was not far from the beach.

"Tell me," I said suddenly, "who is S.K.? I think she must have occupied the room I'm staying in."

Jago wrinkled his brow, then laughed. "You must be referring to Silva Kellaway, your half sister."

"Then I'm the Baby referred to. Oh, you see, I found one of her notebooks, and she had written something about her stepmother and a baby. How strange! My sister!"

"Your half sister."

"You mean we shared the same father, and the stepmother she mentions is my mother?"

"Yes. Poor Silva, her life was tragic. And her death—for it's almost certain that she was drowned."

"*Almost* certain?"

"Her body was never found, although her boat was washed up on the island . . . empty."

"How very sad. How old was she when this happened?"

"It was about a year and a half ago. She'd be twenty-eight now."

"And she lived at the castle—in my room—until then?"

"Yes. No one knew why she took a boat out on such a stormy night, as she did. It was a crazy thing to do, but she was crazy."

"You mean she was . . . *mad?*"

"Oh no, just unbalanced. She'd be very docile for months on end and then suddenly she would create scenes."

"Do go on. I'm longing to hear everything about the family."

"There's not a lot to tell. Your father married twice. His first wife was Effie and she had Silva. Effie and your father used to quarrel violently. He was not fond of Silva. It might have been that he was disappointed because she wasn't a boy. I don't know. In any case, he could hardly bear to look at her. Then Effie died of pneumonia and after a year or two your father went to London on business and came back with your mother. She couldn't settle down either. Then you were born and that seemed to reconcile them, but only for a little while. Your father was not an easy man to live with. She went off, taking you with her. That was a surprise, for she had left no warning."

"Poor little Silva. No wonder she was unbalanced, as you say."

"I wish we could have known why she left, where she was going, and indeed could have some proof that she was drowned."

"If the boat was washed up empty, isn't that proof enough?"

"It is to some. But others will see an unnatural hand even in the most ordinary happenings."

"Well, if she is alive, I want to meet her. All those childhood years when I longed for a sister—and had to do with Esmeralda—I really had one! I wish I'd grown up with her in the castle."

He leaned towards me suddenly and gripped my hand. "So do I, Ellen. Then we'd already be firm friends."

A gull shrieked overhead as though he were mocking us. But Jago did not seem to hear. His expression had grown tender.

384

At that moment I was aware that we were being watched. I turned sharply and saw that a man was standing behind us. Jago noticed him too. "Why, it's our neighbour, the artist who lives on Blue Rock Island," he said.

We rose to our feet as the man advanced. "Ellen," said Jago, "let me present James Manton. Manton, this is Miss Kellaway."

He bowed. "I'm glad to meet you," he said. "I just rowed over here to make a few sketches. The light's so good today, and just look at that sea. I hope you're enjoying the island, Miss Kellaway."

I said I was finding it fascinating.

He watched a bird soar aloft into the distance, and then with a "Good day to you!" he went back the way he had come.

"Manton paints a lot of bird pictures. He's rather good with them. Well, Ellen, are you sufficiently rested to row us back?"

"Yes. I don't feel the least bit tired."

Taking my hand, he ran down the slope with me to our boat.

When we reached the Far Island, Jago said, "Before we go back to the castle I'm going to take you to old Tassie, the wise woman of the island. She'll tell your fortune. You'll like that. All women do."

We walked up the incline to a small cottage surrounded by an herb garden. An old woman appeared at the door.

"Good day, Tassie," said Jago. "I've brought my ward along to see you. This is Miss Ellen Kellaway."

"Good day to 'ee, my lady." Her face was very wrinkled and her bright black eyes reminded me of a monkey's, sharp and shrewd; she wore a grey crocheted shawl, and the black cat who rubbed himself about her skirts fitted the scene perfectly.

We stepped into a cluttered room with a faint pungent odour. There was a chimney seat on either side of the hearth, and the cat, who had followed us in, leaped into a basket and sat watching us. There were pots and pans filled with mysterious substances, and bunches of herbs were hanging from the beams.

"Ellen is anxious to learn about the island, Tassie," said Jago. "And I told her she couldn't know much until she'd visited you. What have you got to tell her?"

"Come close and sit down near me, my dear," said Tassie. She held my hands and gazed into my face. Jago was watching her intently, and I was as much aware of him as of her.

"Oh my life, I do see much here for you. There's good and there's bad. You've had tragedy. Now there's two roads open to 'ee. You must be sure and take the right one."

"How shall I know which is the right one?" I asked.

"There's one beside 'ee to guide 'ee. You'm come home to your family and 'tis a good thing. You'm facing the right way now, but a little while back 'twasn't so. Your fate will soon be settled, for 'tis right at hand."

"You'd better listen to Tassie," said Jago. "She has special powers and is greatly respected here. All the girls come to her."

" 'Tis for the young lady to take the right course and she'll be happy for the rest of her days. She'll have fine sons and a daughter or two to bring comfort to her."

Jago was smiling at me now, his eyes gleaming, and I thought, He is really falling in love with me!

The prospect excited me and at the same time made me apprehensive. I knew that his emotions would be fierce, for there were no half measures about him. From the moment I had seen him at the Carringtons' I had been aware of him . . . physically.

Tassie was telling me what she did for the young people of the island. "If it's a love potion they'll be wanting, I give it to them. And I look into their futures." She moved closer to me. "I can help you to lift a spell that be cast on you, to turn aside an evil wish. So come to me, young maid, if you be in trouble."

"That's more than an invitation, Ellen," said Jago. "It means that Tassie accepts you as an islander." He placed several coins on the table, and I saw an avaricious gleam in the old woman's eyes. Then we came out into the autumn sunshine.

"She's a colourful character, our Tassie, don't you think? And you must admit she gave you a pleasant fortune," said Jago.

"She seemed to be well paid for it."

He looked at me sharply. "Well, didn't she deserve it?"

"If clients are going to pay according to what they're told, isn't that a temptation to the seer to be over optimistic?"

"I don't think she was about you. In fact, I know you're going to have good fortune."

"Don't forget that rests with me."

"But you're a wise woman, Ellen. I knew it from the moment I saw you. Joking aside, Tassie *is* a colourful character."

"Do you really believe in her special powers?"

"I'm like other people. I'm willing to believe that she helped me if I get what I want."

"And if you don't?"

"My dear Ellen, I always make sure I do."

We returned to the castle and I retired to my room. But when I lit the candles and the shadows began to form, I started to brood about the new aspect in my relationship with Jago. He hated my going to the mainland and did not want my friendship with Michael Hydrock to grow any more than Gwennol and Jenifry did; but was I right in thinking it was for a different reason?

Could it really be that Jago Kellaway wanted to be my husband!

THE next day I went to find Slack.

He was in the courtyard feeding an injured sea gull. "Her can't fly, Miss Ellen. Found her cowering on the cliffs, I did. Her wing be damaged and I reckon her had had no food for days. 'Twasn't only that—birds be terrible cruel one to the other. If one be maimed or be different, they peck it to death. People be that way sometimes. They don't always like them as are different."

"What a good thing you found it," I said.

"See, I've splinted her wing. But I don't want her flying yet. I want to feed her . . . slow-like at first. There now, my pretty, Slack 'ull look after 'ee, you see."

"I've come to ask if you'll come out in a boat with me," I said. "I'll do the rowing. I've promised Mr. Jago that I won't take a boat out alone . . . yet."

The fact that I trusted him enough to ask him to go with me delighted him. And as I got to know Slack I realized that his great pleasure in life was looking after people.

I rowed around the island.

"You be proper good with the oars, Miss Ellen," he said. " 'Tis safe enough if you don't go too far out to sea. But you do know how quick a breeze can arise; in fifteen minutes the sea can get all angry and ruffled up. That's what 'ee've got to watch for if 'ee be going to the mainland."

"Do you hear of many people drowning?"

Once again I saw the shutter come down over his eyes. "There have been," he said.

"There was Silva," I suggested. "You knew her, of course."

"Yes, I did know her."

"Just think. She was my half sister and I never knew her. I should love to have you tell me what you know about her."

"She were terrible fond of birds and little things," he said.

"Ah." So there had been a bond between them. I had guessed that. "Did she often come and help you feed them?" I asked.

He looked suddenly happy. "They'd perch on her shoulder. Kind and gentle she were to them. She'd talk and talk, like I wasn't there, and then she'd smile and say, 'I do run on, don't I, Slacky?' "

"And was she very unhappy?"

He looked frightened. "Yes, her used to cry and that was terrible. I never saw anybody cry like Miss Silva did. It was laughing and crying all at once, and she'd say she hated the castle and Mr. Jago and all of them."

"Do you know why she took the boat out that stormy night?"

He nodded, his lips pressed together. I believe he does know something, I thought.

"Did she go out in that boat because she was running away from something? You know, don't you, Slack?"

"You might say she were running away," he said slowly.

"If she went out on a wild night, she must have wanted to kill herself. No boat could survive in such a heavy sea, could it?"

"You can never be sure, Miss Ellen, what can happen to boats on the sea. . . . I pray she be happy in the new life."

His pale face was impassive again. I was convinced he knew more about Silva than he had betrayed. Perhaps when I had won his confidence he would tell me.

The "Ellen" Is Lost

Jago was busy. He personally supervised the farms and arranged the island's business transactions, but he usually managed to spend some time of the day with me. We rode around the island, and he introduced me to the farmers and shopkeepers, the innkeeper, the parson, the doctor and all who made up the life of the island. We were growing closer. Almost against my will I began to feel I needed a strong dose of his society every day.

I had now become a good oarswoman, and he was delighted. One morning he took me down to the cove and there was a freshly painted boat with *Ellen* on the side. I was very proud of her.

After that I took the *Ellen* out by myself every day. I never went far out to sea, but usually skirted the island and put in at some bay which I had not visited before.

The island was growing on me. The people accepted me and I was beginning to feel that I belonged. But I could not help feeling that it was important for me to know what had happened to those vague figures of the past. I believed if I could discover what had happened to Silva, I would have a key to the whole situation.

Jago never wanted to speak of her. He had dismissed her as unbalanced, a foolish girl who had been unable to adjust to life and had found a dramatic way of ending it.

My father—who was hers also—had hated her. In fact, when I thought about it, he seemed to have disliked everyone, except perhaps his secretary-valet, Fenwick. Suddenly I had an idea: if I could have a word with Fenwick, I might discover something about my family. But how could I find him? When I asked Jago where he lived he said merely, "What can Fenwick tell you that I can't?" Perhaps he was right, but secretary-valets often know more about their employers than do their close relations.

Each day, weather permitting, one of the boats went over to the mainland to collect mail. One day, while I was pondering all this, I was delighted to receive a letter from Esmeralda.

She said the castle sounded wonderful and she longed to see it. Her parents had given several balls for her and she had met a very pleasant young man named Freddy Bellings. There was a good deal about Freddy—the colour of his eyes, the kind humour of his manner and the way in which he could make jokes without hurting anyone's feelings. I could see that Esmeralda was delighted with him.

"We see a great deal of the Carringtons," she went on. "No one mentions Philip, but Lady Emily looks a little sad at times. She asks me how you are and hopes you are happy. Someone else asks about you. Rollo. He wanted to know where you had gone and whether you were settling down. I had just received your letter about the castle and everything. He was most interested."

I was so glad Esmeralda had found her Freddy. I was surprised, though, that Rollo should be interested in what I was doing. Perhaps he repented of his harshness to me. However, it was an indication of how much I had grown away from the past when my thoughts were almost immediately back with the problem of the moment: how to find Fenwick and talk to him about my family.

The Pengellys would be likely to know his whereabouts. So I decided to go to the inn and see what I could discover.

The sea was calm and I was now well practiced enough to row myself over to the mainland.

When I reached the inn Mrs. Pengelly brought out the inevitable homemade wine and saffron cakes, and I asked if she had any idea where I might find Mr. Fenwick.

"Well," she said, "he did leave the island when your father died. He retired to a cottage down in Fallerton, a small village but six or seven miles from here."

"I want to talk to him about my father."

She looked alarmed. " 'Twould only distress you, maybe, to hear how very ill he were at the end, Miss Ellen."

"Naturally I want to hear about my family. It seems so difficult to get people to tell me. Surely you must have known Silva."

"Oh yes. She were a strange girl. Wild-like—used to go out in the wind and lose herself for hours so we'd think something had happened to her. Seemed like she wanted to put us all in a turmoil. We did our best, your mother and I, and when you came along Miss Silva were better in a way. She were fond of you. But your father wouldn't have her near him; I never knew such a thing. Sometimes I'd hear her sobbing and I'd go and try to comfort her. Then she'd get up and dance around, laughing at me. My dear life, that were a time!"

"It was very odd that she should go off as she did."

A wary look came into Mrs. Pengelly's eyes, and I realized that even she knew something about Silva's mysterious disappearance, something that she was not going to tell me. But at the moment I was obsessed by the thought of finding Fenwick.

"I'll have one of the horses and go to Fallerton," I said. "What was the name of Fenwick's house, do you remember?"

"I can't tell 'ee that, Miss Ellen, but Fallerton be naught but a village. If you ask, someone will be bound to know."

Outside, as I was about to mount a horse, Michael Hydrock rode by. "Hello, Miss Kellaway, what a pleasant surprise!"

"I'm just off to Fallerton," I told him.

"Why, that's on my way. I'll come with you." He turned his horse alongside mine. It would have been rude not to accept his company, which, had it not been for those unfortunate scenes with Gwennol and Jenifry, I should have been very happy to accept. Well, they would both be on the island today, so I could give myself up to the pleasure.

"What do you want to do in Fallerton?" he asked.

"I'm trying to find a Mr. Fenwick who for many years was secretary-valet to my father. Perhaps I can find out from him why my father never got in touch with me."

"I have heard that Charles Kellaway had rather an unforgiving nature. Wouldn't it be better to let sleeping dogs lie?"

"I don't feel like that. I have a burning desire to know."

"Well, then, let's see if we can find Fenwick."

It was pleasant riding across the country which Michael Hydrock knew so well, and we soon came to the small village of Fallerton.

We saw a man fixing his horse's nose bag, and Michael called to him, "Do you know a Mr. Fenwick hereabouts?"

The man looked up. "Well, sir," he said, "if you do mean John Fenwick as took Mulberry Cottage, he have gone."

"Now where would Mulberry Cottage be?" asked Michael.

"Just follow the street and turn right and you'll see Mulberry. A bit of land there is to that place. He took over the market garden; but he weren't cut out for growing vegetables and flowers, he said. So he sold the place and moved away."

We thanked our informant and went to take a look at Mulberry Cottage. A rosy-faced woman came to the door. Yes, they'd bought the property from Mr. Fenwick, and they'd been here these past six months. No, she had no idea where he had gone.

Michael suggested we refresh ourselves at the local inn, which we found without any trouble. A sign creaking over the door said THE CORN DOLLY. We went in and ordered cider and meat pies.

When the innkeeper's wife brought us our food, Michael asked her about Mr. Fenwick, but she had no idea where he had gone.

"Not a very profitable morning," said Michael. "But never mind, I'll make inquiries. What do you think of the old Corn Dolly?"

"It's charming, but what an odd name."

"You saw the sign as we came in?"

"Yes—it looked like a bundle of corn tied up to look like a doll."

"That's exactly what it is. At the end of the harvest the people make these corn dollies and hang them in their houses. They're supposed to bring a good harvest the next year."

"This reminds me in a way of the Polcrag Inn. The open fireplace, the oak beams . . ."

"They haven't an earthenware lamp like this," said Michael, picking up a candlestick-shaped object from the centre of the table. "See this hole at the top?" he went on. "A cupful of oil can be poured through that and then they insert a wick which they call a purvan. I like to see them keeping up the old customs. You don't see many of these Stonen Chills about now."

I picked it up and examined it. I said it was quaint, but my mind was really on Fenwick. I was bitterly disappointed that our search had been fruitless, and Michael sensed this.

"Cheer up," he said, patting my hand. "I promise I'll find Fenwick for you. When I learn something I'll send you a message by carrier pigeon. Gwennol and I often communicate that way."

392

"Thank you. It's good of you to be so helpful."

We left the Corn Dolly, and when we came in sight of the coast I was dismayed to see that a little way out the white horses were putting in an appearance.

"It's an offshore wind," said Michael. "Nothing much. They'll get you back, but it would be advisable to start at once."

"But I rowed myself over," I said.

"Oh." His expression changed and became anxious.

By the time we reached the Polcrag Inn I could see more of the white-crested waves, and Michael insisted that he would row me back. "You need a man's hands on the oars in this tetchy kind of sea," he said. He organized everything. He arranged for the *Ellen* to be taken to the island by one of the inn men, and he hired a slightly stronger boat than the *Ellen* and in it he rowed me over.

"You'll come to the castle?" I asked after we got out of the boat and were standing together on the shore.

"I don't think I will. I should get back."

"You've been so kind to me. Thank you."

"It's been the greatest pleasure," he said, and took my hand. Then he jumped back into the boat, waved, and took the oars.

As I went up the incline towards the castle I met Jenifry. I knew by her manner that she had seen our arrival and had watched him hold my hand when he said goodbye.

I wondered if Jenifry would tell Gwennol what she had seen.

The next day Gwennol went to the mainland, and it occurred to me that I might call on Tassie. Perhaps she would have different things to tell me if Jago were not present.

She was sitting at the door of her cottage, and her wrinkled old nutcracker face screwed into a smile as I approached. "Come in," she said, and I followed her.

Logs were burning in the fireplace, and the pungent smell of herbs seemed stronger than it had on that previous occasion. "And what can I do for you today, miss?" she said with a smirk. "Would you like me to read the cards or look into the crystal ball?"

"You gave me a very good fortune last time I saw you," I replied. "Today I want you to tell me about someone else."

"Oh?" She cocked her head to one side.

"I want to know about my half sister, Silva," I said.

"Poor maid! Hers was a sad life. She often came to see me. Especially at the end. She had reason to then."

"What reason?" I asked excitedly.

"She was anxious about the future."

"People don't seem to want to talk about her."

" 'Tis natural. She could be lying at the bottom of the sea."

"Is that where you think she is, Tassie?"

She looked at me shrewdly. "The boat came in empty."

"Are you telling me she was really drowned?"

"I didn't say that, miss. I said the boat came back without her."

"What was she like, Tassie? Did she look like me?"

"Nay, she had a lot of yellow hair. She took after her mother. Nothing of the Kellaway in her. Can 'ee keep a secret?"

"Yes," I said eagerly. "I promise to."

"Her mother come to me afore Silva was born. She told me that she didn't want to bear that child. But bear it she did, and Silva was born to be unhappy perhaps and knew it."

"Tell me, Tassie, what happened just before Silva went away?"

"She came to see me, twice, in the week before she left. She said, 'Everything's going to change now. I shan't be here much longer, Tassie.' I read her palm, and I could find little for comfort there. But I didn't tell her that. If I see darkness hovering over someone, I don't always say so. 'You be watchful.' That's what I tell 'em to be. For who can say when the dark shadow of danger isn't hovering over us all, me . . . you . . . yes, you, Miss Ellen. And now there's nothing more I can tell 'ee about Miss Silva."

It was the signal for me to go. I put several coins into a bowl on the table and her shrewd eyes counted. "Come again, me dear, whenever you do feel the need," she said.

I thanked her and went out into the sunshine.

Two days later, as it was calm, I rowed over to the mainland once more. I was walking along the main street when a picture in one of the shop windows caught my eye. It was a seascape—a

394

sapphire-blue sea, and waves edged with white frills rolling gently on a golden shore—but what was so arresting was a cloud of white sea gulls rising and swooping above the water. The contrast of white and blue was dazzling. I must have that picture, I thought. It is so evocative of Sanctuary Island. Then it occurred to me that it would be an ideal Christmas present for Jago, and I was delighted.

I went into the shop and requested a closer look at the picture, entitled *The Gulls*. It was brought from the window and was reasonably priced. I would have it, I said.

While the transaction was taking place a man came from the back. It was James Manton, the artist. "Why, it's Miss Kellaway," he said. "So you are buying *The Gulls*. It's my painting."

"I am fascinated by it and I just felt I had to have it."

"You give me great pleasure. Are you taking it with you?"

"I thought I would."

"Did you come over alone?"

"Yes, and I'm keeping an eye on the sea so I don't get caught."

He laughed. "I have an idea," he said. "They can pack up the picture, and you and I will go and have tea at the inn. Then I'll carry the package to your boat."

So that was how I came to be sitting at the Polcrag Inn chatting with James Manton while we drank Mrs. Pengelly's strong brew and ate scones with jam and clotted cream.

"You knew my father, I believe," I said, for this seemed to me a heaven-sent opportunity to discover all I could.

His face hardened. "Yes, I knew him, but I would prefer not to talk about him to you. You could hardly hope to hear what you obviously want to from one whom he regarded as his enemy."

"He regarded you as such? I am sure he was wrong."

"Your father was a man who thought he was never wrong."

"I know his first wife died. . . ."

"Her life was wretched with him. He was a jealous and vindictive man. You can kill with cruelty, and that's what he did."

I shrank from the vituperation in his voice; he had seemed so placid before, a middle-aged man interested in his art. Now his hatred seemed to endow him with a vitality not apparent earlier.

"I knew his first wife and your mother too," he went on. "Your mother was an artist. She and I had a good deal in common, naturally. She could have been a fine artist, but your father despised that."

"Do you know what happened after my mother took me away?"

"He would never forgive her for running away, just as he never forgave Effie. . . ." He shook his head. "I shouldn't be speaking to you like this about your own father."

"What I want is to get at the truth, even if it's unpleasant."

"You must forgive me," he said. "I was carried away. Your father and I were not on speaking terms. He wouldn't have had me on the island. If I had put a foot there, someone would have been ordered to throw me off."

"Well, I hope that unhappy situation is over now."

"Oh, these family feuds get carried on for generations. They exist when the families don't know the original cause of the quarrel. I wouldn't go to Kellaway Island now. I'm content to stay at Blue Rock. I paint most of the time I'm there and then I go up to London to arrange exhibitions and see other people's."

"Well, I'm glad I saw *The Gulls* in the window and I'm glad it's your picture. I hope my appreciation of your work has done something to break through a little of the feud."

He smiled. "It's miraculous that you could be his daughter."

After I had rowed back I set up the picture in my room and studied it. Then I put it away, for if I was going to give it to Jago it would have to be a secret until Christmas.

IT WAS a golden afternoon later in October. I shipped the oars and let the *Ellen* drift on the tide. The day was so beautiful with the faint breeze on my face and that benign reddish sun up there. But then I began to notice that the clouds drifting slowly in the wind were taking on weird shapes. Dark shadows hovering over all of us, I remembered Tassie saying.

I had drifted nearly a mile out from the island, and as I moved the oars to prepare to go back, I stared down in sudden consternation. Water was seeping in.

I bent forward and ran my hand along the bottom of the boat. The water was still very shallow, and I felt something sticky, like sugar. As I watched, the water started to come in faster. The whole of the bottom was covered now. I seized the oars and frantically started to row for shore. How far off the island seemed!

Before I knew what had happened, the *Ellen* tipped to one side and I was in the water. By great good luck I managed to clutch at the keel as she turned upside down. She was floating and I was clinging to her with all my might. Temporarily I was safe, but I am not a strong swimmer and I could feel the water saturating my skirts. I could manage a few strokes, but could I reach the island, hampered as I was by my clothes?

My hold on the boat was precarious. "Help!" I shouted, but my voice sounded feeble.

"O God," I prayed, "let someone find me." And into my mind there flashed an image of Silva in another boat. I could feel my wet skirts wrapping themselves around my legs and dragging me down. I knew it would be disastrous to try for the shore, and yet with every passing second my hold on the *Ellen* was becoming weaker. My hands were growing numb. I can't cling much longer, I thought. Is this the end? No, no. Someone would come. Jago would come. Yes, it must be Jago. If only I could will him to be taking a stroll along the cliffs.

"Jago!" I called. "Jago!"

I would make an attempt to swim. I wouldn't die; I was going to fight for my life.

A shout came to me over the water. "Hold on, Miss Ellen. I be on the way."

Slack! He was near to me now. He swam like a fish.

" 'Tis all right, Miss Ellen. I be here now. . . . I be taking 'ee to the shore." His voice was soothing, comforting, as though I were a wounded bird.

I released my grip on the boat and for a moment was submerged. Then I was on the surface again and Slack's hand was under my chin, holding my head above the water.

The boat had moved away and the shore seemed a long way off.

397

How can this delicate boy bring me safely ashore? I wondered. Then I heard Jago's voice and knew everything would be all right.

I remember Jago's strong arms about me as he brought me onto the land and carried me to the castle. I remember being laid on my bed, then wrapped in blankets. Hot-water bottles were placed around me. I had had a terrible shock, I was told, and would have to stay in bed for a day or two.

I could not stop thinking of the terrifying moment when I had noticed that the boat was leaking.

Jago came and sat by my bed. "What happened, Ellen?"

"I was drifting away from the shore when suddenly I noticed that the boat was leaking."

"You must have struck something the last time you brought her in. The boats ought to be thoroughly examined before they're taken out. If anything had happened to you, my dear Ellen . . ." His face was distorted with emotion. "It's a lesson. We have to be very careful in future."

"I haven't said thank you for saving my life."

He rose and bent over me. "All the thanks I need is to see you safe." Then he stooped and kissed me.

I was glad that he went out then, for my own emotion was hard to hide.

Gwennol came to see me. "You don't swim very well, do you?" she said. "You must have been born lucky. You'll be more careful next time, won't you?"

"I really didn't realize I was being careless. Who would have thought a boat like the *Ellen* would spring a leak?"

"Any boat might," replied Gwennol. "She hasn't come in yet, so I expect she's drifting out to sea. I doubt she'll ever come back."

I sensed that she was longing to ask about that day I had spent on the mainland in Michael's company, for I was sure Jenifry would have told her she had seen us together. The restraint between us made us both uncomfortable and she didn't stay long.

Jenifry came, her face puckered into an expression of concern. "My goodness, you gave us all a turn. When Jago brought you in I thought you were dead."

398

"It would take a lot to kill me," I said.

"That's a comforting thought," she replied. "I've brought you a concoction of herbs my old nurse used to make. It's said to be very good for shock. Come, drink it. You'll be surprised how well you'll feel afterwards."

I took the glass and set it down on the table beside my bed. "I couldn't drink anything now," I said. "I'm too tired."

"I'll leave you, then," she said. "But do take the tonic."

I nodded sleepily and she went quietly from the room.

There was something stealthy about her. I heard her footsteps going down the corridor and I picked up the glass and put it to my lips. I could smell the herbs and they were not unpleasant. Then I heard old Tassie's voice saying, "Be watchful."

I rose from my bed and took the glass to the window. I tipped out the liquid and watched it trickle down the castle walls.

The Island Necklace

THE next day I felt fully recovered and the first thing I did was to go to the dovecotes. Slack was there, as though expecting me.

I said, "Thank you for coming to my rescue, Slack."

"I may not be big, but I have the Power," he said. "I could have brought you in on my own."

"I'm sure you could, but Mr. Jago happened to be there."

"What happened, Miss Ellen? What did 'ee see?"

"See? Well, I suddenly noticed that the water was coming in. I thought there was something sticky there . . . like sugar."

"Sticky." His brows were wrinkled. "Like sugar, did 'ee say? I wonder what sugar could have been doing in the *Ellen*?"

"I expect I was wrong. I was so frightened. But I'm safe now. I can't tell you, Slack, how pleased I was to hear your voice."

" 'Twas the Power. 'Go along down to the shore. You be needed there,' I heard the voice telling me. 'Tis sometimes so when some little bird needs me. And don't 'ee fret, Miss Ellen. If you do need me, I'll know."

There was an almost fanatical look about the pale eyes.

399

The servants whispered of Slack, "Not all there." But there *was* something there, I was sure. I was glad he was my friend.

Understandably, for a week or more I had no desire to go to sea, certainly not alone. So I stayed on the island and took to going to the dovecotes when Slack was feeding the pigeons.

Once he said, "Did 'ee say sugar, Miss Ellen?"

I wondered what he meant for a moment; then I said, "Oh, you mean when the boat started to sink. Yes, I did think I saw what looked like sugar on the bottom of the boat."

His brow was furrowed. "How did sugar *come* to be there if it hadn't been put there? That's what I want to know."

"Slack, what are you thinking?"

"What if a hole were put there by someone 'as filled it with sugar? There's the Demerara kind . . . brown and coarse-grained, the kind that takes time to dissolve . . . specially in cold salt water. I've heard it said hereabouts more than once that it would hold a leak for a while if you happened to be not too far out to sea and supposing you had a packet of such with you . . . which is hardly likely." His eyes shone with the intensity of his feelings. "You wouldn't see it when you started out and when it did dissolve you have a hole, don't 'ee, what the sugar was bunging up. And the water could get in, couldn't it, where it couldn't before."

"You're suggesting that someone . . ."

"I don't rightly know, but terrible things can happen."

Did he really think that someone had tampered with the boat—*my* boat, which no one took out but me, knowing that sooner or later I should be at sea in it, and almost certainly alone! It was too far-fetched, merely wild conjecture. Who would do such a thing!

"You must be careful, Miss Ellen. Mightn't be a boat next time."

"Next time?"

"I don't know what put that in me mouth, but I want to look after 'ee, you see . . . like I looked after Miss Silva."

"How did you look after her?"

He smiled. "She used to get fits of sadness and wildness, when she wanted to do things that would hurt her. Then she'd come and talk to me and the Power would show me how to soothe her."

400

"And that stormy night when she took a boat and tried to cross to the mainland . . . Did you know she was going?"

He hesitated, then said, "Yes, I knew she were going."

"Something must have happened to make her leave so hurriedly. What, Slack? You *must* know." He was facing my question with silence. I went on. "She was my sister. Just think of that."

"Her weren't like you, Miss Ellen. There couldn't have been two ladies who were so different. Her come to me afore her left and said, 'Slack, I be going away to a place where I'll be happy as I never could be here.' Then her gave me something. Her said, 'Keep these, Slack. Someone might want them someday.' "

"What did she give you?"

"I'll show 'ee."

He took me into the pigeon house, and in the cupboard there was a box which he unlocked and opened. Inside were two notebooks like the one I had found in the desk. A great excitement seized me. "Have you read them, Slack?"

"They be too much for me, Miss Ellen. I can read only little words. Then when you said about the sugar it was as though Miss Silva spoke to me. 'Let her read 'em, Slack.' "

He put the books into my hands. "I hope I be doing right."

"Thank you, Slack. I shall never forget what might have happened to me but for you," I told him earnestly.

"Master Jago were there, were he not? He just happened to be there. But I be mighty glad I were there too."

I did not think about what he meant until later. Meanwhile, I lost no time in shutting myself in my room with the notebooks.

The scrawly handwriting was a little more mature than that in the first notebook. It began: "Those were good days in a way when my stepmother was here with Baby, and when they went I was terribly lonely. At first I thought my father might like me more if there was no competition. How wrong I was! I found that out when he sent for me soon after my stepmother had gone. I was about thirteen. I had let myself imagine that he was going to tell me we would now become friends. All he wanted to tell me was that my latest governess had given notice. I was lazy, stupid and

401

useless, but as he could not allow it to be known that he had a little savage in his household, he would engage a new governess. If he had any complaints from her, she'd be the last."

After a blank page the writing began again: "There is nowhere one can go without being aware of Jago. Since my father's stroke he has taken over completely. Yesterday I was in the garden picking roses. I turned suddenly and Jago was beside me. He always seems to be assessing me and that makes me nervous. He said, 'My sister, Jenifry, is coming to live at the castle with her daughter. They'll be company for you. You'll like that.' Jago has a way of telling you what you are going to like and daring you not to."

Another blank page. Then: "Gwennol is about eight. She is much brighter and prettier than I ever could be. I think Jenifry resents my being the daughter of the house. The idea of anyone's being jealous of me is comic! I'm glad they're here though. Gwennol shares my governess."

There was no more writing in that book. I picked up the second. "My life is so dull and I'm getting old. My father, I have been told, has said that he will not waste money on bringing me out. Jenifry always tries to push Gwennol forward in her social life. She has become quite friendly with Michael Hydrock, the most eligible bachelor in the neighbourhood.

"She came to my room last night. She had been to a garden party at Hydrock Manor and she was all excited because Michael had been particularly nice to her.

" 'You're in love with him,' I said.

" 'Everybody's in love with him. Oh, wouldn't it be nice to have everyone in love with you?'

" 'As not one single person ever has been, I can't say.'

"Gwennol said, 'Poor Silva! I'm going to take you to Hydrock Manor. You know, *you* might meet someone there.'

"It's night and I can't sleep. So I'm writing. This room seems full of shadows. Perhaps that's because I've been so unhappy in it.

"Jago has changed. Two days ago we rode around the island and he talked about things in that way he has—as though it's the most important thing in the world. I was excited when we came back to the castle. Why is Jago suddenly becoming so interested in me?

"Yesterday Fenwick was sitting alone in the garden. 'Where is my father today?' I asked.

" 'He's having a day in bed, Miss Silva. He's a very sick man.'

" 'I'm sorry,' I said. 'I wish he would see me.'

"Fenwick shook his head. 'Whatever you do, miss, don't come to his room. That would just about finish him, the state he's in now.'

" 'Why does he hate me so? Did he want a son?'

" 'Maybe, but he's not one for children.' Fenwick shrugged his shoulders and seemed anxious to end our talk.

"I wouldn't *say* this to anyone, but I can write it. I think Jago is contemplating asking me to marry him."

Jago and Silva! I hadn't thought of that.

I stared at the book in my hand. Why had Silva given the books to Slack? I read on: "I met *him* today. I went over to the mainland and he happened to come to the inn. He is so distinguished and handsome. I can't believe he could be interested in *me*. Why didn't we hire horses and go riding together, he said.

"What a day it was! I am so happy. We had cider and meat pies at the Corn Dolly, a beautiful, romantic place.

"He said, 'We must do this again.'

"Is it possible to be in love so soon, I wonder?"

Was it Michael Hydrock she was in love with? And was he really in love with her? Or was he merely being his charming self?

"Who wants to write when one is happy? He says he loves me. It is all so exciting. He says we shall be together and everything is going to be different."

Then I read: "The artist was on the mainland today. He asked the two of us to Blue Rock Island and he was very hospitable. He showed us his studio and his paintings. It was a lovely day, as it always is when we are together."

The rest of the pages were blank. Although I felt I had come closer to Silva, what had happened on that fateful night of the storm was more than ever a mystery.

He whose name she did not mention had told her he loved her. She was not the kind to imagine that someone loved her. In fact, I

403

think it would be rather difficult for a man to convince her that he did. And then she had gone out in a boat to face almost certain death. Why? Had she, the child who had never felt wanted and who suddenly found someone she believed loved her at last, discovered that she had been bitterly deceived? Or had someone lured her to go out and risk her life?

My disquiet increased as a vision of Jenifry's face, when she had seen me saying goodbye to Michael Hydrock after he had brought me home to the island, rose before me.

I put the books into a drawer and locked it. Then I asked myself if Slack, who knew something of Silva's story, had given them to me as some sort of warning?

Jago rowed me over to Sanctuary Island.

"I've noticed you haven't been on the sea since the accident," he said. "But you don't feel afraid with me, do you, Ellen?"

"I've no doubt that if we overturned you'd bring me safely in."

We came to the island and he helped me out of the boat. He spread the travelling rug on the ground and we sat down.

"Ellen," he said very seriously, "I want to talk about the future."

"Your future?"

"And yours. In fact, I hope they will be intermingled."

I looked startled and he moved nearer to me.

"Since you came here, even the island has taken on a new meaning for me. I've always loved it, always been devoted to making it prosperous, but now everything seems so much more important."

My heart started to beat very fast. He put his arm about me and drew me to him.

"Ellen, I can't believe you're indifferent to me."

"Nobody could be indifferent to you, Jago."

"You mean they must either hate me or love me. Which is it for you, Ellen?"

"Of course I don't hate you."

"Then you must love me."

"I believe there can be a halfway feeling."

"I have no patience with halfway feelings. I love you, Ellen. I

404

want you to marry me without delay. I want to go straight back to the church and put up the banns. I think it has to be three weeks before a wedding. Come."

He had sprung to his feet, but I remained seated. "You go too fast, Jago," I said. "This time last year I had not thought of marrying anyone. Then I became engaged and my fiancé was shot. Now you are suggesting that I marry you in three weeks."

He stared at me in amazement. "What has calculation of a year and weeks to do with it? I love you. You love me. Why wait?"

"Because I'm unsure."

"*You* unsure! You're not some silly simpering female who can be pushed as the wind blows."

"That's exactly so. Please, Jago, listen to me. I'm becoming fascinated by the island, but I don't want to hurry into anything. I don't *know* you well enough. You must understand that."

"Ellen, I thought you knew all you wanted to know about me. However, I know enough for both of us. I know that I love you, that nobody ever meant to me what you do, and that I wasn't really living until you came. Our marriage would be the best thing that could happen to us. Imagine us together for the rest of our lives on the island; we'd make it a paradise."

"Jago," I said, rising, "thank you for asking, but . . ."

He caught me and held me fast. The heavy lids had come down over his eyes, as though he did not want me to see all that was there. He kissed my lips then and I felt an immediate response to his passion. It had never been like that with Philip.

I broke free. "No, Jago," I said. "There's so much to consider. I still can't forget what happened in London."

"You'll soon see it as a fortunate release, my darling."

"It was not very fortunate for Philip."

"Let the past bury itself. You can't mourn him for ever."

"No, I suppose all that will recede eventually, but I must be sure first. I love the island and I have so much enjoyed being with you. If we were never to meet again, I should be unhappy. When I'm with you I think I love you, but give me time to be sure, Jago. Let us go on for a little longer as we have been. Do this for me."

We were standing very close and he held my hands tightly. "Dearest Ellen," he said. "I will do anything you want." He picked up the rug and slung it over one arm; the other he slipped through mine as we went down to the boat.

He rowed me back in silence, and when we entered the castle he said, "Ellen, come to the parlour for a moment. There is something I want to give you." I went with him, and from a drawer he took out a necklace made of roughly hewn stones strung together on a golden chain. "It's the Kellaway Island necklace, and has been worn by our family's women for three hundred years," he said. "These stones—topaz, amethyst, carnelian and agate—were all found on the island, and similar ones can still be picked up if you search the shore at the right time."

I took the necklace in my hands.

"You will give it to our daughter and she will give it to hers, and so it goes on—a link through the ages."

"I think it is too soon for me to accept the necklace."

"That's not so." He took it from me and fastened it about my neck. His hands lingered there. "It becomes you. You are the rightful wearer. So wear it, Ellen. To please me."

I hesitated, for I thought of it as a betrothal ring. And I wasn't sure what I really felt about Jago. I wanted to be with him more than anyone else—yet I didn't really know him.

I left him and went to my room, and the first thing I did was to open my mother's sketchbook and look at the portraits of him. I had seen the kindly, protective Jago often. What of the other one?

Then I turned the pages. The book opened easily at the one I wanted. The room—the homely, pleasant room. Even as I looked at it, depicted so accurately there on paper, the feeling of doom remembered from the dream crept over me.

WHEN I went down to breakfast next morning Gwennol was there alone. She smiled at me in a more friendly fashion than she had done for some time, and I hoped that she realized that her jealousy regarding Michael Hydrock was unfounded. She asked if I had fully recovered from the accident; I told her I had.

"What an ordeal you've been through!" she said. "It's enough to put you off going to sea for a long time, I should imagine."

"Oh, I shall get over it. It doesn't do to give up just because something like that happens."

We chatted easily, and as we came out of the dining room, Slack ran into the hall holding a piece of paper in his hand.

"It's a message for me, is it, Slack?" Gwennol asked eagerly.

"No, Miss Gwennol. Not for you."

She looked bitterly disappointed and Slack stood uncertain for a moment. Then he said, "It be for Miss Ellen."

I took the paper. On it was written: "Fenwick found. I'll be at the inn this morning to take you to him. M.H."

I felt the colour rise to my cheeks. If Fenwick would talk to me about my father, then I really would begin to learn something. I said, "Slack, will you row me over to the mainland this morning?"

"Why yes, Miss Ellen. In half an hour I'll be ready."

"Good." I hesitated, wondering whether to tell Gwennol what the message contained, but she turned and left the hall. It was too late to explain now, so I went to my room and changed.

Slack was ready with a boat and in a short time we were at sea, heading towards the mainland and the inn. Michael was there to greet me. "I've already told them to have a horse waiting," he said. "So we can start at once. The house is about eight miles inland, close to the moors. Shall we go?"

"Yes, I can't wait to see Fenwick."

We rode out of the courtyard together. It was a lovely crisp morning with a touch of frost in the air—rare in these parts.

"He wasn't easy to find. The man seemed determined to hide himself," said Michael. "But he has agreed to talk to you. I felt it best to warn him of your arrival."

We had left the sea behind and all at once the glory of the moors burst upon us. The bright wintry sun shone on the streams, which a few days before had been trickling over the boulders and were now frozen into immobility. We skirted the moor and came to the little hamlet of Karem-on-the-Moor. Fenwick's cottage was small but charming. Ivy climbed its walls, and a small path of

407

crazy paving ran from the front gate to the house. As we tethered the horses, the door was opened by a neatly dressed man.

Michael introduced us, said that he had business in the neighbourhood and would call for me in about an hour.

Fenwick took me into a small room in which a fire was burning. We sat down and he asked, "Now what can I do to help?"

"There is a great deal you can tell me about my family. I can't understand why my father was so indifferent to us . . . to my half sister, to myself, to my mother."

"He was not indifferent to your mother nor to you. . . ."

"Why did she leave him?"

"She could not settle down on the island. She wanted him to take her away, but he said he had his duty there."

"But when she ran away he didn't care."

"He did. She had tried to go before but he stopped her. He ordered that no boat was to leave the island without his permission. We never discovered how she did get away. Obviously someone helped her."

"And what do you know about my half sister, Silva?"

"She was a morose girl who gave a great deal of trouble."

"Did my father not care for her? After all she was his daughter."

Fenwick hesitated, as though he were considering whether he should tell me what he knew.

I prompted him gently. "It is my family, you know. Even if there is something strange, I should like to know it."

He said, "Your father was not sure that Silva was his daughter. He discovered that her mother, his first wife, Effie, had had a lover in his absence on business, and he half believed that Silva was the result of that liaison. Your father was never positive and he could not bear to look at the child. Effie died of pneumonia when Silva was quite young. Self-righteous people are often cruel, Miss Kellaway. And I didn't think you'd really like to hear too much about your father."

"But I want to *know*. Then he married my mother. What of their life together?"

"He met your mother in London and he changed a little when

he brought her back to the island. But she found the place oppressive. They weren't compatible, and I think he was very disillusioned when he realized he had made another mistake. The fact is, Miss Kellaway, he was not a man for marriage. His temper was too short; he expected too much. It was the same with the island. He was not popular with the people. Now the island is a much happier place—and more prosperous—than it was in your father's time."

"Jago is for the island heart and soul," I said.

"Jago is a very ambitious man—in a great many ways more suited to rule the island than your father was. Your father resented him for this, and there was often tension between them. And Jago felt a certain bitterness because he belonged to the illegitimate branch of the family."

"But my father recognized Jago's superior ability to run the island by leaving everything to him."

Fenwick looked at me incredulously. "But by now you must be aware of the contents of the will."

"My father's will, you mean?"

"Certainly. *You* are the heiress of the island. You will be twenty-one next year, and you will come into your inheritance."

"*My* inheritance?"

"Of course. Your father was a man with a strong sense of justice. You were his daughter. He was sure of that. Jago was to hold the estate in trust for you until you were twenty-one, when it would become yours. If you died without heirs, your half sister—because after all he was not entirely certain that she was not his daughter—also was to inherit. In the event of your both dying without heirs, everything was to go to Jago."

I was astounded. I, who had grown up thinking of myself as the Poor Relation, had all the time been an heiress.

"Your father was a very rich man. With the price of land what it is and the prosperity of the island, you stand to inherit at least a million pounds. But surely Jago has informed you of this."

"I have heard nothing of it. Can it be that you are mistaken?"

"I should be very surprised if I were. Your father discussed it with me. I was more than a secretary. He trusted me. He thought

409

it unfortunate that he had not known you since you were three. He said that on his death you must return to the island, learn about it and, he hoped, come to love it. He assumed that Jago's dedication to the place would become known—and necessary—to you. 'Of course,' he once said to me, 'she will marry, no doubt, and if she has a husband he might be able to do for the island all that Jago does. That will be a matter for her to decide.' "

I was speechless. This had completely changed my outlook. I said at length, "I thought I was Jago's guest. I was sure he was lord of the island. I am quite bewildered, not so much because I am an heiress—although I have yet to consider what that will mean. It is the fact that I knew nothing. . . ."

"Perhaps Jago had his covert reasons for not telling."

I felt myself flushing. Why, of course Jago wanted to marry me! The island would be mine, and I fancied he loved it with a passion he might not be able to give to anything—or anyone—else. The scene was falling into place, and my chief feeling was one of hurt.

"Your father was generous to me," Fenwick was saying. "He left me enough money to live on in comfort." He rose and went to a writing desk in the corner. He sat down and wrote something on a piece of paper, which he handed to me. On it was written "Merry, Fair and Dunn" and an address. "Your father's solicitors. It may be that they are looking for you. It's only a year since his death. They will confirm—or deny—all that I have told you."

"How strange that, having made such a will, he made no attempt to find me."

"He didn't want his life complicated at that stage. It's information which you should know now, however."

I thanked him, and told him he'd been ever so much more helpful than I could possibly have hoped. When Michael returned I showed him the address; he said he would take me there immediately. The solicitors' offices were in a town nearby.

And so, that afternoon, I learned that indeed they had been searching for me to inform me that I was the heiress to a considerable fortune which I should inherit when I was twenty-one. That was but a few months away. Until then it was held in trust, and

410

Jago Kellaway had the power to manage the estate; my father had strongly advised allowing him to continue to do so.

There was something else. It was true that in the event of my death without heirs, Silva Kellaway was to inherit the island. Since she was undoubtedly dead, Jago Kellaway was next in succession.

This last piece of news set the alarm bells ringing in my mind, but I didn't want to listen to what they were trying to tell me.

MORE than anything I was eager to confront Jago. I could not get rid of the thought that if I were not there, with Silva presumed dead, it would all belong to him.

Jago was not in the castle when I returned. Jenifry told me that he would not be back until dinner-time, and so I went to my room to change. But it seemed alien and filled with menace. When at last it was time to go down to dinner, my heart beat uncertainly.

Jago was there. "Have you had a pleasant day, Ellen?" he asked.

"Very interesting, thank you. I went to the mainland."

Gwennol was eyeing me coldly.

"What! Deserting our island again!" said Jago.

Our island, Jago, I thought. You mean *my* island.

I wished we were alone. How long the meal seemed. As soon as it was over I said, "Jago, I want to talk to you."

His eyes lit up. Was he thinking that I had come to a decision? And being a man who could not imagine defeat, would he be certain that I wanted to marry him?

I faced him in the parlour. "Today," I said bluntly, "I have been to see Mr. Fenwick and he gave me the address of Merry, Fair and Dunn. Mr. Dunn explained to me the terms of my father's will."

Jago did not seem in the least embarrassed. "Then you know everything," he said easily. "How did you locate Fenwick?"

"Michael Hydrock found him for me."

"Oh? Is he interested in your inheritance?"

"What do you mean?"

"That he goes to a great deal of trouble for you."

"It was a friendly gesture. He is very rich, I should imagine, and would not possibly be interested in my inheritance."

"Don't be too sure. Often those who appear to be rich are in urgent need of money."

Jago is attacking, I thought, when he should be on the defensive. "You knew all this when you came to London," I accused.

"Ellen, let us not be melodramatic. As your guardian I wanted to get to know you and to inspect the man you were to marry. Philip's death made it possible for me to ask you here, so that you could come to love the island before you knew it would be yours."

"Why?"

"Because, my dear Ellen, if you had heard that you were to inherit a remote island which could, if sold, represent a great deal of money, what would you have done?"

"I should have come to see it, of course."

"And very likely have sold it at once—to some unknown person. That was something I dared not risk."

"And you thought I would marry you before I knew that the island was mine."

"That has nothing to do with our marriage, except that it will be profitable for you to have me here to work with you."

I looked into those heavy-lidded eyes; they held secrets. I felt wretched because I could not trust him, and yet I knew that whatever he had done, my life would be meaningless without him.

"Oh, Jago," I began, and he came swiftly to me and held me tightly in his arms.

His lips were on my hair. "I'll look after you, Ellen," he said. "You've nothing to fear with me to protect you."

I broke away from him. "It's all so unnecessary," I said angrily. "Why did you have to come to London so mysteriously—why?"

"I did not want the Carringtons to know that I was around, because, Ellen, I was making inquiries about them."

"About the Carringtons? They are a well-known family not only in England but internationally."

"Exactly. Then why should they be so happy about their son's marriage with a girl who was, it seemed, penniless?"

"They had so much money it was not important."

"Ellen, I believe they knew of your inheritance and that was

412

why they were eager for the marriage. They wanted that money. The island would have been sold and the proceeds would have been used to back up the Carrington empire."

"This is wild speculation."

"Things are not always what they seem, my darling. I'll admit I did not want this island to pass out of my hands. The greatest joy I have ever known was when I met you and loved you on the spot."

"Your joy would have been less had I not been the heiress."

"Of course. But I was determined to have you for my own, and I would have found some means of saving the island too."

My common sense was telling me not to accept what he was saying, but common sense had no chance against such magnetism.

"Now, my dearest Ellen," he went on, "you will look at the island through different eyes. We'll work together. We'll have children, and we'll bring them up to love this place as we do."

"I have not yet said I will marry you."

"You are being perverse; you know you are going to do as I say."

"I think at times you believe you are a god."

"If you don't have a high opinion of yourself, no one else will." He gave me a steady look. "Why aren't you wearing the Kellaway necklace?"

"The clasp is weak. I'll get it repaired," I said, realizing he had talked himself out of a difficult situation.

I said I was very tired. But he held me against him for a time. "Good night, sweet Ellen. Don't be afraid to love."

Very firmly I said, "Good night, Jago." And I retired to my room. I could hear the wind rising and I went to the window and looked out on a sea just visible in starlight. The waves were beginning to have that white-crested ruffled look.

Could it possibly be true that the Carringtons had known I was an heiress? And Philip? I was sure he was without guile, but would his family have used him?

It was inevitable that I should have the dream that night. There was the room again—more familiar than ever. I could hear the whispering voices. The door was opening slowly. Then came the terrible realization that doom was just beyond it.

THE NEXT DAY I avoided Jago. I wanted to be alone to sort out my thoughts. The cool practical side of my nature must take command. I climbed to the top of one of the hills from where I could look down and see most of the island. How beautiful it was—very green, touched with the gold of the gorse bushes; and brooding over it all were the stone walls of the medieval edifice that had housed Kellaways for centuries. And this would soon be mine.

A man was slowly climbing the hill. There was something familiar about him. I must be dreaming. But how like—

"Rollo!" I cried.

"You're surprised," he said as he approached. "I'm staying at the island inn. I have business in Truro and I thought I'd look you up on the way. I've come to ask you to forgive me. I'm afraid I was quite obnoxious the last time we met. I've suffered many a qualm since. After all, Philip's death was worse for you than for any of us. And now that I can look at it more calmly, I agree—he could not have killed himself. I had to come and see you, Ellen, because I wanted to ask you to forgive me."

"I do understand. We were all distraught. I am so glad you no longer believe that I was responsible. How is Lady Emily?"

"The same as ever. She often speaks of you. By the way, the landlady of the inn told me you had an accident."

"Yes, my boat sprang a leak and overturned. I don't swim very well and stood little chance of reaching the shore. Fortunately a boy from the castle and Jago Kellaway rescued me."

"What a terrible thing to happen! Was the boat brought in?"

"No, it hasn't come in yet, and I suppose it won't now."

"My dear Ellen, you must take greater care. Tell me, are you going to stay here long?"

"It seems to have become my home. I never had a real home before. I like this place more and more every day."

"It's a rich and very profitable island, I imagine."

Just then I glanced down at the shore and saw Tassie. "Look," I said, pointing her out. "She's gathering limpets and crabs for her love potions and other concoctions."

"She appears to be a disreputable old crone."

"I hope she hasn't heard that. She'd ill-wish you. Oh, she's seen us." I waved a hand. She waved back and went on her way.

"Did she see me with you, do you think?"

"Certainly. Old Tassie sees everything. That's why her prophecies come true. Her eyes are open."

Rollo took my hand and said, "So I am forgiven? I can go on my way with a good conscience?"

I nodded. "Thank you for coming. Will you call at the castle?"

He shook his head. "No. I have to leave the island shortly. If I have time, I might stop by on my way back."

"That would be pleasant," I said.

As we went our different ways—he to the inn, I to the castle—I thought of Jago's suggestion that the Carringtons had been after my fortune. That seemed quite absurd.

It was two days later when Slack came to me in a state of great excitement. "Miss Ellen," he said. "The *Ellen*. She have come in. I were watching for her. I saw her and I swam out and brought her to my special cove where nobody goes. Come. I have something to show you. I don't like it, but we got to look at it."

He led the way down to the cove where the boat lay.

"That's not the *Ellen*," I said at once. "There's no name on her."

He looked suddenly sly. "I painted it out," he said.

"Why?"

He looked lost. "I can't rightly say. It seemed best. But look 'ee here." And he directed my gaze to the bottom of the boat. A hole was bored there.

"Miss Ellen, you did talk of sugar. Well, if a hole were bored and packed tight with a packet of Demerara sugar, 'twould take a little time to dissolve and that's what it did. 'Tis clear as daylight."

I stood there staring, and then I was aware of Slack beside me, gently laying a hand on my arm. "Miss Ellen, if you do be in trouble, come to me. I'll help you."

"Thank you, Slack," I said. "I'm glad you're my friend."

I can't bear it, I thought. Someone chanced that I would go out in that boat alone and saw to it that I would not come back alive.

415

In the Dungeons

FEAR was stalking me. I was certain now that whoever drilled a hole in my boat wanted to murder me. Could the reason be this beautiful, fertile island?

I went to the room on the ground floor which my mother had used. There was a certain comfort in sitting on the old settle and thinking about her. I could not get Silva out of my mind. Was her story in some way connected with mine?

Silva. Could someone have pretended to be in love with her—perhaps because she was her father's eldest daughter, who, it was thought, would inherit the island? And had that someone discovered that the island had been left to someone else—myself?

Jago's face rose before me, intense, passionate. I almost wished Slack had not found the boat, with the evidence of that hole.

I refused to think of Jago as the one who had made that hole in the boat, and my thoughts went to Michael Hydrock. What if he had been the one with whom Silva had fallen in love?

Then I thought of Jenifry and Gwennol. Jago might want the island, but Gwennol wanted Michael Hydrock.

And as I sat there brooding I heard a sound. A cold shiver ran down my spine. The door was slowly pushed open. It was only Slack.

"Oh, it be you, Miss Ellen," he whispered. "I knew someone was here like. It be a good spot to be when there's trouble about."

"What an odd thing to say. What's so special about this room?"

"Miss Silva, her did come here. You be watchful, won't 'ee?"

"Tassie also said that, Slack. It would be easier if I knew what to watch for."

"If you be feared sometimes, Miss Ellen, I'll be watchful for 'ee. Come to me first and then to this room. Then I'd know you was here. That would be best. 'Twas what I told Miss Silva."

"So she came here and then you came too?" I asked.

He nodded. "Miss Silva, her trusted me, her did. You trust me too, Miss Ellen. So you come here when the time do come."

416

THE SEA WAS BEING roughened up by the wind, and a boat was bobbing about on the waves. I left the cove and climbed the cliff, where I found a spot among the gorse and bracken. It was easier to think up here, away from the castle.

I was wearing a cape of greenish hue, and sitting there in it I almost merged into the landscape.

I watched the boat come in, and as a man stepped out into the shallow water the fancy came to me that I had seen him before.

Suddenly I heard Jago's voice and saw him ride down to the cove. Then he cried out, "How dare you come here like this?"

I couldn't hear the man's answer but could see that Jago was very angry. Then the wind dropped for a moment and I heard the man say, "I have to talk to you."

"What can you be thinking of . . . to come *here?*" said Jago.

The man was gesticulating and speaking earnestly, and I was frustrated because I could not hear his words.

"All right," said Jago. "I'll see you tonight. Keep yourself scarce till then. Meet me in the dungeons. We'll be out of the way there. Be at the west door at nine o'clock, but you're wasting your time. You'll get nothing more from me. Go back to the inn now and stay in your room till tonight. You'll be sorry if you disobey."

With that, Jago turned his horse and rode off. The man stood gazing after him. Then he looked up at the cliff. I shrank into the bracken though I was certain he could not see me. But as he lifted his face I realized with a shock that it was Hawley, the Carrington groom who had watched Philip and me in the park.

I sat still, staring out at the sea. What connection could there be between Jago and Hawley? A feeling of dread assailed me.

That Hawley was afraid of Jago was obvious, but on the other hand, Jago was so angry at the sight of him that he might have something to be afraid of too. Jago must have known he was coming—he had been at the cove to meet him and was anxious that Hawley should not be seen. By whom? By me perhaps. I was the one who had seen him in the Carrington household.

What had Jago to do with those horrifying events in London? And Hawley? He had come here to ask something of Jago. What did he know of Philip's death? It wasn't suicide; and if that was so, then it was *murder*.

I knew that I must be hidden in the dungeons to hear what Jago and Hawley had to say to each other. This was the only way to unravel the terrifying mystery.

It seemed as if evening would never come.

I put on a dress of biscuit-coloured silk, and because Jago always looked to see if I had on the necklace of island stones, I decided to wear it. As I fastened it, I noticed once more that the clasp was not very strong, but it would hold.

Jago did notice the necklace. He said, at dinner, how becoming it was with that coloured silk, but I sensed that his thoughts were elsewhere. When the meal was over, Gwennol and Jenifry went into the parlour to take coffee. Jago did not join them, and I murmured something about having a letter to write.

I did not go to my room but slipped straight out of the castle and quietly made my way across the courtyard. I was terribly afraid that Hawley might already be in the dungeons, in which case I should be discovered.

It was a bright night, for there was a full moon and it touched the castle walls with an eerie light. I was full of trepidation as I descended the spiral staircase to the dungeons.

I stood in the circular enclosure surrounded by doors and looked about me. There was something repelling about the place, but I managed to push open a door and enter one of the cavelike dungeons. A faint shaft of moonlight filtered through a small barred window, but it was enough to show me the moist walls and earth floor. The cell was cold and smelled unwholesome. Nevertheless, I went farther in and half closed the door.

I waited. It must have been nine o'clock when I heard footsteps and the creaking of the enclosure door.

Through the dungeon doorway I saw a ray of light. Jago was carrying a lantern. "Are you there?" he shouted.

I cowered in my dungeon and wondered what his reaction would be if he discovered me.

Footsteps at last.

418

"Well, here you are," said Jago. "What do you mean by sending a message that you were coming to the island?"

"I had to see you," said Hawley. "I'm in debt and I need money. Just a little something. I did a good job for you."

"You were paid for what you did, Hawley. I'm no longer employing you. You made a pretty good mess of it too, I must say."

"It wasn't easy," said Hawley. "And after all the trouble I got into . . . I might have been accused of murder."

"You weren't. There was a verdict of suicide."

"It could have been different. Think what a tricky job I had to do. I had to get friendly with that maid Bessie and find out what your young lady was doing. Then I had to get the key cut for you."

"It was child's play," said Jago.

"I wouldn't call it that when a man was killed."

"You should have managed better than you did. Now listen, Hawley, you're saying, 'You pay me or else.' There's a name for that and it's blackmail. I won't have it, Hawley! I'll lock you up here and hand you over to the courts."

"I don't think you'd like some things to come out, Mr. Kellaway. The young lady—"

Jago interrupted. "If you think you can blackmail me, you've made a big mistake. Just remember what happened in Philip Carrington's bedroom."

"I was only working for you. . . ."

I felt limp with horror. I leaned against the wall, my fingers clutching unconsciously at my necklace. Could it be that Philip had been cold-bloodedly murdered by a man employed by Jago to kill him? And why? Because Jago knew that I was the heiress to the island and wanted to marry me himself.

There was a second or so of silence in the dungeons and during it I heard a slight clatter.

Jago heard it too. "What's that?" he cried sharply. "There's someone here. Did you bring someone with you, Hawley?"

"I didn't. I swear I didn't."

"I'm going to look," said Jago. "I'll search every one of these dungeons. You hold the lantern."

The light shifted and I peeped through the doorway. They had their backs to me and had started searching the dungeons on the other side. I waited, my heartbeats threatening to choke me, until they were as far as they could be from my cell. Then, while their backs were still turned, I slipped out silently. In a flash I was up the staircase, luckily unseen.

I reached the main building and forced myself to join Gwennol and Jenifry in the parlour. I picked up a magazine and leafed through it, my mind busy planning what I ought to do next. What I had heard this night had brought home to me one overwhelming truth: whatever Jago was, whatever he had done, I loved him.

I knew he wanted the island; but he wanted me too.

Jago was coming into the room now. I kept my eyes on the magazine, but I could feel his gaze fixed upon me.

He sat down beside me on the sofa and said, "Have you lost something, Ellen?"

I looked at him in surprise. His eyes were gleaming and there were conflicting emotions there—passion, reproach and a certain amusement. The amusement of a cat playing with a mouse?

He held out his hand and I stared down at it in horror, for there lay the necklace and I knew at once what that clatter in the dungeons had been. The catch was weak; I had grasped the necklace in my agitation and when I had let go it had fallen to the floor. Jago had found it; he knew I had been there and what I had heard.

"Ellen," he said gently, "what on earth were you doing in the dungeons? It takes courage to go there at night."

"I'm not afraid," I said, looking straight at him.

He put his hand over mine and gripped it hard. "I have a good deal to say to you. Will you come into my study?"

"I'll join you there shortly," I said.

"Don't be long."

I must consider what I have heard, I thought. I ran down to the hall and out across the courtyard. Slack was at the dovecotes.

"You look proper scared, Miss Ellen. Have the time come?"

I thought of Philip . . . shot. Had Jago really ordered that?

Slack was saying, "Don't be afraid. It'll be as it was with Miss Silva. Maybe there is no time to lose."

He took my hand and we went into the castle. He picked up a candle in the hall and lighted it as we entered my mother's sitting room. He approached the settle and lifted the lid. "Now you see, Miss Ellen, this ain't no ordinary settle." To my astonishment he raised the base, which came up like another lid. I could see down into darkness. "There be steps. Do 'ee see 'em? Go down 'em . . . very careful-like. I'll follow 'ee."

I got into the settle and lowered myself and my feet found the steps. I went down six of them. Slack handed me the candle and followed me, after shutting the lid and base of the settle.

"Where are we?" I asked fearfully.

"This be a great cave which do go right under the sea. 'Tis where I brought Miss Silva when she did fly away."

"What happened to her?"

"She did live happy ever after, as she told me she would. It goes down deep. Down and down and up again. 'Tis no more than a quarter of a mile long—the distance between Kellaway's Isle and Blue Rock. That's where it comes out. It's what they do call a natural cave, but the entrances was made in the old smuggling days. It weren't much used since then. I know about the cave from my mother, who knew of it from her father, who knew of it from his. Ships could come from France, and liquor would be unloaded and stored here until safe to bring it to the mainland."

"And when we get to Blue Rock, what then?"

"The artist will help us. He helped Miss Silva. He had a real fancy for her. Her went away to live happy ever after."

"And the boat that was washed up?"

"That were a trick like. Her weren't in it. 'Twasn't till later on a dark calm night when she did cross."

"How do you know all this, Slack?"

"Well, I helped her, didn't I? Her father had been terrible cruel to her, and she thought he'd laugh at her and try to stop her if he knew, so she ran away with her own true love."

"Where did she go?"

"That I never heard on, Miss Ellen. Be careful now."

Down we went, down a steep slope below the sea. It was damp and cold and we passed little pools of water; at times my feet sank into the sand and the surface changed to rocks. Fortunately Slack was surefooted and knew the way.

"Now," he said, "we are beginning to go up. It's a climb. But we'll soon be on Blue Rock and then Mr. Manton will be ready to help 'ee get to the mainland, if that be what you want."

I did not want to leave the island. I only wanted a day or two to think clearly about everything. I wanted to talk to Jago, to demand an explanation. But not just yet. First I wanted to try to stand outside the enormity of those emotions which Jago aroused in me and assess the situation dispassionately. I wanted to discover how deeply involved I was with an unscrupulous man who might well have been involved in Philip's murder.

I wouldn't accept the fact that Jago didn't at least love me a little; perhaps in time he would love me even more than the island. How obsessed I must be by him to be so ready to compromise.

But what if he did not love me? What if, after I had married him and willed everything to him, he'd have no further use for me? All I knew of Jago was that I loved him. That was all. But is it possible to love a man whom one can suspect of murder? The answer seemed to thunder in my ears: "Yes, yes."

There was one thing he was unaware of. He thought Silva was dead, but Slack assumed she had eloped with the lover of whom she wrote and continued to live happily ever after. If that were true, then on my death she would be the next in succession.

"Can 'ee hear the sea?" asked Slack. "We be nearly there."

Now we were right out in the open, pushing our way through bushes, and I could feel the fresh air on my face.

"There be the house," said Slack as he took my hand and dragged me forward. The door was open, and he went through, calling, "Mr. Manton. Mr. Manton. I be here with Miss Ellen."

There was no answer. We had stepped into a small hall, and Slack pushed open a door and we entered a room.

I felt my senses reel. There it was—the red curtains tied with

423

gold fringe, the brick fireplace, the rocking chair, the gateleg table, and even the painting of the storm at sea hanging on the wall.

In every detail it was there—the room which had come to me so often in my dreams.

THIS was surely a nightmare. I had somehow strayed into the dream. "Slack," I murmured, "what is this room?"

"You'll be all right here," he said soothingly. "Miss Silva were . . ."

My eyes were fixed on the door which had been the centre of the dream. It was not the one through which we had entered—there were two doors in this room.

The handle slowly turned. The door was beginning to open.

This was it—the moment when the terrible sense of doom had come over me—just as in the dream, except that this was not a dream but the actual moment of revelation. I was terrified of what the opening of the door would reveal. The artist! I thought. What has he to do with my life? Why should I fear him?

The door opened wide. A man was standing on the threshold. Not the artist, though. It was Rollo.

Amazement was quickly overtaking fear. Rollo! What could Rollo possibly be doing at Blue Rock?

"Ellen!" He smiled. "How good to see you here."

I stammered, "I—I had no idea. I thought the artist lived here."

"He's gone to London for a few days. He lent me his place. You look scared out of your wits. Come. Sit down. Let me get you some wine."

"I'm sorry," I said. "I'm so bewildered."

Slack was staring at Rollo. I heard him whisper, "Something terrible have happened to Miss Silva."

Rollo led me to the gateleg table and made me sit down in the chair which I had seen so many times in my dreams.

"You must tell me what happened, Ellen," he said. Then he poured something into a glass and put the glass into my hand. "Drink this. It will steady you. I can see you've had a shock."

"There's a tunnel from here to the castle," I began.

He did not express any surprise. "I was concerned about you,

424

which is why I didn't leave the vicinity. I felt something was going on, and I couldn't get that affair of the boat out of my mind."

"You think someone was trying to murder me?"

He nodded. "I'm sure of it."

Not Jago, I thought. I won't believe it was Jago. "I want to get away to the mainland," I said. "I'll stay at the Polcrag Inn—at least until I've thought all this over."

"Of course. I'll row you across." Suddenly he seemed alert and distressed. "Where's the boy you brought with you?"

I looked behind me. Slack was not there. Rollo stepped into the hall, closing the door behind him and calling Slack.

Now that I was in the room alone I examined it with awed wonder. I went over to touch the window curtains. It was hard to believe that this was more vivid than even my most vivid dream.

My mother must have been in the room often, for she had re-created its every detail in her picture. Why and how it had played such a part in my dreams was what baffled me.

The door opened and the familiar feeling of fear began to creep over me.

It was Rollo, his face distorted in anger.

"I can't find the boy. Why did he run off? What did he say?"

"Something about Silva. She was my half sister. He said something terrible had happened to her."

"He's crazy, that boy."

"I don't think so. His mind works in a strange way, that's all."

"He's an idiot," said Rollo. "You haven't had your drink. You'll feel better for it, you know."

I took a sip. "I want to go to the mainland," I said.

"Finish your drink first, and I'll get the boat."

"I've left everything at the castle," I said.

"Why did you leave in such a hurry?"

"It seemed necessary then. Now . . ."

"You regret it?"

"Yes, I should have waited, should have talked to Jago. . . ."

My voice seemed to be coming from a long way off. Rollo was smiling at me and the room seemed to be dissolving about him.

425

"I feel very strange. Rollo, what's happening?"

"You're getting drowsy. It's the drink. A little sedative. You needed that—and so did I."

"You, Rollo?"

"Come. We're going to the boat. That's what you want, isn't it?"

I stood up, swaying unsteadily. He caught me.

"Now," he said, "it will be easy. Curse that boy, though."

He led me out of the house. The cold air revived me a little. "What happened?" I cried.

I heard Rollo laugh softly. "I didn't expect such luck. It'll be over soon. Come down . . . down the slope to the shore."

Something warned me. The doom feeling I had known in the dream was very strong. "I want to see Jago first. I *must* see Jago."

I slid to the ground. I was lying among the bushes. Rollo was trying to pull me to my feet, but I clung to the nearest bush with all my strength. For a terrible realization had come to me. The dream had been right. My doom had entered through that door, and my doom was Rollo.

The drink had contained more than a little sedative. I knew that now. Rollo meant to overcome my resistance so that he could do with me what he wanted. And something told me that what he wanted was to kill me. But why? Why Rollo?

Even at such a time I was able to feel relief, because I had been wrong about Jago. Oh, Jago, why did I run away from you?

Rollo was dragging me from the bush. He lifted me. "Don't struggle. It won't help you and will only make me angry."

It was hard going for him carrying me. I heard him curse against the sound of the breakers. And somehow I knew that he was going to row out and throw me into the sea; I would be unable to struggle because of increasing drowsiness.

I heard the boat scraping on the sand. He lifted me up and put me roughly inside. I tried to climb out, but he was ready.

"You've had a charmed life, Ellen . . . until now."

"Rollo, you came down here to kill me. Why?"

"You're in the way. That's all. If Philip had lived, this wouldn't have been necessary."

426

This was the end, then. My sleepy body would receive the embrace of the sea and my heavy clothes would drag me down.

But I was wrong.

There was a shout, and I heard Rollo's furious exclamation. And there was Jago himself on the shore, then wading out to sea. He knocked Rollo aside and snatched me out of the boat.

"Ellen." I heard his voice through the waves of sleepiness which swept over me and I was filled with exultation. "My Ellen."

I awoke in my bedroom in the castle. It was daylight and Jago was sitting by my bed. He bent over me and kissed me.

"All's well, Ellen. I love you; you love me, although I must say you didn't show it last night. I waited and waited for you to come to my study as you'd promised. Then I searched everywhere for you. By that time Slack had come back in a state of alarm. He said you were on Blue Rock with a man who intended to harm you."

"How did he know?"

"He'd seen him before on the island. Apparently, Rollo had had the house on Blue Rock for a week or more."

"So he could have tampered with the *Ellen*. Why . . . why did he want to kill me?"

"It's a simple reason. With you out of the way his wife would have come into a great deal of money."

"His wife?"

"Silva. You see, she's not dead. That boy Slack, pretending to be half-baked and knowing so much more than the rest of us!"

"Silva. Rollo's wife! Rollo wanting money. I can't believe it."

"The Carrington empire is tottering. They'd seen it coming and that was presumably why he married Silva. Then he discovered the contents of your father's will and that you came first. So they arranged for you to marry Philip, which would have made them sure of the Kellaway fortune."

"Philip. Oh, Philip! What happened to him? I heard—"

"Yes, I know. You were eavesdropping in the dungeons. The necklace betrayed you. But how could you have doubted me?"

"I had to know. I was afraid you might have done something. . . ."

427

"Which would have stopped your loving me?"

"The one discovery I made was that nothing can do that."

"Then your doubt was worthwhile. But if that devil had been minutes earlier he would have had you at sea. The worst could have happened."

"Tell me everything, please."

"I've had to piece a lot together, but it seems to me your father was not sure that Silva was his daughter; he suspected that she was James Manton's. So did Manton, because he and Silva's mother had been lovers. Rollo, who was interested in art, met Manton at a London exhibition and heard from him about the island and the Kellaways. He came, and met Silva on the mainland. He never crossed over to the island, so I didn't see him before that encounter in the house you were considering in Finlay Square.

"He had discovered that Silva was the elder daughter and naturally believed that she would inherit the island. So he married her secretly—she was worried your father would object—and took her to London. Your father died and only then did the Carringtons discover that you were the heiress, so they devised the plan for you and Philip to marry. In the meantime, I came to London to see you and learned that all was not well with the Carrington interests. I understood why they were so anxious to welcome you. I engaged a private detective—Hawley, rather a shady character—to make a thorough study of their affairs. By serving in their household he found out more than I ever could. I attended the Carrington soiree, where I promptly fell in love with you."

"And what do you know about Philip's death?"

"It was an accident. A disastrous thing to have happened. Hawley was going through some papers in Philip's room when Philip disturbed him. Philip kept a pistol under his pillow and he threatened Hawley with it, demanding to know what he was doing. Hawley lost his head and struggled with Philip to get the pistol from him. It went off, alas, killing Philip. Hawley is a sharp character. He arranged it to look like suicide, and got away with it."

"Then you didn't hire him to kill Philip?"

"Certainly not. I was horrified by his death."

"But he was going to marry me, taking the island with me."

"I was planning to lay before you all the information I had gathered about the Carringtons, and I had a notion that you were at that time questioning the wisdom of rushing into marriage with Philip. I was counting on getting you to postpone the wedding for a while."

"And you got Hawley to have a key cut for you."

"Yes, I did. I thought that if we met in that house by chance I might be able to hint at something. I'd do a great deal to get you, Ellen, but I'd stop at murder. I was so anxious about you. I didn't trust those Carringtons. Then Philip's death changed everything. But that's the past. There's so much to plan for. Just think of it, Ellen . . . the two of us together on the island."

The Outcome

I MARRIED Jago a month later.

Everything was clear to me by that time. Rollo's body was found a few days later. After his encounter with Jago he had had no alternative but to try to reach the mainland. However, the sea was not in a benign mood that night. A few weeks later the collapse of the Carrington interests was announced in the papers; a great many people had lost money in the crash, and there was talk of a prosecution which might have taken place if Rollo had lived. It was presumed that he had deliberately chosen death by drowning.

I owed so much to Slack, who, when he had seen Rollo, had recognized him as the man with whom Silva had run away. But somehow he had instinctively known that this time he was there for no good purpose. So he had hastened back through the tunnel and summoned Jago.

Gwennol eventually married Michael Hydrock, and Jenifry went to live with them. Jenifry and I are quite good friends now—though we could never be close.

And I have found Silva. Her brief honeymoon with Rollo had soon ended and, when she realized that he was not in love with her, she had been more heartbroken than ever before. He had kept her shut away in a lonely country house while he sought to get his hands on the island fortune.

I brought Silva back to the castle. I call her my sister. And although it may well be that James Manton was her father, we both like to think it was otherwise. The artist is a kindly man, and we often row over to his island and have tea in my dream room.

It has not been easy to nurse Silva back to health. She was, at first, furtive and suspicious, and I taught her that there were people who love her. Slack has been helpful too. He is delighted to have her here and looks upon us both as his special protégées.

When my first baby came—Jago, after his father—Silva began to change. She adored the child and the others too. They love her dearly and I think that at last she is happy.

I never dreamed my dream again, but I think I know why it had haunted me. My mother had lived on uneasy terms with my father and was determined to escape. Her maid, Mrs. Pengelly, knew of the tunnel to Blue Rock, and one night, so I later learned from her, they escaped through it with James Manton's help. My mother carried me in the tunnel and to that room, and I would have sensed her fear that my father might come through that door to prevent her escape; I must have felt that fear so intensely that it haunted my dreams in the years ahead.

How I love the island! How I love my life here! Jago and I are full of contentment and plans for the future.

Often we lie on the cliffs and look down on the cove where I saw Hawley come in; we look up at the sky and see the pigeons now and then, perhaps carrying a message to Michael and Gwennol at Hydrock Manor; and sometimes we talk of the past.

"It's all yours now," said Jago.

"Ours," I reminded him. Yes, I thought, ours—this fair island, these beloved children, this good life. Ours.

Victoria Holt

"I chose Victoria because my stories are Victorian, and Holt, for the name of my London bank branch. It seemed a good omen. And, as it turned out, it was."

And so best-selling author Victoria Holt was born—the most successful of a series of pseudonyms used by this author in a writing career spanning more than thirty years. She is almost equally well known as Jean Plaidy and Philippa Carr for books more heavily accented on history, and at the last count well over 30,000,000 copies of her books had been sold worldwide, putting her into the millionaire class in terms not only of dollars but also of fans.

Despite extensive foreign travel, Miss Holt still finds Cornwall one of the most fascinating, inspiring places of all. "I have spent many summers there," she says, "in a house right on the coast. On clear days I could look out my bedroom window and see a rockbound island. I would hear the sea thundering in the caves and wonder what it would be like to live on such an island. And so the story of *Lord of the Far Island* began to take shape in my mind.

"Recently I acquired an ancient house of my own in the town of Sandwich—a vital seaport during the Middle Ages. The house is called the King's Lodging, because Henry VIII stayed there when it was the local inn. In 1572 Queen Elizabeth visited the house and reviewed the fleet from my drawing-room window."

She confesses lightheartedly that it all makes a startling contrast to her modern penthouse flat overlooking Hyde Park, where she lives for most of the year. Her only serious domestic worry in London that she can remember during a lifetime of living there occurred quite recently when it seemed that King Hussein of Jordan might buy the penthouse next door. Miss Holt foresaw endless problems: security checks in the hall every time she went out shopping, getting mistaken for the king and being kidnapped by some terrorist group for ransom . . . Fortunately the king did not take the penthouse. Perhaps he foresaw similar dangers in his being mistaken for a top-selling international author.

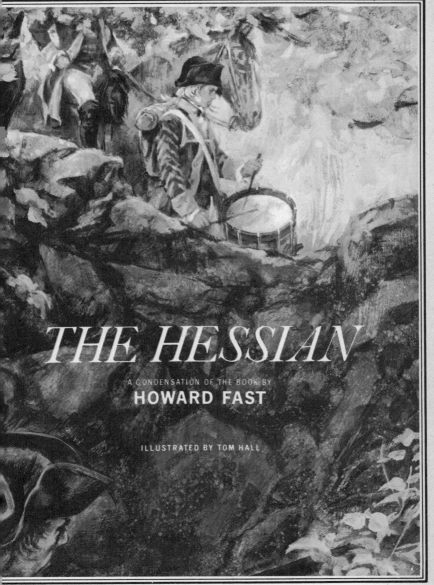

THE HESSIAN

A CONDENSATION OF THE BOOK BY

HOWARD FAST

ILLUSTRATED BY TOM HALL

PUBLISHED BY HODDER & STOUGHTON, LONDON

For Evan Feversham, a country doctor and a Christian, the American War of Independence had been a sad, bitter experience. But now the war was ending. Even the detested Hessians, mercenary soldiers paid by the British, were leaving. There were citizens who would have had mercy on those few who did remain. But there were others who still burned with the need for vengeance.

In this deeply moving book we see events through Dr. Feversham's eyes. We see vengeance in action in one small township, backed by the full, cold panoply of the law. But we see love also, Christian love at its simplest and best, and the tender, courageous love of a woman for a man.

It's a quiet story, yet fired by the passionate involvement of a master storyteller—an utterly unforgettable tale of that historic war two hundred years ago.

Chapter One: The Priest

Toward four o'clock of an afternoon in middle May, 1781, the priest appeared, and the following day the whole thing began. It was the priest who told me about the ship in Long Island Sound.

He came riding up the road from Norwalk on a donkey—so small a donkey that the rider's feet barely topped the ground. It had suddenly turned hot, the first heat of early summer, and momentarily the glowing new green of springtime seemed dusty and old. Somewhere the priest had lost his hat, and the sun was turning his bald head the color of ripe apples.

Mrs. Feversham and I were in the garden, where I was directing Rodney Stephan, our man-about-the-house, how to prune the grape arbor—not that grapes are anything to speak of in this wretched Connecticut soil—when I saw the priest. I walked through the garden to the road and waited for him, watching silently as he climbed down from a makeshift straw saddle. "Dr. Feversham?"

"If you will."

"My name is Father Hesselman, and I am a Roman Catholic priest—if you will—" with a slight smile, "and I am very thirsty."

I nodded understandingly, and my wife meanwhile sent Rodney with a clay mug for cold water out of the well. He returned with a full quart and the priest drained it.

"How did you get to me, Father Hesselman?"

"They told me in Norwalk that there was a Catholic doctor up on the Ridge. I'm passing by on my way to Rhode Island where I am called."

I asked him to stay for dinner. He had a clean cassock with him, and after he had shaved and washed he appeared to be a most pleasant man indeed. He blessed our table and then dug into the roast ham as if he had not eaten in a fortnight.

I had put a good French wine on the table in honor of our guest—the first Catholic priest I had seen in a long, long time—and he drank it with appreciation. It was pleasant to see the little man come to life, admiring all the elements that go to create a little touch of civilization on the Connecticut High Ridge—our silver, linen, china, good food—and with his belly full, he leaned back and ventured to speak of our religion.

"Well," I said, "I have not made my confession for more than five years, I have not prayed with a pure heart, I am married to a Protestant woman"—I nodded toward my wife—"withal a lovely one. For three years I led a regiment against the British, not because I love the colonies but because I hate the damned English, who put my father to death for no other reason than that he was a Catholic; so even if I am not in a state of grace I remain Catholic because the British are not."

"Then you'll be interested to know there's a British frigate in the Sound, at anchor off the river mouth. What do you people call it now, Saugatuck?"

"Right."

"There she was, with ship's boats going back and forth. They were slaughtering meat on shore. Soldiers standing all around and keeping guard."

"Redcoats?"

"No. Soldiers in green coats with yellow facings. Black boots, white knee breeches—"

"Yes, Hessians." I added as kindly as I could, "I am not really interested in Hessians, Father Hesselman, or in the war which should be done with and drags on and on and on."

436

Somewhat diffidently the little man asked me in what I truly was interested?

"My immortal soul, if I have one."

He reassured me. "You fed me and will give me bed, so I shall pray for you in return for the love and kindness from you and your good lady."

THE following morning before sunrise I found the priest praying in the garden; and then we both sat on the bench and he heard my confession. With daylight he was on his way, clutching a basket of bread and meat that Alice had given him.

It was out of that ship Father Hesselman had seen that the Hessian detachment came. Why they had to make their way the fifteen miles up onto the Ridge, I will never know. If I could make up this story, it would be of one piece, but in its truth it is full of gaps, holes and unanswered questions, even though I was privy to more of it than anyone else, and some of it was of my own cause.

For one thing, it was I who insisted to Jenny Perkins, who was schoolteacher over at Ridgefield, that Saul Clamberham could learn. He had come into her school towering over the children there, and while some of them realized that he was harmless, others were terrified of the oversized half-wit with his loose, slobbering speech.

When they brought the matter to me, I said to let him go sit in back of the school. "He wants to learn. He's not mindless, only addled, and what harm does he do if he sits quietly in school?"

Squire Abraham Hunt had come with her to see me. What did I have against Squire Hunt, except my own petulance at the sort of a man he was? He was a commanding man, and I suppose I don't like commanding men who know precisely what is right and what is wrong. He made decisions, and his decision was that a physician should examine Saul Clamberham and bundle him off to the madhouse in Boston.

"Saul's harmless," I said. "And he will not learn to read, Miss Perkins, not ever, but I think he could learn small counting, if you give him just five or ten minutes after school."

437

"And why not give him the lessons yourself, Colonel?" Hunt enjoyed using my military title because he knew I had cast it away.

"I would indeed, but he would have no faith in learning outside the schoolhouse. If Miss Perkins supplies him with an old piece of slate and a bit of chalk, he will be no more a nuisance."

She finally agreed, and that is how Saul Clamberham came to his bit of broken slate and his small skill at addition. So there was the priest and the British frigate and Saul Clamberham, whose mind was addled, but so without hate or resentment or gall that sometimes I felt he had the better of all of us. That's how it began.

Chapter Two: The Hessians

RAYMOND HEATHER was a Quaker who had bought a freehold on half a hundred rocky acres on the Ridge. He had been there seventeen years, cobbling shoes in the wintertime and raising sheep in the summer, but he was still a stranger, a recipient of the grudging grace that Connecticut extended to Quakers, Papists, Jews and others of the damned. He had a daughter of sixteen named Sally, a boy of twelve who bore the name Jacob, Annie who was four, and a toddler of twelve months named Joanna. He had a strong, cheerful wife, Sarah. Since he knew the game of chess—withal a bad player—we spent an occasional winter evening together.

It was his boy, Jacob Heather, who saw what happened between the half-wit, Saul Clamberham, and the Hessians; and except for Hans Pohl, the Hessians' drummer boy, he was the only witness.

The detachment was landed from the frigate; and two squads of them—sixteen men, an officer and the drummer, eighteen in all—were selected to march up onto the High Ridge. Someone suggested that another British warship had sailed up the Hudson River, and perhaps the Hessians were sent to sight it, since there are places on the High Ridge where one can see both the Hudson River and Long Island Sound.

Their first day's march—on the same day that the priest came to my house—was made quietly and carefully, wide of the Post Road to Danbury, and they camped for the night somewhere on the Saugatuck River. No one saw them that day, or if anyone did, they kept quiet about it. And since the war was down in Virginia now, only a damn fool would take any measures to reintroduce it into Connecticut.

So no one bothered the Hessians.

Jacob Heather had gone out to fish before sunrise the next day, and climbing over Hightop, he saw the Hessians coming up the trail from the creek. Saul Clamberham was among them and had a rope around his neck. The Heather boy watched from down in the new fern and dry leaves, and then it happened, no more than fifty yards from where he lay.

They hanged Saul Clamberham.

Sometimes on a warm day Saul would bed down on a pile of dead leaves in the woods. So he must have done on this day, and the beat of the Hessian drum probably awakened him. He had a piece of slate and a butt of chalk, and he decided to make a counting game with the Hessians.

Perhaps he knew that they could see him, and perhaps he felt secure, for everyone knew that he was a half-wit. In any case, the Hessian commander, Captain Wolfgang Hauser, ordered his sergeant to tell off a detail to take the spy. Saul didn't even try to run away, just stood there grinning at them, and when they examined the slate he nodded proudly.

I imagine that they suspected something wrong about him, his loose lips and his shambling walk; but in war men do not think or react as normal men do. They are full of fear and anger. Still, in all fairness to the Hessian officer, Hauser, he did not act at once but led Saul on for two miles while he turned the matter over in his mind. Hans Pohl, the drummer boy, said afterward that he felt the decision the captain was coming to and it made him sick at heart to think about it.

When they were just below Hightop, where Jacob Heather lay hidden, Captain Hauser drew up his horse in front of a tree and said flatly to his sergeant, "This will do. Hang him to this tree."

He spoke in German, but when the sergeant threw a rope over a limb of the great spreading ash which loomed over the road at that point, Saul realized what they were up to. He began to blubber and went down on his knees. He pleaded for his life as best he could, while Hauser sat on his horse, patient, formal and attempting to be very correct. The sergeant detailed four men to drag the rope, and the captain ordered Hans Pohl to beat a roll.

"God have mercy on your soul," the captain said.

Then the four men walked the rope away, and Saul Clamberham was hoisted into the air, where he strangled to death.

It was not a pretty sight for a twelve-year-old boy to see, and Jacob lay frozen in his bed of leaf and fern until the Hessians marched away, leaving poor Saul's body swaying from the tree.

It was the same morning, as I said, that I bade Father Hesselman good-by; and then I mounted my horse and rode off to the village inn. When I arrived I went into the taproom, and there was Abraham Hunt, holding his morning magistracy.

There was never love lost between Hunt and myself, but whatever I hold against him personally, as a magistrate he is fair and objective. He was in the process, that morning, of fining Salem Alan five dollars for poaching Isaac Leeds' land, and Salem Alan was his friend and cousin.

Then suddenly Jacob Heather burst into the taproom, weeping and sobbing and trying to speak. Half a dozen men were there and half a dozen kids who had picked up Jacob's path on their way to school—so it made for quite a crowd.

The boy saw me and buried his face in my coat. I thought it was only the other boys after him to give him more of the endless bullying that came to him because he was a Quaker and therefore sinfully different from themselves. After a moment his sobs were easing, and I held him away from me, asking him, "What is it, Jacob? What is it?"

Then he managed to get the words out. "Saul Clamberham is dead."

440

"Where? How? Speak up now, boy!" Hunt cried, taking command of the situation as he always did. "Stop that blubbering."

"The Hessians caught Saul Clamberham and hanged him."

"The boy is a liar," someone said. "There be no Hessians in all Connecticut."

"He's not lying," I said. "There's a British warship off the Saugatuck across the islands, and they landed Hessians."

"How do you know?" Hunt demanded.

"A Catholic priest stopped by for the night. He told me he saw them. Why don't you listen to the boy?"

"All right, Jacob," Hunt said, his voice flat and dry. "Where were you when you saw them?"

"On Hightop track."

"How many were they?"

"Sixteen and a drummer boy and one on a horse."

"All right." Hunt stood up and said to Salem Alan, "Muster the militia. I want at least thirty men, mounted, and I want them one hour from now at Naham Buskin's place. And tell them to load with heavy bird shot for close range." He turned to me. "Will you go with me to Hightop, Feversham? The poor devil could still be alive."

We rode hard and reached the big ash in no more than twenty minutes, and there was Saul Clamberham's body swaying in the feathery new leaves of the tree.

"He's dead," I said. I knew it without touching him. His neck was broken, his face swollen and purple. I dismounted and took out my pocketknife.

"What are you going to do?" Hunt demanded.

"Cut him down. We'll take him to Buskin's."

"There's no time. Understand me, Feversham—I'm going to stop those Hessians from going back to their ship."

"With the militia? Hunt, you're not serious."

"I've never been more serious in my life, Feversham," he said heatedly. "They've hanged a man—our man. They're up here on our Ridge. What is it, Feversham—are you afraid of them?"

I cut the rope now and lowered Saul's body to the ground before

441

I answered him. "If you want it that way, Squire, I am afraid—yes. I have lived through seventeen battles in my lifetime, in France, Spain—and here too. I have been afraid every time. This war is over, Squire, and they're beaten; but still these Germans are the best soldiers in the world. I say, let them get back on their ship and sail away. Then perhaps we can live the way God meant us to."

I tried to lift Saul's body, but he was more than I could manage.

"Let go of him," Hunt said, shouldering me aside. Abraham Hunt weighed sixteen stone, and most of it bone and muscle. He lifted the body and set it across the saddle of his horse in one easy motion. "All right, Colonel," he said. "We have time to lay Saul out in a Christian manner and meet the Hessians too."

He was not to be shaken by reason or mercy but was wholly directed to the simple fact of revenge. There are times when you have the feeling that no force or argument or plea can alter circumstances; one event moves in the tracks of another with the mindless motion of a great ox. So I felt then, and we went on in silence to Naham Buskin's farm.

His outlying field sloped up to the Indian track and shielded itself behind a long stone wall. On the other side the ground fell away, and I saw what was in Abraham Hunt's mind. I had to admire the man for his scope and imagination.

As we rode past the stone wall and down the hill, we saw the militiamen coming in by ones and twos. They rode through the young grass of Buskin's pastures, framed by the new May leafing, and they made a lovely, almost fanciful picture from the distance. By the time we reached them there were thirty-two present, and during the next few minutes four more rode in.

Abraham Hunt climbed onto the well housing and told the men what he intended to do. I heard it out of one ear, for I was making arrangements with Mrs. Buskin for Saul's burial as well as for bandages, some sharp knives that I could use for instruments— since mine were at home—scissors, needles, clean linen thread and a small saw.

Meanwhile Hunt laid out his plan for an ambush from which there was no escape. The plan was practical and brutal, and in less time than it takes to put this down, the whole lot of them were running behind Hunt, hot on the trail.

I took a few minutes more to complete my supplies and then I followed, but did not run. I still walked with a gimp from a shot I had taken in the leg. When Hunt saw me coming up the slope he waved frantically for me to get down. I chose a spot between two of the militiamen and laid out my collection of makeshift equipment behind the wall. There were thirty-six militiamen against the eighteen Hessians, but most of our men did not think that evened the odds and they did not share Hunt's absolute resolve and confidence. They were farmers and storekeepers, a blacksmith and his two helpers, two carpenters and a cooper, and Saxon, the undertaker. The youngest in the group was fourteen, and the oldest was ninety-one. Hunt walked along our ranks, telling the men to be quiet and to pray silently if they must, and not one blessed word did he want out of them.

"You'll stay down behind that wall until I give the signal"—he hooked his pinkies in his lips and whistled softly—"that signal, and then you up and fire. Once you fire, reload, and if you're still alive and whole, continue firing at anything moving in that road. But remember that it's the first fire that counts and if you botch that, God help you! I want the ten men at each end to box the column—to kill the leaders and the trailers—and the rest of you shoot at whatever is right in front of you. And aim—don't just blow your piece. Aim. You all got scatter shot, so aim on the shoulder halfway to the elbow, and then if you pull your gun, you'll still have your target. Overprime your pieces, and if you don't spark, keep your head and cock and shoot again. That's it."

Silence then—no sound but the breathing and an occasional rustle or crunch as one of the men shifted his position. Hunt came over to me and said half mockingly, "Well, surgeon—ready?"

I looked at Hunt without answering him.

"Feversham," he said, "one day, you and me, we'll have a long talk and get out all the worms that are eating us. If there's nothing else about you I like, you've got guts."

Still I didn't answer, for it was too late to talk any more about

443

the horror he contemplated. Hunt was wrong. I had no guts. I knew too much about war, and Hunt knew too little.

For a full half hour we lay there and nothing happened. I regretted now that I had not had enough presence of mind to get our men to bring along a few buckets of water. If you can't wash a bleeding wound the work is twice as difficult; yet I knew that Hunt would raise all kinds of hell if I even suggested that we send a man back for water.

The thought of water made me realize how dry the men were, how dry their lips which they licked constantly, while their hands were wet with nervousness. They rubbed their hands on their breeches, and sweat beaded their brows and wet their clothes. Yet they remained quiet. The meadow and woods life around us relaxed as the men remained still; the robins came close and the blue jays waxed bold. A chipmunk perched upon the stone wall and regarded us. Overhead the May wind blew and the lovely new foliage rustled with the excitement of spring.

Then we heard the drum. My scalp stiffened and a cold chill raised gooseflesh on my arms. The Hessians' drum said, Here we are and be damned to you! Such was their confidence in themselves and their contempt for the Yankee farmers of Connecticut.

The drumbeat approached, a steady marching beat, and now we could hear the sound of their boots. I glanced at Hunt.

He was in the act of putting his fingers into his mouth. An instant later his piercing whistle cut the air and the militiamen behind the wall stood up and fired their guns—all of them except the Cutler twins, fourteen years old, who remained under the wall, frozen with fear.

I stood up with them, and in that moment of confused, exploded sight—which is all one ever has at the joining of battle—I saw the Hessian detachment cut down. Shooting point-blank at targets only a few feet away, the militiamen could not miss. The Hessian captain's head was blown open and another shot tore his horse's throat, yet it leaped the wall, dragging the officer's body by a stirrup, and then rolled over dead in the meadow. The others lay in the road, some of them twisting and screaming but most of them dead in-

444

stantly, yet our men were reloading like mad and firing again and again. Powder smoke began to blanket the road. They fired into the smoke, and all the time they were screaming and yelling, their screaming mounting in intensity as the sounds from the Hessians died away.

I limped across to Hunt as he was loading his gun again and I shouted, "Hunt, for God's sake, stop it! Some of them may be left alive! It's murder now!"

He never heard me. He was looking past me across the meadow, and in spite of myself I followed his eyes, and there, on the other side of the meadow, where it sloped up again onto a high hill, a Hessian was running. It was the drummer boy, his drum swinging wildly behind him. He paused for a moment, unhooked his drum and flung it away, and then raced on into the woods.

Chapter Three: The Chase

I HAVE seen places of death, but this was more terrible than any I had ever looked at before, and when I walked among the bodies the blood splashed from under my boots and made a ghastly sucking noise with each step. The narrow ditch of the trail was still acrid with the smell of gun smoke, but there was no sound. Even Abraham Hunt held his peace, and the militiamen stood in horrified silence, staring at what they had wrought. I went from body to body—sixteen men in a little river of blood. "Pray God Almighty, let one of them be alive and live!"—the first time I had asked God for anything in a long while, and this time it was for the impossible gift of life where there was no life.

"All dead?" Hunt asked, his voice muted.

"All dead, Squire Hunt, all dead," I replied.

"The officer's in the field with the horse," he said.

I walked away from him then, climbed over Buskin's wall and went to the officer. The sight of him lying there with his brains pouring out was more than I could take, and I began to vomit.

Coughing and gasping, I came out of it to see Hunt watching me.

"We'll have to bury the horse," he said, and then he walked over to the Hessian officer and stared at him for a long moment.

"Do you know the insignia, Feversham?" he asked.

"He's a captain. It's a forester regiment. They call them jägers. They're very good."

"Not good enough. You know only one of them got away?" Hunt was bending over the officer, going through his pockets. He came up with a wallet, which he opened and riffled through. He handed me a letter.

The script was beautifully controlled. There were many words I did not understand, but I could read enough of it to get the drift.

"Squire! Squire!" Isaac Leeds was calling. "Where do you want the rings and money?"

"Lay them out against the wall, and so help me God, if one of you takes a ring or penny, I'll see him in hell!"

Naham Buskin joined us. "Squire—you can't bury them here. I'll never sleep a night through if you bury them here."

"My God, man, they're Christian, and there's room enough in the churchyard. There's room for a hundred," I said to Hunt.

"Isaac," Hunt yelled, "send someone for Pastor Dorset."

He backed out of that. Let Pastor Dorset settle it. People were coming across the meadows from the direction of Buskin's farm. There were children running ahead of the women.

"Keep them all away," Hunt growled. "Don't any of you have any sense? Naham! Where the devil is Naham Buskin?"

"Here! Here!" Buskin shouted. He had gone to the wall and was staring at the carnage.

"Can you give us a wagon to put the bodies in?" Saxon, the undertaker, asked.

"That curses the wagon," Buskin said.

"Don't be such a superstitious fool," Saxon told him. "If you don't give us a wagon, you'll have those poor souls swelling up like sausages in the sun."

Buskin went off toward his house, and Hunt turned to me and asked, "What does the letter say?"

446

"It's a letter to his wife," I said. "He never finished it. It's an intimate kind of thing, and he talks about his love for her and his love for his children—three children, I believe—"

"Feversham, that's out of the whole cloth."

"Go to hell!" I told him, and threw the letter in his face and stalked away.

An hour later I rode through my front gate, gave my horse to Rodney Stephan and went into the surgery to clean myself. While I was undressing, Alice came in and gasped with horror at the pile of bloodstained garments.

"What happened?" she whispered. "I heard the guns."

I stood there naked, looking down at my skinny shanks and the great purple gash in my left thigh from the old wound.

"Please bring me my robe," I said to her.

I washed, and then she came with the robe. I wrapped it around me and sat down on a stool, hunched over and shivering. She took the clothes and my boots away.

She brought me a cup of hot broth, and I drank it and felt somewhat better.

"Get dressed, Evan," she said gently. "There is some meat and bread on the table, and you must eat."

I went up to my room, and while I was dressing I heard men and horses at the front gate. When I came down, they rode off. I stepped outside to ask Rodney Stephan what the commotion was.

"The men on the hunt. They would I went with them," he said, "and I told them no, I cannot. They hunt the Hessian boy. They rouse up the whole neighborhood. There never was such a hunt, Dr. Feversham."

I went inside and sat at the table without appetite but drank coffee greedily, and Alice finally said, "It will be better if you talk about it, Evan."

Then I told her all that had happened since I went to the inn in the morning. She sat there regarding me thoughtfully and with affection.

"What shall I say, Evan?"

I shook my head vainly.

"Strange," Alice said. "When I first knew you, I thought you and Abe Hunt would be good friends. There is so much in both of you that is alike."

"Then you know me very little," I answered with annoyance.

"I am only trying to say that Abe Hunt is not just a murderer. He courted me before I married Alex. Then when Alex died, I leaned on him and he was like a rock." Seeing the look on my face she added, "No, he's not jealous. He's well-married with five children, but I only want you to understand that he isn't entirely the person you think he is. He's honest and loyal. If he says the Hessians' money and jewels will go back to the British, somehow they will—"

I shook my head in agreement. "He will return the money. He's a righteous man. You Puritans are an amazing lot, and most amazing is your corner on righteousness."

"And now you're angry."

"Not at all! Oh, no. Myself angry? No indeed." She looked at me with that expression of inscrutable patience that only a woman can wear. And I slammed my chair back and stamped out of the room.

SERVING at dinner, Rodney Stephan told us that the Hessian, though trapped, had somehow managed to claw his way up the hundred and fifty feet of ragged cliff of the Squeehunk Rockface, and then they had lost him. Later that night I was sitting in front of the fire with Alice, when we heard the hounds calling.

Alice, working over petit point, looked up and asked me how old I thought the Hessian drummer boy might be.

"Fifteen, sixteen perhaps. German regiments enlist them at the age of twelve."

"How dreadful!"

"Indeed? The Cutler twins are what, thirteen, fourteen? And they were at the ambush."

"Oh." Then she went back to her petit point, and again, from far off, we heard the baying of the hounds.

"What will they do if they catch him?" Alice asked me.

"Alive? Try him."

"For what? For running away? For being a Hessian?"

"For the murder of Saul Clamberham."

"You're being vile tonight. I trust you know how perfectly vile you are being."

"It's a vile night."

We went to bed then and slept. In the morning there was no word that the Hessian had been taken. After my morning surgery Rodney Stephan came in and told me that Raymond Heather's boy, Jacob, desired to speak with me. When he brought Jacob into the surgery, the small, freckled, orange-haired lad stood there waiting and licking his lips until I told Rodney Stephan to go and leave us private.

"Well, we're alone, Jacob."

"Yes, sir. My father says, thee must come and the need is very great, sir, Dr. Feversham."

"Who is sick? Not your mother?"

He shook his head. "I cannot tell thee."

"Come now, Jacob," I declared with annoyance. "It's four long miles to your place, and you want me to ride over there without knowing why?"

"Yes, sir."

I stared at him, and then understood. I said gently, "All right, lad, I'll come."

Chapter Four: The Refuge

SITTING next to me in the buggy, the boy asked, "Dr. Feversham, did thee kill any Hessians?"

"No."

"Why?"

He was filled with a kind of small-boy agony that I could only sense, and I answered his question in the most direct way I could. "I had no gun."

We drove on in silence to the Heather place, where Raymond

was standing in front of his house, awaiting me. Heather is a man of middling height, pale blue eyes and a long, gentle face. His strength was not apparent, for his lack of animosity was so consistent that one tended to take it for weakness. He greeted me warmly, trying to find a way into explanations, but I said shortly, "Is it a bullet?"

"Then Jacob—" Raymond began.

"No, Jacob said nothing, but neither am I foolish, Raymond."

"Yes, it is a bullet," he said. "In the back, over the shoulder blade."

Sarah opened the door for us, her lovely round face troubled.

"Take this bottle of rum," I snapped at her. "I want boiling water and clean linen, and I want them as quickly as possible. Where is he?"

Raymond led the way upstairs and into the small room under the eaves where Jacob slept. The bed was low and narrow, and the Hessian lay there, his eyes closed, moaning slightly, while Sally, Raymond's sixteen-year-old daughter, wiped his brow with a damp cloth. The Hessian's long, damp flaxen hair was spread across the pillow, and the freckles stood out sharply on his ashen skin.

He could not have been much older than Sally, the yellow down on his cheeks still unshaven, and his scratched, bruised hands were long-fingered and rather delicate.

I felt his forehead, which was aflame with the kind of heat that bodes no good, and then I told Sally to bring me soap and water. There are doctors who believe otherwise, but to me dirt is evil, in a wound or on a doctor's hands.

"Help me turn him on his belly," I said to Raymond. He had put a pad on the hole in his back and a bandage to hold it there, which had at least stopped the bleeding. Now I cut it away, revealing a hole the size of a farthing.

"That's a spent rifle ball, thank God, and no wound he suffered over by Buskin's. He must have taken the ball before the sun went down and lived with it the night through, and now he's got a wretched fever from the wound. Come on, Sally, where's the soap and water?"

450

She brought in the basin of warm water, and I washed my hands, telling her to bring candles. When she'd done that, I told her to remain. "She's old enough to see this," I said, meeting Raymond's eye. I was probing gently for the bullet when the Hessian boy suddenly came into consciousness and screamed with pain. "Hold him," I snapped at Raymond. "Put your knee in his back and hold him down. Sally, get that candle over here!"

Sarah entered the room and handed Sally a second candle. Now I touched the bullet and was brought back to the hundred times I had probed into the flesh of some poor boy on some blood-stinking battlefield.

I took the forceps and went in, but the hole was too small and I had to open the wound with a scalpel. When I did, yellow pus poured out. I glanced at Sally and said sharply, "Look smart, girl, and learn something, and mind what you're doing!"

Sarah handed me pieces of clean linen, and the boy's screaming became a whimper as I found the bullet and drew it forth. The wound was bleeding freely now, and Sarah handed me piece after piece of the linen to wipe away the blood and pus.

"He'll bleed to death," Sally whispered.

"No he won't, my girl. That's the evil humor bleeding out, God willing. If it festers inside, he won't live to see tomorrow, so you just grit your teeth and keep the light with me."

I cleaned the wound thoroughly, and while I worked, the boy's struggling stopped.

Sally cried out, "He's dead!"

"No more than you are," I said, as I took up my needle and gut. I took five stitches in the wound, and then made a pad for it. The boy had fainted, which made it somewhat easier to bandage across his chest and back, and then we laid him out on the bed and made him easy. When I took his pulse, it was at one hundred and ten, which was only to be expected after the shock of the operation. I cleaned my instruments with hot water from a fresh kettle Sarah brought me and then washed my hands and packed my bag.

"Pull a chair by his bed," I said to Sally. "You must care for him now. There is no more I can do at the moment. The next day or so

452

will tell whether he lives or dies. All we can do is watch him and put cold compresses on his brow."

Then we left them and went down the stairs to the kitchen, where Sarah put coffee, bread, butter and cheese on the table. When I lifted the cup of coffee I saw that my hand was trembling and realized that the Hessian boy meant much to me. Jacob and Annie were there in the kitchen, silent and wide-eyed with fright at the screams they had heard, but the baby, Joanna, had slept peacefully through it all. Raymond joined me at the table and ate hungrily.

"I served no dinner today," Sarah said apologetically. "Thee must know, Dr. Feversham, that we are not with ourselves just now."

Sarah's bread was good and so was her country cheese and fresh-churned sweet butter, and like Raymond I had been the day without food. I ate and considered the irresponsibility of fate—that it should place us here, with the Hessian drummer boy, and I began to think of the consequences, when Raymond asked me, "Will he live, Doctor?"

"As God wills—and if God wills him to live, then so much the greater pleasure for Abraham Hunt when he hangs him."

"Ah, no!" Sarah exclaimed. "Squire Hunt is a just man!"

"Sarah, we are all just men and we make the rules of justice. Hunt will hold a court-martial, and I have no doubt that General Packenham will preside. They will find that the boy participated in the hanging of Saul Clamberham. So they will do justice."

"I am afraid, Sarah, that the doctor is right," Raymond said.

"We will pray," she said calmly.

"No, Sarah—thee don't understand me. We will pray, but the doctor is right. They will take the boy and hang him."

"Then," Sarah said calmly, "they shall not take the boy."

"Oh?" And I looked at Raymond.

Sarah pulled out a chair and sat down facing me now. She studied me for a long moment, her lovely gray eyes fixed upon mine, her honey-colored hair loosened somewhat in the excitement. Almost every time I laid eyes upon her I suffered from a sick feeling of hopelessness and desire.

"Now let me say this to thee, Evan Feversham. There is no Hessian. Up in bed lies my nephew from Pennsylvania, who grew up in the Dutch country there, where there are plenty of our people. Raymond will bury his uniform, and in six months it will all be forgotten."

"Sarah, Sarah," Raymond sighed.

"We will do what we must, and God will provide," Sarah said calmly.

THE following afternoon when I came again to the Heather place, Sarah said to me, "Sally is with him. I'm afraid for the lad." While I washed she told me how Sally had scarcely left his side through the night.

All afternoon it had rained steadily, and as I went up the stairs, the rain beat its tattoo over the little house. In the tiny room where the Hessian lay, Sally greeted me with a face of woe and weariness. Somehow this twenty-four hours had turned her into a woman, and I noticed how like her mother she appeared.

"Evan," she pleaded, calling me by my Christian name as her mother did, "Evan, don't let him die. He's kind and good."

The boy was watching us, his eyes moving from Sally to me. With his clean hair like silk on the pillow, and with the almost translucent pallor of his skin, he appeared strangely childlike.

"Who said he's going to die?" Then I said to him, "Boy, can you turn over?" And I asked Sally, "Does he know English?"

"He knows some English, but he's out of his head. He doesn't know what thee is saying."

"Then help me turn him over."

The boy resisted, but his strength was small and we turned him on his stomach. "Can you hold him?" I asked Sally.

"I can hold him. Perhaps he'll know me." And then she said to him, "Hans—Hans, listen. We help thee. Have faith in me."

"How do you know his name is Hans?" I asked her as I cut away the bandage. "How do you know he's kind and good?"

"Because we spoke this morning."

I took the bandage off. The wound was swollen with pus and

454

when I touched the area the boy groaned with pain. I cut the sutures, opened the wound and let it drain.

"What did you give him to eat?" I asked Sally.

"A little broth. A cup. And he drank a lot of water."

"That's good, good."

The draining of the wound had eased him and he appeared to be sleeping.

"Now, look you, girl, I am going to leave the wound open and let it drain. I'll stay here by his side, and you go eat some food, then have a nap."

"He needs me."

"He does not need you now, Sally. I shall do whatever can be done. So get out of here, and don't put your face through that door until I call you."

Then I sat alone with the Hessian, as I have sat with man, woman and child, sick or dying or finding life, so many times that I cannot remember. I don't know what I bring to them, if indeed anything at all; but perhaps I take something from them. Whatever the case, I found some peace there, a kind of quietude where my thoughts calmed and where some sort of prayer for forgiveness and healing worked itself out in my soul.

It became night, and in the stillness I could hear the shrill cry of an owl, the angry barks of the dogs and in the distance the cries of the loons in the great swamp.

The Hessian groaned. I felt his brow, and the fever burned like fire. Then the door opened and Sally came into the room. She brought new candles, lit them and sat down across the bed from me. She explained quietly, "I know he will live or die now, so it is better that I be here, is it not?"

"Perhaps," I said.

"He will only live if his spirit quickens," she said simply.

"And you will quicken it, Sally?" I asked, not sardonically but with actual curiosity.

"Yes."

"Tell me how."

"With love," she said. "I love him."

"Child, you don't even know him."

"I know him well, Evan Feversham," she replied with great dignity. "His name is Hans Pohl. He is sixteen years and nine months of age, and he has been in America three years. His father was a sergeant. I found him, so his life is in my hands, is it not?"

"How do you mean, you found him?"

"He came out of the swamp and hid himself in our barn. When I went in the morning to feed the chickens, I saw his hand under the hay. I took the hay away and wakened him. There was no fear between us. Then I went for my father, who carried him into the house."

"But why do you say you love him?" I insisted. "Unless you speak of your faith, which I suppose is to love everyone if you can."

"That is one way," she said as calmly as if she were talking about the weather. "I love him another way. I love him as a woman loves a man."

"Aren't you being foolish?" I asked, irritated by her calm and certainty. "He's not a man. He's a boy, and you're only a child. How can you love him? You don't know him. He's a stranger."

"There are no strangers to us."

"Have you spoken of this to your mother or father?"

"No, only to thee, to explain why I must stay here. Thee will let me stay here?"

"If you wish. But I must say I think you are talking romantic nonsense, and if you were my own daughter I would shake some sense into your foolish head."

"Then I must be grateful I am not thy daughter, Dr. Feversham, as much as I admire thee."

"I thank you for your admiration, Sally Heather. Now we'll say no more about it. I am a physician and used to confidences, so don't feel that yours are misplaced."

Time passed, and when I finally took out my watch and looked at it, it was half past four in the morning. The boy was breathing easier now. I laid my hand against his forehead. He was cool.

"That's it," I whispered to Sally. "The fever has broken. He's asleep now. It's real sleep." I stood up. "You can leave him."

She shook her head.

"As you wish."

I went downstairs. There was hot water in a kettle and I made myself a cup of coffee, mixing the cold leftovers of the night before with the hot water. I was full of that good feeling a doctor has when someone he is treating draws back from the doors of death.

I stepped out into the cool, rain-washed morning air, remaining there for a moment or two, breathing deeply, staring with pleasure at the east, where pink and rose color flamed in advance of the sun. Raymond came from the cow barn carrying two pails of frothy milk. He set them down carefully in his cold pit and then joined me at the door.

"The boy will live," I said.

"Thank God."

Chapter Five: Hans Pohl

I N THE ordinary course of things Abraham Hunt was not a patient of mine. He preferred to take his infrequent ailments to Toby Benson, the town barber, who knew two things about what he called "medicine"—namely, leeching and bleeding. This local monstrosity had bled half a dozen citizens into an early grave, but since Squire Hunt was by no means unintelligent, he came to me when he contracted gout.

A few hours after I had returned home from Raymond Heather's place, Hunt limped into my surgery. It took the help of Rodney Stephan to get the boot off his swollen foot. When I asked him why on earth he didn't wear a slipper, he looked at me with cold disdain.

"Gout?" he asked me.

I prodded his foot a bit more than necessary and then agreed with his diagnosis.

"What can you do for me?" he demanded.

"Did you catch the Hessian?" I couldn't help asking him.

"Oh? We shall—we shall indeed, Feversham."

"Who knows? He could be off the Ridge and back down to Saugatuck, couldn't he? Time enough by now."

"With a bullet in his back?" Hunt said.

"What?"

"A bullet, Feversham. He caught a bullet, and we found a nice, likely sum of blood. He went into the great swamp and he'll come out, or there he'll die. I can wait. No Hessian will leave this ridge alive—not while I'm here, Feversham."

I prodded his gout again, and he winced. "About this foot of yours. It's a wretched mess."

"You're a physician, Feversham. Do something about it."

"Oh, no. That's up to you, Squire. You go on eating meat three times a day and filling your belly full of port and rum and beer— well, you'll have two gouty legs, not one. A fortnight without meat or drink; gruel and bread twice a day and clean water, and you'll have a normal foot again."

"Gruel twice a day?"

"Gruel twice a day—precisely."

It was poor revenge and I felt quite disgusted with myself. I looked up at Hunt and he was smiling at me.

"You have me, Feversham."

"There's no other cure for it. I'm sorry."

"I believe you are sorry," he said.

At dinner Alice was quiet and seemed lost in melancholy. First I felt that she had taken umbrage at my staying the night at Raymond's place; but when I attempted to explain that the very thought of anything between myself and Sarah Heather was of the stuff of fevered imagination, she snapped at me, "Don't be a fool, Evan, or take me for one. You've been in love with that woman since the first day you laid eyes upon her. But believe me, I am not troubled by any thoughts of yours concerning Sarah Heather. Underneath that saintly face of hers a very dull woman resides. I only wish you could spend a week with her and be properly bored."

"Then what are you so morose about?"

She didn't answer immediately, but a little while later she admitted that she had talked with Abraham Hunt. "I asked him what he would do if they took the Hessian."

"To which he said?"

"They would try him and hang him."

"How splendid! They will not try him and attempt to discover just what he is guilty of. No. They will try him and hang him."

"Evan," she said, "through the long years of this war eighteen boys have gone out of our little township and have never returned. Do you wonder that we feel a certain bitterness toward men who fight and kill for hire? Is it so strange?"

"Perhaps not. I don't know. I can't judge."

"Do you imagine I enjoy thinking that they'll hang this man?"

"He's only a boy, not a man."

"And boys fight the war, don't they?"

I nodded.

"Will he live?" she asked.

"I think so. Yes, he'll live."

Then she dropped the subject and would say no more.

THE following day, when I had finished with the single patient in my morning surgery, I had Rodney Stephan saddle my horse, and I rode off to the Heather place. Raymond was cleaning the barn. He came out to take my horse and to greet me with a query as to whether I preferred black or brown boots.

"It's a damn curious question, Raymond, and if you are thinking of making boots for me let me tell you plain out that I will not accept payment for treating the Hessian. Don't you understand why?"

"I think I do"—Raymond nodded—"but thee are gone to such bitter trouble."

"As you are. And by the way, how is he?"

"Well, he is fretting to get out and about. How can I get the boy away? Where can he go?"

"Back onto that British frigate in the Sound."

"I rode down to Saugatuck yesterday, and the frigate is gone."

"Now that's a devil's mess, isn't it?"

I moved to enter the house, but Raymond laid a hand on my arm and said gently, "Thee will not give him the feeling that we fear for his presence here or that he is a dangerous burden to us?"

"Good Lord, Raymond, I am not afraid for you. Hunt will do nothing very awful to you, but if he ever lays hands on that boy he intends to hang him."

Then I went into the house. Sarah was sitting by the hearth nursing the baby, and I stood there, staring at her breast, suddenly so speechless and forlorn that she was moved to say, "Evan, what ails thee?"

I shook my head hopelessly. She rose, handed me the child, now asleep, and then hooked her bodice over her breast.

"Is there trouble at home? Is Alice well?"

I gave the child back and she placed her in the cradle. "Thee, Evan Feversham, is the strangest of any man I have ever known, but I suppose that being a Papist and a doctor and a devotee of that incredible game called chess all combine to make thee so."

"That's an excellent if somewhat superficial analysis of my character and defects."

"Thee mock me, and it be not kind of thee."

"How can I mock you?" I asked her. "I only envy you."

"Ha! I cook and clean and sew and nurse one child and scold three. Thee has traveled the whole world, been to war, live in a great fine house, and thee is wed to a lovely lady of quality. Well, I do not give a fig for thy envy. Thee is very glib, Evan Feversham, but I love thee, and so enough of that. Will thee look at the boy?"

"Did he eat?" I asked.

"This morning, a bowl of wheatmeal, two slices of bread, two pieces of bacon and a cup of hot milk and treacle."

"Well, that's encouraging, isn't it?" I said, and went up the stairs.

The boy was sitting up in bed. Sally sat in a chair beside him. He broke off speaking as I entered, starting with alarm, but Sally took my hand so eagerly that his fear went, and she told him who I was.

"Dr. Feversham," he said. His English was only fairly good.

460

"I know. I think about it very much. You save my life, so my life belongs to you."

"Your life belongs to nobody but you, Hans Pohl. And as for saving your life, this lassie here and her father and mother—they saved your life. Enough of that. Let me feel your brow."

His forehead was cool. Some color had returned to his cheeks, and he was rather pleasant looking.

"Well, Hans Pohl," I said to him, "you're a lucky lad for the time being. Now I'll look at your wound." Sally helped the boy off with his shirt without any hint of girlish embarrassment. I cut the bandage away, and to my amazement the wound had not only ceased to fester but had already begun to heal. I told him that he could dress that same afternoon and be on his feet.

"Thank you, sir," he said. "I thank you with my whole heart."

"Blessed mercy!" Sally exclaimed, and then bent over the bed and kissed him with delight. When he looked at Sally, his expression was as near to worship as I have ever seen on a human face.

I started toward the door, but the boy stopped me. "Doctor," he said, "listen, please. I have nobody in the world because my father—" He paused, choked up, and then fought to compose himself. "My father was sergeant," he said. "By the stone wall, he died with the others. I did not try to help him. I ran away. I know it is not manly."

"You could not have helped him. It was too late. He was dead."

He nodded at me, unable to say anything else. Then I asked Sally to step out and have a word with me. I took her to her mother's room and closed the door behind us.

"What on earth are you up to, child?" I demanded of her.

"Do thee think I am a child, Evan Feversham? Look at me. I think I am a woman."

"I have no intention of arguing the degree of your puberty," I said with annoyance. "I am only trying to drive some sense into that silly pretty head of yours. Don't you Quakers know anything about war? War is not a game, not a question of ethics or Christianity—war is a bloody damned insanity. Do you know what hate is? Well, of all the things hated by these bluenosed Puritans here,

461

the Hessians are hated the most. I have seen Hessians beaten to death and I have seen their women raped with delight. You don't believe me? Well, as senseless as it might appear, it is just an application of that fine old principle, an eye for an eye and a tooth for a tooth. The Hessians have cut them to pieces, not once but ten times. The Hessians pinned your Connecticut farm boys up against trees and emptied out their guts. That is why, if your militia takes Hans Pohl, they will hang him by the neck until he is dead, and that is why this love, this faith of yours is utterly childish and absurd."

"Have thee finished, Dr. Feversham?" she inquired quietly.

"I am quite finished."

"Since I have asserted that I am a woman, I will answer thee as a woman answers a man. Thee appear to be an authority on hate, but what do thee know of love, sir? Thee make such a small thing of my love. Not for my life would I offend thee, but why do thee offend me?"

"I did not intend to offend you."

"I am sure thee did not, and I am not taking offense at what thee said of my faith, because thee do not know. Jesus Christ said, *Love thy neighbour as thyself*, and this we try to do. But since I was a child I knew that one day I would love a man. This Hessian is simple and plain and homely. Will thee make it sinful or senseless that I love him? This is where thee offend me."

"Sally, Sally," I begged her, "we must get this boy away from here and we must not be hindered by your feelings."

"Do thee think my feelings hinder thee, Evan Feversham? It was I who urged my father to ride to Saugatuck and look for the British ship. But now there is no way to take him away. Is there? Tell me how thee will take him to safety, and see how I hinder thee." With that, she walked out of the room.

Back in my own home, I told all of this to Alice, and she asked, "What is the boy like?"

"Well, I've seen a thousand in the army who could be twin to him: middling tall, fair skin, blue eyes, straw-colored hair. I might

462

say that he has an honest face, if I were given to that kind of defi-
nition. The sergeant who was shot down with the others was his
father."

"Oh, poor lad!" Alice exclaimed. "Do you believe that Sally
Heather is truly in love with him?"

"I am not sure that I know what truly in love means."

"It means the feeling I had the first time I saw you, Evan."

"And what was that feeling?"

"Evan—that you should ask me!"

It was ever that way. We would begin and come toward each
other and then reach a point and find that it was all dust in our
fingers. It was always myself who closed the gate. Looking at her
now—the pale, lovely face under the black hair, a face alert, intelligent and yearning—I felt a deep loathing for myself.

"Evan?" She called me back to myself. "I would like Abraham
Hunt and his wife to dinner."

"You know how I feel about him?"

"Of course I do. But, Evan, there's no way to save the Hessian
boy, is there? So he will die. If he dies, he will live always between
us. Don't you see that?"

I shook my head.

"Well, it's something I feel deeply, and I think that if Abraham
Hunt comes here we can talk to him about this thing. We might
be able to reach out and touch him."

"Reach out and touch Abraham Hunt?" I asked incredulously.

"Evan, Evan, did you ever try to understand us here? Sometimes
I think you feel we are barbarians. We are not, Evan; we are plain
Christian people who were persecuted and driven for a hundred
years before we came to this land. If we hadn't been hard and
narrow and righteous, how would we have endured? Think of what
a will it took to scratch a living out of this wretched Connecticut
soil, the will that raised up the hundreds of miles of stone wall you
see here on the Ridge. If you think about what we were and what
we had to become—you might not consider us so rigid and bigoted
as you do."

"And you want Abraham Hunt here?"

"Yes."

"All right," I said. "We'll try." Then I reached out and took her hand. "Believe me, I will try, Alice."

Later we walked together in the garden hand in hand. It was one of those lovely May evenings, with the air as sweet as honey and the sunset piling up into layers of pink and violet and gold. When we built the house, I laid out a garden of paths and hedges to remind me of the gardens in England, and in the time since then Alice had filled the beds with jonquils and lilies and phlox and roses and beddings of every annual she could beg or buy in seed. The jonquils and tulips were with us now, with pale borders of nasturtium, and the lilies thrusting up fat out of the soil not yet in bloom, but still lovely. The garden was Alice's refuge, her wall against me and the world and her childlessness, and she took me there tonight as one takes a lover into the innermost recesses of the heart. I had found a bench of Italian alabaster in a dockside warehouse in Philadelphia when we had turned that place into a hospital. The two most precious furnishings of her garden were the bench and a marble cupid that I had bought in Madrid. When we sat down, she reminded me of that, and said, "Do you know, Evan, I always wanted to return in kind, and it had to be a horse of Arab blood, English-trained for fast pacing. I think though that I will wait forever before one can buy a horse out of Britain and have it shipped here."

I did not know what to say, and so I said as lamely as a foolish boy, "You must know that I never touched Sarah Heather, never kissed her, never addressed a single word of affection to her, not a word of what a man might say to a woman—and never will."

"And do you think that makes it better, Evan?"

THE following day I stopped by at the Heather place to take the sutures out of the wound. The boy, Hans Pohl, sat in the kitchen by the hearth, dressed in Raymond's old clothes, his hair now cropped short in the Quaker fashion. Sally was there churning butter while she tried to rid his English of that curious mixture of German and cockney accent that he had acquired among the red-

464

coats. I listened with interest for a minute or two before I told him to take off his shirt.

The wound was beautifully healed. There was no heat on the skin, and I could not help but have the neat pride of a surgeon who conquers a bullet as I pulled out the sutures.

"How do you feel?" I asked him.

"Very good, Dr. Feversham." He paused, then asked, "Can I work, Doctor?"

"He wants to work with my father," Sally explained.

I stared at him thoughtfully. "Yes, you can work."

Outside the house, I met Sarah returning from the chicken house with a basket of eggs.

"Did thee see Hans, Evan?" she asked.

"He's well now. He tells me he wants to work."

"He's a good lad, Evan, and he says that if he eats our food he must earn the bread."

"And where will he stay?"

"Raymond made him a bed in the empty stall. In summertime it's no hardship to sleep in the barn."

"Sleep in the barn, work in the fields," I said unhappily. "Sarah, you and Raymond are quite out of your minds." I shook my head and mounted my horse. "At least keep him out of sight when people come by," I told her.

"Thee is a dear, strange man," she replied, smiling.

THE next morning I rode over to Redding to set the broken leg of a farmer named Caleb Winters. I took a shortcut back, through the woods and down to the Norwalk Run, a pretty little stream that rises in the great swamp and flows south into the Sound.

At the edge of the run I dismounted and sprawled in the grass on the riverside while my horse drank. I was stretched out there when I saw Hans Pohl and Sally Heather across the stream, walking hand in hand with no thought or eye for anyone in the world except each other.

My horse came to nudge me, but I remained there quietly until the boy and the girl were out of sight.

Chapter Six: Squire Hunt

S QUIRE HUNT's wife, Abigail, accepted Alice's dinner invitation
immediately.

She was a gracious and well-educated woman, and distant kin
to her husband. Hunt's father had settled on the Ridge with a gift
of the magistracy, but his money came from a large interest in the
ropewalks in Boston.

The day before we expected them for dinner, Hunt rode over to
the Heather farm, ostensibly to speak with Jacob again. Sally saw
him coming from afar. She ran to the barn, which Hans Pohl was
cleaning, and then the two of them climbed up into the loft. As I
heard it from Sally long afterward, they hid under the hay more to
be together than out of any real fear that Hunt would come poking
around the barn.

And together they were, body to body and breath to breath,
clinging to each other. It seems to me that in those moments they
faced that awful punishment of maturity, the knowledge that man's
life is fraught with mortality. That Sally had to tell it to me one
day is evidence of how poignantly the moment touched both of
them. Even though Hans Pohl had lived his life in camp and bar-
racks, he was as virgin as she, and they clung to each other with
fear and excitement, the world exploding into that wonderful moment of insight and understanding that only first love brings.

Squire Hunt dismounted at the kitchen door, knocked and was
admitted by Sarah, who managed to greet him quite calmly. "A
good morning to thee, Squire Hunt, and what would thee?"

Raymond ran all the way to the house, Jacob at his heels, to face
Hunt. The squire apologized for his abrupt appearance and explained that all he desired was to talk to Jacob.

"About what would thee speak to him?" Raymond asked, realizing that he had never told Jacob to lie or dissemble about Hans.

"About the Hessian," Hunt replied.

Sarah said, smiling, "Sit thee down, Squire Hunt. I have hot water on the hearth; will thee have coffee?"

He shook his head. "No, thank you, only a word with Jacob. Here, lad," he said to Jacob, "when you saw the Hessians did you mark the one with the drum?"

Jacob nodded.

"Was he a boy or a man?"

"He was a man," Jacob said evenly.

"How old a man?"

"Sixteen or seventeen years."

"Then he was a boy."

"I will be a man when I am sixteen or seventeen years," Jacob said calmly. "I will do what a man must do."

"By God, you will," Hunt cried. "I like him. He's a damn fine boy, Heather. Was he tall, Jacob?"

"Like a man," Jacob said.

"Well, I suppose that's all I will get out of him," Hunt said, and Raymond knew that he should never have doubted his son.

More or less of this was told by Hunt at my dinner table. Alice had asked John Dorset, the Congregational minister, and his wife to join us. Dorset was one of those lively and imaginative men who fill conversational holes so easily. His wife, Ziporah, was a pale blond lady who had suffered thirty-six years with an impossible name, and nineteen of those with impossible poverty as the wife of a minister on the Ridge.

We had made small talk, which Alice directed as carefully as if she walked upon a carpet of shattered glass, until Hunt told the story of his visit to the Heathers; and that raised the question of those curious people who called themselves Quakers. There were at least twenty families of them among us. They had a meeting-house of their own and had lived through the years of the war with quiet resignation, accepting the general climate of contempt with patience and without rancor.

Pastor Dorset pointed out to Hunt that, annoying as their attitude was, if they rendered us no assistance, they certainly were of no comfort to the British either.

Hunt was in a more relaxed mood than I had seen him enjoy in a long time. He reminded Dorset that at the great battle on the Ridge the Quakers had taken the British wounded into their homes and attended them.

"As they took in our own wounded," his wife reminded him.

"War and charity go poorly together," he said; and then to the minister, "You, John, will disagree with me, but we reason from our calling, don't we? You are a preacher. I am a soldier."

"War without charity is a ghastly thing," Dorset replied. "If we cease to be Christians on the battlefield, then God help us. Don't you agree with me, Dr. Feversham?" he asked.

"Yes, but I have never seen evidence of Christianity on a battle-field."

"Anyway, Abraham, you will admit that the Heathers are pleasant people?" Alice said.

"They were pleasant enough to me. But damned if I understand any man who will not fight for what is his. When the British burn my home and slaughter my stock am I to turn the other cheek? A man can't live that way without degrading himself."

I couldn't help remarking that the Quakers appeared to live that way without any particular degradation. Alice caught my eye. I had promised to make no issue with Hunt.

"Do they now? I would say they live in peace and comfort because others were willing to fight their battles," he replied.

"And Dr. Feversham," Abigail Hunt said sweetly, "do you think there was ever a cause more just than ours?"

"I don't know," I replied. "Perhaps Cromwell's cause was as just as ours. But since I am a Catholic, I could hardly be expected to look at it in that light. You see, my dear Abigail, when nations quarrel, each considers her cause just and God to be on her side."

"Now hold on here," said Hunt. "Let me put this to you, Feversham. If you feel as you do, why did you join our side?"

"I chose this side, Squire, for a few obvious reasons. For one thing, I married an American girl whom I care for deeply. For another, my house stands here and the people in this region are my patients. For a third, I felt that the British had behaved abom-

468

inably; and for a fourth, I am a Catholic and the British have not been kind to me or mine. I don't know whether those are reasons enough, but neutrality is not my nature. I do not admire it."

"Yet your Quaker friends are neutral, are they not, Doctor?"

"Perhaps. Or perhaps not."

"Pray how are they both?" Dorset insisted.

"Possibly they consider that they are on the side of mankind."

So THE evening went, and when they had left I sat down beside the embers that remained of the fire. Alice came and stood behind a wing chair and stared at me quizzically. I made my apology. I had been rude and altogether a poor host.

"I thought you were marvelously restrained. Abraham Hunt overeats, belches and has absolutely no sense of humor," she said.

"I thought you were once in love with him."

"Who told you that?" she demanded.

"Abigail Hunt."

"Abigail is a stupid cat."

"I think I love you," I said to her.

"You have a remarkably controlled way of demonstrating it. Also, you are vindictive."

"Am I? In what way?"

"You know he has gout. And you let him stuff himself with roast beef."

"The truth of it is that we don't really know that roast beef causes gout. But you must admit that he refrained from mentioning the Hessian."

"He mentioned the Hessian," she said, rather sadly.

"When?"

"When he kissed me good-night and got into that ridiculous carriage of his. He said that I should be sure to tell you that as certainly as the Pope sits in Rome the Hessian will hang."

IT RAINED the following morning, and when it rains people who have put off attending to their ailments in fair weather to do their plowing and planting come to see me. Not until after our midday meal was I able to tell Rodney Stephan to saddle up my horse.

The rain had blown away by then. The trees in their new green were radiant and jewel-like, and the meadow grass was as sparkling bright as if God had just laid it down. I thought that day, as I had on so many occasions, that the Ridge was the most beautiful place in all the world. In a single mile of one of its narrow, wretched, twisting roads there was an infinite variety of scenery, a deep bog, a high cliff, a great pile of mighty boulders heaped haphazardly as if some childish giants had played with them and then heaped them up.

Before I reached the Heather place I came upon Jacob on his way back from school at the meetinghouse. His dark, somber clothes were at odds with the song he sang as he hopped and skipped along.

"Ride me, please, sir, Dr. Feversham," he called out. I swung him up behind me, finding pleasure in the clutch of his arms around my waist.

We came to the farm, and Jacob took my horse to drink. When I went into the house Sarah turned a face to me so bleak that my whole body tensed.

"What happened?"

"Have I no right to be sad, Evan?"

I nodded. "The squire was here, wasn't he?"

"Yes, he was here. Sit down, and I will give thee some refreshment."

"I did not come for refreshment, Sarah. I came because you and I must talk forthrightly. The boy must go. Now. Not tomorrow, not the next day—but now."

"What has the boy become to thee, Evan?"

"I can take him down to Saugatuck myself. Then he must make his way to New York as best he may. We have done what we can do."

She did not answer immediately. She sat down by the table and began to cut through old swede turnips. They were as hard as stone, and I watched the play of muscle in her strong forearms. Then she looked up at me, her gray eyes calm.

"We have no churches in our faith, Evan," she said gently. "We have a meetinghouse, but it is no more sacred than any other house. My own house is like a church to me, and if it is not a place of refuge, then God help me, how can I live here?"

"I don't know," I answered, almost brutally. And then I left.

Chapter Seven: The Dog

SALEM ALAN was a Vermont man who had paused in his wandering on the Ridge because he took a fancy to one of the Bullett sisters. He was a tall, lean, laconic man, and because he was shiftless and indifferent to most of our "virtues," he was looked down upon, regarded as a thief—for which there was no evidence— and as a poacher, for which there was evidence enough. He married Nancy Bullett and they lived on game; and then he fathered five children who lived as best they could. He never bathed, and generally he was as gamy as a bear a month dead.

The only thing Salem Alan was fond of was his Pennsylvania rifle, and the only thing he appeared to know anything about was hunting. Along with his red setter, Duklik, he could be found prowling after game anywhere and everywhere.

I must mention that Duklik was the best hunting dog on the Ridge, and thereby he came into the business of the Hessian. But I am not much of a believer in accidents, and if it had not been Salem Alan it would have been someone else.

He and his dog meandered through the woods, up from the great swamp for perhaps a mile to the edge of Raymond Heather's place. Annie, Raymond's four-year-old, had climbed on the wall and was mincing along the top of it when she saw the man and his dog. She paused, intrigued by the dog's behavior. The dog had apparently found a scent and was digging for it. As Salem Alan and Annie Heather watched, Duklik dug away at the ground, found what he was after and pulled back. His teeth were locked on the sleeve of the Hessian jacket which Raymond Heather had buried there.

471

What happened after that is hard to piece out exactly. Evidently the child sensed that something deeply significant was taking place and certainly she was frightened. You would have to understand how thoroughly the word *Hessian* had impressed the imagination of every child in Connecticut to sense what she felt. There was a surge of fear in her mind that sent her leaping off the wall and racing across the meadow toward home.

Salem Alan claimed that he called out to her, "Hey you, girl— who are you? What the devil are you running for?"

He swore he did nothing to set Duklik on her, but his dog was certainly sensitive to his voice and alert to his desires.

The dog was over the fence in a moment and loping after the child. Salem Alan insisted that Duklik had no intention of harming her, but Annie had turned on the animal in terror. That's as it may be. The result, however, was that Jacob Heather came to me in my surgery and told me breathlessly that his little sister had been bitten by a dog.

"Why didn't your father bring her here?"

"I don't know. I think there's trouble over Hans Pohl."

I threw my instruments into my bag and ran out of the surgery without even waiting for the boy to finish his story. I rode hard, and I don't think it was much more than half an hour between Jacob's appearance and my reaching the Heather place. Raymond and Sally were in front of the house. I threw my reins to the girl and then followed Raymond inside.

Annie, her arm swathed in bandages, lay on the kitchen table, over which Sarah had spread a quilt. The baby was crying woefully, and Sarah, utterly distracted, turned to me and cried, "Oh, thank God thee is here—thank God."

"Wash my instruments and put them on clean linen. All the needles. Quick now—where do I wash my hands?"

She had soap and a bowl of hot water waiting, and I washed hurriedly. The wound in the child's arm was not serious in itself. I had feared to find one of those long, ugly tears that happen when a dog slashes with a will to kill, but here were only four tooth marks, bleeding hardly at all.

"Whose dog was it? We must find the dog."

But neither Sarah nor Raymond knew and they stared at me voiceless with terror.

"If the dog was mad—" Sarah began, her eyes filling with tears.

I took my scalpel in hand. "I must cut a bit and make the holes bleed, for only the blood can cleanse it. Did you ask her? Did you try to find out who owns the dog?"

Raymond said, "Whosever dog it was dug up the Hessian's uniform."

"What!"

Raymond nodded woefully.

"Annie, Annie," I said gently, "what was the dog like?"

No answer.

"Was the dog's mouth white? Tell me, Annie." I took a silver shilling out of my pocket. "You shall have this. A whole silver shilling. You can buy a doll at Miss Crocus's shop in Norwalk. But you must be a smart girl and answer me."

Her eyes were fixed on the coin. She smiled slightly.

"Did you ever watch your father shave?" I asked her. "Did you see him make a lather out of soap and put it on his face?"

"Yes."

"Did the dog have white soap on his face? Now think, darling. You must answer truthfully, and then I will give you this."

"No," she whispered.

"You mean there was no soap on the dog's face?"

She sat up now and nodded.

"Good girl. Oh, you're a wonderful girl, Annie. Now you must think again. Was there soap in the dog's mouth?"

"It was a red dog."

"But did he have soap in his mouth?" I insisted. "Was there foamy soap dripping from his mouth?"

"No, he was a red dog."

"Damned if I don't think it Salem Alan's beast." I gave her the coin. "Hold tight on this. I must prick your arm a little."

A few minutes later the cuts were clean, her arm was bandaged and I had decided that it was hopeless to rage at Raymond for

burying the uniform when he could have burned it. Sarah had retreated into a corner, where she let herself sob out her terror against the wall. She was herself again in a few moments and then I said to Raymond, "The odds are that I am right and it was Salem Alan's dog. If that's so, how long do you think it will be before they are here? Where is the Hessian?"

"He hides in the hayloft."

You fool, I thought, and then I realized that he and Sarah were both half out of their minds with the belief that their child had been bitten by a mad dog.

"All right. We must get him out of here. Saddle your horse, Raymond, and I'll lead him down to Norwalk and work out something."

I don't know what I would have thought of, but it was too late. Raymond opened the door, and there was Sally staring at Squire Hunt and half a dozen militiamen riding up to the farm.

In answer to Sally's wordless question, I said, "You do nothing, Sally—and don't go to the barn. Believe me, there's no way out now unless a miracle happens. But I don't want the boy hurt either, so be still and let me talk to Hunt."

It was midday now, a gentle, sunny day in May—a day of the kind of sweet charm that appears to embrace tragedy—and I remembered such a day when my father was buried and the graveyard a garden of old roses and sweet-smelling grass.

They dismounted. One of them held the horses. The rest followed Hunt as he strode up and greeted me.

"Good day, Feversham. What brings you here?"

"A dog ripped their child's arm."

"I'm sorry to hear that."

"What do you want here, Hunt?"

"You know what I want," Hunt said. "I want the Hessian. I'll find him if I have to pull this place to pieces."

"Suppose I said he isn't here."

"Don't be a fool, Feversham. I have had a notion he's been here for days. Now I have the proof." He lifted the flap of his saddlebag, pulled out Hans Pohl's dirty uniform coat and flung it at Raymond's feet.

It lay there a moment and then Sally picked it up. She walked over to Hunt and said to him, "Take this and get out of here, sir. This is our land and thee has no place here."

Hunt passed the coat to one of his men and nodded with approval at Sally. "Well spoken. But it's pointless. Will you tell her that it's pointless, Feversham?"

"What will you do with him?" I asked Hunt.

"You know what I will do with him, Feversham. We're not going to beat him or torture him. We'll lock him up, and when General Packenham gets here we'll hold a trial. Now understand me"—he came close and spoke quietly—"I want no trouble with the Heathers. There are those who hate the Friends; I don't. I don't give a damn what they are. I want the Hessian, and there's no one here who can stop me from taking him."

I nodded.

"Where is he?"

"I have your word for what you say—as between us, Hunt, as between two men who have respect for each other?"

"Yes."

I walked over to Sally then and took her a few paces away. I said to her, "You must bring him out, Sally."

"No—oh, no, please, Evan. They will kill him."

"No. They are going to try him in a court. Believe me, Squire Hunt will not hurt him now. So go to him and make him understand that he must give himself up."

"Oh, my God."

"You must do it, Sally, because there is no other way."

For a long, long moment we stood facing each other; then Sally turned and walked off toward the barn.

"She's going for the boy," I said to Hunt. "In God's name, will you remember that he's just a boy?"

Hunt made no reply, and we stood there and waited. The door opened and Sarah appeared, her broad, lovely face calm under the mass of her honey-colored hair. She walked over to Raymond and took his hand.

No one moved, no one spoke. Time passed, and finally Hunt said,

"Oh, I do dearly hope you're not playing a game with me, Feversham."

"You see the barn," I said, pointing to it. "Where could they go? You'll have him long enough, Hunt. Be patient."

"Squire Hunt?" Raymond said.

Hunt turned away from the barn to face him. He appeared to turn toward Raymond with a sort of pity; and to give the devil his due, he never raised the question of punishment for Raymond or myself—perhaps because he sensed our anguish.

"What need thee the boy," Raymond asked, "when all the rest of his company have died and paid the price? His own father perished. He is a good boy. He works hard—"

I don't know where Jacob had been until then, but now the boy appeared from behind the house and went to stand close to his father. Raymond paused, looked down at his son and then touched his hair gently.

"Go on," Hunt said.

"I will take him in for my own," Raymond pleaded. "Others have bought Hessian prisoners into bondage. I will pay thee up to the whole value of my worldly goods and give thee mortgage on my home and fields."

"That cannot be," Hunt said, a note of weariness in his voice. "He hanged Saul Clamberham, who had done him no wrong."

"Not him! His officer!"

"I will not argue it, Heather!"

What had transpired between Hans Pohl and Sally Heather in the barn during all of this I don't know and most likely will never know. Most of my own youth I have forgotten, but the taste of my first love, when I was no older than this Hessian boy, I will never forget as long as I live. It was one of the few moments in my life when I knew that God existed, and I thought of this when I saw the boy and girl come out of the barn. Sally seemed suddenly like her mother, not a girl any longer but a woman of beauty and dignity, her head held high. The boy held her hand and walked straight and proud.

Not a sound now from any of the militiamen, nor from Raymond or Sarah or their children. Sally and the boy walked over to where the militiamen were. One of them tied the boy's hands behind his back, and they lifted him into the saddle so that he rode double with a militiaman behind him. Then the rest of them mounted and they rode away.

Chapter Eight: General Packenham

"ARE YOU awake?" my wife asked me.
I had thought her long asleep. "Yes, I am awake."
"You were awake last night. Try to sleep."
"If I could sleep, I would."
"I was with Abigail today."
"Oh? What did Abigail say?"
"That her husband doesn't listen to her, that he hasn't heard a word she's said for more years than she cares to remember. Still I begged her to talk to him."
"Will she?"
"She says that the Hessian boy is his burden now."
Alice said no more, and in time I felt her body gently against mine, and then I slept.

THE next day Raymond Heather brought Annie to my surgery, and I changed the dressing on her arm. I had seen the dog, Duklik, and satisfied myself that he was not rabid; and when I exposed the wound I saw that the bite was healing rapidly and cleanly.
"How is Sally?" I asked Raymond.
"Somber. She keeps her peace. Will they hang the boy, Evan?"
"I don't know."
The day after that I asked Rodney Stephan when they would hold the trial.
He said General Packenham would arrive during the next day or two, and then the trial would be held. I remembered Packenham only too well. I had been at Saratoga when he had his quarrel with

Colonel Stark and when Stark had been close to killing him in his anger at what he felt was Packenham's cowardice. Packenham was a vain and pompous man, well-fleshed, with an imposing manner and a florid complexion. The fact that he would preside at the trial gave me no great hope for the boy.

The next day my patients were full of the news that General Packenham and his aide, Colonel St. August, had arrived in town and had taken rooms at the inn. The talk I heard was for the most part of their splendid uniforms. The best that we on the Ridge had ever put together in the way of uniform was eight blue coats with sashes for the leaders to wear in militia parades. If St. August was there for the defense, then who would prosecute? I somehow felt that Abraham Hunt would avoid the post.

That night Alice asked me who would defend the boy.

"I don't know. Possibly St. August."

"Everyone says he's the prosecutor."

I shook my head hopelessly.

"Would you defend him, Evan?"

"No, it's impossible. I'm a doctor, not a lawyer."

"You're a colonel in the army. You still have your rank. Certainly you are peer to Colonel St. August. Why could you not defend the boy?"

"No," I insisted. "It's wrong. He must have a lawyer."

"And do you really think they'll find him a lawyer? The trial is tomorrow."

So it was that an hour later I knocked at the door of Squire Hunt's house. Abigail opened the door herself, surprised and patently pleased to see me. "I am sure the squire will be delighted to see you. He is in his study with General Packenham."

She led me through the sitting room into the study. Theirs was a fine and well-appointed house, the fireplaces framed in white Italian marble and the floors of polished hardwood. The study had a wall of calfbound books which, read or unread, gave the place an aspect of culture and civilization.

Abigail knocked, and then we entered at Hunt's bidding. Hunt introduced me to Packenham as Colonel Feversham.

"Ah, a colleague. Always pleased to meet a patriot, Colonel," Packenham said, thrusting out a meaty hand. He squinted at me. "Haven't we met before?"

"At Saratoga, General."

"Oh? Were you with Gates?"

"No, sir." I hesitated. "I was with Stark."

The general stared at me coldly. "Are you a Vermonter, sir?"

"I am English," I replied. "I led the Eleventh Connecticut Volunteer Riflemen—or what was left of them—only thirty-two men. So they put me with Stark."

"Feversham here is a physician," Hunt said. "I spoke about him. He tended the Hessian's wound."

Packenham cleared his throat. "I see. This is the man who took it upon himself to give aid and comfort to a malignant enemy of our cause."

"General," I said quietly, "I have performed that same function on many battlefields and I have yet to be reprimanded for it."

"Then perhaps the time is at hand, Feversham. The squire tells me that with every loyal militiaman hunting this Hessian, you laughed up your sleeve with the knowledge of who he was and where he was. I would not sleep easily, if I were you. Who knows whether this trial might not be broadened?"

"Are you threatening me, sir?"

"Informing you, sir."

"I don't threaten, I don't inform," I said very softly. "But I must remind you, General, that I was very close to Colonel John Stark. We were like brothers. I also have in my desk at home a personal letter from General Washington, thanking me for the reorganization of his medical service and begging me to call upon him if the need be. I simply cite this so that when you make your threats—"

"I make no threats!" he interrupted me.

"Good. Now if I may take up my business with Squire Hunt?"

"As you please, sir."

Hunt, who was watching this byplay with interest, nodded at me and said, "Go on, Feversham. I am listening."

My behavior reminded me of that of a petulant boy. I had done

nothing to help the Hessian. I had antagonized General Packenham, perhaps beyond apology, for I had called to mind his own
cowardice and the humiliation he received at the hands of Colonel
Stark. My falling back upon the security granted by a relationship
with famous personalities was a bluff and a lie—I was like a brother
to Stark for one day in the heat of combat and doubt that now he
even remembered my name. My letter from General Washington
was one of hundreds of similar letters and of as little moment.

I was not proud of myself, not by any means, and I said to the
general now, "Forgive me for my show of temper, sir."

Hunt watched with acute attention. He had never heard me
apologize before. I said to him, "Squire, while the general has
ample credentials to sit as military judge and prosecutor—"

"Colonel St. August will sit with me as prosecutor," Packenham
interrupted.

"As prosecutor," I said. "But who will defend the Hessian?"

"The court will defend him," Packenham replied.

It was not unheard of—I could recall precedent—but never
where the court consisted of two officers only, and now I asked if
Squire Hunt would sit on the court.

"He is chief witness, as I understand it, sir."

"Then only yourself—"

He interrupted me again. "I do not understand your concern,
Colonel Feversham. Do you doubt my ability to conduct a just
court?"

"No, sir."

"Do you come here to plead for the Hessian?"

"I came because I believe that a military lawyer should sit and
defend."

Packenham shrugged. Hunt said nothing.

"Would you allow me to sit on the court?" I asked.

"You, sir," Packenham replied, "are even more involved than
Squire Hunt, who is at least the commander of your local militia.
I know of no command you hold, sir."

I turned to Hunt, pleading silently.

"There is nothing I can do, Feversham."

"Would you allow me at least to talk with the boy, to help him with his defense?" I begged of Packenham. "He is only a boy of sixteen years."

"What kind of talk is this, sir? Have you never seen boys of sixteen, fifteen, fourteen even in our own ranks? Have you never seen them lying dead, having paid the highest price a lad can pay?"

"Still, that doesn't change the fact—"

"I know one fact, Feversham. The man is a Hessian. He wore a Hessian uniform and he took Hessian pay. He killed for hire."

"Damn that," I cried. "Every soldier who ever set foot on our soil killed for hire—Hessian, British, French, Scot! This whole filthy game is played for hire! I'm only asking you to show some Christian mercy!" I turned on my heel and left the place.

Chapter Nine: The Trial

WHEN Alice and I arrived in the village on the morning of the trial, we found a great crowd assembled in front of the inn. There must have been two or three hundred people there, and I recognized faces from Redding and Danbury. Others, I am sure, rode up from Saugatuck and Norwalk. All hoped to get into the big pipe room, which at best could hold no more than fifty.

I do not blame them. Little enough happens on the Ridge, and here in this lovely springtime was that fiercest of all drama, a man on trial for his life. And he was not just an ordinary man but the most hated of all men in those strange years—a Hessian.

Not that people called for blood; it was not their way. They were religious and deeply proud people, whose God was just and unforgiving, who not only read the Old Testament but who lived it too, and named their children after the same ancient people whose prayers they recited.

Alice found Raymond and his daughter Sally. Sarah had remained at home with the other children. Only Raymond had been called as a witness, but he told me Sally had insisted that she come with him. I wondered whether this was anything she should see.

Abraham Hunt came through the crowd and found us. He was curiously gentle. He had put on his militia uniform, his blue coat and white trousers, and wore a wig and a wide sword sash. He was not at ease in his uniform. At least a hundred men and boys from the Ridge had gone off to the war at one time or another and not one of them had ever worn a uniform.

Hunt greeted Raymond, not ungraciously, and asked where Jacob was.

"At home," Raymond said.

"But he must testify."

"There was no warrant for him," Raymond said. I had begun to appreciate how different Raymond's response to the affair was from mine. Somewhere inside of him there was an ultimate calm and acceptance.

At least a dozen Quaker men were outside the inn, grouped behind Raymond. Their coats were buttoned high in spite of the heat, their round hats straight upon their heads. I had assured myself that I had great intimacy with the Heather family, but now I realized how little I knew of their way of life. I was struck with the fact that they—unlike other settlers—had not come to this place with grim courage, gun in hand, to wrest it from the savage and the wilderness, but in a sort of nakedness. So did I comprehend suddenly what love meant to Sally Heather, and I felt myself full of a kind of melancholy I had not known before.

Perhaps Alice felt something of the same, for she took her place beside Sally as Hunt told Raymond, "Then you must go for the boy, Heather. I am sorry, but we must have him here."

Raymond nodded and went off, leaving Sally with us. Hunt cleared a way through the crowd to the inn and we went out of the sunlight into the crowded taproom. At one end of the room a long table had been set up. Behind it were seated General Packenham, Colonel St. August and Bosley Crippit, the town clerk and recorder.

Colonel St. August wore a brown coat with yellow facings, the uniform of an artillery regiment that he had organized somewhere in northern Connecticut. The colonies were full of men of wealth and social position who had beautiful uniforms and organized companies of their own, but somehow one rarely remembered them from a battlefield.

For a little while the confusion continued. At least a dozen men were ejected forcibly, and the air was full of arguments, name-calling and catcalls. In one case an actual scuffle broke out between the militiamen and someone who claimed he had ridden all the way from New Haven to see the trial. It was at least fifteen or twenty minutes after we had entered before some kind of order was achieved out of the drumming of Packenham's gavel upon the table.

Hunt had placed the three of us, Alice, myself and Sally, on a bench across the open space from the witnesses. There were chairs on one side where Miss Perkins, the schoolmistress, Mr. Saxon, the undertaker, and Salem Alan were already seated. I guessed that the Hessian was held in the inn's kitchen or pantry.

Having achieved a sort of order, Packenham asked the witnesses to identify themselves. There was little form about a court-martial in those days, each presiding officer setting the rules more or less as he pleased, with no appeal and no rein on his actions. Crippit read the names of the witnesses, and each one stood for identity. When the clerk came to Raymond's name there was no response, and Packenham said with irritation, "Why is he not here, Squire Hunt? I warranted him."

"He was here. I sent him back for his son. He will be here within the hour, I am sure."

Packenham tapped with his gavel again. I glanced at Sally, who sat primly erect, apparently oblivious to the stares, the grins and the whispering. Gossip had dealt with her swiftly and cruelly.

"We will come to order," Packenham announced. "I hereby convene a military court in the name of the Sovereign State of Connecticut and the Continental Congress."

"General Jonah Packenham presiding," Crippit called out. "Colonel Albert St. August sitting with him. These are summary proceedings under a state of war. The accused is one Hans Pohl, a

484

soldier from Hesse, sworn to action under the flag of King George the Third of England."

I could imagine the hours Bosley Crippit had spent putting together the pompous and ridiculous phrases that made up the charge. In all his years of writing and rewriting the details of land titles and boundaries he had never had such an opportunity as this and he was making the most of it.

"Bring the prisoner before the court," General Packenham said.

Two militiamen pushed through the crowd, bringing Hans Pohl with them. The boy had been dressed in his filthy, bloodstained uniform—at his own desire, I learned—and his hands were bound behind his back.

"Untie him!" Hunt ordered.

The two militiamen obeyed, and then the boy stood stiffly at attention in front of the table. From the moment he had come into the room, Sally had not taken her eyes from him; yet he avoided hers and stared straight ahead at General Packenham.

"You stand before a legally constituted military court of this sovereign state," Packenham said. "Do you understand that, sir?"

The boy nodded.

"What is your name?" the general asked.

"Hans Pohl."

"Your regiment?"

"Sixteenth Jäger."

"Your rank?"

"Private soldier."

The answers were soft but firm, the accent hardly discernible in the few words he spoke.

"Read the charge," Packenham said to Crippit. The little clerk, his hands shaking with excitement, picked up a long sheet of foolscap, cleared his throat and proceeded to read:

"Accused, one Hans Pohl, private soldier in the service of the King of England. It is charged that on the sixteenth day of May, in the year of our Lord, 1781, the accused, Hans Pohl, was one of a detachment of Hessian soldiers who made an incursion into the territory of the township of Ridgefield. In the course of this in-

cursion they met with a citizen, one Saul Clamberham, unarmed and dressed in civilian clothes. Without cause of any kind, they made the said Saul Clamberham prisoner, and without trial or reason hanged him by the neck until he was dead. The court charges that every member of the detachment of Hessian soldiers was equally guilty of this cruel and wanton murder and so deserves the punishment in kind. How does the prisoner before the court plead to this charge?"

The boy appeared not to understand. The courtroom had become very quiet now, and then suddenly there was a bustle of movement and voices. Those men in front of the outer door pushed aside to allow Raymond and his son, Jacob, to enter. They saw us and moved slowly to where we were. Sally rose, giving her father the seat, and sat down cross-legged on the floor, Jacob beside her.

St. August stood up and said to the Hessian, "How do you plead, sir? You must give an answer. Are you guilty or not guilty?"

"I don't understand," Hans Pohl said.

"What is there that defies your understanding?" St. August demanded. "The charge was simple and plain. Are you guilty of the murder of one Saul Clamberham or are you not guilty?"

Hans shook his head.

"Then if you will not plead, I must accept your silence as a statement of guilt."

"You will not, sir!" I cried out, rising. "This is damnable! The boy speaks kitchen English and no more. He doesn't understand half the words in that charge."

"Who are you, sir?" St. August shouted. "How do you dare interrupt this trial? Who gave you permission to speak?"

Hunt rose and stood facing Packenham, who was pounding with his gavel. The gabble of voices in the background stilled, and Hunt said coldly, "This is a misunderstanding, is it not, Colonel St. August? As I understand it, you were going to plead him not guilty. I think there is nothing else you can do, sir. He has not yet been tried or heard."

"If he pleads guilty, he pleads guilty," St. August insisted. "There is no illegality in that."

488

"Then make it clear to him," Hunt said and sat down.

St. August said, "Hans Pohl, did you murder Saul Clamberham?"

"No," the boy replied. "I don't murder him."

"Then you plead not guilty."

"I don't murder him," the boy repeated.

"You may call your first witness," Packenham said to St. August.

The colonel glanced at Crippit, who riffled ostentatiously through his papers until he found his list of witnesses and then sang out, "Call Miss Jenny Perkins!"

"I'm right here, Bosley," Miss Perkins replied, sitting as she was no more than six feet from him.

"Rise and put your hand on the Book."

Miss Perkins went up and placed her hand on the Bible.

"Do you swear to tell the truth, the whole truth and nothing but the truth? Say I do."

"I'll say nothing of the sort," Miss Perkins replied. "I am not given to lying. I have never taken an oath and I have no intentions of taking one now. It's an unchristian thing."

Crippit turned to the general, who was pounding his gavel to still the laughter. St. August said, "So long as she places her hand on the Book."

"You see that I have," she said.

"What is your name, madam?"

"I am unmarried, sir. My name is Jenny Perkins."

"Did you know one Saul Clamberham?"

"I did."

"Did you know his family?"

"He had no family. He was a foundling. He was left with Goody Allison by people passing through. Worthless people. I think he was five years old. Goody Allison took care of him until her death. He was eleven years old then. After that he just lived hand to mouth and no one took care of him, God forgive us."

"Why do you say God forgive us?" St. August asked.

"If he had proper care or love or home, he would not have been down on the trail playing foolish games with the Hessians."

"Do you mean he was irresponsible?"

"He was a half-wit, sir. He couldn't learn anything, not to read or write even the simplest thing."

"Did you try to teach Saul Clamberham?"

"Yes, I tried. It was hopeless. He would come to school, then stay away for months, then come to the school again."

"Why would he come back?"

"Because he wanted so desperately to learn."

"Was he dangerous?"

"Dangerous? How could he be dangerous?" She looked at Hans Pohl now. She was an intelligent, principled woman, but Hans Pohl was from the outside. She had never seen a German before, and for six years she had listened to the terrible barbarisms that were attributed to the Hessians and had shivered at night, alone in her house, at the creaking of wood, asking herself whether it was not a Hessian come to murder her in her sleep.

"I mean," St. August explained, "did Saul Clamberham molest the children or try to hurt people?"

"He could not hurt a fly." She dabbed at her eyes. "He was gentle."

"Thank you, Miss Perkins. That will do," St. August said.

She went back to her chair and began to weep into her kerchief.

"It's very hot here," General Packenham said, and indeed by now he was perspiring profusely. "Can't we have a window opened? There are delicate women and little children in this room."

The windows were opened, and then Bosley Crippit called Jacob Heather.

"Put your hand on the Book and swear to tell the truth," Crippit told him.

Jacob shook his head. "We do not swear," he said, his voice a bit shaky. "I must not."

Packenham declared that the boy would damn well take the oath or he'd know the reason why.

"Let him be, General," Hunt said tiredly, "and let him tell his story. What difference does it make?"

St. August sighed in acknowledgment of the strangeness of people who lived on the Ridge and asked Jacob to state his name.

"Jacob Heather."

"Well, Jacob, you're a fine-looking lad. How old are you?"

"Twelve years."

"Now will you tell us where you were on the sixteenth of May?"

Jacob looked at Hans now. Hans did not move, and, like a shadow, woe crept over the small boy's face.

"Do you remember the day?"

"Yes," Jacob whispered.

"Where were you when you saw the Hessians?"

"On Hightop."

"Why weren't you at school?"

"It was a meditation day."

"What do you mean, a meditation day?"

"Thee remain at home and look into thy heart."

"But you were at Hightop?"

Packenham hammered with his gavel to still the laughter.

"Yes, sir."

"And what did you see there?"

"The Hessians."

"Was Saul Clamberham with the Hessians?"

"Yes—yes, sir." He looked at Hans again.

"What were they doing to him?"

Jacob shook his head.

"Then why didn't he run away?"

"They had a rope around his neck and his hands were tied."

"Come now, Jacob, don't be afraid. No Hessian can hurt you here. Tell us what they did to Saul Clamberham."

"They threw—they threw—" His face was tight with agony; and he turned then to look at his sister Sally.

Alice asked me, "Must they do this to him? Everyone knows what he saw."

"Everyone wants to hear it again," I murmured. "Death is very special. See how everyone listens." It was so still in the room that the buzzing of flies against the windowpanes sounded as loud as the rasp of a wood saw.

"Come now, Jacob. Be a man. Speak up."

Slowly Jacob said, "They threw the rope over a tree and pulled him up into the tree."

"Who did they pull up into the tree?"

"Saul Clamberham!" Jacob cried desperately.

"Saul Clamberham was a large man. Did one Hessian pull him up into the tree?"

Jacob stood silent.

"Come, Jacob. You must answer my question. Now, how many men pulled the rope and hanged Saul Clamberham?"

"Why do you torture him?" my wife burst out.

Packenham pounded his gavel. "I will not have interruptions, madam! That is plain!"

"Was it three men, four men? Five men? Or was it the whole detachment on the rope?" St. August loomed over the boy. "How many?"

"I don't remember," Jacob pleaded.

"Didn't you tell Squire Hunt that there were sixteen men, an officer and a drummer?"

"Yes," Jacob admitted.

"How did you know that?"

"I counted them."

"And you were right!" St. August cried, a note of triumph in his voice. "Good lad! Now let me ask you this, Jacob, do you refuse to answer now because every last one of those men put their hands on the rope and dragged Saul Clamberham to his death?"

"No," Jacob burst out. "There were four men."

"Ah, now you know there were four men. You are sure? Will you swear to that?"

Jacob shook his head miserably. He was crying now.

"Let the boy be," Hunt said. "What does it matter how many men pulled the rope? The detachment hanged him."

"I think it matters very much indeed, sir," St. August said. "I think that this man here"—pointing to Hans Pohl—"pulled the rope with the others, and I intend to have the truth."

"Then get it from someone else and let the boy be."

Packenham nodded and said, "Let the boy sit down."

Jacob ran to Sally and plopped down in front of her, putting his head in her lap. Crippit picked up his list and called Raymond Heather.

"State your name," St. August said.

"Raymond Heather."

"Are you the father of Jacob Heather?"

"Yes."

"Did he tell you how many men were on the rope when the Hessians hanged Saul Clamberham?"

"Yes. He told me that four men dragged the rope, God forgive them and rest their souls."

Then St. August demanded, "Does your religion forbid you to lie, or does it give you license to lie when the mood takes you?"

"It forbids me to lie," Raymond answered, "for when I lie there is no refuge for me or place to conceal it."

"You gave this Hessian, Hans Pohl, shelter in your house, did you not?"

"I sheltered him. He was sick and wounded."

"If your religion forbids you to lie, why did you lie about the Hessian you sheltered?"

Raymond was silent.

"You live in peace and safety because others take up arms to fight and die, and yet when a word would mean safety to those who protect you—you chose to be silent. If that is no lie, then I don't know what falsehood is."

"I chose between a man's life and a lie. Thus I lied," Raymond admitted.

Sitting where she was, her brother's head buried in her skirts, Sally said quietly, "It's enough, it's enough, please."

Raymond looked at St. August, and St. August knew enough not to press it. "You may go back to your seat, sir," he said.

Hunt was the next witness. He stood near the Hessian boy, his bulk making the Hessian appear smaller than he was.

"You were here at this inn when Jacob Heather came with the word about the Hessians?"

"Yes, sir."

"Did he tell you how many dragged the rope that hanged Saul Clamberham?"

"No."

"Why not?"

"I didn't ask him. It makes no difference who held the rope. The Hessians hanged him."

"I agree with you, Squire Hunt. The Hessians hanged him."

Then Salem Alan told the story of how his dog, Duklik, had dug up the uniform.

All through this Hans Pohl had been standing stiffly in front of the table. I marveled at his control.

"You do not have to testify if you do not wish to," St. August said to the boy. "We do not force men to testify against their will. But if you want to answer my questions we will be glad to listen."

The boy nodded.

"Where did your detachment come from?"

"From New York."

"How did you come to Connecticut?"

"On British frigate."

"Why was your detachment landed and sent up to the Ridge?"

"I do not know that. Such things are not for me."

"How did they come to take Saul Clamberham prisoner?"

"He follow us—maybe a mile. We see him in woods, and sergeant ask captain what to do. Captain Hauser say pace one-half mile, one thousand pace, and then take him. Sergeant tell off four men and tell them when signal is called, they go into woods and take the Yankee man."

"What did you do then?"

"We stand at ease and wait for captain's decision."

"And what was his decision?"

"He say the Yankee man is spy."

"Why? What evidence did he have?"

"This man, Clamberham, he has piece of—" He groped for the word. "From schoolhouse, you write with chalk. Slate. On slate are marks, one for each man. So captain tells him he is making intelligence and only spies make intelligence."

"Did Captain Hauser speak in German or in English?"

"Captain Hauser knows no English. My father—"

"Your father? What has your father got to do with this?"

"My father is sergeant," the boy said, his voice breaking. "My father speak English, but not good."

St. August paused. I felt my wife's hand gripping my wrist.

"My father told the Yankee man."

"And then?"

"He did not want to die," the boy said woefully.

Packenham broke in at this point. "You heard the testimony here to the effect that this man, Saul Clamberham, was a half-wit. Do you feel proud because you hanged a half-wit?"

Hans Pohl shook his head. "We don't know that."

"Were there numbers on the slate?" St. August demanded.

"Marks."

"And it did not strike you as strange that a grown man could not write numbers?"

"Even some men in my regiment—they cannot write down numbers, no? They don't read or write."

"But you, yourself, Hans Pohl, did you see nothing strange in the foolish behavior of this man, Clamberham?"

"I think he is a little crazy, yes."

"But you did nothing?"

"What could I do?" Hans Pohl asked. "If I talk to Captain Hauser, I am punished."

"You could talk to your father."

The boy shook his head again.

"Then you did nothing. You stood by while this unspeakable murder took place and raised no hand to stop it."

The boy remained still, stiff as a ramrod, silent.

"How many men dragged the rope and hanged him?"

"Four."

"Who were those four? Can you name them?"

"Private Schwartz, Private Messerbaum, Private Schimmel—I think, I am not sure."

"And the fourth?"

"I don't remember."

"Was it you?"

"No!" he cried.

"Are you a Christian?" St. August demanded.

"Yes."

"You understand what it means to take an oath, to put your immortal soul in jeopardy?"

"Yes, I understand."

"And you still maintain that you did not act as hangman?"

"No, I am not hangman."

"Then let us suppose your Captain Hauser had ordered you to act as hangman—what would you have done?"

"I am good soldier," the boy replied. "I obey orders."

Chapter Ten: The Verdict

THE COURT had adjourned for three hours, until four o'clock in the afternoon, at which time, General Packenham had announced, he would deliver the verdict. I had sent Alice home in the buggy, for she felt she could bear no more of it.

The crowd had emptied out of the inn, for while the verdict was still to come, no one had any question as to what it might be. I made my way down the street to where Raymond had hitched his wagon. He saw me coming and waited. Sally and Jacob sat in the wagon, their backs straight, their faces set. Ebenezer Calvil, who was mostly drunk and always foul-mouthed, stood a few feet from them, swaying back and forth. As I came by he was saying, "—not young, sissy, but on four sides I be a better man than any Hessian—" He turned to me, grinning, large, dirty, the purple veins standing out on his nose and cheeks. "Think I got a future with the lassie, Doc?"

"You don't have much of a future with anything," I told him coldly, "and if you don't stop drinking, you'll be dead before the year's end. Now get out of here."

Sally's lips were trembling, and Jacob held himself still, fighting the tears that rolled down his cheeks.

"She wanted to stay," Raymond explained, "but it's no use to stay, is it?"

"No, I don't think so."

"Will thee come to us and tell us?"

"Yes, I'll come."

Raymond drove off, Calvil flinging curses after him, and I walked back to the inn. I went into the taproom where I had left my hat. In the semidarkness I thought that it was deserted, and then I noticed Hunt sitting at one side of the room.

I would have passed through without speaking to him, but he called to me, and I walked over to him. He was sprawled in his chair, his coat off and his waistcoat open.

"What can I do for you?" I asked him.

"Did the Heathers go home?"

"Yes."

"That's the best thing they could have done. I wouldn't have wanted them here when the verdict is said."

"I imagine you wouldn't."

"Damn you, Feversham, I've been fair. Give me a nod for that. I could have made life hell for those people. In your eyes they've done nothing. In my eyes and in the eyes of most people around here they've betrayed our cause."

"I never said they did nothing. In my eyes they performed an act of human kindness."

"You amaze me, Feversham." There was a long pause, Hunt watching me in the gloom, and then he asked, "Was that Calvil yelling out there?"

"Yes."

"I'll remember that. I'll break his back."

"Defender of womanhood," I said with approval.

"Don't go out of your way to be nasty, Feversham. It comes naturally enough. I suppose you're off to plead with Packenham now."

"Do you object?"

"No. Go ahead, for all the difference it will make. Personally, I think he hates your guts. After what you said to him, I don't blame him. What happened at Saratoga?"

"He lost his nerve and decided to run away."

"Did he?"

"No. Stark caught him and beat him half to death with the flat of his sword. Have you ever seen a man whipped with a sword?"

"And you're going to ask him for favors?" Hunt smiled and shook his head. "Go ahead, Feversham, go ahead."

"Where is he?"

"Upstairs, in the big double room. He's having a bite of dinner with the charming St. August."

"I admire the company you keep," I said as I walked toward the door, and he snapped at me:

"Feversham!"

I paused.

"I do what I must, Feversham. I don't give a damn what else you think of me, but I want to make that plain. I do what I must."

"As we all do, Squire."

When I knocked at the door upstairs, St. August sang out cheerfully, "Come in, come in!"

Packenham and St. August were in their shirt sleeves. On the table was a platter with two roast ducks and a great apple pastry. They were eating with determination, tearing pieces out of the ducks and spooning eagerly from the depths of the pastry. It was a long moment before they turned to examine their visitor, and then their bright faces darkened.

"What do you want, Feversham?" the general asked.

"I want to plead."

"Nonsense," he said, sputtering through a mouthful of duck. "Men like you don't plead. Trouble with your kind, Feversham, is that you take everyone else for a fool."

"Don't hang the boy. I ask you that with all my heart, General Packenham. Sell him out as a chattel. That's punishment enough."

"For murder? Come, come, Feversham."

"No, no—he's no more guilty of murder than I am."

"Indeed?"

"Please—I beg it of you, as an officer and a gentleman."

"I return the compliment, Feversham, although damned if I know how an officer and a gentleman survives up here on this ridge. Have a beer with us, Feversham, and let bygones be bygones. Pleading doesn't become you. You heard the evidence, did you not?"

I closed the door behind me and went downstairs. The kitchen of the inn was packed with men. It was noisy and smelled of food and beer. I went through to the courtroom, where Hunt still sprawled in his chair. He raised an arm to salute me and asked, "Did you soften the general's heart, Feversham?"

"He would listen to you."

"Let the Hessian hang, Feversham. You ask for mercy—but do you think we took this continent and made it ours with mercy? Like hell we did! We paid with blood every inch of the way. My grandmother had eleven children and two survived. We cleared these fields with our own hands and fought the Indians because what was ours had to be ours. Now we've fought the British six years and we'll fight them another six or sixty if we have to. So I can't explain to you what happened inside of me when I saw Saul Clamberham's body hanging there."

"You didn't give two damns for Saul Clamberham," I said.

"You're right; but I will tell you what I give two damns about— the Hessians. When they marched up here onto the Ridge, my stomach turned as sour as bad wine. There's a difference between us, Feversham. I know how to hate, and you don't, and hate is a lovely thing. A man is strong with hate, stronger than you imagine. Do you think I knew what the outcome would be when I took those men down to Buskin's place? I did not. These are no soldiers, these militia here on the Ridge, and they were so frightened of Hessians that they shook at the thought of them. How many imagined that they would live through that day at Buskin's? And you want me to mourn the Hessians? No, sir. You fail to understand me."

"Yes, I fail to understand you, Squire Hunt," I admitted.

"Then let it be at that, and plead no more, Feversham."

I was thinking, I plead only for myself. But it was no use to say that to him. In some ways, he knew me better than I knew myself.

Now people were beginning to drift back into the room, but no more than a few dozen men had taken their places when General Packenham and Colonel St. August and Clerk Crippit took their seats. General Packenham, the buttons on his waistcoat open to accommodate duck and pastry, pounded his gavel. Crippit rose, called the court into session and then looked at the general.

"Have them stand."

"Everybody rise," Crippit called out.

We stood up.

The Hessian entered the room, the two militiamen on either side of him. He stood at attention in front of the table.

"Do you have anything to say, Hans Pohl, before this court passes sentence upon you?"

The boy's voice thickened with emotion as he forced the words out. "I do not murder any man. But I am a Hessian soldier. I am a jäger. If I must die, I will die like a jäger."

He must have rehearsed the words over and over.

"Then hear the sentence of this court. You have been found guilty of premeditated murder of an American citizen. We have heard all the evidence given and we have pondered upon it. We find no extenuating circumstances. Therefore, we sentence you to be hanged by the neck until dead, and may God have mercy on your soul."

The boy fought to maintain his dignity, but he was only a boy, and the tears rolled down his cheeks.

Chapter Eleven: The Gallows

THERE was still an hour of daylight left when I finally returned home that day, and when Rodney Stephan had taken my horse, I was so tired I could barely stand. Alice was in the garden, tying the grapevine into place over the arbor. I sat on our bench and stretched my legs gratefully. It was a warm, kind June evening, with only a gentle breeze to move the air. Alice went on working, watching me, and then she asked me about the Heathers.

"Did they take it badly?"

"I'm afraid so."

"And Sally?"

"I don't know," I said. "They left before the verdict, so I stopped by on my way home to tell them what happened. She appears to have walled herself off—but then I don't know those people. I thought I did, but I don't."

"Rodney Stephan says Packenham and St. August hardly discussed the verdict. He says they sat in their rooms at the inn and stuffed themselves with food."

"There's very little Rodney Stephan misses, is there? Did he also tell you that I saw them?"

"That you pleaded with them and then had a bitter argument with Abraham Hunt."

"Not bitter and hardly any argument at all."

She looked at me strangely then.

"He is what he is." I shrugged.

She ceased her work on the vine and sat down beside me, placing her hand over mine. "What did Sally do when you told her that it was a death sentence?"

"She went to her father and embraced him," I answered, thinking of how that curious family of Quakers were knit together with something that I did not know but yearned for desperately.

"Evan," Alice said, "if you had known Sarah Heather eighteen years ago, before she was married, would you have asked her to marry you?"

"That's a damn foolish question, isn't it? I was not even in America eighteen years ago."

"Please—try to answer me."

"Then the answer is no. I would not have married her."

"Why?"

"Because it's not enough to share love. There's agony to be shared, and I don't think she could ever sense what my agony is. They are all so removed from it."

"As I am not?"

"As you are not."

She was crying now, and I said to her, "Come to bed, and we'll hold each other for a while."

The next day was Sunday, and at lunch Alice told me about the sermon she'd heard at church that morning. Dorset had taken for his text, *Judge not, that ye be not judged.*

"It was a very good sermon," she said. "I wish you had heard it, Evan."

"You Puritans are an incredible people," I told her. "I think you are the most incredible people that ever appeared on this earth. Do you know that they will hang the Hessian tomorrow?"

"Then is it wrong for me to sit in church and weep inside?"

"I am not talking about what is right and what is wrong, Alice. If ever there was a man who did not know what is right or wrong, you are looking at him now."

"I have heard," she said, "that in your country they will hang a man for stealing a purse."

"Yes," I agreed, "or for stealing a crust of bread. There are three hundred and eighty-two offenses in England for which a man may be hanged, but it's not my country. Will you never understand that this is my country, that this rocky ridge of land in Connecticut is the only place I ever loved?"

She remained silent for a little while, and then she asked me, "Will you have surgery tomorrow?"

"No."

"What shall I tell the people who come?"

"Tell them that it's a day of penance and that Dr. Feversham has gone to see a man hanged."

"Why will you go?"

"Because I must."

I AWAKENED in the early dawn and crept silently down to the surgery, where I dressed myself. Then I went into the kitchen and took some water, but I could not bear the thought of food. When I came to the barn Rodney Stephan was already there. The sun was just tipping the hills, dropping its lovely pink warmth into the mist-filled bottoms. We stood for a few minutes without a word being said, and then Rodney Stephan asked me what horse I desired.

"Give me the bay."

She was a gentle, intelligent beast, and when I rode out she moved in a dreamlike way through the mist and past the endless stone walls that lined the road.

When I reached town, the Benton brothers, who were the best carpenters in Ridgefield, were already at work on the gallows. They had framed out a platform about five feet high in the middle of the common, and now, with help from the boys who had paused to watch on their way to school, they were sliding the gallows post into the hole they had dug to receive it.

I dismounted and stood watching for a while, and presently I noticed that Abraham Hunt stood beside me.

"Good morning," he said.

I nodded. Then he said, not unkindly, "Will the Heathers claim the body?"

"I don't know."

"Will you ask them, Feversham?"

"I'll ask them."

I rode down the street to the Congregational church, tied my horse and went to the parsonage. Ziporah Dorset opened the door for me. "John is in the study, Dr. Feversham," she whispered. "I'll tell him you are here."

Her husband must have heard our voices, for he opened the door and came into the parlor.

"Come in, please, Dr. Feversham," he said.

I followed him into the little room he called his study. The rug was threadbare, the few pieces of pine furniture worn and rickety. I wondered whether anyone in these colonies was quite as poor as a Congregational minister on the Ridge. He motioned me to a seat and then sat down behind the old table he used as a desk.

I told him of my few words with Hunt. "You will allow him to be buried in the churchyard with the Hessians?"

"Oh, of course, of course."

"Did you mark the Hessian graves?"

"We will. I must go to Danbury and talk to the stonecutters. I thought of a stone with all the names of the men inscribed upon it. But we are not a wealthy church, and the truth is—" He shook his head. "We just don't have the money."

"How much will it cost?"

"A hundred dollars Spanish or ten pounds sterling. It would have to be a large stone."

I took two five-guinea gold pieces out of my pocket and laid them on the table.

"Add the boy's name to it, please."

"Of course." Then he said uneasily, "Should I have some small service here at the church?"

"I am going to ask Raymond Heather what to do. Do the Quakers have any special ritual for the dead? I'm afraid I don't know."

"They're good Christians," Dorset said miserably. "If they want to, it might be better that they do it. It's not easy for me to say this, Dr. Feversham, but it might be better."

"You will have the grave dug?"

"Yes. Oh, yes, indeed."

I rose to go, and Dorset walked with me to the door. "Dr. Feversham," he said, "don't judge us too harshly. You have been a soldier and you know how merciless war is."

"Is war merciless?" I asked him. "Or are men merciless?"

I WENT out to Raymond Heather's place then. I rode slowly, for I was not eager to go there, and I had much to think about. When I reached the farm they had just finished their midday meal, or what small part of it they were able to eat, and I stood with Sarah while Raymond bent his head and offered their silent thanksgiving for their bread.

When Sally raised her head she said, "It's good to see thee, Evan." Her face was wan and drawn, but her voice was calm.

"Have thee had food, Evan?" Sarah asked me.

"I am not hungry."

Jacob got up suddenly and bolted from the house.

504

"Sit here," Sarah said. She put bread in front of me, and cheese and butter, and poured me a mixture of warm coffee and milk.

I ate a little, and then said to Raymond, "I must talk about some painful things. Shall we be by ourselves?"

"Evan," Sally said quietly, "if thee will talk about Hans Pohl, I would hear what you have to say."

"All right. I spoke to the squire this morning, and he asked me whether you would want to claim the body."

"I thought of that," Raymond said. "If they will allow it, we would take the body to our meetinghouse."

"They will. I also spoke to Pastor Dorset. He will have a grave dug where the other Hessians are buried in his churchyard."

"I considered that we might bury him in our own place."

"No," Sally said. "He would want to lie with his father."

"As thee will," Raymond agreed.

"Where should he lie until he is buried?" I asked.

"In our meetinghouse. We'll take him in my wagon," Raymond said. "Sally will go with me, and we will be there when the thing is done."

"No," I said. "It's not a thing that a child should see."

"Evan," Sally said, "must I always remind thee that I am not a child?"

"Let her go, Evan," Sarah said. "We don't turn our eyes away from the world. We accept it as it is. Otherwise, even our own faith will not save us."

"What has faith got to do with this murderous act?"

"More than thee might imagine. Please, Evan, don't reason with us today."

"And I must see Hans before he dies," Sally said.

"Thee must make it possible," Raymond said.

"All right." I sighed and stood up. "Let's harness your horses now, Raymond." I looked at my watch. "There are only about three hours remaining."

I rode behind the wagon into the town. We tied the horses at the church, and then the three of us walked to the inn, where the Hessian was being held. In the big kitchen Hunt and Packenham and

St. August and a half-dozen militiamen were drinking beer and munching bread and cheese. A sudden silence fell when I appeared. I nodded at Hunt.

"A word with you, Squire?"

I stepped into the pantry, and he followed me there.

"I have Raymond Heather and his daughter outside."

"Now that was a damn fool thing to do, to bring them here!"

"She wants to see the Hessian."

"Be damned, Feversham! What good will it do for them to see each other now?"

"No good as far as you and I are concerned. But it is something she wants and she wants it desperately. As far as I can see, it's the most important thing in the world to her right now."

"Tell her no."

"Hunt, I can't tell her no."

"I know what Packenham will say."

"I don't think you give a damn what Packenham will say. I think you despise him as much as I do. You did this thing, not Packenham. Haven't you enough guts to stand up to it?"

I thought he was going to explode at me, but he held onto himself. He stood and stared at me.

"Do it, Hunt. Do this one thing."

He took a deep breath and said, "Bring her around to the taproom. I don't want her coming through the kitchen."

I went outside then and told Raymond to wait for us. Then I took Sally into the taproom. We stood there for a few minutes, until Hunt appeared from the kitchen and said brusquely, "Follow me."

He took us up the serving stairs to the second floor, where two militiamen stood in front of a door.

"Open it," Hunt said.

They opened the door to reveal the boy lying on his back on a low trundle bed. The room was one of those tiny cubbyholes under the eaves that Latham, the innkeeper, rented out to travelers. The boy did not move.

"Hans," Sally said softly.

506

He jumped up, amazement and despair on his face, and Sally went into the room.

"Fifteen minutes," Hunt said.

I closed the door. The militiamen stood grinning foolishly until Hunt told them that he saw nothing amusing for two idiots to grin at. He took a fat turnip watch out of his waistcoat and stared at it.

"Fifteen minutes, twenty minutes—what difference does it make?" I asked him.

"Don't push me too far, Feversham," he said, and left.

A beam of sunlight came into the narrow hallway from a half-moon window, and I watched the dust motes dance and whirl as the minutes passed.

Then Sally opened the door. The Hessian boy stood with his back to her. He did not turn around as she left the room, and I guessed that he had been crying.

I took her downstairs and outside into the sunlight, where Raymond was waiting. Her face was dry and set. Her father kissed her, but she made no response.

A crowd had gathered around the gallows now, and three militiamen, wearing blue coats and white sashes, kept pushing them back. On the other side of the field, across from the crowd and farther away from the gallows, half a dozen Quakers stood in their long dark coats and flat-brimmed hats. The three of us, Raymond, Sally and myself, walked across the field and joined them. At the other side of the field, over a hundred people stood, mostly men, but with a good sprinkling of women, boys and girls. There was a chatter of noise and excitement out of them.

Saxon, the undertaker, drove up with his high-walled wagon, which he used as a hearse, and he and his assistant took out a plain pine coffin, which they carried over to the gallows. I glanced at Sally. She did not avert her eyes, nor did her face change. The long hitching rail in front of the inn was now crowded with horses and wagons. There were people there who must have come a considerable distance to see the Hessian hanged, many of them well-dressed, some women in expensive silk, with sun umbrellas.

We stood waiting, the afternoon sun still high in the sky, and then, from behind the inn, there came the rattle of a trap drum. That would be old Seth Harkness, who had played his drum for every parade on the Ridge since the war began. Presently he came into sight, playing a mournful roll. He was followed by the hangman, who carried a black scarf in his hand, and after him a dozen militiamen, marching six and six on either side of the Hessian. Following them came Packenham, St. August and Hunt.

The Hessian boy marched with his head upright, his pale hair blowing in the wind, his step firm and sure; and my heart went out to him as never before for his indomitable courage. He could only justify his meaningless death to himself by being brave; and there came to my mind a memory of all the other boys I had seen who went to kill or be killed because they must be brave.

He stood before the gallows now, and an almost terrifying stillness settled over the common. Pastor Dorset came walking across from the church, his prayer book in his hands, went to where Hans Pohl stood and began to speak softly. Yet such was the stillness that here and there a word of the whispered plea could be made out— *life everlasting, I am the resurrection and the life*—but it could not drive the sour smell of death away.

Then the boy climbed the ladder, the hangman holding him, for his hands were bound, and he shook his head wildly when the hangman tried to cover his eyes. Then the rope was put around his neck, tightened, and he was pushed into the open pit.

Sally stood there, weeping, her eyes upon the place where the boy had been.

Chapter Twelve: The Meetinghouse

THEY cut down the body and I pronounced the boy dead. Then the Quakers carried the coffin to Dorset's house, the crowd trailing after us and then drifting away. Ziporah Dorset took Sally into her parlor to comfort her as best she might; and we took the body into the kitchen and washed it and cleaned the boy's uniform. Dorset gave us a quilt to place under the body and a hammer and nails to close the coffin.

Then we placed it in Raymond's wagon, and the other Quakers went to their own horses. Sally came out of the house with Ziporah, her face dry and controlled. I helped Sally up to the seat next to Raymond and watched them drive off.

Dorset stood beside me. "Would they take umbrage if I came to the meetinghouse?" he asked me.

"They do not appear to take umbrage at anything."

"Before, I could think of nothing that I could do, and now there seems to be so much that I could have done."

"We all feel that way, I suppose," I said.

I walked across to the inn. The common was empty now, the gallows standing in naked ugliness. As I took the reins of my horse, Abraham Hunt came out of the inn and walked over to me.

"Well, Feversham?" he challenged me.

There was nothing I desired to say. I looked at him without hate and without wonder. Then I mounted my horse and rode off.

It was just before twilight when I reached the meetinghouse, a small frame building sitting off the road near the top of Peaceable Ridge. At least a dozen horses and wagons were already outside, and I could see others coming up the road.

I went into the meetinghouse. There was no cross, no ornamentation, just a room with pine benches, and a lectern at the front. Having never been inside before, although I had passed it many times, I was unprepared for its plainness. The coffin had been laid in the space behind the lectern, but with not a single flower on it, just the plain pine boards.

There were about twenty people in the place already, men, women, some boys and girls, and others were coming in and sitting down quietly. The people on the benches sat, eyes cast down and hands folded in their laps.

Sarah had come from her home with Jacob and the baby, and Raymond and Sally sat on the bench beside them. I sat down next to Raymond, who put his hand on my arm and said, "Thank thee for coming here in our time of grief."

I sat there then as they did, feeling strangely out of place among these people, finding no answers, no hint of any grace that could touch me. We stayed there thus until there were about thirty people in the room.

Then Raymond rose and walked up to the lectern and opened the Bible that lay there.

"I will read from the fourth chapter of Genesis," he said. "*And Cain talked with Abel his brother: and it came to pass, when they were in the field, that Cain rose up against Abel his brother, and slew him. And the Lord said unto Cain, Where is Abel thy brother? And he said, I know not: Am I my brother's keeper?*

"*I know not,*" he repeated, closing the book. "I am my brother's keeper, and yet I know not."

The moon rose as my horse took me home, a great, wide moon that shed its pale light all over the landscape. The day had been eternity, and I think that more than anything else in the world I wished for the small priest to be waiting for me, so that I might go down on my knees and beg him, "Father, hear my confession." Yet I knew that even if he were there it would change nothing, that for me there was neither salvation nor damnation but only the purgatory wherein a stranger lives, knowing that he will always be a stranger, coming naked and going naked, and knowing no more at the moment of his death than he knew at the moment of his birth.

Howard Fast

Howard Fast was born in New York in 1914. He published his first story when he was only seventeen and since then has repeatedly shown a unique talent for dramatizing vivid moments in America's history. He is particularly intrigued by the American War of Independence: it was, he says, a time when moral issues seemed clearer than they do today. Although the action in *The Hessian* centres around the religious beliefs of the Quakers, he feels that all religions have things in common to say about violence and war. His conviction is that the killing of human beings is the greatest horror of civilized man.

He and his wife spend much of their time in their handsome New York apartment. Mrs. Fast is a talented sculptor and children's book illustrator. At weekends they travel to their country home in Connecticut. Once there they have simple pleasures: walking, gardening, and cutting firewood for the long cold winters.

Howard Fast's books have been translated into eighty-two languages and have sold more than twenty million copies. When working on a book he writes at fever pitch, typing far into the night. And he cares passionately about what happens to his characters. His wife recalls their early days in a two-roomed apartment. "Howard was working on his latest book, day and night. I couldn't sleep with the typewriter going. Finally I woke up from a light doze, and I heard Howard crying. It tore him apart to see the main character die at the end. I felt sad too, but I have to admit I also thought to myself: now I'll finally get some sleep."

But she knows it is the white-hot fever and the caring that matter. For only so can he make his readers care also.

The Sir Alfred Munnings painting on p. 6, "Under Starter's Orders", photographed at Castle House, Dedham, by kind permission of the Trustees.

Photograph of Dick Francis on p.127 by Fay Godwin.

BRING ON THE EMPTY HORSES: Picture Credits: Pages 238 (top centre), 239: courtesy of Metro-Goldwyn-Mayer, Inc.; Culver Pictures. Page 238 (top left): courtesy of National Film Archive, London. Page 238 (top right): Samuel Goldwyn Productions; Culver Pictures. Page 238 (bottom left): copyright 1941 by Warner Bros. Pictures, Inc., copyright © renewed 1969; The Museum of Modern Art/Film Stills Archive. Page 238 (bottom right): courtesy of Metro-Goldwyn-Mayer Inc.; The Museum of Modern Art/Film Stills Archive. Page 240: United Press International. Pages, 251, 261, 270, 277, 286: Culver Pictures. Page 249: copyright 1936 by Warner Bros. Pictures, Inc., and The Vitaphone Corp., copyright © renewed 1964; Culver Pictures. Pages 253, 275: collection of David Niven. Page 265: Edward Steichen. Page 279: Murray Garrett/Graphic House. Page 294: courtesy of National Film Archive, London.

Photograph of Victoria Holt on p.431 by Godfrey Argent.

Photograph of Howard Fast on p.511 by Bill Mason.